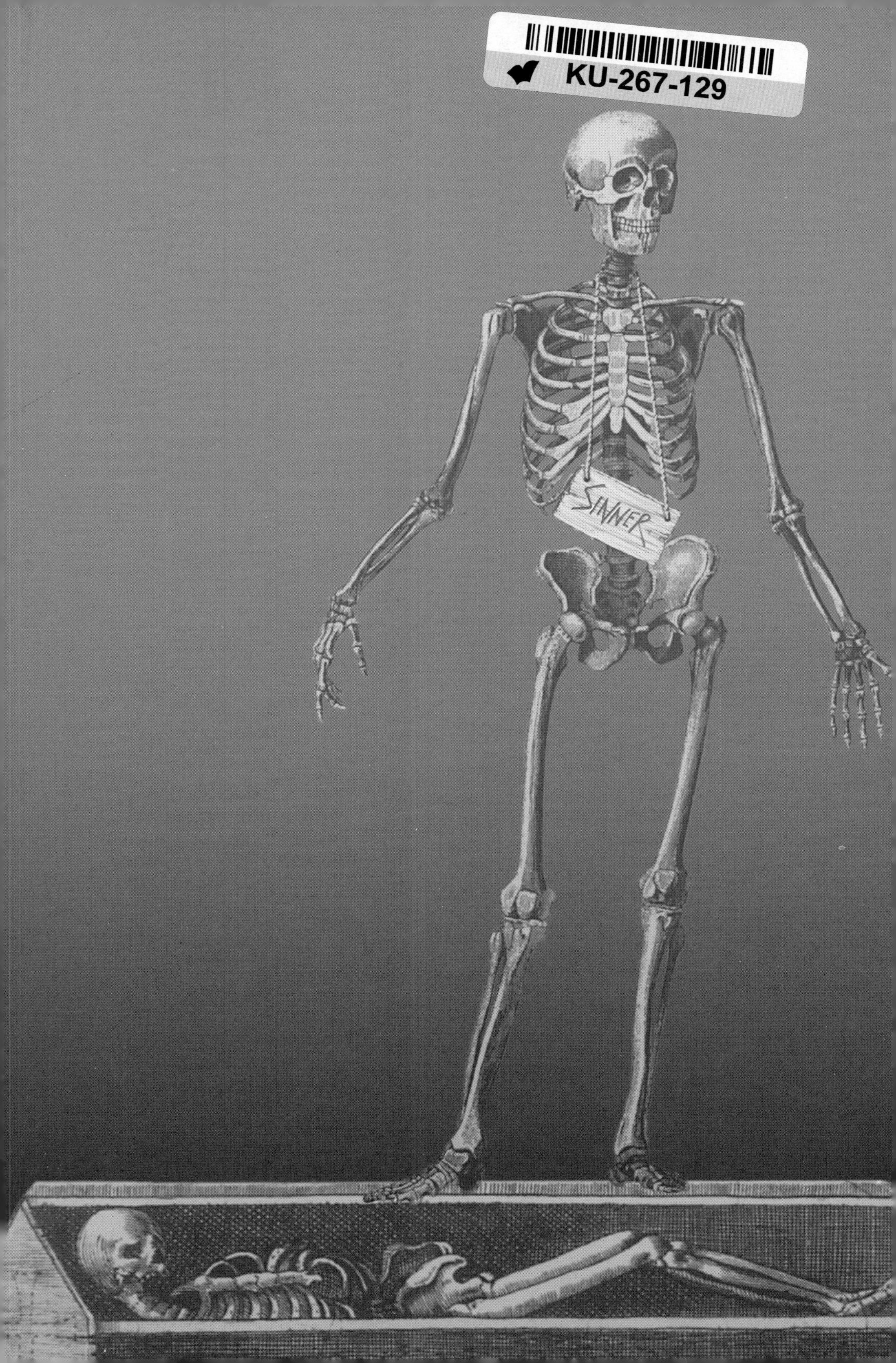
SINNER

THE KILLING KIND

Also by John Connolly

EVERY DEAD THING
DARK HOLLOW

THE KILLING KIND

John Connolly

Hodder & Stoughton

First published in 2001 by Hodder and Stoughton
A division of Hodder Headline

10 9 8 7 6 5 4 3 2 1

British Library Cataloguing in Publication Data
Connolly, John, 1968–
The Killing Kind
1.Suspense fiction
I.Title
823.9'14 [F]

ISBN 0 340 77120 8 HARDBACK
ISBN 0 340 77121 6 TRADE PAPERBACK

Typeset by Hewer Text Ltd, Edinburgh
Printed and bound in Great Britain by
Clays Ltd, St Ives plc

Hodder and Stoughton
A division of Hodder Headline
338 Euston Road
London NW1 3BH

For my Mother

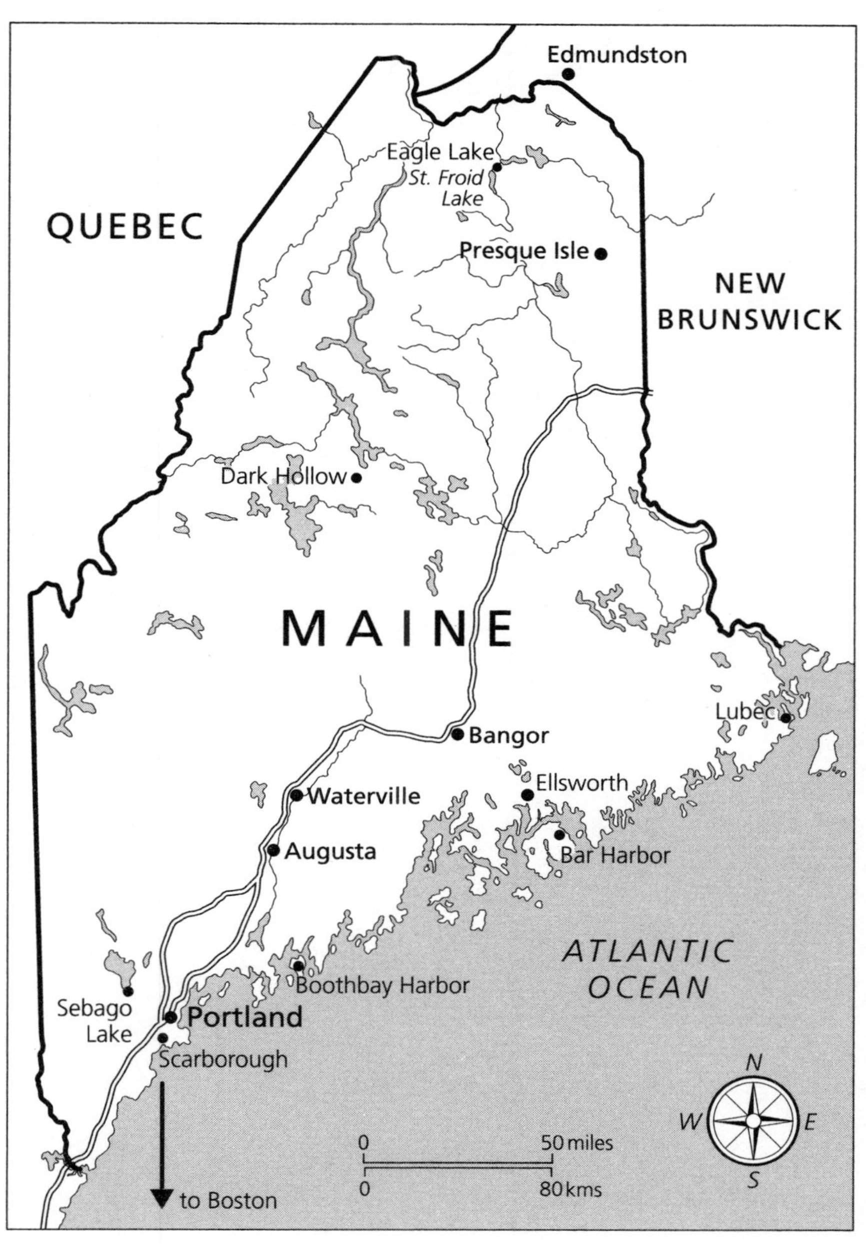

Edmundston
QUEBEC
Eagle Lake
St. Froid
Lake
Presque Isle
NEW
BRUNSWICK
Dark Hollow
MAINE
Lubec
Bangor
Ellsworth
Waterville
Augusta
Bar Harbor
ATLANTIC
OCEAN
Boothbay Harbor
Sebago
Lake
Portland
Scarborough
N
W
E
S
0
50 miles
0
80 kms
to Boston

Part One

And heavy is the tread
Of the living; but the dead
Returning lightly dance . . .

Edward Thomas,
'Roads'

PROLOGUE

This is a honeycomb world. It hides a hollow heart.

The truth of nature, wrote the philosopher Democritus, lies in deep mines and caves. The stability of what is seen and felt beneath our feet is an illusion, for this life is not as it seems. Below the surface, there are cracks and fissures and pockets of stale, trapped air; stalagmites and helactites and unmapped dark rivers that flow ever downward. It is a place of caverns and stone waterfalls, a labyrinth of crystal tumors and frozen columns where history becomes future, then becomes now.

For in total blackness, time has no meaning.

The present is imperfectly layered on the past; it does not conform flawlessly at every point. Things fall and die and their decay creates new layers, thickening the surface crust and adding another thin membrane to cover what lies beneath, new worlds resting on the remains of the old. Day upon day, year upon year, century upon century, layers are added and the imperfections multiply. The past never truly dies. It is there, waiting, just below the surface of the now. We stumble into it occasionally, all of us, through remembrance and recall. We summon to mind former lovers, lost children, departed parents, the wonder of a single day when we captured, however briefly, the ineffable, fleeting beauty of the world. These are our memories. We hold them close and call them ours, and we can find them when we need them.

But sometimes that choice is made for us: a piece of the present simply falls away, and the past is exposed like old bone. Afterward, nothing can ever be the same again, and we are forced to reassess the form of what we believed to be true in the light of new revelations about its substance. The truth is revealed by a misstep and the fleeting sense that something beneath our feet rings false. The past bubbles out like molten lava, and lives turn to ash in its path.

This is a honeycomb world. Our actions echo through its depths.

Down here, dark life exists: microbes and bacteria that draw their energy from chemicals and natural radioactivity, older than the first plant cells that brought color to the world above. Every deep pool is alive with them, every mine shaft, every ice core. They live and die unseen.

But there are other organisms, other beings: creatures that know only hunger, entities that exist purely to hunt and kill. They move ceaselessly through the hidden cavities, their jaws snapping at the endless night. They come to the surface only when they are forced to do so, and all living things flee from their path.

They came for Alison Beck.

Dr. Beck was sixty and had been performing abortions since 1974, in the immediate aftermath of *Roe v. Wade*. As a young woman she had become involved in Planned Parenthood following the rubella epidemic of the early 1960s, when thousands of American women delivered babies with serious birth defects. She had progressed to outspoken membership of NOW and the National Association for the Repeal of Abortion Laws before the changes for which they fought enabled her to establish her own clinic in Minneapolis. Since then, she had defied Joseph Scheidler's Pro-Life Action Network, his sidewalk counselors and bullhorn mafia, and had stood head-to-head with Randall Terry when Operation Rescue tried to blockade her clinic in 1989. She had fought against the Hyde amendment of '76, which cut off Medicaid funding for abortions, and had cried when the antiabortionist C. Everett Koop became U.S. surgeon general. On three separate occasions butyric acid had been injected into the clinic walls by antiabortion activists, forcing it to close its doors for days until the fumes had dispersed. The tires on her car had been slashed more times than she could count, and only the toughened glass on the clinic window had prevented an incendiary device housed in a fire extinguisher from burning the building to the ground.

But in recent years the strain of her profession had begun to tell, and she now looked much older than her years. In almost three decades, she had enjoyed the company of only a handful of men. David had been the first, and she had married him and loved him, but David was gone now. She had held him as he died, and she still kept the shirt he had worn on that day, the bloodstains like the shadows of dark clouds floating across its once pristine whiteness. The men who followed offered many excuses for departing, but in the end, all the excuses could be distilled down to one simple essence: fear. Alison Beck was a marked woman. She lived each day in the knowledge that there were those who would rather see her dead than have her continue her work, and few men were willing to stand beside such a woman.

She knew the statistics off by heart. There had been twenty-seven cases of extreme violence against American abortion clinics in the previous year, and two doctors had died. Seven abortion doctors and assistants had been killed in the preceding five years, and many others injured in bombings and shootings. She knew all of this because she had spent over twenty years documenting the incidences of violence, tracing common factors, establishing connections. It was the only way that she could cope with the loss of David, the only means she had of making sure that some small good might arise from the ashes of his death. Her research had been used to support the abortion providers' successful invocation of the RICO antiracketeering laws in their fight against their opponents, alleging a nationwide conspiracy to close down clinics. It had been a hard-won victory.

But slowly, another, more indistinct pattern had begun to emerge: names recurring and echoing down the canyons of the years, figures half glimpsed in the shadows of violent acts. The convergences were visible in barely half a dozen cases, but they were there. She was certain of it, and the others seemed to agree. Together, they were drawing closer and closer to the truth.

But that brought with it its own dangers.

Alison Beck had an alarm system in her home, linked directly to a private security firm, and two armed guards were always on duty at the clinic. In her bedroom closet was an American Body Armor bullet-proof vest, which she wore while traveling to and from the clinic despite the discomfort involved. Its twin hung on a steel rail in her consulting room. She drove a red Porsche Boxster, her only true indulgence. She collected speeding tickets the way other people collected stamps.

Alison was a conservative dresser. She typically wore a jacket, unbuttoned, which hung to midthigh level. Beneath the jacket she wore pants with either a brown or a black belt, depending on the color of her ensemble. Attached to the belt was an Alessi holster containing a Kahr K40 Covert pistol. The Kahr held a five-round magazine of .40 caliber ammunition. Beck had tried using six rounds for a time but found that the extended magazine sometimes caught in the folds of her shirt. The Kahr had an abbreviated grip that suited her small hands, for Alison Beck was just a shade over five feet tall and slightly built. On a range, with the Kahr's smooth double-action trigger pull, she could put the five rounds through the heart of a target thirty feet away in under ten seconds.

Her shoulder bag contained a can of Mace and a stun gun that could send a 20,000-volt charge through a man and leave him gasping and quivering on the ground like a stranded fish. While she had never fired her gun in anger, she had been forced to use the Mace on one occasion, when an antiabortion protester had tried to force his way into her home. Later she recalled, with a twinge of shame, that Macing him had felt good. She had chosen her life – that she simply could not deny – but the fear and the anger at the restrictions it had imposed upon her, and the hatred and animosity of those who despised her for what she did, had affected her in ways she did not like to admit. That November evening, with the Mace in her hand and the short, bearded man howling and crying in her hallway, all of that tension and anger had exploded from her through the simple action of pressing a plastic button.

Alison Beck was a familiar figure, a public figure. Although based in a leafy street in Minneapolis, she traveled twice each month to South Dakota, where she conducted a clinic at Sioux Falls. She appeared regularly on local and national television, campaigning against what she perceived as the gradual erosion of women's right to choose. Clinics were closing, she had pointed out on the local NBC affiliate only the previous week, and now 83 percent of U.S. counties had no abortion services. Three dozen congressmen, a dozen senators, and four governors were openly antichoice. Meanwhile, the Roman Catholic Church was now the largest private health care provider in America, and access to abortion services, sterilization, birth control, and in vitro fertilization was becoming increasingly limited.

Yet faced with a pleasant, soft-spoken young woman from Right to Life of Minnesota, who concentrated on the health issues for women and the changing attitudes of a younger generation that could not remember the days before *Roe v. Wade*, Alison Beck had begun to feel that it was she, the campaigning doctor, who now sounded strident and intolerant, and that perhaps the tide was turning more than she realized. She admitted as much to friends in the days before she died.

But something else had given her cause to feel afraid. She had seen him again, the strange red-haired man, and she knew that he was closing in on her, that he intended to move against her and the others before they could complete their work.

But they can't know, Mercier had tried to reassure her. We've made no move against them yet.

I tell you, they know. I have seen him. And . . .

Yes?

I found something in my car this morning.

What? What did you find?

A skin. I found a spider skin.

Spiders grow by shedding their old exoskeleton and replacing it with a larger, less constraining hide, a process known as ecdysis. The discarded skin, or exuvium, that Alison Beck had found on the passenger seat of her car belonged to a Sri Lankan ornamental tarantula, *Poecilotheria fasciata*, a beautifully-colored but temperamental arachnid. The species had been specifically selected for its capacity to alarm: its body was about two and a half inches in length, marked with grays, blacks and creams, and its legspan was almost four inches. Alison had been terrified, and that terror had only slightly abated when she realized that the shape beside her was not a living, breathing spider.

Mercier had gone silent then, before advising her to go away for a time, promising that he would warn their associates to be vigilant.

And so Alison Beck had, in that final week, decided to take her first vacation in almost two years. She intended to drive to Montana, stopping off along the way for the first week, before visiting an old college friend in Bozeman. From there the two of them planned to travel north to Glacier National Park if the roads were passable, for it was only April and the snows might not yet have completely melted.

When Alison did not arrive on that Sunday evening as she had promised, her friend was mildly concerned. When, by late Monday afternoon, there was still no word from her, she phoned the headquarters of the Minneapolis PD. Two patrol officers, Ames and Frayn, familiar with Alison from previous incidents, were assigned to check on her home at 604 West Twenty-sixth Street.

Nobody answered the doorbell when they rang, and the garage entrance was firmly locked. Ames cupped his hands and peered through the glass into the hallway. In the open doorway leading into the kitchen were two suitcases, and a kitchen chair lay on the floor with its legs toward the wall. Seconds later, Ames had slipped on his gloves, broken a side window, and, his gun drawn, entered the house. Frayn made his approach from the rear and came in through the back door. The house was a small two-story, and it didn't take the policemen long to confirm that it was empty. From the kitchen, a connecting door led into the garage. Through the frosted glass, the lines of Alison Beck's Boxster were clearly visible.

Ames took a breath and opened the door.

The garage was dark. He removed his flashlight from his belt and twisted it on. For a moment, as its beam hit the car, he wasn't sure what he was seeing. He believed initially that the windshield was cracked, for thin lines spread in all directions across it, radiating from irregular clumps dotted like bullet holes across the glass and making it impossible to see the interior of the car. Then, as he drew nearer the driver's door, he thought instead that the car had somehow filled with cotton candy, for the windows appeared to be coated on the inside with soft white strands. It was only when he shined the light close to the windshield and something swift and brown darted across the pane that he recognized it for what it was.

It was spiderweb, its filaments gilded with silver by the flashlight's beam. Beneath the weave, a dark shape sat upright in the driver's seat.

'Dr. Beck?' he called. He placed his gloved hand on the door handle and pulled.

There came the sound of sticky strands breaking, and the silken web flailed at the air as the door opened. Something dropped at Ames's feet with a soft, barely audible thud. When he looked down, he saw a small brown spider making its way across the concrete floor toward his right foot. It was a recluse, about half an inch in length, with a dark groove running down the center of its back. Instinctively, Ames raised his steel-capped shoe and stamped down on it. For a brief moment he wondered if his action constituted a destruction of evidence, until he looked into the interior of the car and realized that, for all its effect, he might just as easily have stolen a grain of sand from the seashore or pilfered a single drop of water from the ocean.

Alison Beck had been stripped to her underwear and tied to the driver's seat. Gray masking tape had been wrapped around her head, covering her mouth and anchoring her to the seat. Her face was swollen almost beyond recognition, her body mottled with decay, and there was a square of exposed red flesh just below her neck where a section of skin had been removed.

Yet the disintegration of her body was masked by the fragments of web that covered her in a tattered white veil, her face almost concealed beneath the dense pockets of thread. All around her, small brown spiders moved on arched legs, their palps twitching as they sensed the change in the air; others remained huddled in dark recesses, orange egg sacs dangling beside them like bunches of poisonous fruit. The husks of drained insects speckled the snares, interspersed with the bodies of spiders who had been preyed upon by their own kind. Fruit flies flitted around the seats, and Ames could see decaying oranges and pears on the floor by Alison Beck's feet. Elsewhere invisible crickets chirped, part of the small ecosystem that had been created inside the doctor's car, but most of the activity came from the compact brown spiders who busied themselves around Alison Beck's face, dancing lightly across her cheeks and her eyelids, continuing the construction of the irregular webs that coated the inside of the car with thread.

But there was one last surprise for those who found

Alison Beck. When the masking tape was removed from her face and her mouth was opened during the autopsy, small black-and-red balls tumbled from her lips and lay like misshapen marbles on the steel table. There were more lodged in her thorax and trapped beneath her tongue. Some had caught in her teeth, crushed as her mouth convulsed when the biting began.

Only one was still alive: it was discovered in her nasal cavity, its long, black legs curled in upon itself. When the tweezers gripped the spherical abdomen it struggled feebly against the pressure, the red hourglass on its underside like the relic of a life suddenly stopped.

And in the harsh light of the autopsy room, the eyes of the black widow gleamed like small, dark stars.

This is a honeycomb world. History is its gravity.

In the far north of Maine, figures move along a road, silhouetted against the early-morning sun. Behind them are a bulldozer and a cherry picker and two small trucks, the little convoy making its way along a county road toward the sound of lapping water. There is laughter and swearing in the air, and plumes of cigarette smoke rising to join with the morning fog. There is room for these men and women in the bed of the truck but they choose instead to walk, enjoying the feel of the ground beneath their feet, the clean air in their lungs, the camaraderie of those who will soon perform hard physical labor together but are grateful for the sun that will shine gently upon them, the breeze that will cool them in their work, and the friendship of those who walk by their side.

There are two groups of workers here. The first are line clearers, jointly employed by the Maine Public Service Company and the New England Telephone and Telegraph Company to cut back the trees and brush alongside the road. This is work that should have been completed in the autumn, when the ground was dry and clear, not at the end of April, when frozen, compacted snow still lay on the high ground and the first buds had already begun to sprout from the branches. But the line clearers have long since ceased to wonder at the ways of their employers and are content simply that there is no rain falling upon them as they traipse along the blacktop.

The second group consists of workmen employed by one Jean Beaulieu to clear vegetation from the banks of St. Froid Lake in preparation for the construction of a house. It is simply coincidence that both groups of men have taken to the same stretch of road on this bright morning, but they mingle as they go, exchanging comments about the weather and lighting one another's cigarettes.

Just outside the little town of Eagle Lake, the workers turn west onto Red River Road, the Fish River flowing at their left, the red brick edifice of the Eagle Lake Water and Sewage District building to their right. A small wire fence ends where the river joins St. Froid Lake, and houses begin to appear along the bank. Through the branches of the trees, the glittering surface of the water can be glimpsed.

Soon the noise of their passing is joined by another sound. On the ground above them, shapes appear from wooden kennels: gray animals with thick fur and keen, intelligent eyes. They are wolf hybrids, each chained to a iron ring outside its kennel, and they bark and howl as the men and women walk below them, their chains jangling as they strain to reach the intruders. The breeding of such hybrids is relatively common in this part of the state, a regional peculiarity surprising to strangers. Some of the workers stop and watch, one or two taunting the beasts from the safety of the road, but the wiser ones move on. They know that it is better to let these animals be.

The work commences, accompanied by a chorus of engines and shouts, of picks and shovels breaking the ground, of chain saws tearing at branches and tree trunks; and the smells of diesel fumes and sweat and fresh earth mingle in the air. The sounds drown out the rhythms of the natural world: the wood frogs clearing their throats, the calls of hermit thrushes and winter wrens, the crying of a single loon out on the water.

The day grows short, the sun moving west across the lake. On Jean Beaulieu's land a man removes his yellow hard hat, wipes his brow on his sleeve, and lights a cigarette before making his way back to the bulldozer. He climbs into the cab and slowly starts to reverse, the harsh buzz of the engine adding its guttural notes to the sounds of men and nature. The howling from above begins again, and he shakes his head wearily at the man in the cherry picker nearby.

This ground has lain undisturbed for many years. The grass is wild and long, and the bushes cling tenaciously to the hard earth. There is no reason for the man in the cab to doubt that the bank upon which he stands is solid, until an alien clamor intrudes on the rustling of the evergreens and the sawing of the clearers. The bulldozer makes a high, growling din, like an animal in panic, as huge quantities of earth shift. The howling of the hybrids increases in intensity, some turning in circles or wrenching again at their chains as they register the new sounds.

The roots of a white spruce are exposed as a section of the riverbank collapses, and the tree topples slowly into the water, sending ripples across the still surface of the lake. Beside it, the bulldozer seems to hang suspended for a moment, one track still clinging to the ground, the other poised over empty space, before it tumbles sideways, its operator leaping to safety, falling away from the vehicle as it turns and lands with a loud splash in the shallows. Men drop their tools and start running. They scramble to the new verge, where brown water has already rushed in to exploit the sudden expansion of the banks. Their colleague raises himself, shivering and soaked, from the lake, then grins embarrassedly and raises a hand to let them know that he is okay. The men crowd the bank, looking at the stranded bulldozer. One or two cheer desultorily. To their left, another huge slab of earth crumbles and falls into the water, but they hardly notice, their efforts are so focused on helping their comrade out of the cold water.

But the man in the cherry picker is not looking at the bulldozer, or at the arms reaching out to pull the drenched figure from the water. He stands unmoving, the chain saw in his hands, and looks down on the newly exposed bank. His name is Lyall Dobbs. He has a wife and two children and, at this moment, he desperately wishes that he were with them. He desperately wishes he were anywhere but staring down at the banks of St. Froid, at the darkened bones revealed among the tree roots and broken earth, and the small skull slowly disappearing beneath the cold waters of the lake.

'Billy?' he shouts.

Billy Laughton, the foreman of the clearing crew, turns away from the crowd of men by the shore, shaking his head in bemusement.

'Yeah?'

There is no further word for a moment. Lyall Dobbs's throat is suddenly too dry to produce sound. He swallows, then resumes.

'Billy, we got a cemetery round here?'

Laughton's brow furrows. From his pocket he takes a folded map and examines it briefly. He shakes his head at the other man.

'No,' he replies simply.

Dobbs looks at him, and his face is pale.

'Well, we do now.'

This is a honeycomb world.

You must be careful where you step.

And you must be ready for what you might find.

Chapter One

It was spring, and color had returned to the world.

The distant mountains were transforming, the gray trees now cloaking themselves in new life, their leaves a faded echo of fall's riot. The scarlets of the red maples were dominant, but they were being joined now by the greenish-yellow leaves of the red oaks, the silver of the bigtooth aspens, and the greens of the quaking aspens, the birches, and the beeches. Poplars and willows, elms and hazelnuts were all bursting into full bloom, and the woods were ringing with the noise of returning birds.

I could see the woods from the gym at One City Center, the tips of the evergreens still dominating the landscape amid the slowly transforming seasonals. Rain was falling on the streets of Portland, and umbrellas swarmed on the streets below, glistening darkly like the carapaces of squat black beetles.

For the first time in many months, I felt good. I was in semiregular employment. I was eating well, working out three or four days each week, and Rachel Wolfe was coming up from Boston the next weekend, so I would have someone to admire my improving physique. I hadn't had bad dreams for some time. My dead wife and my lost daughter had not appeared to me since the previous Christmas, when they touched me amid the falling snow and gave me some respite from the visions that had haunted me for so long.

I completed a set of military presses and laid the bar down, sweat dripping from my nose and rising in little wisps of steam from my body. Seated on a bench, sipping some water, I watched the two men enter from the reception area, glance around, then fix on me. They wore conservative dark suits with somber ties. One was large, with brown wavy hair and a thick mustache, like a porn star gone to seed, the bulge of the gun in the cheap rig beneath his jacket visible to me in the mirror behind him. The other was smaller, a tidy, dapper man with receding, prematurely graying hair. The big man held a pair of shades in his hand while his companion wore a pair of gold-rimmed eyeglasses with square frames. He smiled as he approached me.

'Mr. Parker?' he asked, his hands clasped behind his back.

I nodded and the hands disengaged, the right extending toward me in a sharp motion like a shark making its way through familiar waters.

'My name is Quentin Harrold, Mr. Parker,' he said. 'I work for Mr. Jack Mercier.'

I wiped my own right hand on a towel to remove some of the sweat, then accepted the handshake. Harrold's mouth quivered a little as my still-sweaty palm gripped his, but he resisted the temptation to wipe his hand clean on the side of his trousers. I guessed that he didn't want to spoil the crease.

Jack Mercier came from money so old that some of it had jangled on the *Mayflower*. He was a former U.S. senator, as his father and grandfather had been before him, and lived in a big house out on Prouts Neck overlooking the sea. He had interests in timber companies, newspaper publishing, cable television, software, and the Internet. In fact, he had interests in just about anything that might ensure the Merciers' old money was regularly replenished with injections of new money. As a senator he had been something of a liberal and he still supported various ecological and civil rights groups through generous donations. He was a family man; he didn't screw around – as far as anyone knew – and he had emerged from his brief flirtation with politics with his reputation enhanced rather than tarnished, a product as much of his financial independence as of any moral probity. There were rumors that he was planning a return to politics, possibly as an independent candidate for governor, although Mercier himself had yet to confirm them.

Quentin Harrold coughed into his palm, then used it as an excuse to take a handkerchief from his pocket and discreetly wipe his hand. 'Mr. Mercier would like to see you,' he said, in the tone of voice he probably reserved for the pool cleaner and the chauffeur. 'He has some work for you.'

I looked at him. He smiled. I smiled back. We stayed like that, grinning at each other, until the only options were to speak or start dating. Harrold took the first option.

'Perhaps you didn't hear me, Mr. Parker,' he said. 'Mr. Mercier has some work for you.'

'And?'

Harrold's smile floundered. 'I'm not sure what you mean, Mr. Parker.'

'I'm not so desperate for work, Mr. Harrold, that I run and fetch every time somebody throws a stick.' This wasn't entirely true. Portland, Maine, wasn't such a wellspring of vice and corruption that I could afford to look down my nose at too many jobs. If Harrold had been better looking and a different sex, I'd have fetched the stick and then rolled onto my back to have my belly rubbed if I thought it might have earned me more than a couple of bucks.

Harrold glanced at the big guy with the mustache. The big guy shrugged, then went back to staring at me impassively, maybe trying to figure out what my head would look like mounted over his fireplace.

Harrold coughed again. 'I'm sorry,' he said. 'I didn't mean to offend you.' He seemed to have trouble forming the words, as if they were part of someone else's vocabulary and he was just borrowing them for a time. I waited for his nose to start growing or his tongue to turn to ash and fall to the floor, but nothing happened. 'We'd be grateful if you'd spare the time to talk to Mr. Mercier,' he conceded with a wince.

I figured that I'd played hard to get for long enough, although I still wasn't sure that they'd respect me in the morning. 'When I've finished up here, I can probably call out and see him,' I said.

Harrold craned his neck slightly, indicating that he believed he might have misheard me. 'Mr. Mercier was hoping that you could come with us now, Mr. Parker. Mr. Mercier is a very busy man, as I'm sure you'll understand.'

I stood up, stretched, and prepared to do another set of presses. 'Oh, I understand, Mr. Harrold. I'll be as quick as I can. Why don't you gentlemen wait downstairs, and I'll join you when I'm done? You're making me nervous. I might drop a weight on you.'

Harrold shifted on his feet for a moment, then nodded. 'We'll be in the lobby,' he said.

'Enjoy,' I replied, then watched them in the mirror as they walked away.

I took my time finishing my workout, then had a long shower and talked about the future of the Pirates with the guy who was cleaning down the changing room. When I figured that Harrold and the porn star had spent enough time looking at their watches, I took the elevator down to the lobby and waited for them to join me. The expression on Harrold's face, I noticed, was oscillating between annoyance and relief.

Harrold insisted that I accompany him and his companion in their Mercedes, but despite their protests I opted to follow them in my own Mustang. It struck me that I was becoming more wilfully perverse as I settled into my mid-thirties. If Harrold had told me to take my own car, I'd probably have chained myself to the steering column of the Mercedes until they agreed to give me a ride.

The Mustang was a 1969 Boss 302, and replaced the Mach 1 that had been shot to pieces the previous year. The 302 had been sourced for me by Willie Brew, who ran an auto shop down in Queens. The spoilers and wings were kind of over the top, but it made my eyes water when it accelerated, and Willie had sold it to me for $8,000, which was about $3,000 less than a car in its condition was worth. The downside was that I might as well have had ARRESTED ADOLESCENCE painted on the side in big black letters.

I followed the Mercedes south out of Portland and on to U.S.1. At Oak Hill, we turned east and I stayed behind it at a steady thirty all the way to the tip of the Neck. At the Black Point Inn, guests sat at the picture windows, staring out with drinks in their hands at Grand Beach and Pine Point. A Scarborough PD cruiser inched along the road, making sure that everybody stayed under thirty and nobody unwanted hung around long enough to spoil the view.

Jack Mercier had his home on Winslow Homer Road, within sight of the painter's former house. As we approached, an electronically operated barrier opened and a second Mercedes swept toward us from the house, headed for Black Point Road. In the backseat sat a small man with a dark beard and a skullcap on his head. We exchanged a look as the two cars passed each other, and he nodded at me. His face was familiar, I thought, but I couldn't place it. Then the road was clear and we continued on our way.

Mercier's home was a huge white place with landscaped gardens and so many rooms that a search party would have to be organized if anybody got lost on the way to the bathroom. The man with the mustache parked the Mercedes while I followed Harrold through the large double front doors, down the hallway, and into a room to the left of the main stairs. It was a library, furnished with antique couches and chairs. Books stretched to the ceiling on three walls; on the east-facing wall, a window looked out on the grounds and the sea beyond, a desk and chair beside it and a small bar to the right.

Harrold closed the door behind me and left me to

examine the spines on the books and the photographs on the wall. The books ranged from political biographies to historical works, mainly examinations of the Civil War, Korea, and Vietnam. There was no fiction. In one corner was a small, locked cabinet with a glass front. The books it contained were different from those on the open shelves. They had titles like *Myth and History in the Book of Revelation*; *Apocalypse and Millennium in English Romantic Poetry*; *The Book of Revelation: Apocalypse and Empire*; and *The Apocalyptic Sublime*. It was cheerful stuff: bedtime reading for the end of the world. There were also critical biographies of the artists William Blake, Albrecht Dürer, Lucas Cranach the Elder, and Jean Duvet, in addition to facsimile editions of what appeared to be medieval texts. Finally, on the top shelf were twelve almost identical slim volumes, each bound in black leather with six gold bands inset on the spine in three equidistant sets of two. At the base of each spine was the last letter of the Greek alphabet: Ω, for omega. There was no key in the lock, and the doors stayed closed when I gave them an experimental tug.

I turned my attention to the photographs on the walls. There were pictures of Jack Mercier with various Kennedys, Clintons, and even a superannuated Jimmy Carter. Others showed Mercier in an assortment of athletic poses from his youth: winning races, pretending to toss footballs, and being carried aloft on the shoulders of his adoring teammates. There were also testimonials from grateful universities, framed awards from charitable organizations headed by movie stars, and even some medals presented by poor but proud nations. It was like an underachiever's worst nightmare.

One more recent photograph caught my eye. It showed Mercier sitting at a table, flanked on one side by a woman in her sixties wearing a smartly tailored black jacket and a string of pearls around her neck. To Mercier's right was the bearded man who had passed me in the Mercedes, and beside him was a figure I recognized from his appearances on prime-time news shows, usually looking triumphant at the top of some courthouse steps: Warren Ober, of Ober, Thayer & Moss, one of Boston's top law firms. Ober was Mercier's attorney, and even the mention of his name was enough to send most opposition running for the hills. When Ober, Thayer & Moss took a case they brought so many lawyers with them to court that there was barely enough room for the jury. Even judges got nervous around them.

Looking at the photograph, it struck me that nobody in it seemed particularly happy. There was an air of tension about the poses, a sense that some darker business was being conducted and the photographer was an unnecessary distraction. There were thick files on the table before them, and white coffee cups lay discarded like yesterday's roses.

Behind me the door opened and Jack Mercier entered, laying aside on the table a sheaf of papers speckled with bar charts and figures. He was tall, six-two or six-three, with shoulders that spoke of his athletic past and an expensive gold Rolex that indicated his present status as a very wealthy man. His hair was white and thick, swept back from a perma-tanned forehead over large blue eyes, a Roman nose, and a thin, smiling mouth, the teeth white and even. I guessed that he was sixty-five by now, maybe a little older. He wore a blue polo shirt, tan chinos, and brown Sebagos. There was white hair on his arms, and tufts of it peeked out over the collar of his shirt. For a moment the smile on his face faltered as he saw my attention focused on the photograph, but it quickly brightened again as I moved away from it. Meanwhile, Harrold stood at the door like a nervous matchmaker.

'Mr. Parker,' said Mercier, shaking my hand with enough force to dislodge my fillings. 'I appreciate you taking the time to see me.' He waved me to a chair. From the hallway, an olive-skinned man in a white tunic appeared with a silver tray and set it down. Two china cups, a silver coffeepot, and a matching silver creamer and sugar bowl jangled softly as the tray hit the table. The tray looked heavy, and the servant seemed kind of relieved to be rid of it.

'Thank you,' said Mercier. We watched as he left, Harrold behind him. Harrold gently closed the door, giving me one last pained look before he departed, then Mercier and I were alone.

'I know a lot about you, Mr. Parker,' he began as he poured the coffee and offered me cream and sugar. He had an easy, unaffected manner, designed to put even the most fleeting of acquaintances at ease. It was so unaffected that he must have spent years perfecting it.

'Likewise,' I replied.

He frowned good-naturedly. 'I don't imagine you're old enough to have ever voted for me.'

'No, you retired before it became an issue.'

'Did your grandfather vote for me?'

My grandfather Bob Warren had been a Cumberland County sheriff's deputy and had lived in Scarborough all his life. My mother and I had come to stay with him after my father died. In the end, he outlived his own wife and daughter, and I had buried him one autumn day after his great heart failed him at last.

'I don't believe he ever voted for anyone, Mr. Mercier,' I said. 'My grandfather had a natural distrust of politicians.' The only politician for whom my grandfather ever had any regard was President Zachary Taylor, who never voted in an election and didn't even vote for himself.

Jack Mercier grinned his big white grin again. 'He might have been right. Most of them have sold their souls ten times over before they're even elected. Once it's sold, you can never buy it back. You just have to hope that you got the best price for it.'

'And are you in the business of buying souls, Mr. Mercier, or selling them?'

The grin stayed fixed, but the eyes narrowed. 'I take care of my own soul, Mr. Parker, and let other people do as they wish with theirs.'

Our special moment was broken by the entrance of a woman into the room. She wore a deceptively casual outfit of black pants and a black cashmere sweater, and a thin gold necklace gleamed dully against the dark wool. She was about forty-five, maybe a little older. Her hair was blond, fading to gray in places, and there was a hardness to her features that made her seem less beautiful than she probably thought she was.

This was Mercier's wife, Deborah, who had some kind of permanent residency in the local society pages. She was a Southern belle, from what I could recall, a graduate of the Madeira School for Girls in Virginia. The Madeira's principal claim to fame, apart from producing eligible young women who always used the correct spoon and never spat on the sidewalk, was that its former headmistress Jean Harris had shot dead her lover, Dr. Herman Tarnower, in 1980, after he left her for a younger woman. Dr. Tarnower was best known as the author of *The Scarsdale Diet*, so his death seemed to provide conclusive evidence that diets could be bad for your health. Jack Mercier had met his future wife at the Swan Ball in Nashville, the most lavish social occasion in the South, and had introduced himself to her by buying her a '55 Coupe de Ville with his AmEx card at the postdinner auction. It was, as someone later commented, love at first swipe.

Mrs. Mercier held a magazine in her hand and assumed a look of surprise, but the expression didn't reach her eyes.

'I'm sorry, Jack. I didn't know you had company.' She was lying, and I could see in Mercier's face that he knew she was lying, that we both knew. He tried to hide his annoyance behind the trademark smile but I could hear his teeth gritting. He rose, and I rose with him.

'Mr. Parker, this is my wife, Deborah.'

Mrs. Mercier took one step toward me, then waited for me to cross the rest of the floor before extending her hand. It hung limply in my palm as I gripped it, and her eyes bored holes in my face while her teeth gnawed at my skull. Her hostility was so blatant it was almost funny.

'I'm pleased to meet you,' she spat, before turning her glare on her husband. 'I'll talk to you later, Jack,' she said, and made it sound like a threat. She didn't look back as she closed the door.

The temperature in the room immediately rose a few degrees, and Mercier regained his composure. 'My apologies, Mr. Parker. Tensions in the house are a little high. My daughter Samantha is to be married early next month.'

'Really. Who's the lucky man?' It seemed polite to ask.

'Robert Ober. He's the son of my attorney.'

'At least your wife will get to buy a new hat.'

'She's buying a great deal more than a hat, Mr. Parker, and she is currently occupied by the arrangements for our guests. Warren and I may have to take to my yacht to escape the demands of our respective wives, although they are such excellent sailors themselves that I imagine they will insist upon keeping us company. Do you sail, Mr. Parker?'

'With difficulty. I don't have a yacht.'

'Everybody should have a yacht,' remarked Mercier, his good humor returning in earnest.

'Why, you're practically a socialist, Mr. Mercier.'

He laughed softly, then put his coffee cup down and arranged his features into a sincere expression. 'I hope you'll forgive me for prying into your background, but I wanted to find out about you before I requested your help,' he continued.

I acknowledged his comments with a nod. 'In your position, I'd probably do the same,' I said.

He leaned forward and said gently: 'I'm sorry about your family. It was a terrible thing that happened to them, and to you.'

My wife, Susan, and my daughter, Jennifer, had been taken from me by a killer known as the Traveling Man while I was still a policeman in New York. He had killed a lot of other people too, until he was stopped. When I killed him, a part of me had died with him.

Over two years had passed since then, and for much of

that time the deaths of Susan and Jennifer had defined me. I had allowed that to be so until I realized that pain and hurt, guilt and regret, were tearing me apart. Now, slowly, I was getting my life back together in Maine, back in the place where I had spent my teens and part of my twenties, back in the house I had shared with my mother and my grandfather, in which I now lived alone. I had a woman who cared for me, who made me feel that it was worth trying to rebuild my life with her beside me and that maybe the time to begin the process had now arrived.

'I can't imagine what such a thing must be like,' continued Mercier. 'But I know someone who probably can, which is why I've asked you here today.'

Outside, the rain had stopped and the clouds had parted. Behind Mercier's head, the sun shone brightly through the window, bathing the desk and chair in its glow and replicating the shape of the glasswork on the carpet below. I watched as a bug crawled across the patch of bright light, its tiny feelers testing the air as it went.

'His name is Curtis Peltier, Mr. Parker,' said Mercier. 'He used to be my business partner, a long time ago, until he asked me to buy him out and followed his own path. Things didn't work out so well for him; he made some bad investments, I'm afraid. Ten days ago his daughter was found dead in her car. Her name was Grace Peltier. You may have read about her. In fact, I understand you may have known her once upon a time.'

I nodded. Yes, I thought, I knew Grace once upon a time, when we were both much younger and thought that we might, for an instant, even be in love. It was a fleeting thing, lasting no more than a couple of months after my high school graduation, one of any number of similar summer romances that curled up and died like a leaf as soon as autumn came. Grace was pretty and dark, with very blue eyes, a tiny mouth, and skin the color of honey. She was strong – a medal-winning swimmer – and formidably intelligent, which meant that despite her looks, a great many young men shied away from her. I wasn't as smart as Grace but I was smart enough to appreciate something beautiful when it appeared before me. At least I thought I was. In the end, I didn't appreciate it, or her, at all.

I remembered Grace mostly because of one morning spent at Higgins Beach, not far from where I now sat with Jack Mercier. We stood beneath the shadow of the old guest house known as the Breakers, the wind tossing Grace's hair and the sea crashing before us. She had missed her period, she told me over the phone: five days late, and she was never late. As I drove down to Higgins Beach to meet her, my stomach felt like it was slowly being crushed in a vise. When a fleet of trucks passed by at the Oak Hill intersection, I briefly considered flooring the accelerator and ending it all. I knew then that whatever I felt for Grace Peltier, it wasn't love. She must have seen it in my face that morning as we sat in silence listening to the sound of the sea. When her period arrived two days later, after an agonizing wait for both of us, she told me that she didn't think we should see each other anymore, and I was happy to let her go. It wasn't one of my finer moments, I thought, not by a long shot. Since then, we hadn't stayed in touch. I had seen her once or twice, nodding to her in bars or restaurants, but we had never really spoken. Each time I saw her I was reminded of that meeting at Higgins Beach and of my own callow youth.

I tried to recall what I had heard about her death. Grace, now a graduate student at Northeastern in Boston, had died from a single gunshot wound in a side road off U.S. 1, up by Ellsworth. Her body had been discovered slumped in the driver's seat of her car, the gun still in her hand. Suicide: the ultimate form of self-defense. She had been Curtis Peltier's only child. The story had merited more coverage than usual only because of Peltier's former connections to Jack Mercier. I hadn't attended the funeral.

'According to the newspaper reports, the police aren't looking for anyone in connection with her death, Mr.

Mercier,' I said. 'They seem to think Grace committed suicide.'

He shook his head. 'Curtis doesn't believe that Grace's wound was self-inflicted.'

'It's a common enough reaction,' I replied. 'Nobody wants to accept that someone close might have taken his or her own life. Too much blame accrues to those left behind for it to be accommodated so easily.'

Mercier stood, and his large frame blocked out the sunlight. I couldn't see the bug anymore. I wondered how it had reacted when the light disappeared. I guessed that it had probably taken it in stride, which is one of the burdens of being a bug: you pretty much have to take everything in stride, until something bigger stamps on you or eats you and the matter becomes immaterial.

'Grace was a strong, smart girl with her whole life ahead of her. She didn't own a gun of any kind and the police don't seem to have any idea where she might have acquired the one found in her hand.'

'Assuming that she killed herself,' I added.

'Assuming that, yes.'

'Which you, in common with Mr. Peltier, don't.'

He sighed. 'I agree with Curtis. Despite the views of the police, I think somebody killed Grace. I'd like you to look into this matter on his behalf.'

'Did Curtis Peltier approach you about this, Mr. Mercier?'

Jack Mercier's gaze shifted. When he looked at me again, something had cloaked itself in the darkness of his pupils.

'He came to visit me a few days ago. We discussed it, and he told me what he believed. He doesn't have enough money to pay for a private investigator, Mr. Parker, but thankfully, I do. I don't think Curtis will have any difficulty in talking this over with you, or allowing you to look into it further. I will be paying your bill, but officially you will be working for Curtis. I would ask you to keep my name out of this affair.'

I finished my coffee and laid the cup down on the saucer. I didn't speak until I had marshaled my thoughts a little.

'Mr. Mercier, I didn't mind coming out here but I don't do that kind of work anymore.'

Mercier's brow furrowed. 'But you *are* a private investigator?'

'Yes sir, I am, but I've made a decision to deal only with certain matters: white-collar crime, corporate intelligence. I don't take on cases involving death or violence.'

'Do you carry a gun?'

'No. Loud noises scare me.'

'But you used to carry a gun?'

'That's right, I used to. Now, if I want to disarm a white-collar criminal, I just take away his pen.'

'As I told you, Mr. Parker, I know a great deal about you. Investigating fraud and petty theft doesn't appear to be your style. In the past you have involved yourself in more . . . *colorful* matters.'

'Those kinds of investigations cost me too much.'

'I'll cover any costs you may incur, and more than adequately.'

'I don't mean financial cost, Mr. Mercier.'

He nodded to himself, as if he suddenly understood. 'You're talking moral, physical cost, maybe? I understand you were injured in the course of some of your work.'

I didn't reply. I'd been hurt, and in response I had acted violently, destroying a little of myself each time I did so, but that wasn't the worst of it. It seemed to me that as soon as I became involved in such matters, they caused a fissure in my world. I saw things: lost things, dead things. It was as if my intervention drew them to me, those who had been wrenched painfully, violently from this life. Once I had thought it was a product of my own incipient guilt, or an empathy I felt that passed beyond feeling and into hallucination.

But now I believed that they really did know, and they really did come.

Jack Mercier leaned against his desk, opened his drawer, and drew a black, leather-bound folder from within. He wrote for a few seconds, then tore the check from the folder.

'This is a check for ten thousand dollars, Mr. Parker. All I want you to do is talk to Curtis. If you think that there's nothing you can do for him, then the money is yours to keep and there'll be no hard feelings between us. If you do agree to look into this matter, we can negotiate further remuneration.'

I shook my head. 'Once again, it's not the money, Mr. Mercier—,' I began.

He raised a hand to stop me. 'I know that. I didn't mean to offend you.'

'No offense taken.'

'I have friends in the police force, in Scarborough and Portland and farther afield. Those friends tell me that you are a very fine investigator, with very particular talents. I want you to utilize those talents to find out what really happened to Grace, for my sake and for that of Curtis.'

I noticed that he had placed himself above Grace's father in his appeal, and once again I was conscious of a disparity between what he was telling me and what he knew. I thought too of his wife's unveiled hostility, my sense that she had known exactly who I was and why I was in her house, and that she bitterly resented my presence there. Mercier proffered the check, and in his eyes I saw something that I couldn't quite identify: grief maybe, or even guilt.

'Please, Mr. Parker,' he said. 'Talk to him. I mean, what harm can it do?'

What harm can it do? Those words would come back to haunt me again and again in the days that followed. They came back to haunt Jack Mercier as well. I wonder if he thought of them in his final moments as the shadows drew around him, and those he loved were drowned in redness.

Despite my misgivings I took the check. And in that instant, unbeknownst to us both, a circuit was completed, sending a charge through the world around and beneath us.

Far away, something broke from its hiding place beneath the dead layers of the honeycomb. It tested the air, probing for the disturbance that had roused it, until it found the source.

Then, with a lurch, it began to move.

The Search for Sanctuary: Religious Fervor in the State of Maine and the Disappearance of the Aroostook Baptists

Extract from the postgraduate thesis of Grace Peltier, submitted posthumously in accordance with the requirements of the Masters Sociology Program, Northeastern University

To understand the reasons for the formation and subsequent disintegration of the religious group known as the Aroostook Baptists, it is important to first understand the history of the state of Maine. To comprehend why four families of well-intentioned and not unintelligent people should have followed an individual such as the Reverend Faulkner into the wilderness, never to be seen again, one must recognize that for almost three centuries, men such as Faulkner have gathered followers to them in this state, often in the face of challenges from larger churches and more orthodox religious movements. It may be said, therefore, that there is something in the character of the state's inhabitants, some streak of individualism dating back to pioneer times, that has led them to be attracted to preachers like the Reverend Faulkner.

For much of its history, Maine was a frontier state. In fact, from the time when the first Jesuit missionaries arrived, in the seventeenth century, to the mid part of the twentieth century, religious groups regarded Maine as mission territory. It provided fertile, if not always profitable, ground for itinerant preachers, unorthodox religious movements, and even charlatans for the best part of three hundred years. The rural economy did not allow for the maintenance of permanent churches and clergymen, and religious observance was oftentimes a low priority for families who were undernourished, insufficiently clothed, and lacking proper shelter.

In 1790, General Benjamin Lincoln observed that few of those in Maine had been properly baptized, and there were some who had never taken Communion. The Reverend John Murray of Boothbay wrote, in 1763, of the inhabitants' 'inveterate habits of vice and no remorse' and thanked God that he had found 'one prayerful family, and a humble professor at the head of it'. It is interesting to note that the Reverend Faulkner was given to quoting this passage of Murray's in the course of his own sermons to his congregations.

Itinerant preachers ministered to those who lacked their own churches. Some were outstanding, frequently having trained at York or Harvard. Others were less praiseworthy. The Reverend Mr. Jotham Sewall of Chesterville, Maine, is reported to have preached 12,593 sermons in 413 settlements, mostly in Maine, between 1783 and 1849. By contrast, the Reverend Martin Schaeffer of Broad Bay, a Lutheran, comprehensively cheated his flock before eventually being run out of town.

Orthodox preachers found it difficult to achieve a foothold in the state, Calvinists being particularly unwelcome as much for their unyielding doctrines as for their associations with the forces of government. Baptists and Methodists, with their concepts of egalitarianism and equality, found more willing converts. In the thirty years between 1790 and 1820, the number of Baptist churches in the state rose from seventeen to sixty. They were joined, in time, by Free Will Baptists, Free Baptists, Methodists, Congregationalists, Unitarians, Universalists, Shakers, Millerites, Spiritualists, Sandfordites, Holy Rollers, Higginsites, Free Thinkers, and Black Stockings.

Yet the tradition of Schaeffer and other charlatans still remained: in 1816, the 'delusion' of Cochranism grew up around the charismatic Cochrane in the west of the state, ending with charges of gross lewdness being leveled at its founder. In the 1860s, the Reverend Mr. George L. Adams persuaded his followers to sell their homes, stores, even their fishing gear, and to pass the money on to him to help found a colony in Palestine. Sixteen people died in the first weeks of the Jaffa colony's foundation in 1866. In 1867, amid charges of excessive drinking and misappropriation of funds, Adams and his wife fled the short-lived Jaffa colony, Adams later reemerging in California, where he tried to persuade people to invest money in a five cent savings bank until his secretary exposed his past.

Finally, at the turn of this century, the evangelist Frank Weston Sandford founded the Shiloh community in Durham. Sandford is worthy of particular attention because the Shiloh community clearly provided a model for what the Reverend Faulkner attempted to achieve more than half a century later.

Sandford's cultlike sect raised huge sums of money for building projects and overseas missions, sending sailing vessels filled with missionaries to remote areas of the planet. His followers were persuaded to sell their homes and move to the Shiloh settlement at Durham, only thirty miles from Portland. Scores of them later died there from malnutrition and disease. It is a testament to the magnetism of Sandford, a native of Bowdoinham, Maine, and a graduate of the divinity school at Bates College, Lewiston, that they were willing to follow him and to die for him.

Sandford was only thirty-four when the Shiloh settlement was officially dedicated, on October 2, 1896, a date apparently dictated to Sandford by God himself. Within the space of a few years, and funded largely by donations and the sale of his followers' property, there were over $200,000 worth of buildings on the land. The main building, Shiloh itself, had 520 rooms and was a quarter of a mile in circumference.

But Sandford's increasing megalomania – he claimed that God had proclaimed him the second Elijah – and his insistence on absolute obedience began to cause friction. A harsh winter in 1902-3 caused food supplies to shrink, and the community was swept by smallpox. People began to die. In 1904 Sandford was arrested and charged on five counts of cruelty to children and one charge of manslaughter as a result of that winter's depredations. A guilty verdict was later overturned on appeal.

In 1906 Sandford sailed for the Holy Land, taking with him a hundred of the faithful in two vessels, the *Kingdom* and the *Coronet*. They spent the next five years at sea, sailing to Africa and South America, although their conversion technique was somewhat unorthodox: the two ships cruised the coast while Sandford's followers prayed continuously for God to bring the natives to him. Actual contact with potential converts was virtually nil.

The *Kingdom* was eventually wrecked off the west coast of Africa, and when Sandford tried to force the crew of the *Coronet* to sail on to Greenland, they mutinied, forcing him to return to Maine. In 1911 Sandford was sentenced to jail for ten years on charges of manslaughter arising from the deaths of six crewmen. Released in 1918, he set up home in Boston and allowed subordinates to take care of the day-to-day running of Shiloh.

In 1920, after hearing testimony of the terrible conditions being endured by the children of the community, a judge ordered their removal. Shiloh disintegrated, its membership falling from four hundred to one hundred in an incident that became known as the Scattering. Sandford announced his retirement in May 1920 and retreated to a farm in upstate New York, from which he attempted, unsuccessfully, to rebuild the community. He died, aged eighty-five, in 1948. The Shiloh community still exists today, although in a very different form from its original inception, and Sandford is still honored as its founder.

It is known that Faulkner regarded Sandford as a particular inspiration: Sandford had shown that it was possible to build an independent religious community using donations and the sale of the assets of true believers. It is therefore both ironic and strangely apt that Faulkner's attempt at establishing his own religious utopia, close to the small town of Eagle Lake, should have ended in bitterness and acrimony, near starvation and despair, and finally the disappearance of twenty people, among them Faulkner himself.

Chapter Two

The next morning I sat in my kitchen shortly after sunrise, a pot of coffee and the remains of some dry toast lying beside my PowerBook on the table. I had a report to make to a client that day, so I put Jack Mercier to the back of my mind. Outside, rainwater dripped from the beech tree that grew by my kitchen window, beating an irregular cadence on the damp earth below. There were still one or two dry, brown leaves clinging to the tree's branches but they were now surrounded by green buds, old life preparing to make way for the new. A nuthatch puffed out its red breast and sang from its nest of twigs. I couldn't see its mate, but I guessed that he was close. There would be eggs laid in the nest before the end of May and soon a whole family would be waking me in the mornings.

By the time the main news commenced on WPXT, the local Fox affiliate, I had finished a pretty satisfactory draft and ejected the disk so that I could print from my desktop. The news led with the latest report on the remains unearthed at St. Froid Lake the day before. Dr. Claire Gray, the state's newly appointed ME, was shown arriving at the scene, wearing fireman's boots and a set of overalls. Her dark hair was long and curly, and her face betrayed no emotion as she walked down to the lakeshore.

Sandbag levees had already been built to hold back the waters, and the bones now rested in a layer of thick mud and rotting vegetation, over which a tarpaulin had been stretched to protect them from the elements. A preliminary examination had been conducted by one of the state's two hundred part-time MEs, who confirmed that the remains were human, and the state police had then e-mailed digital images of the scene to the ME's office in Augusta so that she and her staff would be familiar with the terrain and the task they faced. They had already alerted the forensic anthropologist based at the University of Maine at Orono: she was due to travel up to Eagle Lake later that day.

According to the reporter, the danger of further weakening the bank and the possibility of damaging the remains had ruled out the use of a backhoe to uncover the bodies and it was now likely that the task would have to be completed entirely by hand, using shovels and then small Marshalltown trowels in a painstaking, inch-by-inch dig. As the reporter spoke, the howling of the wolf hybrids was clearly audible from the slopes above her. Maybe it had to do with the sound from the live broadcast, but the howls seemed to have a terrible, keening tone to them, as if the animals somehow understood what had been found on their territory. The howling increased in intensity as a car pulled up at the edge of the secured area and the deputy chief ME, known to one and all as Dr. Bill, climbed out to talk to the trooper. In the back of his car sat his two cadaver dogs: it was their presence that had set off the hybrids.

A mobile crime scene unit from the state police barracks at Houlton stood behind the reporter, and members of CID III, the Criminal Investigation Division of the state police with responsibility for Aroostook, mingled with state troopers and sheriff's deputies in the background. The reporter had obviously been talking to the right people. She was able to confirm that the bodies had been underground for some time, that there were children's bones among them, and there was damage to some of the visible skulls consistent with the kind of low-velocity impact caused by a blunt instrument. The transportation of the first of the bodies to the morgue in Augusta would probably not begin for another day or two; there they would be cleaned with scalpels and a mix of heated water and detergents, then laid out on metal trays beneath a fume hood to dry them for analysis. It would then be up to the forensic anthropologist to rearticulate the bodies as best she could.

But it was the reporter's concluding comment that was particularly interesting. She said that detectives believed they had made a preliminary identification of at least three of the bodies, although they declined to give any further details. That meant they had found something at the scene, something they had chosen to keep to themselves. The discovery aroused my curiosity – mine and a million other people's – but no more than that. I did not envy the investigators who would have to wade through the mud of St. Froid in order to remove those bones with their gloved hands, fighting off the early blackflies and trying to blank out the howls of the hybrids.

When the report ended, I printed off my own work and then drove to the offices of PanTech Systems to deliver my findings. PanTech operated out of a three-story smoked-glass office in Westbrook and specialized in making security systems for the networks of financial institutions. Their latest innovation involved some kind of complex algorithm that made the eyes of anyone with an IQ of less than 200 glaze over with incomprehension but was reckoned by the company to be a pretty surefire thing. Unfortunately, Errol Hoyt, the mathematician who understood the algorithm best and who had been involved in its development from the start, had decided that PanTech didn't value him enough and was now trying to sell his services, and the algorithm, to a rival company from behind the backs of his current employers. The fact that he was also screwing his contact at the rival firm – a woman named Stacey Kean, who had the kind of body that caused highway pileups after Sunday services – made the whole business slightly more complicated.

I had monitored Hoyt's cell phone transmissions using a Cellmate cellular radio monitoring system, aided by a cellular gain antenna. The Cellmate came in a neat brushed-aluminum case containing a modified Panasonic phone, a DTMF decoder, and a Marantz recorder. I simply had to enter the number of Hoyt's cellular and the Cellmate did the rest. By monitoring his calls, I had traced Hoyt and Kean to a rendezvous at the Days Inn out on Maine Mall Road. I waited in the parking lot, got photos of both of them entering the same room, then checked into the room on their right and removed the Penetrator II surveillance unit from my leather bag. The Penetrator II sounded like some kind of sexual aid but was simply a specially designed transducer that attached to the wall and picked up vibrations, converting them into electrical impulses that were then amplified and became recognizable audio. Most of the audio was recognizable only as grunts and groans, but when they'd finished the pleasure part they got down to business, and Hoyt provided enough incriminating detail of what he was offering, and the how and when of its transfer, to enable PanTech to fire him without incurring a major damages suit for unlawful dismissal. Admittedly, it was a kind of sordid way to earn a few bucks, but it had been painless and relatively easy. Now it was simply a matter of presenting the evidence to PanTech and collecting my check.

I sat in a conference room on one side of an oval glass table while the three men across from me examined the photographs, then listened to Hoyt's telephone conversations and the recording of his romantic interlude with the lovely Stacey. One of the men was Roger Axton, PanTech's vice president. The second was Philip Voight, head of corporate security. The third man had introduced himself as Marvin Gross, the personnel director. He was short and reedily built, with a small belly that protruded over the belt of his pants and made him look like he was suffering from malnutrition. It was Gross, I noticed, who held the checkbook.

Eventually, Axton reached across with a plump finger and killed the tape. He exchanged a look with Voight, then stood.

'That all seems to be in order, Mr. Parker. Thank you for your time and efforts. Mr. Gross will deal with the matter of payment.'

I noticed that he didn't shake my hand but simply departed from the room with a swish of silk like a wealthy dowager. I guessed that if I'd just listened to the sounds of two strangers having sex, I wouldn't want to shake hands with the guy who'd made the tape either. Instead, I sat in silence while Gross's pen made a scratching noise on the checkbook. When he had finished, he blew softly on the ink and carefully tore away the check. He didn't hand it over immediately but looked at it for a time before peering out from under his brow and asking:

'Do you like your work, Mr. Parker?'

'Sometimes,' I replied.

'It seems to me,' Gross continued languidly, 'that it's somewhat . . . *sleazy*.'

'Sometimes,' I repeated, neutrally. 'But usually that's not the nature of the work, but the nature of some of the people involved.'

'You're referring to Mr. Hoyt?'

'Mr. Hoyt had sex in the afternoon with a woman. Neither of them is married. What they did wasn't sleazy, or at least it was no sleazier than a hundred other things most people do every day. Your company paid me to listen in on them, and that's where the sleaze part came in.'

Gross's smile didn't waver. He held the check up between his fingers as if he was expecting me to beg for it. Beside him, I saw Voight look down at his feet in embarrassment.

'I'm not sure that we are entirely to blame for the manner in which you conducted your task, Mr. Parker,' said Gross. 'That was your own choice.'

I felt my fist tighten, partly out of my rising anger at

Gross but also because I knew that he had a point. Sitting in that room, watching those three besuited men listening to the sounds of a couple's lovemaking, I had felt ashamed at them, and at myself. Gross was right: this was dirty work, marginally better than repos, and the money didn't make up for the filthy sheen it left on the clothes, on the skin, and on the soul.

I sat in silence, my eyes on him, until he stood and gathered up the material relating to Hoyt, returning it to the black plastic folder in which I had brought it. Voight stood too, but I remained seated. Gross took one more look at the check, then dropped it on the table in front of me before leaving the room.

'Enjoy your money, Mr. Parker,' he concluded. 'I believe you've earned it.'

Voight gave me a pained look, then shrugged and followed Gross. 'I'll wait for you outside,' he said.

I nodded and began replacing my own notes in my bag. When I was done, I picked up the check, examined the amount, then folded it and put it in the small zipped compartment at the back of my wallet. PanTech had paid me a bonus of 20 percent. For some reason, it made me feel even dirtier than before.

Voight walked me to the lobby, then made a point of shaking my hand and thanking me before I left the building. I walked through the parking lot, past the lines of reserved spaces with the names of their owners marked on small tin plates nailed to the parking lot's surrounding wall. Marvin Gross's car, a red Impala, occupied space number 20. I removed my keys from my pocket and flicked open the little knife I kept on the key chain. I knelt down beside his left rear tire and placed the tip of the blade against it, ready to slash the rubber. I stayed like that for maybe thirty seconds, then stood and closed the knife, leaving the tire undamaged. There was a tiny indentation where the blade had touched it, but nothing more.

As Gross had intimated, following couples to motel

rooms was the poor cousin of divorce work, but it paid the bills and the risks were minimal. In the past I had taken on jobs out of a sense of charity, but I quickly realized that if I kept doing things for charity, then pretty soon charities would be doing things for me. Now Jack Mercier was offering me good money to look into Grace Peltier's death, but something told me that the money would be hard earned. I had seen it in Mercier's eyes.

I drove into the center of Portland and parked in the garage at Cumberland and Preble, then headed into the Portland Public Market. The Port City Jazz Band were playing in one corner and the smells of baking and spices mingled in the air. I bought some skim milk from Smiling Hill Farm and venison from Bayley Hill, then added fresh vegetables and a loaf of bread from the Big Sky Bread Company. I sat for a time by the fireplace, watching the people go by and listening to the music. Rachel and I would come here next weekend, I thought, browsing among the stalls, holding hands, and the scent of her would linger on my fingers and palms for the rest of the day.

With the arrival of the lunchtime crowds I headed back toward Congress, then cut down Exchange Street toward Java Joe's in the Old Port. As I reached the junction of Exchange and Middle, I saw a small boy seated on the ground at Tommy's Park on the opposite side of the street. He was wearing only a check shirt and short pants, despite the fact that it was a cool day. A woman leaned over him, obviously talking to him, and he stared up at her intently. Like the boy, the woman was dressed for very different weather. She wore a pale summer dress decorated with small pink flowers, the sunlight shining through the material to reveal the shape of her legs, and her blond hair was tied back with an aquamarine bow. I couldn't see her face, but something tightened in my stomach as I drew nearer.

Susan had worn just such a dress, and had tied her blond hair back with an aquamarine bow. The memory made me stop short as the woman straightened and began to walk away from the boy in the direction of Spring Street. As she walked, the boy looked up at me and I saw that he was wearing old black-rimmed eyeglasses, one lens of which was obscured by black masking tape. Through the other, clear lens his single visible eye stared unblinkingly at me. Around his neck hung a wooden board of some sort, held in place by a length of thick rope. There was something carved into the wood, but it was too faint to see from where I stood. I smiled at him and he smiled back as I stepped from the sidewalk and straight into the path of a delivery truck. The driver slammed on the brakes and blew his horn, and I was forced to jump back quickly as the truck shot past. By the time the driver had finished giving me the finger and proceeded on his way, both the woman and the boy were gone. I could find no trace of them on Spring Street, or Middle, or Exchange. Despite that, I could not shake off the sense that they were near and they were watching.

It was almost four o'clock when I returned to the Scarborough house, after depositing my check at the bank and completing various errands. I padded around in my bare feet as some Jim White played on my stereo. It was 'Still Waters' and Jim was singing about how there were projects for the dead and projects for the living, but sometimes he got confused by that distinction. On the kitchen table lay Jack Mercier's check, and once again that unease returned. There was something about the way he looked at me when he offered me the money in return for talking to Curtis Peltier. The more I thought about it, the more I believed that Mercier was paying for my services out of guilt.

I wondered too what Curtis Peltier might have on Mercier that would cause him to hire an investigator to look into the death of a girl he barely knew. There were a lot of people who said that the collapse of their business partnership had been an acrimonious one, bringing to an end not only a long-established professional association but also more than a decade of friendship. If Peltier was looking for help, Jack Mercier seemed to me to be a curious choice.

But I couldn't refuse the job either, I thought, because I, too, felt a nagging sense of guilt over Grace Peltier, as if I somehow owed her at least the time it would take to talk to her father. Maybe it was the remains of what I had felt for her years before and the way I had reacted when she believed herself to be in trouble. True, I was young then, but she was younger still. I recalled her short dark hair, her questioning blue eyes, and even now, the smell of her, like freshly cut flowers.

Sometimes life is lived in retrospect. I sat at the kitchen table and looked at Jack Mercier's check for a long time. Finally, still undecided, I folded it and placed it on the table beneath a vase of lilies I had bought on impulse as I was leaving the market. I cooked myself a dinner of chicken with chilis and ginger and watched TV while I ate, but I barely took in a fraction of what I was seeing. When I had finished, and the dishes were washed and dried, I called the number Jack Mercier had given to me the day before. A maid answered on the third ring, and Mercier was on the line seconds later.

'It's Charlie Parker, Mr. Mercier. I've decided. I'll look into that matter.'

I heard a sigh on the other end of the phone. It might have been relief. It might also have been resignation.

'Thank you, Mr. Parker,' was all he said.

Maybe Marvin Gross had done me a favor by calling me a sleazebag, I thought.

Maybe.

That night, as I lay in bed thinking of the small boy with the darkened lens and the blond-haired woman who had stood over him, the scent of the flowers in the kitchen seemed to fill the house, becoming almost oppressive. I smelled them on my pillow and on the sheets. When I rubbed my fingers together, I seemed to feel grains of pollen like salt on my skin. Yet when I awoke the next morning the flowers were already dead.

And I could not understand why.

The day of my first meeting with Curtis Peltier dawned clear and bright. I heard cars moving by my house on Spring Street, cutting from Oak Hill to Maine Mall Road, a brief oasis of calm between U.S. 1 and I-95. The nuthatch was back and the breeze created waves in the fir trees at the edge of my property, testing the resilience of the newly extended needles.

My grandfather had refused to sell any of his land when the developers came to Scarborough looking for sites for new homes in the late seventies and early eighties, which meant that the house was still surrounded by forest until the trees ended at the interstate. Unfortunately, what remained of my semirural idyll was about to come to an end. The U.S. Postal Service was planning to build a huge mail processing center off nearby Mussey Road, on land including the Grondin Quarry and the Neilson Farm parcels. It would be nine acres in size, and over a hundred trucks a day would eventually be entering and leaving the site; in addition there would be air traffic from a proposed air freight facility. It was good for the town but bad for me. For the first time, I had begun to consider selling my grandfather's house.

I sat on my porch, sipping coffee and watching lapwings flit, and thought of the old man. He had been dead for almost six years now, and I missed his calm, his love of people, and his quiet concern for the vulnerable and the underprivileged. It had brought him into the law enforcement community and had just as surely forced him out of it again, when his empathy for the victims became too much for him to bear.

A second check for $10,000 had been delivered to my house during the night, but despite my promise to Mercier I was still uneasy. I felt for Curtis Peltier, I truly did, but what he wanted I didn't think I could give him; he wanted his daughter back, the way she used to be, so that he could hold her to him forever. His memory of her had been tainted by the manner of her death, and he wanted that stain removed.

I thought too of the woman on Exchange.

Who wears a summer dress on a cold day? When the answer came to me, I pushed it away as a thing unwanted.

Who wears a summer dress on a cold day?

Someone who doesn't feel the cold.

Someone who *can't* feel the cold.

I finished my coffee and caught up on some paperwork at my desk, but Curtis Peltier and his dead daughter kept intruding on my thoughts, along with the small boy and the blond woman. In the end it all came to weights on a scale: my own inconvenience measured against Curtis Peltier's pain.

I picked up my car keys and drove into Portland.

Peltier lived in a big brownstone on Danforth Street, close by the beautiful Italianate Victoria Mansion, which his home resembled in miniature. I guessed that he had bought it when times were good, and now it was probably all that he had left. This area of Portland, encompassing parts of Danforth, Pine, Congress, and Spring Streets, was where prosperous citizens made their homes in the nineteenth century. It was natural, I supposed, that Peltier should have gravitated toward it when he became a wealthy man.

The house looked impressive from the outside, but the gardens were overgrown and the paint was peeling from the door and window frames. I had never been inside the house with Grace. From what I understood, her relationship with her father floundered during her teens and she kept her home life separate from all other aspects of her existence. Her father doted on her but she appeared reluctant to reciprocate, as if she found his affection for her almost suffocating. Grace was always extraordinarily strong willed, with a determination and inner strength that sometimes led her to behave in ways that were hurtful to those around her, even if she had not intended to cause them pain. When she decided to ostracize her father, then ostracized he became. Later I learned from mutual friends that Grace had gradually overcome her resentment and that the two had become much closer in the years before her death, but the reason for the earlier distance between them remained unclear.

I rang the bell and heard it echo through the big house. A shape appeared at the frosted glass and an old man opened the door, his shoulders too small for his big red shirt and a pair of black suspenders holding his tan trousers up over his thin hips. There was a gap between his trousers and his waist. It made him look like a small, sad clown.

'Mr. Peltier?' I asked.

He nodded in reply. I showed him my ID. 'My name is Charlie Parker. Jack Mercier said you might be expecting me.'

Curtis Peltier's face brightened a little and he stood aside to let me in, while tidying his hair and straightening his shirt collar with his free hand. The house smelled musty. There was a thin layer of dust over some of the furniture in the hall and in the dining room to the left. The furnishings looked good but not that good, as if the best items had already been sold and what remained was used only to fill up what would otherwise have been vacant space. I followed him into a small, bright kitchen, with old magazines scattered on the chairs, three watercolor landscapes on the walls, and a pot of coffee filling the air with the scent of French vanilla. The landscape in the paintings looked vaguely familiar; they seemed to consist of views of the same area, painted from three different angles in subdued hues of brown and red. Skeletal trees converged on an expanse of dark water, hills fading into the distance beneath cloudy skies. In the corner of each painting were the initials *GP*. I never knew that Grace had painted.

There were paperbacks yellowing on the windowsill and an easy chair sat beside an open cast-iron fireplace packed with logs and paper so that it wouldn't brood emptily when not in use. The old man filled two cups with coffee and produced a plate of cookies from a cupboard, then raised his hands from his sides and smiled apologetically.

'You'll have to forgive me, Mr. Parker,' he said, indicating his shirt and his faded pants, and the sandals on his stockinged feet. 'I wasn't expecting company so early in the day.'

'Don't worry about it,' I replied. 'The cable guy once found me trying to kill a roach while wearing nothing but sneakers.'

He smiled gratefully and sat. 'Jack Mercier tell you about my little girl?' he asked, cutting straight to the chase. I watched his face while he said Mercier's name and saw something flicker, like a candle flame suddenly exposed to a draft.

I nodded. 'I'm sorry.'

'She didn't kill herself, Mr. Parker. I don't care what anybody says. She was with me the weekend before she died, and I have never seen her happier. She didn't do drugs. She didn't smoke. Hell, she didn't even drink, at least nothing stronger than a Bud Light.' He sipped at his coffee, the thumb of his left hand worrying his forefinger in a constant, rhythmic movement. There was a white callus on his skin from the repeated contact.

I took out my notebook and my pen and wrote while Peltier spoke. Grace's mother had died when she was thirteen. After a succession of dead-end jobs, Grace had returned to college and had been preparing her postgraduate thesis on the history of certain religious movements in the state. She had recently returned to live with her father, traveling down to Boston to use library facilities when necessary.

'You know who she might have been talking to?' I asked.

'She took her notes with her, so I couldn't say,' said Peltier. 'She had an appointment in Waterville, though, a day or two before . . .'

He trailed off.

'With whom?' I prompted him gently.

'Carter Paragon,' he replied. 'That fella who runs the Fellowship.'

The Fellowship was a pretty low-end operation, hosting shows on late-night cable and paying little old ladies a nickel a shot to stuff Bible pamphlets into envelopes. Paragon's pitch involved claiming to cure minor ailments by asking viewers to touch the TV screen with their hands, or one hand at least, the other hand being occupied ringing the Fellowship's toll-free number and pledging whatever they could afford for the greater glory of the Lord. The only thing Carter Paragon ever cured was an excess of cash in a bank balance.

Unsurprisingly, Carter Paragon wasn't his real name. He had been born Chester Quincy Deedes: that was the name on his birth certificate and his criminal record, a record that consisted mainly of minor credit card and insurance fraud, peripheral involvement in a pension scam, and a couple of DUIs. When hostile journalists brought this up, the newly monikered Carter Paragon admitted that he had been a sinner, that he hadn't even been searching for God but God had found him anyway. It still wasn't exactly clear why God had been looking for Chester Deedes in the first place, unless Chester had somehow managed to steal God's wallet.

Mostly the Fellowship was kind of a joke, but I'd heard rumors – unsubstantiated, mostly – that the Fellowship supported extremist religious and right-wing groups financially. Organizations believed to have received funding from the Fellowship had been linked to pickets and attacks on abortion clinics, AIDS help lines, family planning institutes, even synagogues. Very little had ever been proved: checks from the Fellowship had been deposited in the accounts of the American Coalition of Life Activists, an umbrella organization for some of the more extreme anti-abortion groups, and Defenders of the Defenders of Life, a support group for convicted clinic bombers and their families. Phone records seized in the aftermath of various incidents of violence also revealed that assorted fascists, rednecks, and cracker militants had contacted the Fellowship on a regular basis.

The Fellowship usually issued swift condemnations of any illegal actions by groups alleged to have received funding from it, but Paragon had still felt compelled to turn up on respectable newsmagazine programs on a couple of occasions uttering denials like St. Peter on a Thursday night, dressed in a suit that shimmered oilily, a small gold cross pinned discreetly to his lapel as he attempted to be charming, apologetic, and manipulative all at the same time. Trying to pin down Carter Paragon was like trying to nail smoke.

Now it seemed that Grace Peltier had been due to meet with Paragon shortly before she died. I wondered if she had made the meeting. If so, Paragon might be worth talking to.

'Do you have any notes she might have made for her thesis, any computer disks?' I continued.

He shook his head. 'Like I said, she took everything with her. She was planning to stay with a friend after she'd met with Paragon and do some work on her thesis there.'

'You know who the friend was?'

'Marcy Becker,' he said immediately. 'She's a history grad, friend of Grace's from way back. Her family lives up in Bar Harbor. They run a motel there. Marcy's been living with them for the last couple of years, helping them to run the place.'

'Was she a good friend?'

'Pretty good. Or I used to think she was.'

'What do you mean?'

'I mean that she never made it to the funeral.' I felt that little lance of guilt again. 'That's kinda strange, don't you think?'

'I guess it is,' I said. 'Did she have any other close friends who didn't show for the service?'

He thought for a moment. 'There's a girl called Ali Wynn, younger than Grace. She came up here a couple of times and they seemed to get on well together. Grace shared an apartment with her when she was in Boston, and she used to stay with her when she traveled down to study. She's a student at Northeastern too, but works part-time in a fancy restaurant in Harvard, the Pudding something.'

'"Upstairs at the Pudding"?'

He nodded. 'That's the one.'

It was on Holyoke Street, close by Harvard Square. I added the name to my notebook.

'Did Grace own a gun?' I asked.

'No.'

'Are you sure?'

'Positive. She hated guns.'

'Was she seeing anybody?'

'Not that I know of.'

He sipped his coffee and I found him watching me closely over the rim of the cup, as if my last question had caused a shift in his perception of me.

'I recall you, you know,' he said softly.

I felt myself flush red, and instantly I was a more than a decade and a half younger, dropping Grace Peltier off outside this same house and then driving away, grateful that I would never have to look at her or hold her again. I wondered what Peltier knew about my time with his daughter, and was surprised and embarrassed at my concern.

'I told Jack Mercier to ask for you,' he continued. 'You knew Grace. I thought maybe you might help us because of that.'

'That was a long time ago,' I answered gently.

'Maybe,' he said, 'but it seems like only yesterday to me that she was born. Her doctor was the worst doctor in the world. He couldn't deliver milk, but somehow, despite him, she managed to come wailing into the world. Everything since then, all of the little incidents that made up her life, seem to have occurred in the blink of an eye. You look at it like that and it wasn't so long ago, Mr. Parker. For me, in one way, she was barely here at all. Will you look into this? Will you try to find out the truth of what happened to my daughter?'

I sighed. I felt as if I was heading into deep waters just as I had begun to like the feel of the ground beneath my feet.

'I'll look into it,' I said at last. 'I can't promise anything, but I'll do some work on it.'

We spoke a little more of Grace and of her friends, and Peltier gave me copies of the phone records for the last couple of months, as well as Grace's most recent bank and credit card statements, before he showed me to her bedroom. He left me alone in there. It was probably too soon for him to spend time in a room that still smelled of her, that still contained traces of her existence. I went through the drawers and closets, feeling awkward as my fingers lifted and then replaced items of clothing, the hangers in the closets chiming sadly as I patted down the jackets and coats they held. I found nothing except a shoe box containing the mementos of her romantic life: cards and letters from long-departed lovers, and ticket stubs from dates that had obviously meant something to her. There was nothing recent, and nothing of mine among them. I hadn't expected that there would be. I checked through the books on the shelves and the medicines in the cabinet above the small sink in the corner of the room. There were no contraceptives that might have indicated a regular boyfriend and no prescription drugs that might have suggested she was suffering from depression or anxiety.

When I returned to the kitchen there was a manila file of papers lying in front of Peltier on the table. He passed it across to me. When I opened it, the file contained all of the state police reports on the death of Grace Peltier, along with a copy of the death certificate and the ME's report. There were also photographs of Grace in the car, printed off a computer. The quality wasn't so good, but it didn't have to be. The wound on Grace's head was clearly visible, and the blood on the window behind her was like the birth of a red star.

'Where did you get these, Mr. Peltier?' I asked, but I knew the answer almost as soon as the words were out of my mouth. Jack Mercier always got what he wanted.

'I think you know,' he replied. He wrote his telephone

number on a small pad and tore the page out. 'You can usually get me here, day or night. I don't sleep much these days.'

I thanked him. Then he shook my hand and walked me to the door. He was still watching me as I climbed into the Mustang and drove away.

I parked on Congress and took the reports into Kinkos to photocopy them, a precaution that I had recently started to take with everything from tax letters to investigation notes, with the originals retained at the house and the copies put into storage in case the originals were lost or damaged. Copying was a small amount of trouble and expense to go to for the reassurance that it offered. When I had finished, I went to Coffee by Design and started to read the reports in detail. As I did, I found myself growing more and more unhappy with what they contained.

The police report listed the contents of the car, including a small quantity of cocaine found in the glove compartment and a pack of cigarettes that was lying on the dashboard. Fingerprint analysis revealed three sets of prints on the pack, only one of them belonging to Grace. The only prints on the bag of coke were Grace's. For someone who didn't smoke or take drugs, Grace Peltier seemed to be carrying a lot of narcotics in her car.

The certificate of death didn't add much else to what I already knew, although one section did interest me. Section 42 of the state of Maine certificate of death requires the ME to ascribe the manner of death to one of six causes. In order, these are: 'natural', 'accident', 'suicide', 'homicide', 'pending investigation', and 'could not be determined.'

The ME had not ticked 'suicide' as the manner of Grace Peltier's death. She had, instead, opted for 'pending investigation.' In other words, she had enough doubts about the circumstances to require the state police to continue their enquiries into the death. I moved on to the ME's own report.

The report noted Grace's body measurements, her clothing, her physique and state of nutrition at the time of death, and her personal cleanliness. There were no signs of self-neglect indicative of mental disorder or drug dependency of any kind. The analysis of her ocular fluid found no traces of drugs or alcohol taken in the hours before her death, and urine and bile analysis also came up negative, indicating that she had not ingested drugs in the three days preceding her death either. Blood taken from a peripheral vein beneath her armpit had been combined in a tube with sodium fluoride, which reduces the microbiologic action that may increase or decrease any alcohol content in the blood after collection. Once again, it came up negative. Grace hadn't been drinking before she died.

It's a difficult thing to do, taking one's own life. Most people require a little Dutch courage to help them on their way, but Grace Peltier had been clean. Despite the fact that her father said she was happy, that she had no alcohol or drugs in her system when she died, and the autopsy revealed none of the telltale signs of a disturbed, distracted personality of the type likely to attempt suicide, Grace Peltier had still apparently put a gun close to her head and shot herself.

Grace's fatal injury had been caused by a .40 caliber bullet fired from a Smith & Wesson at a range of not more than two inches. The bullet had entered through the left temple, burning and splitting the skin and singeing Grace's hair above the wound, and shattering the sphenoid bone. The bullet hole was slightly smaller than the diameter of the bullet, since the elastic epidermis had stretched to allow its passage and then contracted afterward. There was an abrasion collar around the hole, caused by the friction, heating, and dirt effect of the bullet, as well as surrounding bruising.

The bullet had exited above and slightly behind the right temple, fracturing the orbital roof and causing bruising around the right eye. The wound was large and everted, with an irregular stellate appearance. Its irregularity was due to the damage caused to the bullet by contact with the skull, which had distorted its shape. The only blood in the car had come from Grace, and the bloodstain pattern analysis was consistent with the injury received. A ballistics examination of the recovered bullet also matched up. Chemical and scanning electron microscope analysis of skin swabs taken from Grace's left hand revealed propellant residues, indicating that the gun had been fired by Grace. The gun was found hanging from Grace's left hand. On the seat, beside her right hand, was a Bible.

It is an established fact that women rarely commit suicide with guns. Although there are exceptions, women don't seem to have the same fascination with firearms as men and tend to pick less obviously violent ways to end their lives. There is a useful rule in police work: a shot woman is a murdered woman unless proved otherwise. Suicides also shoot themselves in certain sites of election: the mouth, the front of the neck, the forehead, the temple, or the chest. Discharges into the temple usually occur on the side of the dominant hand, although that is not an absolute. Grace Peltier, I knew, was right handed, yet she had elected to shoot herself in the left temple, using her left hand and holding what I assumed to be an unfamiliar weapon. According to Curtis, she didn't even own a gun, although it was possible that she had decided to acquire one for reasons of her own.

There were three additional elements in the reports that struck me as odd. The first was that Grace Peltier's clothes had been soaked with water when her body was found. Upon examination, the water was found to be salt water. For some reason, Grace Peltier had taken a dip in the sea fully clothed before shooting herself.

The second was that the ends of Grace's hair had been cut shortly before, or possibly after, her death, using not a scissors but a blade. Part of her ponytail had been severed, leaving some loose hairs trapped between her shirt and her skin.

The third was not an inclusion but an omission. Curtis Peltier had told me that Grace had brought all of her thesis notes with her, but there were no notes found in the car.

The Bible was a nice touch, I thought.

I was walking back to my car when the cell phone rang.

'Hi, it's me,' said Rachel's voice.

'Hi, you.'

Rachel Wolfe was a criminal psychologist who had once specialized in profiling. She had joined me in Louisiana as the hunt for the Traveling Man came to its end, and we had become lovers. It had not been an easy relationship: Rachel had been hurt badly both physically and emotionally in Louisiana, and I had spent a long time coming to terms with the guilt my feelings for her had provoked. We were now slowly establishing ourselves together, although she continued to live in Boston, where she was doing research and tutorial work at Harvard. The subject of her moving up to Maine had been glanced upon once or twice, but never pursued.

'I've got bad news. I can't come up next weekend. The faculty has called an emergency meeting for Friday afternoon over funding cuts, and it's likely to pick up again on Saturday morning. I won't be free until Saturday afternoon at the earliest. I'm really sorry.'

I found myself smiling as she spoke. Lately, talking to Rachel always made me smile. 'Actually, that might work out okay. Louis has been talking about heading up to Boston for a weekend. If he can convince Angel to come along I can link up with them while you're tied up in meetings, then we can spend the rest of the time together.'

Angel and Louis were, in no particular order, gay, semiretired criminals, silent partners in a number of restaurants and auto shops, a threat to decent people everywhere and possibly to the fabric of society itself, and polar opposites in just about every imaginable way, with the exception of a shared delight in mayhem and occasional homicide. They were also, not entirely coincidentally, my friends.

'*Cleopatra* opens at the Wang on the fourth,' probed Rachel. 'I think I can probably hustle a pair of tickets.'

Rachel was a huge fan of the Boston Ballet and was trying to convert me to its joys. She was kind of succeeding, although it had led Angel to speculate unkindly on my sexuality.

'Sure, but you owe me a couple of Pirates games when the hockey season starts.'

'Agreed. Call me back and let me know what their plans are. I can book a table for dinner and join the three of you after my meeting. And I'll look into those tickets. Anything else?'

'How about lots of rampant, noisy sex?'

'The neighbors will complain.'

'Are they good looking?'

'Very.'

'Well, if they get jealous I'll see what I can do for them.'

'Why don't you see what you can do for *me* first?'

'Okay, but when I wear you out I may have to go elsewhere for my own pleasure.'

I couldn't be sure, but I thought her laughter had a distinctly mocking tone as she hung up.

When I got back to the house, I called a number on Manhattan's Upper West Side using the landline. Angel and Louis didn't like being called on a cell phone, because – as the unfortunate Hoyt was about to learn to his cost – cell phone conversations could be monitored or traced, and Angel and Louis were the kind of individuals who sometimes dealt in delicate matters upon which the law might not smile too gently. Angel was a burglar, and a very good one, although he was now officially "resting" on the joint income he had acquired with Louis. Louis's current career position was murkier: Louis killed people for money, or he used to. Now he sometimes killed people, but money was less of a concern for him than the moral imperative for their deaths. Bad people died at Louis's hands, and maybe the world was a better place without them. Concepts like morality and justice got a little complicated where Louis was concerned.

The phone rang three times and then a voice with all the charm of a snake hissing at a mongoose said, 'Yeah?' The voice also sounded a little breathless.

'It's me. I see you still haven't got to the chapter on phone etiquette in that Miss Manners book I gave you.'

'I put that piece of shit in the trash,' said Angel. 'Guy who laces his shoes with string is probably still trying to sell it on Broadway.'

'Your breathing sounds labored. Do I even want to know what I interrupted?'

'Elevator's busted. I heard the phone on the stairs. I was at an organ recital.'

'What were you doing, passing around the tin cup?'

'Funny.'

I don't think he meant it. Louis was obviously still engaged in an unsuccessful attempt to expand Angel's cultural horizons. You had to admire his perseverance, and his optimism.

'How was it?'

'Like being trapped with the phantom of the opera for two hours. My head hurts.'

'You up for a trip to Boston?'

'Louis is. He thinks it's got class. Me, I like the order of New York. Boston is like the whole of Manhattan below Fourteenth Street, you know, with all them little streets that cross back over one another. It's like the Twilight Zone down in the Village. I didn't even like visiting when you lived there.'

'You finished?' I interrupted.

'Well, I guess I am now, Mr. Fucking Impatient.'

'I'm heading down next weekend, maybe meet Rachel for dinner late on Friday. You want to join us?'

'Hold on.' I heard a muffled conversation, and then a deep male voice came on the line.

'You comin' on to my boy?' asked Louis.

'Lord no,' I replied. 'I like to be the pretty one in my relationships, but that's taking it a little too far.'

'We'll be at the Copley Plaza. You give us a call when you got a restaurant booked.'

'Sure thing, boss. Anything else?'

'We let you know,' he said, then the line went dead.

It was a shame about the Miss Manners book, really.

Grace Peltier's credit card statement revealed nothing out of the ordinary, while the telephone records indicated calls to Marcy Becker at her parents' motel, a private number in Boston which was now disconnected but which I assumed to be Ali Wynn's, and repeated calls to the Fellowship's office in Waterville. Late that afternoon I called the Fellowship at that same number and got a recorded message asking me to choose *one* if I wanted to make a donation, *two* if I wanted to hear the recorded prayer of the day, or *three* to speak to an operator. I pressed *three* and when the operator spoke I gave my name and asked for Carter Paragon's office. The operator told me she was putting me through to Paragon's assistant, Miss Torrance. There was a pause and then another female voice came on the line.

'Can I help you?' it said, in the tone that a certain type of secretary reserves for those whom it has no intention of helping at all.

'I'd like to speak to Mr. Paragon, please. My name is Charlie Parker. I'm a private investigator.'

'What is it in connection with, Mr. Parker?'

'A young woman named Grace Peltier. I believe Mr. Paragon had a meeting with her about two weeks ago.'

'I'm sorry, the name isn't familiar to me. No such meeting took place.' If spiders apologized to flies before eating them, they could have managed more sincerity than this woman.

'Would you mind checking?'

'As I've told you, Mr. Parker, that meeting never took place.'

'No, *you* told me that you weren't familiar with the name, and *then* you told me that the meeting never took place. If you didn't recognize the name, how could you remember whether or not any meeting took place?'

There was a pause on the end of the line, and I thought the receiver began to grow distinctly chilly in my hand. After a time, Miss Torrance spoke again. 'I see from Mr. Paragon's diary that a meeting was due to be held with a Grace Peltier, but she never arrived.'

'Did she cancel the appointment?'

'No, she simply didn't turn up.'

'Can I speak to Mr. Paragon, Miss Torrance?'

'No, Mr. Parker, you cannot.'

'Can I make an appointment to speak to Mr. Paragon?'

'I'm sorry. Mr. Paragon is a very busy man, but I'll tell him you called.' She hung up before I could give her a number, so I figured that I probably wasn't going to be hearing from Carter Paragon in the near future, or even the distant future. It seemed that I might have to pay a personal call on the Fellowship, although I guessed from Miss Torrance's tone that a visit from me would be about as welcome as a whorehouse in Disneyland.

Something had been nagging at me since reading the police report on the contents of the car, so I picked up the phone and called Curtis Peltier.

'Mr. Peltier,' I asked, 'do you recall if either Marcy Becker or Ali Wynn smoked?'

He paused before answering. 'Y'know, I think they both did, at that, but there's something else you should know. Grace's thesis wasn't just a general one: she had a specific interest in one religious group. They were called the Aroostook Baptists. You ever hear of them?'

'I don't think so.'

'The community disappeared in nineteen sixty-four. A lot of folks just assumed they'd given up and gone somewhere else, somewhere warmer and more hospitable.'

'I'm sorry, Mr. Peltier, I don't see the point.'

'These people, they were also known as the Eagle Lake Baptists.'

I recalled the news reports from the north of the state, the photographs in the newspapers of figures moving behind crime scene tape, the howling of the animals.

'The bodies found in the north,' I said quietly.

'I'd have told you when you were here, but I only just saw the TV reports,' he said. 'I think it's them. I think they've found the Aroostook Baptists.'

Chapter Three

They come now, the dark angels, the violent ones, their wings black against the sun, their swords unsheathed. They move remorselessly through the great mass of humanity: purging, taking, killing.

They are no part of us.

The Manhattan North Homicide Squad is regarded as an elite group within the NYPD, operating out of an office at 120 East 119th Street. Each member has spent years as a precinct detective before being handpicked for homicide duty. They are experienced detectives, their gold shields bearing the hallmarks of long service. The most junior members probably have twenty years behind them. The more senior members have been around for so long that jokes have accreted to them like barnacles to the prows of old ships. As Michael Lansky, who was the senior detective on the squad when I was a rookie patrolman, used to say, 'When I started in homicide, the Dead Sea was just sick.'

My father was himself a policeman, until the day he took his own life. I used to worry about my father. That was what you did when you were a policeman's son, or anyway, that was what I did. I loved him; I was envious of him – of his uniform, of his power, of the camaraderie of his friends; but I also worried about him. I worried about him all the time. New York in the 1970s wasn't like New York now:

policemen were dying on the streets in ever-greater numbers, exterminated like roaches. You saw it in the newspapers and on the TV, and I saw it reflected in my mother's eyes every time the doorbell rang late at night while my father was supposed to be on duty. She didn't want to become another PBA widow. She just wanted her husband to come home, alive and complaining, at the end of every tour. He felt the strain too; he kept a bottle of Mylanta in his locker to fight the heartburn he endured almost every day, until eventually something snapped inside him and it all came to a violent end.

My father had only occasional contact with Manhattan North Homicide. Mostly, he watched them as they passed by while he held the crowds back or guarded the door, checking shields and IDs. Then, one stiflingly hot July day in 1980, shortly before he died, he was called to a modest apartment on Ninety-fourth Street and Second Avenue rented by a woman named Marilyn Hyde, who worked as an insurance investigator in midtown.

Her sister had called on her and smelled something foul coming from inside the apartment. When she tried to gain entry using a spare key given to her by Marilyn, she found that the lock had been jammed up with adhesive and informed the super, who immediately notified the police. My father, who had been eating a sandwich at a diner around the corner, was the first officer to reach the building.

It emerged that two days before she died, Marilyn Hyde had called her sister. She had been walking up from the subway at Ninety-sixth and Lexington when she caught the eye of a man descending. He was tall and pale, with dark hair and a small, thin mouth. He wore a yellow squall jacket and neatly pressed jeans. Marilyn had probably held his glance for no more than a couple of seconds, she told her sister that night, but something in his eyes caused her to step back against the wall as if she had been slammed in the chest by a fist. She felt a dampness on the legs of her pantsuit, and when she looked down, she realized that she had lost control of herself.

The following morning she called her sister again and expressed concern that she was being followed. She couldn't say by whom, exactly; it was just a feeling she had. Her sister told her to talk to the police but Marilyn refused, arguing that she had no proof that she was being shadowed and had seen nobody acting suspiciously in her vicinity.

That day she left work early, pleading sickness, and returned to her apartment. When she didn't turn up for work the next morning and didn't answer her phone, her sister went to check on her, setting in train the chain of events that led my father to her door. The hallway was quiet, since most of the other tenants were at work or out enjoying the summer sun. After knocking, my father unholstered his weapon and kicked the door in. The A/C in the apartment had been turned off and the smell hit him with a force that made his head reel. He told the super and Marilyn Hyde's sister to stay back, then made his way through the small living area, past the kitchen and the bathroom, and into the apartment's only bedroom.

He found Marilyn chained to her bed, the sheets and the floor below drenched with blood. Flies buzzed around her. Her body had swollen in the heat, the skin stained a light green at her belly, the superficial veins on the thighs and shoulders outlined in deeper greens and reds like the tracery in autumn leaves. There was no longer any way to tell how beautiful she had once been.

The autopsy found one hundred separate knife wounds on her body. The final cut to the jugular had killed her: the preceding ninety-nine had simply been used to bleed her slowly over a period of hours. There was a container of salt by the bed, and a jar of fresh lemon juice. Her killer had used them to rouse her when she lost consciousness.

That evening, after my father returned home, the smell of the soap he had used to wash away the traces of Marilyn Hyde's death still strong upon him, he sat at our kitchen table and opened a bottle of Coors. My mother had left as soon as he came home, anxious to meet up with friends whom she had not seen in many weeks. His dinner was in the oven, but he did not touch it. Instead, he sipped from the bottle and did not speak for a long time. I sat across from him and he took a soda from the refrigerator and handed it to me, so that I would have something to drink with him.

'What's wrong?' I asked him at last.

'Somebody got hurt today,' he replied.

'Somebody we know?'

'No, son, nobody we know, but I think she was a good person. She was probably worth knowing.'

'Who did it? Who hurt her?'

He looked at me, then reached out and touched my hair, the palm of his hand resting lightly on my head for a moment.

'A dark angel,' he said. 'A dark angel did it.'

He did not tell me what he had seen in Marilyn Hyde's apartment. It was only many years later that I would hear of it – from my mother, from my grandfather, from other detectives – but I never forgot the dark angels. Many years later, my wife and child were taken from me, and the man who killed them believed that he, too, was one of the dark angels, the fruit of the union between earthly women and those who had been banished from heaven for their pride and their lust.

St. Augustine believed that natural evil could be ascribed to the activity of beings who were free and rational but nonhuman. Nietzsche considered evil to be a source of power independent of the human. Such a force of evil could exist outside of the human psyche, representing a capacity for cruelty and harm distinct from our own capabilities, a malevolent and hostile intelligence whose aim was, ultimately, to undermine our own essential humanity, to take away our ability to feel compassion, empathy, love.

I think my father saw certain acts of violence and cruelty, such as the terrible death of Marilyn Hyde, and wondered if there were some deeds that were beyond even the potential of human beings to commit; if there were creatures both more and less than human that preyed upon us.

They were the violent ones, the dark angels.

Manhattan North, the best homicide squad in the city, maybe even in the whole country, investigated the Marilyn Hyde case for seven weeks but found no trace of the man in the subway. There were no other suspects. The man at whom Marilyn Hyde had simply looked for a second too long and who had, it was believed, bled her to death for his own pleasure had returned to the hidden place from which he came.

Marilyn Hyde's murder remains unsolved, and detectives in the squad still catch themselves staring at the faces on the subway, sometimes with their own wives, their own children beside them, trying to find the dark-haired man with the too-small mouth. And some of them, if you ask, will tell you that perhaps they experience a moment of relief when they find that he is not among the crowds, that they have not caught his eye, that they have not made contact with this man while their families are with them.

There are people whose eyes you must avoid, whose attention you must not draw to yourself. They are strange, parasitic creatures, lost souls seeking to stretch across the abyss and make fatal contact with the warm, constant flow of humanity. They live in pain and exist only to visit that pain on others. A random glance, the momentary lingering of a look, is enough to give them the excuse that they seek. Sometimes it is better to keep your eyes on the gutter, for fear that by looking up you might catch a glimpse of them, black shapes against the sun, and be blinded forever.

And now, on a patch of damp, muddy ground by a cold lake in northern Maine, the work of the dark angels was slowly being exposed.

The grave had been discovered at the boundary of the public reserved lands known as Winterville. The integrity of the scene had been compromised somewhat by the activities of the maintenance and construction crews, but there was nothing that could now be done except to ensure that no further damage was caused.

On that first day, the emergency team had taken the names of all of the workers at the lake site, interviewed each briefly, and then secured the scene with tape and uniformed officers. Initially there had been some trouble from one of the timber companies that used the road, but the company had agreed to postpone its truck runs until the extent of the grave had been determined.

Following the initial examination the sandbag levees were strengthened, while a command post, including the mobile crime scene unit, was established in a turnaround by the side of the Red River Road, with a strict sign-in policy in place to ensure that no further contamination of the area occurred. A pathway through the scene was created and marked with tape, after which a walking tour of the ground was made with a video camera to indoctrinate the police officers who would take no direct role in the investigation.

The scene was photographed: overall views first, to preserve the essential history of the scene at the moment of discovery, then orientation shots of the visible bones, followed by close-ups of the bones themselves. The camcorder was brought into play again, this time detailing the scene instead of merely recording it. Sketches were made, a three-foot-long metal stake indicating the center point from which all measurements of distance and angles would be made. The boundaries of Red River Road were marked and recorded, in case any widening might occur in the future to alter the territory, and GPS equipment was used to make a satellite estimation of the crime scene location.

Then, the light by now almost gone, the investigative team dispersed following a final meeting, leaving state troopers and sheriff's deputies to guard the scene. The autopsy team would arrive at first light, when the investigation into the deaths of the Aroostook Baptists would begin in earnest.

And in all that they did and in all that would follow, the sound of the hybrids stayed with them, so that each night, when they returned home and tried to sleep, they would wake to imagined howls and think that they were once again standing by the shores of the lake, their hands cold and their boots thick with mud, surrounded by the bones of the dead.

That night, for the first time in many months, I dreamed, as memories of Grace and my own father followed me from waking to sleeping. In my dream I stood on a patch of cleared land with bare trees at its verge and frozen water glittering coldly beyond. There were fresh mounds of earth scattered randomly on the ground and the dirt seemed to shift as I watched, as if something was moving beneath it.

And in the trees, shapes gathered; huge, black, birdlike figures with red eyes that gazed with hunger upon the shifting earth below. Then one unfurled its wings and dived, but instead of making for the earth it flew toward me, and I saw that it was not a bird but a man, an old man with flowing gray hair and yellow teeth and nodes on his back from which the leathery wings erupted. His legs were thin, his ribs showed through his skin, and his wrinkled male organ bobbed obscenely as he flew down. He hovered before me, the dark wings beating at the night. His gaunt cheeks stretched and he spat the word at me:

'*Sinner!*' he hissed. His wings still flapping, he tore at a pile of earth with his clawlike feet until he revealed a patch of white skin that glowed translucently in the moonlight. His mouth opened and his head descended toward the body, which writhed and twisted against him as he bit into it, blood flowing over his chin and pooling on the ground below.

Then he smiled at me, and I turned away from the sight to find myself reflected in the waters before me. I saw my own face twinned with the moon, bleeding whitely into my naked shoulders and chest. And from my back, huge dark wings unfurled themselves and spread behind me, covering the surface of the lake like thick, black ink and stilling all life beneath.

The Search for Sanctuary

Extract from the postgraduate thesis of Grace Peltier

In April 1963, a group of four families left their homes on the eastern seaboard and journeyed north in a collection of automobiles and trucks for two hundred miles, to an area of land close by the town of Eagle Lake, twenty miles south of the border between New Brunswick and Maine. The families were the Perrsons, from Friendship, south of the coastal town of Rockland; the Kellogs and the Cornishes, from Seal Cove; and the Jessops, from Portland. Collectively, they became known as the Aroostook Baptists, or sometimes as the Eagle Lake Baptists, although there is no evidence to suggest that any families other than the Perrsons and the Jessops were, in fact, originally members of that faith.

Once they reached their final destination, all of the automobiles were taken and sold, the money raised being used to buy essential supplies for the families over the coming year until the settlement could become self-sufficient. The settlement land, approximately forty acres, was rented on a thirty-year lease from a local landowner. Following the desertion of the settlement, this land eventually reverted to the family of the original owner although until recently a dispute over boundaries has prevented any development of the site.

In total, sixteen people journeyed north that month: eight adults and eight children, all equally divided between the sexes. At Eagle Lake they were met by the man they knew as Preacher (or sometimes Reverend Faulkner), his wife, Louise, and their two children, Leonard and Muriel, aged seventeen and sixteen respectively.

It was at Faulkner's instigation that the families, mainly poor farmers and blue-collar workers, had sold their properties, pooled the money made, and traveled north to establish a community based on strict religious principles. A number of other families had also been willing to make the journey, motivated variously by their persistent fears of the perceived communist threat, their own fundamentalist religious beliefs, poverty, and an inability to cope with what they saw as the moral deterioration of the society around them, and perhaps subconsciously by the tradition of adherence to nonmainstream religious movements that was so much a part of the state's history. These additional applicants had been rejected on the basis of family size and the ages and sexes of their children. Faulkner stipulated that he wanted to create a community where families could intermarry, strengthening the bonds between them over generations, and that he therefore required equal numbers of male and female partners of similar age. The families he chose were, to a greater or lesser degree, estranged from their own relatives and appeared to be untroubled by the thought of being cut off from the outside world.

The Aroostook Baptists arrived in Eagle Lake on April 15, 1963. By January 1964, the settlement had been abandoned. No trace of the founding families or of the Faulkners was ever found again.

Chapter Four

I slept late the next morning but didn't feel refreshed when I woke. The memory of my dream was still vivid, and despite the cool of the night, I had sweated under the sheets.

I decided to grab breakfast in Portland before paying a visit to the Fellowship's offices, but it wasn't until I was in my car that I noticed that the red marker on the mailbox had been raised. It was a little early for a delivery, but I didn't think anything more of it. I walked down the drive and was about to reach for the mailbox when something lithe and dark scurried across the tin. It was a small brown spider, with an odd violin-shaped mark on its body. It took me a moment or two to recognize it for what it was: a fiddleback, one of the recluses. I drew my hand away quickly. I knew that they could bite, although I'd never seen one this far north before. I used a stick to knock it away, but as I did so another set of thin legs pushed at the crack of the mailbox flap, and a second fiddleback squeezed its way out, then a third. I moved around the mailbox carefully and saw more spiders, some creeping along its base, others already rappelling slowly to the ground on lengths of silken thread. I took a deep breath and flipped the mailbox catch open with the stick.

Hundreds of tiny spiders tumbled out, some falling instantly to the grass below, others crawling and fighting their way across the inside of the flap, clinging to the bodies of those below them. The interior was alive with them. In the center of the box itself stood a small cardboard packing crate with airholes in its side, spiders spilling from the holes as the sunlight hit them. I could see dead spiders lying curled in the crate or littered around the corners of the mailbox, their legs curled into their abdomens as their peers fed on them. I backed away in disgust, trying not to think of what would have happened had I thrust my hand unthinkingly into the semidarkness.

I went to my car and took the spare gas can from the trunk, then retrieved a Zippo from the glove compartment. I sprinkled the gas both inside and outside the mailbox, and on the dry earth surrounding it, before lighting a roll of newspaper and tossing it in. The mailbox went up instantly, tiny arachnids falling aflame from the inferno. I stepped back as the grass began to burn and moved to the garden hose. I attached it to the outside faucet and wet the grass to contain the fire, then stood for a time and watched the mailbox burn. When I was content that nothing had survived, I doused it in water, the tin hissing at the contact and steam rising into the air. After it had cooled, I put on a pair of calfskin gloves and emptied the remains of the spiders into a black bag, which I threw in the garbage can outside my back door. Then I stood for a long time at the edge of my property, scanning the trees and striking at the invisible spiders I felt crawling across my skin.

I ate breakfast in Bintliff's on Portland Street and plotted my plan of action for the day. I sat in one of the big red booths upstairs, the ceiling fan gently turning as blues played softly in the background. Bintliff's has a menu so calorific that Weight Watchers should place a permanent picket on the door; gingerbread pancakes with lemon sauce, Orange Graham French toast, and lobster Benedict are not the kind of breakfast items that contribute to a slim waistline, although they're guaranteed to raise the eyebrows of even the most jaded dietician. I settled for fresh fruit, wheat toast, and coffee, which made me feel very virtuous but also kind of sad. The sight of the spiders had taken away most of my appetite anyhow. It could have been kids playing a joke, I supposed, but if so, then it was a vicious, deeply unpleasant one.

Waterville, the site of the Fellowship's office, was midway between Portland and Bangor. After Bangor I could head east to Ellsworth and the area of U.S. 1 where Grace Peltier's body had been discovered. From Ellsworth, Bar Harbor, home of Grace's good friend but funeral absentee Marcy Becker, was only a short drive to the coast. I finished off my coffee, took a last lingering look at a plate of apple cinnamon and raisin French toast that was heading toward a table by the window, then stepped outside and walked to my car.

Across the street, a man sat at the base of the steps leading up to the main post office. He wore a brown suit with a yellow shirt and a brown-and-red tie beneath a long, dark brown overcoat. Short, spiky red hair, tinged slightly with gray, stood up straight on his head as if he were permanently plugged into an electrical outlet. He was eating an ice cream cone. His mouth worked at the ice cream in a relentless methodical motion, never stopping once to savor the taste. There was something unpleasant, almost insectlike, about the way his mouth moved, and I felt his eyes upon me as I opened the car door and sat inside. When I pulled away from the curb, those eyes followed me. In the rearview, I could see his head turn to watch my progress, the mouth still working like the jaws of a mantid.

The Fellowship had its registered office at 109A Main Street, in the middle of Waterville's central business district. Parts of Waterville are pretty but downtown is a mess, largely because it looks like the ugly Ames shopping mall was dropped randomly from the sky and allowed to remain where it landed, reducing a huge tract of the town center to a glorified parking lot. Still, enough brownstone blocks remained to support a sign welcoming visitors to the joys of downtown Waterville, among them the modest offices of the Fellowship. They occupied the two top floors over an otherwise vacant storefront down from Joe's Smoke Shop, nestled between the Head Quarters hairdressing salon and Jorgensen's Cafe. I parked in the Ames lot and crossed at Joe's. There was a buzzer beside the locked glass door of 109A, with a small fish-eye lens beneath it. A metal plate on the door frame was engraved with the words *The Fellowship – Let the Lord Guide You.* A small shelf to one side held a sheaf of pamphlets. I took one and slipped it into my pocket, then rang the buzzer and heard a voice crackle in response. It sounded suspiciously like that of Miss Torrance.

'Can I help you?' it said.

'I'm here to see Carter Paragon,' I replied.

'I'm afraid Mr. Paragon is busy.' The day had hardly begun and already I was experiencing déjà vu.

'But I let the Lord guide me here,' I protested. 'You wouldn't want to let Him down, would you?'

The only sound that came from the speaker was that of the connection between us being closed. I rang again.

'Yes?' The irritation in her voice was obvious.

'Maybe I could wait for Mr. Paragon?'

'That won't be possible. This is not a public office. Any contact with Mr. Paragon should be made in writing in the first instance. Have a good day.'

I had a feeling that a good day for Miss Torrance would probably be a pretty bad day for me. It also struck me that in the course of our entire conversation, Miss Torrance had not asked me my name or my business. It might simply have been my suspicious nature, but I guessed that Miss Torrance already knew who I was. More to the point, she knew what I looked like.

I walked around the block to Temple Street and the rear of the Fellowship's offices. There was a small parking lot, its concrete cracked and overgrown with weeds, dominated by a dead tree beneath which stood two tanks of propane. The back door of the building was white and the windows were screened, while the black iron fire escape looked so decrepit that any occupants might have been better advised to take their chances with the flames. It didn't look like the back door to 109A had been opened in some time, which meant that the occupants of the building entered and left through the door on Main Street. There was one car in the lot, a red 4x4 Explorer. When I peered in the window I saw a box on the floor containing what looked like more religious pamphlets bound with rubber bands. Using my elementary deduction skills, I guessed that I'd found the Fellowship's wheels.

I went back onto Main Street, bought a couple of newspapers and the latest issue of *Rolling Stone*, then headed into Jorgensen's and took a seat at the raised table by the window. From there I had a perfect view of the doorway to 109A. I ordered coffee and a muffin, then sat back to read and wait.

The newspapers were full of the discovery at St. Froid, although they couldn't add much to the news reports I'd seen on television. Still, somebody had dredged up an old photograph of Faulkner and the original four families that had journeyed north with him. He was a tall man, plainly dressed, with long dark hair, very straight black eyebrows, and sunken cheeks. Even in the photograph there was an undeniable charisma to him. He was probably in his late thirties, his wife a little older. Their children, a boy and a girl aged about seventeen and sixteen respectively, stood in front of him. He must have been comparatively young when they were born.

Despite the fact that I knew the photograph had been taken in the sixties, it seemed that these people could have been frozen in their poses at any time over the previous hundred years. There was something timeless about them and their belief in the possibility of escape, twenty people in simple clothes dreaming of a utopia dedicated to the greater glory of the Lord. According to a small caption, the land for the community had been granted to them by the owner, himself a religious man, for the sum of $1 per acre per annum, paid in advance for the term of the lease. By moving so far north the congregation's privacy was virtually guaranteed. The nearest town was Eagle Lake to the north, but it was then already in decline, the mills closing and the population depleted. Tourism would eventually rescue the area, but in 1963, Faulkner and his followers would have been left largely to their own devices.

I turned my attention to the Fellowship's pamphlet. It was basically one long sales pitch designed to elicit the appropriate response from any readers: namely, to hand over all of the loose change they might have on their person at the time, plus any spare cash that might be making their bank statements look untidy. There was an interesting medieval illustration on the front, depicting what looked like the Last Judgment: horned demons tore at the naked bodies of the damned while God looked on from above, surrounded by a handful of presumably very relieved good folk. I noticed that the damned outnumbered the saved by about five to one. All things considered, those didn't look like very good odds on salvation for most of the people I knew. Beneath the illustration was a quotation: 'And I saw the dead, small and great, stand before God; and the books were opened: and another book was opened, which is the book of life: and the dead were judged out of those things which were written in the books, according to their works (Revelation 20:12).'

I laid aside the pamphlet, kind of relieved that I'd bought *Rolling Stone*. I spent the next hour deciding who among the good and not-so-good of modern music was unlikely to be taking up salvation space in the next world. I had made a pretty comprehensive list when, shortly after one-thirty, a woman and a man came out of the Fellowship's offices. The man was Carter Paragon: I recognized the slicked-back dark hair, the shiny gray suit, and the unctuous manner. I was just surprised that he didn't leave a trail of slime behind him as he walked.

The woman with him was tall and probably about the same age as Paragon; early forties, I guessed. She had straight dark brown hair that hung to her shoulders, and her body was hidden beneath a dark blue wool overcoat. Her face was hardly conventionally pretty; the jaw was too square, the nose too wide, and the muscles at her jaws looked overdeveloped, as if her teeth were permanently gritted. She wore white pancake makeup and bright red lipstick like a graduate of clown school, although if she was, nobody was laughing. Her shoes were flat, but she was still at least five-ten or five-eleven and towered over Paragon by about four inches. The look that passed between them as they made their way toward Temple Street was strange. It seemed that Paragon deferred to her and I noticed that he stepped back quickly when she turned away from the door after checking the lock, as if afraid to get in her way.

I left $5 on the table, then walked out onto Main and strolled over to the Mustang. I had been tempted to tackle them on the street but I was curious to see where they were going. The red Explorer emerged onto Temple, then drove past me through the lot, heading south. I followed it at a distance until it came to Kennedy Memorial Drive, where it turned right onto West River Road. We passed Waterville Junior High and the Pine Ridge Golf Course before the Explorer took another right onto Webb Road. I stayed a couple of cars behind as far as Webb, but the Explorer was the only car to make the right. I hung back as much as I could and thought that I'd lost them when an empty stretch of road was revealed after I passed the airfield. I made a U-turn and headed back the way I had come, just in time to see the Explorer's brake lights glow about two hundred yards on my right. It had turned up Eight Rod Road and was now entering the driveway of a private house. I arrived in time to see the black steel gates close and the red body of the 4x4 disappearing around the side of a modest two-story white home with black shutters on the windows and black trim on the gable.

I parked in front of the gates, waited for about five minutes, and then tried the intercom on the gatepost. I noticed that there was another fish-eye lens built in, so I covered it with my hand.

'Yes?' came Miss Torrance's voice.

'UPS delivery,' I said.

There was silence for a few moments as Miss Torrance tried to figure out what had gone wrong with her gate camera, before her voice told me that she'd be right out. I was kind of hoping that she might have let me in, but I settled for keeping my hand on the camera and my body out of sight. It was only when Miss Torrance was almost at the gate that I stepped into view. She didn't look too pleased to see me, but then I couldn't imagine her looking too pleased to see anyone. Even Jesus would have got a frosty reception from Miss Torrance.

'My name is Charlie Parker. I'm a private detective. I'd like to see Carter Paragon, please.' Those words were assuming the status of a mantra, with none of the associated calm.

Miss Torrance's face was so hard it could have mined diamonds. 'I've told you before, Mr. Paragon isn't available,' she said.

'Mr. Paragon certainly is elusive,' I replied. 'Do you deflate him and put him in a box when he's not needed?'

'I'm afraid I have nothing more to say to you, Mr. Parker. Please go away or I'll call the police. You are harassing Mr. Parragon.'

'No,' I corrected. 'I *would* be harassing Mr. Paragon, if I could find him. Instead, I'm stuck with harassing you, Miss Torrance. It is Miss Torrance, isn't it? Are you unhappy, Miss Torrance? You sure look unhappy. In fact, you look so unhappy that you're starting to make me unhappy.'

Miss Torrance gave me the evil eye. 'Go fuck yourself, Mr. Parker,' she said softly.

I leaned forward confidentially. 'You know, God can hear you talk that way.'

Miss Torrance turned on her heel and walked away. She looked a whole lot better from the back than she did from the front, which wasn't saying much.

I stood there for a time, peering through the bars like an unwanted party guest. Apart from the Explorer there was only one other vehicle in the driveway of the Paragon house, a beat-up blue Honda Civic. It didn't look like the kind of car a man of Carter Paragon's stature would drive, so maybe it was what Miss Torrance used to get around when she wasn't chauffeuring her charge. I went back to my car, listened to a classical music slot on PBS, and continued reading *Rolling Stone*. I had just begun to wonder if I was optimistic enough to buy one hundred rubbers for $29.99 when a white Acura pulled up behind me. A big man dressed in a black jacket and blue jeans, with a black silk-knit tie knotted over his white shirt, strode up to my window and knocked on the glass. I rolled down the window, looked at his shield and the name beside his photo, and smiled. The name was familiar from the police report on Grace Peltier. This was Detective John Lutz, the investigating officer on the case, except Lutz was attached to CID III and operated out of Machias, while Waterville was technically in the territory of CID II.

Curiouser and curiouser, as Alice liked to say.

'Help you, Detective Lutz?' I asked.

'Can you step out of the car, please, sir?' he said, standing back as I opened the door. The thumb of his right hand hung on his belt, while the rest of his fingers pushed his jacket aside, revealing the butt of his .45 caliber H&K as he did so. He was six-two or six-three and in good condition, his stomach flat beneath his shirt. His eyes were brown and his skin was slightly tanned, his brown hair and brown mustache neatly trimmed. His eyes said he was about mid-forties.

'Turn around, put your hands against the car, and spread your legs,' he told me.

I was about to protest when he gave me a sharp push, spinning me round and propelling me against the side of the car. His speed and his strength took me by surprise.

'Take it easy,' I said. 'I bruise.'

He patted me down, but he didn't find anything of note. I wasn't armed, which I think kind of disappointed him. All he got was my wallet.

'You can turn around now, Mr. Parker,' he said when he had finished. I found him looking at my license, then back at me a couple of times, as if trying to sow enough doubt about its validity to justify hauling me in.

'Why are you loitering outside Mr. Paragon's home, Mr. Parker?' he said. 'Why are you harassing his staff?'

He didn't smile. His voice was low and smooth. He sounded a little like Carter Paragon himself, I thought.

'I was trying to make an appointment,' I said.

'Why?'

'I'm a lost soul, looking for guidance.'

'If you're trying to find yourself, maybe you should go look someplace else.'

'Wherever I go, there I am.'

'That's unfortunate.'

'I've learned to live with it.'

'Doesn't seem to me like you have much choice, but Mr. Paragon does. If he doesn't want to see you, then you should accept that and be on your way.'

'Do you know anything about Grace Peltier, Detective Lutz?'

'What's it to you?'

'I've been hired to look into the circumstances of her death. Someone told me that you might know something about it.' I let the double meaning hang in the air for a time, its ambivalence like a little time bomb ticking between us. Lutz's fingers tapped briefly on his belt, but it was the only indication he gave that his calm might be under threat.

'We think Ms. Peltier took her own life,' he said. 'We're not looking for anyone else in connection with the incident.'

'Did you interview Carter Paragon?'

'I spoke to Mr. Paragon. He never met Grace Peltier.'

Lutz moved a little to his left. The sun was behind him and he stood so that it shone over my shoulder and directly into my eyes. I raised a hand to shade myself and his hand nudged for his gun again.

'Ah-ah,' he said.

'A little jumpy, aren't you, Detective?' I lowered my hand carefully.

'Mr. Paragon sometimes attracts a dangerous element,' he replied. 'Good men often find themselves under threat for their beliefs. It's our duty to protect him.'

'Shouldn't that be the job of the police here in Waterville?' I asked.

He shrugged. 'Mr. Paragon's secretary preferred to contact me. Waterville police have better things to be doing with their time.'

'And you don't?'

He smiled for the first time. 'It's my day off, but I can spare a few minutes for Mr. Paragon.'

'The law never rests.'

'That's right, and I sleep with my eyes open.' He handed my wallet back to me. 'You be on your way now, and don't let me see you round here again. You want to make an appointment with Mr. Paragon, then you contact him during business hours, Monday to Friday. I'm sure his secretary will be happy to help you.'

'Your faith in her is admirable, Detective.'

'Faith is always admirable,' he replied, then started to walk back to his car.

I had pretty much decided that I didn't like Detective Lutz. I wondered what would happen if he was goaded. I decided to find out.

'Amen,' I said. 'But if it's all the same to you, I'd prefer to stay here and read my magazine.'

Lutz stopped, then walked quickly back to me. I saw the punch coming, but I was against the car and all I could do was curl to one side to take the blow to my ribs instead of my stomach. He hit me so hard I thought I heard a rib crack, the pain lancing through my lower body and sending shock waves right to the tips of my toes. I slid down the side of the Mustang and sat on the road, a dull ache spreading across my stomach and into my groin. I felt like I was going to vomit. Then Lutz reached down and applied pressure from his thumbs and forefingers just below my ears. He was using pain compliance techniques and I yelped in agony as he forced me to rise.

'Don't mock me, Mr. Parker,' he said. 'And don't mock my faith. Now get in your car and drive away.'

The pressure eased. Lutz walked over to his car and sat on the hood, waiting for me to leave. I looked over at the Paragon house and saw a woman standing at an upstairs window, watching me. Before I got back into the car, I could have sworn that I saw Miss Torrance smile.

Lutz's white Acura stayed behind me until I left Waterville and headed north on I-95, but the pain and humiliation I felt meant that the memory of him was with me all the way to Ellsworth. The Hancock County Field Office, home of Troop J of the state police, had dealt with the discovery of Grace Peltier's body. It was a small building on U.S. 1, with a pair of blue state trooper cars parked outside. A sergeant named Fortin told me that her body had been found by Trooper Voisine on a site named Happy Acres, which was scheduled to be developed for new housing. Voisine was out on patrol but Fortin told me that he'd contact him and ask him to meet me at the site. I thanked him, then followed his directions north until I came to Happy Acres.

A company called Estate Executives was advertising it as the future setting for 'roads and views', although currently there were only rutted tracks and the main view was of dead or fallen trees. There was still some tape blowing in the wind where Grace's car had been found, but that apart, there was nothing to indicate that a young woman's life had come to an end in this place. Still, when I looked around, something bothered me: I couldn't see the road from where I was standing. I went back to the Mustang and drove it up the track until it was in more or less the same position that Grace's car must have occupied. I turned on the lights, then walked down to the road and looked back.

The car still wasn't visible, and I couldn't see its lights through the trees.

As I stood by the roadside, a blue cruiser pulled up beside me and the trooper inside stepped out.

'Mr. Parker?' he asked.

'Trooper Voisine?' I extended a hand and he took it.

He was about my height and age, with receding hair, an 'aw shucks' smile, and a small triangular scar on his forehead. He caught me looking at it and reached up to rub it with his right hand.

'Lady hit me on the head with a high-heeled shoe after I pulled her over for speeding,' he explained. 'I asked her to step from the car, she stumbled, and when I reached over to help her I caught her heel in my forehead. Sometimes it just don't pay to be polite.'

'Like they say,' I said, 'shoot the women first.'

His smile faltered a little, then regained some of its brightness.

'You from away?' he asked.

'From away.' I hadn't heard that phrase in quite some time. Around these parts, 'from away' meant anyplace more than a half-hour's drive from wherever you happened to be standing at the time. It also meant anyone who couldn't trace a local family connection back at least a hundred years. There were people whose grandparents were buried in the nearest cemetery who were still regarded as 'from away,' although that wasn't quite as bad as being branded a 'rusticator', the locals' favorite term of abuse for city folks who came Down East in order to get in touch with country living.

'Scarborough,' I answered.

'Huh.' Voisine sounded unimpressed. He leaned against his car, removed a Quality Light from a pack in his shirt pocket, then offered the pack to me. I shook my head and watched as he lit up. Quality Lights: he'd have been better off throwing the cigarettes away and trying to smoke the packaging.

'You know,' I said, 'if we were in a movie, smoking a cigarette would automatically brand you as a bad guy.'

'Is that so?' he replied. 'I'll have to remember that.'

'Take it as a crime stopper's tip.'

Somehow, largely through my own efforts, the conversation appeared to have taken a slightly antagonistic turn. I watched while Voisine appraised me through a cloud of cigarette smoke, as if the mutual dislike we instinctively felt had become visible between us.

'Sergeant says you want to talk to me about the Peltier woman,' said Voisine at last.

'That's right. I hear you were the first on the scene.'

He nodded. 'There was a lot of blood, but I saw the gun in her hand and thought: suicide. First thing I thought, and it turns out I was right.'

'From what I hear, the verdict may still be open.'

He blanked me, then shrugged. 'Did you know her?' he asked.

'A little,' I replied. 'From way back.'

'I'm sorry.' He didn't even try to put any emotion into the words.

'What did you do after you found her?'

'Called it in, then waited.'

'Who arrived after you?'

'Another patrol, ambulance. Doc pronounced her dead at the scene.'

'Detectives?'

He flicked his head back like a man who suddenly realizes he has left out something important. It was a curiously theatrical gesture.

'Sure. CID.'

'You remember his name?'

'Lutz. John Lutz.'

'He get here before, or after, the second patrol?'

Voisine paused. I saw him watching me carefully through the cigarette smoke before he replied. 'Before,' he said at last.

'Must have got here pretty fast,' I said, keeping my tone as neutral as possible.

Voisine shrugged again. 'Guess he was in the area.'

'Guess so,' I said. 'Was there anything in the car?'

'I don't understand, sir.'

'Purse, suitcase, that kind of thing?'

'There was a bag with a change of clothes and a small purse with makeup, a wallet, that kind of stuff.'

'Nothing else?'

Something clicked in Voisine's throat before he spoke. 'No.'

I thanked him and he finished off his cigarette, then tossed the butt on the ground, stamping it out beneath his heel. Just as he was about to get back into his car I called to him.

'Just one more thing, Trooper,' I said.

I walked down to join him. He paused, half in and half out of the car, and stared at me.

'How did you find her?'

'What do you mean?'

'I mean, how did you see the car from the road? I can't see my car from here and it's parked in pretty much the same spot. I'm just wondering how you came to find her, seeing as how she was hidden by the trees.'

He said nothing for a time. The professional courtesy was gone now, and I wasn't sure what had replaced it. Trooper Voisine was a difficult man to read.

'We get a lot of speeding on this road,' he said at last. 'I sometimes pull in here to wait. That's how I found her.'

'Ah,' I said. 'That explains it. Thanks for your time.'

'Sure,' he replied. He closed the door and started the engine, then turned onto the road and headed north. I walked out onto the blacktop and made sure that I stayed in his mirror until he was gone from my sight.

There was little traffic on the road from Ellsworth to Bar Harbor as I drove through the gathering dusk of the early evening. The season had not yet begun, which meant that the locals still had the place pretty much to themselves. The streets were quiet, most of the restaurants were closed, and there was digging equipment on the site of the town's park, piles of earth now standing where there used to be green grass. Sherman's bookstore was still open on Main Street, and it was the first time that I had ever seen Ben & Bill's Chocolate Emporium empty. Ben & Bill's was even offering 50 percent off all candies. If they tried that after Memorial Day, people would be killed in the stampede.

The Acadia Pines Motel was situated by the junction of Main and Park. It was a pretty standard tourist place, probably operating at the lower end of the market. It consisted of a single two-story, L-shaped block painted yellow and white, numbering about forty rooms in total. When I pulled into the lot there were only two other cars parked and there seemed to be a kind of desperation about the ferocity with which the VACANCIES sign glowed and hummed. I stepped from the car and noticed that the pain in my side had faded to a dull ache, although when I examined my body in the dashboard light I could still see the imprint of Lutz's knuckles on my skin.

Inside the motel office, a woman in a pale blue dress sat behind the desk, the television tuned to a news show and a copy of *TV Guide* lying open beside her. She sipped from a Grateful Dead mug decorated with lines of dancing teddy bears, chipped red nail polish showing on her fingers. Her hair was dyed a kind of purple-black and shined like a new bruise. Her face was wrinkled and her hands looked old, but she was probably no more than fifty-five, if that. She tried to smile as I entered, but it made her look as if someone had inserted a pair of fishhooks in her upper lip and pulled gently.

'Hi,' she said. 'Are you looking for a room?'

'No, thank you,' I replied. 'I'm looking for Marcy Becker.'

There was a pause that spoke volumes. The office stayed silent but I could still hear her screaming in her head. I watched her as she ran through the various lying options open to her. You have the wrong place. I don't know any Marcy Becker. She's not here and I don't know where she is. In the end, she settled for a variation on the third choice.

'Marcy isn't here. She doesn't live here anymore.'

'I see,' I said. 'Are you Mrs. Becker?'

That pause came again, then she nodded.

I reached into my pocket and showed her my ID. 'My name is Charlie Parker, Mrs. Becker. I'm a private investigator. I've been hired to investigate the circumstances surrounding the death of a woman named Grace Peltier. I believe Marcy was a friend of Grace's, is that correct?'

Pause. Nod.

'Mrs. Becker, when was the last time you saw Grace?'

'I don't recall,' she said. Her voice was dry and cracked, so she coughed and repeated her answer with only marginally more assurance. 'I don't recall.' She took a sip of coffee from her mug.

'Was it when she came to collect Marcy, Mrs. Becker? That would have been a couple of weeks ago.'

'She never came to collect Marcy,' said Mrs. Becker quickly. 'Marcy hasn't seen her in . . . I don't know how long.'

'Your daughter didn't attend Grace's funeral. Don't you think that's strange?'

'I don't know,' she said. I watched her fingers slide beneath the counter and saw her arm tense as she pressed the panic button.

'Are you worried about Marcy, Mrs. Becker?'

This time the pause went on for what seemed like a very long time. When she spoke, her mouth answered no but her eyes whispered yes.

Behind me, I heard the door of the office open. When I turned, a short, bald man in a golf sweater and blue polyester pants stood before me. He had a golf club in his hand.

'Did I interrupt your round?' I asked.

He shifted the club in his hand. It looked like a nine iron. 'Can I help you, mister?'

'I hope so, or maybe I can help you,' I said.

'He was asking about Marcy, Hal,' said Mrs. Becker.

'I can handle this, Francine,' her husband assured her, although even he didn't look convinced.

'I don't think so, Mr. Becker, not if all you've got is a cheap golf club.'

A rivulet of panic sweat trickled down from his brow and into his eyes. He blinked it away, then raised the club to shoulder height in a two-armed grip. 'Get out,' he said.

My ID was still open in my right hand. With my left, I took one of my business cards from my pocket and laid it on the counter. 'Okay, Mr. Becker, have it your way. But before I go, let me tell you something. I think someone may have killed Grace Peltier. Maybe you're telling me the truth, but if you're not, then I think your daughter has some idea who that person might be. If I could figure that out, then so could whoever killed her friend. And if that person comes asking questions, then he probably won't be as nice about it as I am. You bear that in mind after I'm gone.'

The club moved forward an inch or two. 'I'm telling you for the last time,' he snarled, 'get out of this office.'

I flipped my wallet closed, slipped it into my jacket pocket, then walked to the door, Hal Becker circling me with his golf club to keep some swinging distance between us. 'I have a feeling you'll be calling me,' I said as I opened the door and stepped into the lot.

'Don't you bet on it,' replied Becker. As I started my car and drove away, he was still standing at the door, the golf club still raised, like a frustrated amateur with a huge handicap stuck in the biggest, deepest bunker in the world.

On the drive back to Scarborough I ran through what I had learned, which wasn't much. I knew that Carter Paragon was being kept under wraps by Miss Torrance and that Lutz seemed to have more than a professional interest in keeping him that way. I knew that something about Voisine's discovery of Grace's body made me uneasy, and Lutz's involvement in that discovery made me uneasier still. And I knew that Hal and Francine Becker were scared. There were a lot of reasons why people might not want a private detective questioning their child. Maybe Marcy Becker was a porn star, or sold drugs to high school kids. Or maybe their daughter had told them to keep quiet about her whereabouts until whatever she was worried about had blown over. I still had Ali Wynn, Grace's Boston friend, to talk to, but already Marcy Becker was looking like a woman worth pursuing.

It seemed that Curtis Peltier and Jack Mercier were right to suspect the official version of Grace's death, but I also felt that everybody I had met over the past couple of days was either lying to me or holding something back. It was time to rectify that situation, and I had an idea where I wanted to start. Despite my tiredness, I didn't take the Scarborough exit. Instead, I first took Congress Street, then headed onto Danforth and pulled up in front of Curtis Peltier's house.

The old man answered the door wearing a nightgown and bedroom slippers. Inside, I could hear the sound of the television in the kitchen, so I knew I hadn't woken him.

'You find out something?' he asked as he motioned me into the hallway and closed the door behind me.

'No,' I replied, 'but I hope to pretty soon.'

I followed him into the kitchen and took the same seat I had occupied the day before, while Peltier hit the mute button on the remote. He was watching *Night of the Hunter*,

Robert Mitchum oozing evil as the psychotic preacher with the tattooed knuckles.

'Mr. Peltier,' I began, 'why did you and Jack Mercier cease to be business partners?'

He didn't look away, but his eyes blinked closed for slightly longer than usual. When they opened again, he seemed tired. 'What do you mean?'

'I mean, was it for business, or personal, reasons?'

'When you're in partnership with your friend, then all business is personal,' he replied. This time, he did look away when he said it.

'That's not answering the question.'

I waited for a further reply. The silence of the kitchen was broken only by the sound of his breathing. On the screen to my left, the children drifted down the river on a small boat, the preacher tracking them along the bank.

'Have you ever been betrayed by a friend, Mr. Parker?' he asked at last.

Now it was my turn to flinch. 'Once or twice,' I answered quietly.

'Which was it – once, or twice?'

'Twice.'

'What happened to them?'

'The first one died.'

'And the second?'

I heard my heart beating in the few seconds it took me to reply. It sounded impossibly loud.

'I killed him.'

'Either he betrayed you badly or you're a harsh judge of men.'

'I was pretty tense, once upon a time.'

'And now?'

'I take deep breaths and count to ten.'

He smiled. 'Does it work?'

'I don't know. I've never made it as far as ten.'

'I guess it don't, then.'

'I guess not. Do you want to tell me what happened between you and Jack Mercier?'

He shook his head. 'No, I don't want to tell you, but I get the feeling you have your own ideas about what might have happened.'

I did, but I was as reluctant to say them out loud as Peltier was to tell me. Even thinking them in the company of this man who had lost his only child so recently seemed like an unforgivable discourtesy.

'It was personal, wasn't it?' I asked him softly.

'Yes, it was very personal.'

I watched him carefully in the lamplight, took in his eyes, the shape of his face, his hair, even his ears and his Grecian nose. There was nothing of him in Grace, nothing that I could recall. But there was something of Jack Mercier in her. I was almost certain of it. It had struck me most forcefully after I stood in his library and looked at the photographs on the wall, the images of the young Jack triumphant. Yes, I could see Grace in him, and I could see Jack in her. Yet I wasn't certain, and even if it was true, to say it aloud would hurt the old man. He seemed to sense what I was thinking, and my response to it, because what he said next answered everything.

'She was my daughter, Mr. Parker,' he said, and his eyes were two deep wells of hurt and pride and remembered betrayal. 'My daughter in every way that mattered. I raised her, bathed her, held her when she cried, collected her from school, watched her grow, supported her in all that she did, and kissed her good night every time she stayed with me. He had almost nothing to do with her, not in life. But now, I need him to do something for her and for me, maybe even for himself.'

'Did she know?'

'You mean, did I tell her? No, I didn't. But you suspected, and so did she.'

'Did she have contact with Jack Mercier?'

'He payed for her graduate research because I couldn't

afford to. It was done through an educational trust he established, but I think it confirmed what Grace had always believed. Since the funding began, Grace had met him on a few occasions, usually at events organized by the trust. He also let her look at some books he had out at the house, something to do with her thesis. But the issue of her parentage was never discussed. We'd agreed that: Jack, my late wife, and I.'

'You stayed together?'

'I loved her,' he said simply. 'Even after what she'd done, I still loved her. Things were never the same because of it, but yes, we stayed together and I wept for her when she died.'

'Was Mercier married at the time of . . .' I allowed the sentence to peter out.

'The time of the affair?' he finished. 'No, he met his wife a few years later, and they were married a year or so after that again.'

'Do you think she knew about Grace?'

He sighed. 'I don't know, but I guess he must have told her. He's that kind of man. Hell, it was him who confessed to me, not my wife. Jack just had to relieve himself of the burden. He has all the weaknesses that come with a conscience, but none of the strengths.' It was the first hint of bitterness he had revealed.

'I have another question, Mr. Peltier. Why did Grace choose to research the Aroostook Baptists?'

'Because she was related to two of them,' he replied. He said it matter-of-factly, as if it had never occurred to him that it might be relevant.

'You didn't mention it before,' I said, keeping my voice even.

'I guess it didn't seem important.' His voice faltered and he sighed. 'Or maybe I thought that if I told you that, I'd have to tell you about Jack Mercier and . . .' He waved a hand dispiritedly.

'The Aroostook Baptists were what brought Jack Mercier and me together,' he began. 'We weren't friends then. We met at a lecture on the history of Eagle Lake, first and last we ever attended. We went out of curiosity more than concern. My cousin was a woman called Elizabeth Jessop. Jack Mercier's second cousin was Lyall Kellog. Do any of those names mean anything to you, Mr. Parker?'

I thought back to the newspaper report the previous day and the picture of the assembled families taken before they departed for northern Aroostook.

'Elizabeth Jessop and Lyall Kellog were members of the Aroostook Baptists,' I replied.

'That's right. In a way, Grace had links with both of them through Jack and me. That's why she was so interested in their disappearance.' He shook his head. 'I'm sorry. I should have been open with you from the start.'

I rose and put my hand on his shoulder, squeezing gently. 'No,' I replied. 'I'm sorry that I had to ask.'

I released my hold on him and moved toward the door, but his hand reached out to stop me.

'You think that her death has something to do with the bodies in the north?' Seated before me, he seemed very small and frail. I felt a strange kind of empathy with him; we were two men who had been cursed to outlive their daughters.

'I don't know, Mr. Peltier.'

'But you'll keep looking? You'll keep looking for the truth?'

'I'll keep looking,' I assured him.

I could hear again the soft rattle of his breathing as I opened the door and stepped out into the night. When I looked back he was still seated, his head down, his shoulders shaking gently with the force of his tears.

Chapter Five

Curtis Peltier's confession not only explained a great deal about Jack Mercier's actions; it also made things a whole lot more difficult for me. The blood link between Mercier and Grace was bad news.

There was more bad news waiting for me when I got back to the Scarborough house. I couldn't tell why, exactly, but something seemed wrong with the place as soon as I pulled up in front of the door. At first I put it down to that feeling of dislocation you get when you return home after being away, however briefly, but it was more than that. It was as if someone had taken the house and shifted it slightly on its axis, so that the moonlight no longer shone on it in quite the way that it once had and the shadows fell differently along the ground. The smell of gas from the mailbox served as a reminder of what had taken place that morning. Spiders in the mailbox was bad enough, but I wasn't sure that I could handle recluses in my house.

I approached the door, opened the screen, and tested the lock, but it remained secure. I inserted the key and pushed the front door, expecting to see some scene of desolation before me, but there was nothing at first. The house was quiet and the doors stood slightly ajar to allow the flow of air through the rooms. In the hallway, an old coat stand that I used for keeping mail and as a place to lay my keys had been pulled slightly away from the wall. I could see the clear marks on the floor where the legs had once stood, now slightly tarnished with speckles of dust. In the living room, I had the same sensation, as if someone had gone through my house and moved everything marginally out of kilter. The couch and chairs had been lifted, then imperfectly replaced. In the kitchen, crockery had been shifted, foodstuffs in the fridge removed and then returned in a haphazard manner. Even the sheets on my bed were tossed, the top sheet pulled loose at the end. I went to my desk at the back of the living room and thought I knew then what they had come for.

The copy of the file on the case had been taken from me.

I spent the next hour doing something that was unexpected but, upon reflection, natural. I went through the house, cleaning it, vacuuming and brushing, dusting and polishing. I took the sheets from my bed and threw them in a laundry bag, along with the small selection of clothes in my closet. Then I washed all of the cups and plates, the knives and forks, in boiling water and left them on the draining board. By the time I had finished, sweat was running down my face, my hands and face were filthy, and my clothes were stuck to my back, but I felt that I had reclaimed my space a little from those who had intruded upon it. Had I not done so, everything in my house would have felt tarnished by their presence.

When I had showered and changed into the last of the clothes in my overnight bag, I tried calling Curtis Peltier's house, but there was no reply. I wanted to warn him that whoever had searched my house might try to do the same to his, but his machine clicked on. I left a message, asking him to call me.

I drove down to Oak Hill and dropped off my laundry, then turned back and headed for the Kraft Mini-Storage on Gorham Road, close by my house. I used my key to open one of the storage bays I kept there, still filled with some old possessions of my grandfather's, along with items I had kept from the Brooklyn home I had shared briefly with Susan and Jennifer. In the bright light, I sat on the edge of a packing crate and went through the police reports one by one, concentrating in particular on those prepared by Lutz as the detective responsible for the investigation into Grace Peltier's death. His involvement in the case didn't fill me with a great sense of reassurance, but I could still find nothing in his reports to justify my suspicions of him. He had done a perfectly adequate job, even to the extent of interviewing the elusive Carter Paragon.

When I returned to the house, I went to my bedroom and removed an eighteen-inch section of the baseboard from behind the chest of drawers. I took a bundle wrapped in oilcloth from out of the gap I had made. Two other bundles, one larger, one smaller, also lay inside, but I didn't touch them. I took the bundle into the kitchen, lay a newspaper on the table, and unwrapped the gun.

It was a Third Generation Smith & Wesson Model 1076, a 10-millimeter version developed especially for the FBI. I had owned a similar model for a year, until I lost it in a lake in northern Maine while running for my life. In some ways I had been glad to see the last of that gun. I had done terrible things with it, and it had come to represent all that was worst in me.

Yet two weeks after I lost it, a new 1076 had arrived for me, sent by Louis and delivered by one of his emissaries, a huge black man in a *Klan Killer* T-shirt. Louis called me an hour or two after its delivery.

'I don't want it, Louis,' I told him. 'I'm sick of guns, and especially this gun.'

'You feel that way now, but this your gun,' he said. 'You used it because you had to use it, and you was good with it. Maybe a day will come when you be glad you have it.'

Instead of throwing it away, I had wrapped it in oilcloth. I did the same thing with my father's .38 Colt Detective Special and a 9-millimeter Heckler & Koch semiautomatic, for which I didn't have a permit. Then I had cut away the section of baseboard and placed the guns safely in the space I had made for them. Out of sight, out of mind.

Now I released the magazine, using the catch at the left side of the butt. I pulled back the slide in case there was a round in the chamber, still sticking to the old safety routine. I inspected the chamber through the ejection port, then released the slide and pulled the trigger. For the next thirty minutes I cleaned and oiled the gun, then loaded it and sighted at the door. Even fully loaded, it weighed a little over two and a half pounds. I tested its lines with my thumb, ran my finger over the serial number on the left-hand side of the frame, and felt inexplicably afraid.

There is a dark resource within all of us, a reservoir of hurt and pain and anger upon which we can draw when the need arises. Most of us rarely, if ever, have to delve too deeply into it. That is as it should be, because dipping into it costs, and you lose a little of yourself each time, a small part of all that is good and honorable and decent about you. Each time you use it you have to go a little deeper, a little further down into the blackness. Strange creatures move through its depths, illuminated by a burning light from within and fueled only by the desire to survive and to kill. The danger in diving into that pool, in drinking from that dark water, is that one day you may submerge yourself so deeply that you can never find the surface again. Give in to it and you're lost forever.

Looking at the gun, feeling the power of it, its base, unarguable lethality, I saw myself standing at the verge of those dark waters and felt the burning on my skin, heard the cool lapping of the waves calling me to fall into their depths. I did not look down, for fear of what I might see reflected on the surface.

In an effort to pull myself away, I rose and checked my messages. There was one from Rachel phoning to say 'Hi.' I returned her call immediately, and she picked up on the second ring.

'Hey, you,' she said. 'I got those tickets for the Wang.'

'Great.'

'That doesn't sound very enthusiastic.'

'I haven't had such a good day. I got assaulted by a policeman for mocking his belief system, and someone threatened to take my head off with a nine iron.'

'And you're usually so naturally charming,' she said, before her voice grew serious. 'You want to tell me what's going on?'

I told her a little of what I knew, or suspected, so far. I didn't mention Marcy Becker, Ali Wynn, or the two policemen. I didn't like talking about it over the phone, or in a house so recently violated by strangers.

'Are you going to continue with this?'

I paused before answering. Beside me, the Smith & Wesson gleamed dully in the moonlight.

'I think so,' I answered quietly.

She sighed. 'Guess I should cancel those tickets, then.'

'No, don't do that.' Suddenly I wanted to be with Rachel more than anything else in the world, and anyway, I still had to talk to Ali Wynn. 'We'll meet up, as arranged.'

'You're sure?'

'Never been more sure of anything.'

'Okay, then. You know I love you, Parker, don't you?' She had taken to calling me Parker sometimes, simply because nobody else close to me ever called me that.

'I love you too.'

'Good. Then take care of your damned self.'

And with that she hung up.

The second message on the machine was distinctly unusual.

'Mr. Parker,' said a male voice, 'my name is Arthur Franklin. I am an attorney. I have a client who is anxious to speak with you.' Arthur Franklin sounded kind of nervous, as if there was somebody standing in the shadows behind him brandishing a length of rubber hose. 'I'd appreciate it if you'd call me as soon as you can.'

He'd left a home telephone number, so I called him back.

When I told him who I was, relief burst from him like air from a punctured tire. He must have said 'thank you' three times in as many seconds.

'My client's name is Harvey Ragle,' he explained, before I had a chance to say anything further. 'He's a filmmaker. His studio and distribution arm is in California but he has recently come to live and work in Maine. Unfortunately, the state of California has taken issue with the nature of his art, and extradition proceedings are now in train. More to the point, certain individuals outside the law have also taken some offense at Mr. Ragle's art, and my client now believes that his life is in danger. We have a preliminary hearing tomorrow afternoon at the federal courthouse, after which my client will be available to talk to you.'

He came up for air at last, giving me an opportunity to interrupt.

'I'm sorry, Mr. Franklin, but I'm not sure that your client is my concern, and I'm not taking on any new cases.'

'Oh no,' replied Franklin. 'You don't understand. This is not a new case. This is in the nature of assistance with your current case.'

'What do you know about my caseload?'

'Oh dear,' said Franklin. 'I knew this wasn't a good idea. I told him, but he wouldn't listen.'

'Told whom?'

Franklin let out a deep breath that quivered on the verge of tears. Perry Mason he wasn't. Somehow, I got the feeling that Harvey Ragle was going to be getting some California sunshine in the near future.

'I was told to call you,' continued Franklin, 'by a certain individual from Boston. He's in the comic book business. I think you know the gentleman to whom I am referring.'

I knew the gentleman. His name was Al Z, and for all intents and purposes he ran the Boston mob from above a comic book store on Newbury Street.

Suddenly I was in real trouble.

Chapter Six

The sun shone brightly through my windows when I awoke, the thin material of the curtains speckled with thousands of tiny points of light. I could hear the buzzing of bees, attracted by the trilliums and hepaticas growing at the end of my yard and the pink buds of the single wild apple tree that marked the start of my driveway.

I showered and dressed, then took my training bag and headed into One City Center to work out for an hour. In the lobby I passed Norman Boone, one of the ATF agents based in Portland, and nodded a hello. He nodded back, which was something, Boone ordinarily being about as friendly as a cat in a bag. The feds, the U.S. marshals, and the ATF all occupied offices at One City Center, which was the kind of knowledge that made you feel pretty safe and secure while using the gym, as long as some freak with a grudge against the government didn't get it into his head to make his mark on the world with a vanload of Semtex.

I tried to concentrate on my workout but found myself distracted by the events of the past days. Thoughts of Lutz and Voisine and the Beckers flashed through my mind, and I was conscious of the Smith & Wesson, in its Milt Sparks Summer Special holster, which now lay in my locker. I was also acutely aware that Al Z was taking an interest in my affairs, which, on the 'Good Things That Can Happen to a

Person' scale, registered somewhere between contracting leprosy and having the IRS move into your house.

Al Z had arrived in Boston in the early nineties, following some fairly successful FBI moves against the New England mob involving video and tape surveillance and a small army of informants. While Action Jackson Salemme and Baby Shanks Manocchio (of whom it was once said that if there were any flies on him, they were paying rent) ostensibly jostled for control of the outfit, each dogged by surveillance and whispered rumors that one or both of them could be informing for the feds, Al Z tried to restore stability behind the scenes, dispensing advice and impartial discipline in roughly equal measures. His formal position in the hierarchy was kind of nebulous, but according to those with more than a passing interest in organized crime, Al Z was the head of the New England operation in everything but name. Our paths had crossed once before, with violent repercussions; since then I'd been very careful where I walked.

After I left the gym I headed up Congress to the library of the Maine Historical Society, where I spent an hour going through whatever they had on Faulkner and the Aroostook Baptists. The file was close at hand and still warm from the latest round of media photocopying, but it contained little more than sketchy details and yellowed newspaper clippings. The only article of any note came from an edition of *Down East* magazine, published in 1997. The author was credited only as "G.P." A call to *Down East*'s office confirmed that the contributor had been Grace Peltier.

In what was probably a dry run for her thesis, Grace had gathered together details of the four families and a brief history of Faulkner's life and beliefs, most of it accumulated from unpublished sermons he had given and the recollections of those who had heard him preach.

To begin with, Faulkner was not a real minister; instead, he appeared to have been "ordained" by his flock. He was not a premillenarianist, one of those who believe that chaos on earth is an indication of the imminence of the Second Coming and that the faithful should therefore do nothing to stand in its way. Throughout his preaching, Faulkner had shown an acute awareness of earthly affairs and encouraged his followers to stand against divorce, homosexuality, liberalism, and just about anything else the sixties were likely to throw up. In this he showed the influence of the early Protestant thinker John Knox, but Faulkner was also a student of Calvin. He was a believer in predestination: God had chosen those who were saved before they were even born, and it was therefore impossible for people to save themselves, no matter what good deeds they did on earth. Faith alone led to salvation; in this case, faith in the Reverend Faulkner, which was seen to be a natural consequence of faith in God. If you followed Faulkner, you were one of the saved. If you rejected him, then you were one of the damned. It all seemed pretty straightforward.

He adhered to the Augustinian view, popular among some fundamentalists, that God intended his followers to build a 'City on the Hill', a community dedicated to his worship and greater glory. Eagle Lake became the site of his great project: a town of only six hundred souls that had never recovered from the exodus provoked by World War II, when those who returned from the war opted to remain in the cities instead of returning to the small communities in the north; a place with one or two decent roads and no electricity in most of the houses that didn't come from private generators; a community where the meat store and dry goods store had closed in the fifties, where the town's main employer, the Eagle Lake Lumber Mill, which manufactured hardwood bowling pins, had gone bankrupt in 1956 after only five years in operation, only to stagger on in various guises until finally closing forever in 1977; a hamlet of mostly French Catholics, who regarded the newcomers as an oddity and left them to their own devices, grateful for whatever small sums they spent on seeds and supplies. This was the place Faulkner chose, and this was the place in which his people died.

And if it seems strange that twenty people could just arrive somewhere in 1963 and be gone less than a year later, never to be seen again, then it was worth remembering that this is a big state, with 1 million or so people scattered over its 33,000 square miles, most of it forest. Whole New England towns had been swallowed up by the woods, simply ceasing to exist. They were once places with streets and houses, mills and schools, where men and women worked, worshiped, and were buried, but they were now gone, and the only signs that they had ever existed were the remnants of old stone walls and unusual patterns of tree growth along the lines of what were formerly roads. Communities came and went in this part of the world; it was the way of things.

There was a strangeness to this state that was sometimes forgotten, a product of its history and the wars fought upon the land, of the woods and their elemental nature, of the sea and the strangers it had washed up on its shores. There were cemeteries with only one date on each headstone, in communities founded by Gypsies, who had never officially been born yet died as surely as the rest. There were small graves set apart from family plots, where illegitimate children lay, the manner of their passing never questioned too deeply. And there were empty graves, the stones above them monuments to the lost, to those who had drowned at sea or gone astray in the woods and whose bones now lay beneath sand and water, under earth and snow, in places that would never be marked by men.

My fingers smelled musty from turning the yellowed clippings, and I found myself rubbing my hands on my trousers in an attempt to rid myself of the odor. Faulkner's world didn't sound like any that I wanted to live in, I thought as I returned the file to the librarian. It was a world in which salvation was taken out of our hands, in which there was no possibility of atonement; a world peopled by the ranks of the damned, from whom the handful to be saved stood aloof. And if they were damned, then they didn't matter to anyone; whatever happened to them, however awful, was no more or less than they deserved.

As I headed back to my house, a UPS truck shadowed me from the highway and pulled up behind me as I entered the drive. The deliveryman handed me a special delivery parcel from the lawyer Arthur Franklin, while casting a wary glance at the blackened mailbox.

'You got a grudge against the mailman?' he asked.

'Junk mail,' I explained.

He nodded without looking at me as I signed for the package. 'It's a bitch,' he agreed, before hurrying into his truck and driving quickly onto the road.

Arthur Franklin's package contained a videotape. I went back to the house and put the tape in my VCR. After a few seconds some cheesy easy-listening music began to play and the words *Crushem Productions presents* appeared on the screen, followed by the title, *A Bug's Death*, and a director's credit for one Rarvey Hagle. Let the Orange County prosecutor's office chew on that little conundrum for a while.

For the next thirty minutes I watched as women in various stages of undress squashed an assortment of spiders, roaches, mantids and small rodents beneath their high-heeled shoes. In most cases, the bugs and mice seemed to have been glued or stapled to a board and they struggled a lot before they died. I fast-forwarded through the rest, then ejected the tape and considered burning it. Instead I decided to give it right back to Arthur Franklin when I met him, preferably by jamming it into his mouth, but I still couldn't understand why Al Z had put Franklin and his client in touch with me in the first place, unless he thought my sex life might be getting a little staid.

I was still wondering while I made a pot of coffee, poured a cup, and took it outside to drink at the tree stump that my grandfather, years before, had converted into a table by adding a cross section of an oak to it. I had an hour or so to kill before I was due to meet with Franklin and I found that sitting at the table, where my grandfather and I used to sit together, sometimes helped me to relax and think. The *Portland Press Herald* and the *New York Times* lay beside me, the pages gently rustling in the breeze.

My grandfather's hands had been steady when he made this rude table, planing the oak until it was perfectly flat, then adding a coat of wood protector to it so that it shined in the sun. Later, those hands were not so still and he had trouble writing. His memory began to fail him. A sheriff's deputy, the son of one of his old comrades on the force, brought him back to the house one evening after he found him wandering down by the Black Point cemetery on Old County Road, searching fruitlessly for the grave of his wife, so I hired a nurse for him.

He was still strong in body; each morning he would do push-ups and bench presses. Sometimes he would do laps around the yard, running gently but consistently until the back of his T-shirt was soaked in sweat. He would be a little more lucid for a time after that, the nurse would tell us, before his brain clouded once again and the cells continued to blink out of existence like the lights of a great city as the long night draws on. More than my own father and mother, that old man had guided me and tried to shape me into a good man. I wondered if he would have been disappointed at the man I had become.

My thoughts were disturbed by the sound of a car pulling into my drive. Seconds later a black Cirrus drew up at the edge of the grass. There were two people inside, a man driving and a woman sitting in the passenger seat. The man killed the engine and stepped from the car, but the woman remained seated. His back was to the sun so he was almost a silhouette at first, thin and dark like a sheathed blade. The Smith & Wesson lay beneath the arts section of the *Times*, its butt visible only to me. I watched him carefully as he approached, my hand resting casually inches from the gun. The approaching stranger made me uneasy.

Maybe it was his manner, his apparent familiarity with my property; or it could have been the woman, who stared at me through the windshield, straggly gray-brown hair hanging to her shoulders.

Or perhaps it was because I recalled this man eating an ice cream on a cool morning, his lips sucking busily away like a spider draining a fly, watching me as I drove down Portland Street.

He stopped ten feet from me, the fingers of his right hand unwrapping something held in the palm of his left, until two cubes of sugar were revealed. He popped them into his mouth and began to suck, then folded the wrapper carefully and placed it in the pocket of his jacket. He wore brown polyester trousers held up with a cheap leather belt, a once-bright yellow shirt that had now faded to the color of a jaundice victim's face, a vile brown-and-yellow tie, and a brown check polyester jacket. A brown hat shaded his face, and now, as he paused, he removed it and held it loosely in his left hand, patting it against his thigh in a slow, deliberate rhythm.

He was of medium height, five-ten or so, and almost emaciated, his clothes hanging loosely on his body. He walked slowly and carefully, as if he were so fragile that a misstep might cause his leg to snap. His hair was wiry, a combination of red and gray through which patches of pink skin showed. His eyebrows were also red, as were the lashes. Dark brown eyes that were far too small for his face peered out from beneath strange hoods of flesh, as if the skin had been pulled down from his forehead and up from his cheeks, then stitched in place by the corners of his eyes. Blue-red bags swelled up from below, so that his vision appeared to be entirely dependent on two narrow triangles of white and brown by the bridge of his nose. That nose was long and elongated at the tip, hanging almost to his upper lip. His mouth was very thin and his chin was slightly cleft. He was probably in his fifties, I thought, but I sensed that his apparent fragility was deceptive. His eyes were not those of a man who fears for his safety with every footstep.

'Warm today,' he said, the hat still slapping softly against his leg.

I nodded but didn't reply.

He inclined his head back in the direction of the road. 'I see you had an accident with your mailbox.' He smiled, revealing uneven yellow teeth with a pronounced gap at the front, and I knew immediately that he had been responsible for the recluses.

'Spiders,' I replied. 'I burnt them all.'

The smile died. 'That's unfortunate.'

'You seem to be taking it kind of personally.'

His mouth worked at the sugar lumps while his eyes locked on mine. 'I like spiders,' he said.

'They certainly burn well,' I agreed. 'Now, can I help you?'

'I do hope so,' he said. 'Or perhaps I can help you. Yes sir, I feel certain that I can help you.'

His voice had an odd nasal quality that flattened his vowels and made his accent difficult to place, a task complicated further by the formal locutions of his speech. The smile gradually reappeared but those hooded eyes failed to alter in response. Instead, they maintained a watchful, vaguely malevolent quality, as if something else had taken over the body of this odd, dated-looking man, hollowing out his form and controlling his progress by looking through the empty sockets in his head.

'I don't think I need your help.'

He waggled a finger at me in disagreement, and for the first time, I got a good look at his hands. They were thin, absurdly so, and there was something insectlike about them as they emerged from the sleeves of his jacket. The middle finger seemed to be about five inches long and, in common with the rest of his digits, tapered to a point at the tip: not only the nail but the entire finger appeared to grow narrower and narrower. The fingernails themselves looked to be a quarter of an inch at their widest point and were stained a kind of yellow-black. There were patches of short red hair below each of the knuckles, gradually expanding to cover most of the back of his hand and disappearing in tufts beneath his sleeve. They gave him a strange, feral quality.

'Now, now, sir,' he said, his fingers waving the way an arachnid will sometimes raise its legs when it finds itself cornered. Their movements appeared to be unrelated to his words or to the language of the rest of the body. They were like separate creatures that had somehow managed to attach themselves to a host, constantly probing gently at the world around them.

'Don't be hasty,' he continued. 'I admire independence as much as the next man, indeed I do. It is a laudable attribute in a man, sir, a laudable attribute, make no mistake about that, but it can lead him to do reckless things. Worse, sir, worse; it can cause him to interfere with the rights of those around him, sometimes without him even knowing.' His voice assumed a tone of awe at the ways of such men, and he shook his head slowly. 'There you are, living your own life as you see fit, and you are causing pain and embarrassment to others by doing so. It's a sin, sir, that's what it is, a sin.'

He folded his slim fingers across his stomach, still smiling, and waited for a response.

'Who are you?' I said. There was an element of awe in my own voice as well. He was both comical yet sinister, like a bad clown.

'Permit me to introduce myself,' he said. 'My name is Pudd, Mr. Pudd. At your service, sir.' He extended his right hand in greeting, but I didn't reach out to take it. I couldn't. It revolted me. A friend of my grandfather's had once kept a wolf spider in a glass case and one day, on a dare from the man's son, I had touched its leg. The spider had shot away almost instantly, but not before I had felt the hairy, jointed nature of the thing. It was not an experience I wanted to repeat.

The hand hung in midair for a moment, and once again

the smile faltered briefly. Then Mr. Pudd took back his hand, and his fingers scuttled inside his jacket. I eased my right hand a few inches to the left and took hold of the gun beneath the newspapers, my thumb flicking the safety off. Mr. Pudd didn't appear to notice the movement. At least, he gave no indication that he had, but I felt something change in his attitude toward me, like a black widow that believes it has cornered a beetle only to find itself staring into the eyes of a wasp. His jacket tightened around him as his hand searched and I saw the telltale bulge of his gun.

'I think I'd prefer it if you left,' I said quietly.

'Sadly, Mr. Parker, personal preference has nothing to do with this.' The smile faded, and Mr. Pudd's mouth assumed an expression of exaggerated sorrow. 'If the truth be known, sir, I would *prefer* not to be here at all. This is an unpleasant duty, but one that I am afraid you have brought upon yourself by your inconsiderate actions.'

'I don't know what you're talking about.'

'I am *talking* about your harassment of Mr. Carter Paragon, your disregard for the work of the organization that he represents, and your insistence on attempting to connect the unfortunate death of a young woman with that same organization. The Fellowship is a religious body, Mr. Parker, with the rights accruing to such bodies under our fine Constitution. You are aware of the Constitution, are you not, Mr. Parker? You have heard of the First Amendment, have you not?'

Throughout this speech Mr. Pudd's tone did not vary from one of quiet reasonableness. He spoke to me the way a parent speaks to an errant child. I made a note to add 'patronizing' to 'creepy' and 'insectlike' where Mr. Pudd was concerned.

'That, and the Second Amendment,' I said. 'It seems like you've heard of that one too.' I removed my hand from beneath the newspaper and pointed the gun at him. I was glad to see that my hand didn't shake.

'This is most unfortunate, Mr. Parker,' he said in an aggrieved tone.

'I agree, Mr. Pudd. I don't like people coming onto my property carrying guns, or watching me while I conduct my business. It's bad manners, and it makes me nervous.'

Mr. Pudd swallowed, took his hand from inside his jacket, and moved both hands away from his body. 'I meant you no offense, sir, but the servants of the Lord are afflicted with enemies on all sides.'

'Surely God will protect you better than a gun?'

'The Lord helps those who help themselves, Mr. Parker,' he replied.

'I don't think the Lord approves of breaking and entering,' I said, and Mr. Pudd's eyebrow raised slightly.

'Are you accusing me of something?'

'Why, do you have something to confess?'

'Not to you, Mr. Parker. Not to you.'

Once again his fingers danced slowly in the air, but this time there appeared to be purpose in the movement and I wondered what it meant. It was only when I heard the car door open and the shadow of the woman advanced across the lawn that I knew. I stood quickly and moved back, raising the gun to shoulder height in a two-handed grip and aiming it at Mr. Pudd's upper body.

The woman approached from behind his left shoulder. She didn't speak, but her hand was inside her thigh-length black coat. She wore no makeup and her face was very pale. Beneath her coat she wore a black pleated skirt that hung almost to her ankles, and a simple white blouse unbuttoned at the top, with a black scarf knotted around her neck. There was something deeply unpleasant about her looks, an ugliness from within that had seeped through her pores and blighted her skin. The nose was too thin for the face, the eyes too big and too white, the lips strangely bloated. Her chin was weak and receded into layers of flesh at her neck. No muscles moved in her face.

Mr. Pudd turned his head slightly toward her but kept his eyes on me. 'You know, my dear, I think Mr. Parker is frightened of us.'

The woman's expression didn't change. She just kept moving forward.

'Tell her to back off,' I said softly, but I found that it was I who was taking another step back.

'Or?' asked Mr. Pudd softly. 'You won't kill us, Mr. Parker.' But he raised the fingers of his left hand in a halting gesture, and the woman stopped.

If Mr. Pudd's eyes were watchful, his essential malevolence clouded with a thin fog of good humor, his partner's eyes were like those of a doll, glassy and expressionless. They remained fixed on me and I realized that, despite the gun in my hand, I was the one in danger of harm.

'Take your hand out of your coat, slowly,' I told her, my aim now shifting from the man to the woman, then back again as I tried to keep them both under the gun. 'And it better be empty when it appears.'

She didn't move until Mr. Pudd nodded once. 'Do as he says,' he said. She responded immediately, taking her empty hand from her coat carefully but without any fear.

'Now tell me, *Mr.* Pudd,' I said, 'just exactly who are you?'

'I represent the Fellowship,' he said. 'I am asking you, on its behalf, to cease your involvement in this matter.'

'And if I don't?'

'Then we may have to take further action. We could involve you in some very expensive and time-consuming litigation, Mr. Parker. We have excellent lawyers. Of course, that is only one of the options open to us. There are others.' This time the warning was explicit.

'I see no reason for conflict,' I said, mimicking his own tone and mannerisms. 'I simply want to find out what happened to Grace Peltier, and I believe Mr. Paragon could help me toward that end.'

'Mr. Paragon is occupied with the work of the Lord.'

'Things to do, people to fleece?'

'You are an irreverent man, Mr. Parker. Mr. Paragon is a servant of God.'

'It's hard to get good staff these days.'

Mr. Pudd made a strange hissing noise, an audible release of the pent-up aggression I felt within him.

'If he talks to me and answers my questions, then I'll leave him alone,' I said. 'Live and let live, that's my motto.'

I grinned, but he didn't return the favor.

'With respect, Mr. Parker, I don't believe that is your motto.' His mouth opened a little wider, and he almost spat. 'I don't believe that is your motto at all.'

I cocked the pistol. 'Get off my property, Mr. Pudd, and take your chatterbox friend with you.'

That was a mistake. Beside him, the woman shifted to her left suddenly and made as if to spring at me, her left hand tensed like the talons of a hawk while her right hand made a move for her coat. I lowered the gun and fired a shot into the ground between Mr. Pudd's feet, sending a spray of dirt into the air and causing birds to scatter from the surrounding trees. The woman stopped as his hand shot out and gripped her arm.

'Take off your scarf, my dear,' he said, his eyes never leaving mine. The woman paused, then unknotted her black scarf and held it limply in her left hand. Her exposed neck was crisscrossed with scars, pale pink welts that had left her so badly mutilated that to allow them to remain uncovered would be to invite stares from every passerby.

'Open wide, dear,' said Mr. Pudd.

The woman's mouth opened, revealing small yellow teeth, pink gums, and a tattered red mass at the back of her throat that was all that remained of her tongue.

'Now sing. Let Mr. Parker hear you sing.'

She opened her mouth and her lips moved, but no sound came. Yet she continued to sing a song heard only in her own head, her eyes half closed in ecstasy, her body swaying slightly in time to the unheard music, until Mr. Pudd raised his hand and she closed her mouth instantly.

'She used to have such a beautiful voice, Mr. Parker, so

fine and pure. It was throat cancer that took it from her: throat cancer and the will of God. Perhaps it was a strange blessing, a visitation from the Lord sent to test her faith and confirm her on the one true path to salvation. In the end, I think it just made her love the Lord even more.'

I didn't share his faith in the woman. The rage inside her was palpable, a fury at the pain she had endured, the loss she had suffered. It had consumed any love that once existed within her, and now she was forced to look beyond herself to feed it. The pain would never ease, but the burden could be made more bearable by inflicting a taste of it on others.

'But,' Mr. Pudd concluded, 'I like to tell her it was because her voice made the angels jealous.'

I had to take his word for it. I didn't see anything else about her that might have aroused the envy of angels.

'Well,' I said, 'at least she still has her looks.'

Mr. Pudd didn't respond, but for the first time, real hatred appeared in his eyes. It was a passing thing, gone as quickly as a mayfly, to be replaced with his habitual look of false good humor. But what had flickered briefly in his eyes burst into glorious, savage flame in those of the woman; in her eyes I saw churches burn, with the congregations still inside. Mr. Pudd seemed to sense the waves of contained violence rolling from her, because he turned and touched her cheek gently with the hairy back of one finger.

'My Nakir,' he whispered. 'Hush.'

Her eyes fluttered briefly closed at the caress, and I wondered if they were lovers.

'Go back to the car, my dear. Our business here is concluded, for the present.' The woman looked at me once more, then walked away. Mr. Pudd seemed about to follow her, then stopped and turned back.

'You are unwise to pursue this. I advise you for the last time to cease your involvement in this affair.'

'Sue me,' I said.

But Mr. Pudd only shook his head. 'No, it's gone far

beyond that, I'm afraid. I fear we shall be seeing each other again, under less favorable circumstances for you.'

He raised his hands.

'I am going to reach into my pocket, Mr. Parker, for my business card.' Without waiting for a reply, he took a small silver case from the right hand pocket of his jacket. He flipped open the case and removed a white business card, holding it gently by one corner.

Once again, he extended his hand, but this time it didn't falter. He waited patiently until I was forced to reach for it.

As I took it, he shifted his hand slightly and the tips of his fingers brushed against mine. Involuntarily, I shied away from the contact and Mr. Pudd nodded slightly, as if I had somehow confirmed a suspicion he had.

The card said only ELIAS PUDD in black Roman letters. There was no telephone number, no business address, no occupation. The back of the card was completely blank.

'Your card doesn't say a lot about you, Mr. Pudd,' I remarked.

'On the contrary, it says *everything* about me, Mr. Parker. I fear that you are simply not reading it correctly.'

'All it tells me is that you're either cheap or a minimalist,' I responded. 'You're also irritating, but it doesn't say that on your card either.'

For the first time, Mr. Pudd truly smiled, his yellow teeth showing and his eyes lighting up. 'Oh, but it does, in its way,' he said, and chuckled once. I kept the gun trained on him until he had climbed into the car and the strange pair had disappeared in a cloud of dust and fumes that seemed to taint the very sunlight that shone through it.

My fingers began to blister almost as soon as they had driven away. At first there was just a feeling of mild irritation but it quickly became real pain as small raised bumps appeared on my fingertips and the palm of my hand. I applied some hydrocortisone but the irritation persisted for most of the day, an intense, uncomfortable itching where

Mr. Pudd's card, and his fingers, had touched my skin. Using tweezers, I placed the card in a plastic envelope, sealed it, and placed it on my hall table. I would ask Rachel to have someone take a look at it while I was in Boston.

Chapter Seven

I left my gun beneath the spare tire in the trunk of the Mustang before walking to the granite masonry bulk of the Edward T. Gignoux Courthouse at Newbury and Market. I passed through the metal detector, then climbed the marble stairs to courtroom 1, taking a seat in one of the chairs at the back of the court.

The last of the five rows of benches was filled with what, in less enlightened times, might have been referred to as the cast of a freak show. There were five or six people of extremely diminished stature, two or three obese women, and a quartet of very elderly females dressed like hookers. Beside them was a huge, muscular man with a bald head who must have been six-five and weighed in at three hundred pounds. All of them seemed to be paying a great deal of attention to what was going on at the front of the courtroom.

The court was already in session and a man I took to be Arthur Franklin was arguing some point of law with the judge. His client, it appeared, was wanted in California for a range of offences including copyright theft, animal cruelty, and tax evasion, and was about as likely to avoid a jail term as turkeys were to see Christmas. He was released on $50,000 bail and was scheduled to appear later that month before the same judge, when a final decision would be made on his extradition. Then everybody stood and the judge departed through a door behind his brown leather chair.

I walked up the center aisle, the muscular man close behind me, and introduced myself to Franklin. He was in his early forties, dressed in a blue suit, under which he was sweating slightly. His hair was startlingly black and the eyes beneath his bushy brows had the panic-stricken look of a deer faced with the lights of an approaching truck.

Meanwhile Harvey Ragle, who was seated beside Franklin, wasn't what I had expected. He was about forty and wore a neatly pressed tan suit, a clean, white, open-necked shirt, and oxblood loafers. His hair was brown and curly, cut close to his skull, and the only jewelry he wore was a gold Raymond Weil watch with a brown leather strap. He was freshly shaven and had splashed on Armani aftershave like it was being given away free. He rose from his seat and extended a well-manicured hand.

'Harvey Ragle,' he said. 'CEO, Crushem Productions.' He smiled warmly, revealing startlingly white teeth.

'A pleasure, I'm sure,' I replied. 'I'm sorry, I can't shake hands. I seem to have picked up something unpleasant.'

I lifted my blistered fingers and Ragle blanched. For a man who made his living by squashing small creatures, he was a surprisingly sensitive soul. I followed them both out of the courtroom, pausing briefly while the old ladies, the obese women, and the midgets took turns hugging him and wishing him well, before we crossed into attorney conference room 223, beside courtroom 2. The huge man, whose name was Mikey, waited outside, his hands crossed before him.

'Protection,' explained Franklin as he closed the door behind us. We sat down at the conference table and it was Ragle who spoke first.

'You've seen my work, Mr. Parker?' he said.

'The crush video, Mr. Ragle? Yes, I've seen it.'

Ragle recoiled a little, as if I'd just breathed garlic on him.

'I don't like that term. I make erotic films, of every kind, and I am a father to my actors. Those people in court today are stars, Mr. Parker, stars.'

'The midgets?' I asked.

Ragle smiled wistfully. 'They're little people, but they have a lot of love to give.'

'And the old ladies?'

'Very energetic. Their appetites have increased rather than diminished with age.'

Good grief, I thought.

'And now you make films like the one your attorney sent me?'

'Yes.'

'In which people step on bugs.'

'Yes.'

'And mice.'

'Yes.'

'Do you enjoy your work, Mr. Ragle?'

'Very much,' he said. 'I take it that you disapprove.'

'Call me a prude, but it seems kind of sick, besides being cruel and probably illegal.'

Ragle leaned forward and tapped me on the knee with his index finger. I resisted breaking it, but only just.

'But people kill insects and rodents every day, Mr. Parker,' he began. 'Some of them may even derive a great deal of pleasure from doing so. Unfortunately, as soon as they admit to that pleasure and attempt to replicate it in some form, our absurdly censorious law enforcement agencies step in and penalize them. Don't forget, Mr. Parker, we put Reich in jail to die for selling his sex boxes from Rangeley, in this very state. We have a record of penalizing those who seek sexual gratification by unorthodox means.'

He sat back and smiled his bright smile.

I smiled back at him. 'I believe it's not only the state of California that has strong feelings about the legitimacy of what you do.'

Ragle's veneer crumbled and he seemed to grow pale beneath his tan.

'Er, yes,' he said. He coughed, then reached for a glass of water that was resting on the table before him. 'One gentleman in particular seems to have serious objections to some of my more, um, *specialized* productions.'

'Who might that be?'

'He calls himself Mr. Pudd,' interjected Franklin.

I tried to keep my expression neutral.

'He didn't like the spider movies,' he added.

I could guess why.

Ragle's veneer finally crumbled, as if the mention of Pudd's name had finally brought home the reality of the threat he was facing. 'He wants to kill me,' he whined. 'I don't want to die for my art.'

So Al Z knew something about the Fellowship, and Pudd, and had seen fit to point me in Ragle's direction. It seemed that I had another good reason for going to Boston besides Rachel and the elusive Ali Wynn.

'How did he find out about you?'

Ragle shook his head angrily. 'I have a supplier, a man who provides me with rodents and insects and, when necessary, arachnids. It's my belief that he told this individual, this Mr. Pudd, about me.'

'Why would he do that?'

'To divert attention away from himself. I think Mr. Pudd would be just as angry with whoever sold me the creatures as he is with me.'

'So your supplier gave Pudd your name, then claimed not to know what you were planning to do with the bugs?'

'That is correct, yes.'

'What's the supplier's name?'

'Bargus. Lester Bargus. He owns a store in Gorham, specializing in exotic insects and reptiles.'

I stopped taking notes.

'You know the name, Mr. Parker?' asked Franklin.

I nodded. Lester Bargus was what people liked to call "two pounds of shit in a one-pound bag." He was the kind of guy who thought it was patriotic to be stupid and took his mother to Denny's to celebrate Hitler's birthday. I recalled him from my time in Scarborough High, when I used to stand at the fence that marked the boundary of the football field, the big Redskins logo dominating the board, and get ready to face a beating. Those early months were the hardest. I was only fourteen and my father had been dead for two months. The rumors had followed us north: that my father had been a policeman in New York; that he had killed two people, a boy and a girl – shot them down dead and they weren't even armed; that he had subsequently put his gun in his mouth and pulled the trigger. They were made worse by the fact that they were true; there was no way of avoiding what my father had done, just as there was no way of explaining it. He had killed them, that was all. I don't know what he saw when he pulled the trigger on them. They were taunting him, trying to make him lose his temper with them, but they couldn't have known what they would cause him to do. Afterward my mother and I had run north, back to Scarborough, back to her father, who had once been a policeman himself, and the rumors had snapped at our heels like black dogs.

It took me a while to learn how to defend myself, but I did. My grandfather showed me how to block a punch and how to throw one back in a single controlled movement that would draw blood every time. But when I think back on those first months, I think of that fence, and a circle of young men closing on me, and Lester Bargus with his freckles and his brown, square-cut hair, sucking spit back into his mouth after he had begun to drool with the joy of striking out at another human being from the security of the pack. Had he been a coyote, Lester Bargus would have been the runt that hangs at the margins of the group, lying down on its back when the stronger ones turned on it yet always ready to fall on the weak and the wounded when the frenzy struck. He tortured and bullied and came close to rape in his senior year. He didn't even bother to take his SATs; a new scale would have been needed to measure the depths of Bargus's ignorance.

I had heard that Bargus now ran a bug store in Gorham but it was believed to be merely a front for his other interest, which was the illegal sale of weapons. If you needed a clean gun quickly, then Lester Bargus was your man, particularly if your political and social views were so right wing they made the Klan look like the ACLU.

'Are there a lot of stores that supply bugs, Mr. Ragle?'

'Not in this state, no, but Bargus is also regarded as a considerable authority nationally. Herpetologists and arachnologists consult with him on a regular basis.' Ragle shuddered. 'Although not, I should add, in person. Mr. Bargus is a particularly unpleasant individual.'

'And you're telling me all this because . . . ?'

Franklin intervened. 'Because my client is certain that Mr. Pudd will kill him if someone doesn't stop him first. The gentleman in Boston, who has acted as a conduit for some of my client's more mainstream products, believes that a case with which you are currently involved may impinge upon my client's interests. He suggested that any assistance we might be able to provide could only help our cause.'

'And all you have is Lester Bargus?'

Franklin shrugged unhappily.

'Has Pudd tried to contact you?'

'In a way. My client had been sequestered in a safe house in Standish. The house burnt down; somebody threw an incendiary device through the bedroom window. Fortunately, Mr. Ragle was able to escape without injury. It was after that incident that we took Mikey on as security.'

I closed my notebook and stood up to leave. 'I can't promise anything,' I said.

Ragle leaned toward me and gripped my arm. 'If you find this man, Mr. Parker, squash him,' he hissed. 'Squash him like a bug.'

I gently removed my arm from his grasp. 'I don't think stiletto heels come that big, Mr. Ragle, but I'll bear it in mind.'

I drove over to Gorham that afternoon. It was only a

couple of miles but it was still a wasted trip, as I knew it would be. Bargus was aging badly, his hair and teeth almost gone and his fingers stained yellow with nicotine. He wore a *No New World Order* T-shirt, depicting a blue United Nations helmet caught in the crosshairs of a sniper's sight. In his dimly lit store, spiders crouched in dirt-filled cases, snakes curled around branches, and the hard exoskeletons of cockroaches clicked as they crawled against one another. On the counter beside him a four-inch-long mantid squatted in a glass case, its spiked front legs raised before it. Bargus fed it a cricket, which skipped across the dirt at the bottom of the case as it tried vainly to evade destruction. The mantid turned its head to watch it, as if amused by its presumption, then set off in pursuit.

It took Bargus a few moments to recognize me as I approached the counter.

'Well, well,' he said. 'Look what just rose to the lip of the bowl.'

'You're looking well, Lester,' I answered. 'How do you stay so young and pretty?'

He scowled at me and picked at something jammed between two of his remaining teeth. 'You a fag, Parker? I always thought you was queer.'

'Now, Lester, don't think I'm not flattered, but you're not really my type.'

'Huh.' He didn't sound convinced. 'You here to buy something?'

'I'm looking for some information.'

'Out the door, turn right, and keep going till you hit the asshole of hell. Tell 'em I sent you.'

He went back to reading a book, which, judging from the illustrations, appeared to be a guide to making a mortar out of beer cans.

'That's no way to talk to an old high school buddy.'

'You ain't my buddy, and I don't like you being in my store,' he said without looking up from his book.

'Can I ask why?'

'People have a habit of dying around you.'

'You look hard enough, people have a habit of dying around everybody.'

'Maybe, 'cept around you they die a whole lot quicker and a whole lot more regular.'

'Then the sooner I leave, the safer you'll be.'

'I ain't holdin' you.'

I tapped lightly at the glass of the mantid case, directly in the insect's line of vision, and the triangular head drew back as it flinched. A mantid is the most humanlike of insects; it has its eyes arranged so that it can see forward, allowing it depth perception. It can see a certain amount of color, and it can turn its head to look over its "shoulder." Also, like humans, it will eat just about anything it can subdue, from a hornet to a mouse. As I moved my finger, the mantid's head carefully followed the motion while its jaws chomped at the cricket. The top half of its body was already gone.

'Quit botherin' it,' said Bargus.

'That's quite a predator.'

'That bitch would eat you, she thought you'd stay still long enough.' He grinned, revealing his rotting teeth.

'I hear they can take a black widow.'

The beer-can-mortar book now lay forgotten before him. 'I seen her do it,' nodded Bargus.

'Maybe she's not so bad after all.'

'You don't like spiders, you just walked into the wrong store.'

I shrugged. 'I don't like them as much as some. I don't like them as much as Mr. Pudd.'

Lester's eyes suddenly returned to the page before him, but his attention remained focused on me.

'Never heard of him.'

'Ah, but he's heard of you.'

Lester looked up at me and swallowed. 'The fuck you saying?'

'You gave him Harvey Ragle. You think that's going to be enough?'

'I don't know what you're talking about.' In the warm, dank-smelling store, Lester Bargus began to sweat.

'My guess is that he'll take care of Ragle, then come back for you.'

'Get out of my store,' hissed Lester. He tried to make it sound menacing, but the tremor in his voice gave him away.

'Are spiders the only things you sold him, Lester? Maybe you helped him with some of his other needs, too. Is he a gun-lovin' man?'

His hands scrambled beneath the counter and I knew he was reaching for a weapon. I tossed my card on the counter and watched as he grabbed it with his left hand, crushed it in his palm, and threw it into the trash can. His right hand came up holding a shotgun sawed off at the stock. I didn't move.

'I've seen him, Lester,' I said. 'He's a scary guy.'

Lester's thumb cocked the shotgun. 'Like I said, I don't know what you're talking about.'

I sighed and backed away.

'Your call, Lester, but I get the feeling that sooner or later, it's going to come back to haunt you.'

I turned my back on him and headed for the door. I had already opened it when he called my name.

'I don't want no trouble. Not from you, not from him, you understand?' he said.

I waited in silence. The struggle between his fear of saying nothing and the consequences of giving too much away was clear on his face.

'I never had no address for him,' he continued, hesitantly. 'He'd contact me when he needed something, then pick it up hisself and pay in cash. Last time he came he was asking about Ragle, and I told him what I knew. You see him again, you tell him he's got no call to come bothering me.'

Confessing seemed to have restored some of his confidence, because his habitual ugly sneer returned. 'And, I was you, I'd find me another line of work. The kind of fella you're asking about don't like being asked about, you get my meaning. The kind of fella you're asking about, he kills people get involved in his business.'

That evening I felt no desire to be in the house or to cook for myself. I secured all of the windows, placed a chain on the back door and put a broken matchstick above the front door. If anyone tried to gain entry, I would know.

I drove into Portland and parked at the junction of Cotton and Forest in the Old Port, then walked down to Sapporo on Commercial Street, the sound of the sea in my ears. I ate some good teriyaki, sipped green tea, and tried to get my thoughts straight. My reasons for going to Boston were rapidly multiplying: Rachel, Ali Wynn, and now Al Z. But I still hadn't managed to corner Carter Paragon, I was still concerned about Marcy Becker, and I was sweating under my jacket since I couldn't take it off without exposing my gun.

I paid the check and left the restaurant. Across Commercial, crowds of kids lined up to get into Three Dollar Dewey's, the doorman checking IDs with the skepticism of a seasoned pro. The Old Port was buzzing, and noisy crowds congregated at the corner of Forest and Union, the edge of the main drag. I walked among them for a while, not wanting to be alone, not wanting to return to the house in Scarborough. I passed the Calabash Cigar Cafe and Gritty McDuffs, glancing down the pedestrian strip of Moulton Street as I passed.

The woman in the shadows was wearing a pale summer dress patterned with pink flowers. Her back was to me, and her blond hair hung in a ponytail against the whiteness of her back, held in place by an aquamarine bow. Around me, traffic stopped and footsteps hung suspended, passersby frozen briefly in their lives. The only sound I heard was my own breath; the only movement I saw came from Moulton.

Beside the woman stood a small boy, and the woman's left hand was clasped gently over his right. He wore the same check shirt and short pants as he had on the day when I had first seen him on Exchange Street. As I watched, the woman leaned over and whispered something to him. He nodded and his head turned as he looked back at me, the single clear lens gleaming in the darkness. Then the woman straightened, released his hand, and began to walk away from us, turning right at the corner onto Wharf Street. When she left my sight it was as if the world around me released its breath, and movement resumed. I sprinted down Moulton, past the shape of the little boy. When I reached the corner the woman was just passing Dana Street, the street lamps creating pools of illumination through which she moved soundlessly.

'Susan.'

I heard myself call her name, and for a moment it seemed to me that she paused as if to listen. Then she passed from light into shade and was gone.

The boy was now sitting at the corner of Moulton, staring at the cobblestones. As I approached him he looked up, and his left eye peered curiously at me from behind his black-rimmed glasses. Dark tape had been wrapped inexpertly around the lens, obscuring the right eye. He was probably no more than eight years old, with light brown hair parted at one side and flicked loosely across his forehead. His pants were almost stiff with mud in places and his shirt was filthy. Most of it was obscured by the block of wood – maybe eighteen inches by five inches, and an inch thick – that hung from the rope around his neck. Something had been hacked into the wood in jagged, childish letters, probably with a nail, but the grooves were filled with dirt in places, conspiring with the darkness to make it almost impossible to read.

I squatted down in front of him. 'Hi,' I said.

He didn't seem scared. He didn't look hungry or ill. He was just . . . there.

'Hi,' he replied.

'What's your name?' I asked.

'James,' he said.

'Are you lost, James?'

He shook his head.

'Then what are you doing out here?'

'Waiting,' he said simply.

'Waiting for what?'

He didn't reply. I got the feeling that I was supposed to know, and that he was a little surprised I didn't.

'Who was the lady you were with, James?' I asked.

'The Summer Lady,' he answered.

'Does she have a name?'

He waited for a moment or two before replying. When he did, all the breath seemed to leave my body and I felt light headed, and afraid.

'She said you'd know her name.' Again he seemed puzzled, almost disappointed.

My eyes closed for an instant and I rocked back on my heels. I felt his hand on my wrist, steadying me, and the hand was cold. When I opened my eyes, he was leaning close to me. There was dirt caught between his teeth.

'What happened to your eye, James?' I asked.

'I don't remember,' he said.

I reached toward him and he released his grip on my wrist as I rubbed at the dirt and filth encrusted on the board. It fell to the ground in little clumps, revealing the words:

James Jessop
Sinner

'Who made you wear this, James?'

A small tear trickled from his left eye, then a second. 'I was bad,' he whispered. 'We were all bad.'

But the tears fell only from one eye, and only the dirt on his left cheek was streaked with moisture. My hands were trembling as I reached for his glasses. I took the frames gently in each hand and slowly removed them. He didn't try to stop me, his single visible eye regarding me with absolute trust.

And when I took the glasses away, a hole was revealed where his right eye had been, the flesh torn and burnt and the wound dry as if it were an old, old injury that had long since stopped bleeding, or even hurting.

'I've been waiting for you,' said James Jessop. 'We've all been waiting for you.'

I rose and backed away from him, the glasses dropping to the ground as I turned.

And I saw them all.

They stood watching me, men and women, young boys and girls, all with wooden boards around their necks. There were a dozen at least, maybe more. They stood in the shadows of Wharf Street and at the entrance to Commercial, wearing simple clothes, clothes designed to be worn on the land: pants that wouldn't tear at the first misstep in the dirt, and boots that would not let in the rain or be pierced by a stone.

Katherine Cornish, Sinner.

Vyrna Kellog, Sinner.

Frank Jessop, Sinner.

Billy Perrson, Sinner.

The others were farther back, their names on the boards harder to read. Some of them had wounds to their heads. Vyrna Kellog's skull had been split open, and the open wound extended almost to the bridge of her nose; Billy Perrson had been shot through the forehead; a flap of Katherine Cornish's skin hung forward from the back of her head, obscuring her left ear. They stood and regarded me, and the air around them seemed to crackle with a hidden energy.

I swallowed, but my throat was dry and the effort made it ache.

'Who are you?' I asked, but even as they faded away, I knew.

I stumbled backward, the bricks behind me cold against my body, and I saw tall trees and men wading through mud and bone. Water lapped against a sandbag levee, and animals howled. And as I stood there trembling, I closed my eyes tight and heard my own voice start to pray.

Please Lord, it said.

Please don't let this begin again.

Chapter Eight

The next day, I drove down to Boston in about two hours but got snarled up in the city's horrific traffic for almost another hour. They were calling Boston's never-ending roadworks 'the Big Dig,' and signs dotted around various large holes in the ground promised: *It'll be worth it.* If you listened hard enough, you could hear millions of voters hissing that it had better be.

Before I left, I called Curtis Peltier at home. He had been out to dinner with some friends the night before, he told me, and when he got back the police were at his house.

'Someone tried to break in the back door,' he explained. 'Some kids heard the noise and called the police. Probably damn junkies from Kennedy Park or Riverton.'

I didn't think so. I told him about the missing notes.

'You think there was something important in them?'

'Maybe,' I replied, although I couldn't think what it might be. I suspected that whoever took them – Mr. Pudd or some other person as yet unknown – simply wanted to make things as difficult as possible for me. I told Curtis to look after himself and he assured me that he would.

Shortly before noon I reached Exeter Street, just off Commonwealth Avenue, and parked outside Rachel's building. She was renting in a four-story brownstone across the street from where Henry Lee Higginson, the founder of the Boston Symphony Orchestra, once lived. On Commonwealth, people jogged and walked their dogs or sat on the benches and took in the traffic fumes. Close by, pigeons and sparrows fed before paying their respects to the statue of the sailor-historian Samuel Eliot Morison, who sat on his plinth with the vaguely troubled look of a man who has forgotten where he parked his car.

Rachel had given me my own key to the apartment, so I dumped my overnight bag, bought some fruit and bottled water in Deluca's Market at Fairfield, and headed up Commonwealth Avenue until I reached the Public Garden between Arlington and Charles. I drank my water, ate my fruit, and watched children playing in the sunlight and dogs chasing Frisbees. I wanted a dog, I thought. My family had always had them, my grandfather too, and I liked the idea of having a dog around the house. I guessed that I wanted the company, which made me wonder why I wasn't asking Rachel to move in with me. I thought that Rachel might have been wondering about it herself. Lately there seemed to be an edge to her voice when the subject came up, a new urgency to her probings. She had been patient for over fourteen months now, and I guessed that she was feeling the strain of being trapped in relationship limbo. That was my fault: I wanted her near me, yet I was still afraid of the potential consequences. She had almost died once because of me. I did not want to see her hurt again.

At 2 P.M. I took the red line out to Harvard and headed for Holyoke Street. Ali Wynn was due to finish her lunchtime shift at two-thirty and I'd left a message to say that I'd be coming by to talk to her about Grace. The redbrick building in which the restaurant was housed had ivy growing across its face and the upstairs windows were decked with small white lights. From the room below came the sound of tap dancers practising their steps, their rhythms like the movements of fingers on the keys of an old Underwood typewriter.

A young woman of twenty-three or twenty-four stood on the steps of the building, adjusting a stud in her nose. Her hair was dyed a coal black, she wore heavy blue-black makeup around her eyes, and her lipstick was so red it could have stopped traffic. She was very pale and very thin, so she couldn't have been a regular eater at her own restaurant. She looked at me with a mixture of expectancy and unease as I approached.

'Ali Wynn?' I asked.

She nodded. 'You're the detective?'

'Charlie Parker.' She reached out and shook my hand, her back remaining firmly against the brickwork of the building behind her.

'Like the jazz guy?'

'I guess.'

'He was pretty cool. You listen to him?'

'No. I prefer country music.'

She wrinkled her forehead. 'Guess your mom and dad had to be jazz fans to give you a name like that?'

'They listened to Glenn Miller and Lawrence Welk. I don't think they even knew who Charlie Parker was.'

'Do people call you Bird?'

'Sometimes. My girlfriend thinks it's cute. My friends do it to irritate me.'

'Must be kind of a drag for you.'

'I'm used to it.'

The deconstruction of my family's naming procedures seemed to make her a little less wary of me, because she detached herself from the wall and fell into step beside me. We walked down to the Au Bon Pain at Harvard Square, where she smoked four cigarettes and drank two espressos in fifteen minutes. Ali Wynn had so much nervous energy she made electrons seem calm.

'Did you know Grace well?' I asked when she was about halfway through cigarette number two.

She blew out a stream of smoke. 'Sure, pretty well. We were friends.'

'Her father told me that she used to live with you and that she stayed with you sometimes even after she moved out.'

'She used to come down at weekends to use the library and I let her crash on my couch. Grace was fun. Well, she used to be fun.'

'When did she stop being fun?'

Ali finished number two and lit number three with a matchbook from the Grafton Pub. 'About the time she started her graduate thesis.'

'On the Aroostook Baptists?'

The cigarette made a lazy arc. 'Whatever. She was obsessed with them. She had all of these letters and photographs belonging to them. She'd lie on the couch, put some mournful shit on the stereo, and stay like that for hours, just going through them over and over again. Can you get me another coffee?'

I did as I was asked. I figured that she wasn't going to run away until she'd finished her cigarette.

'You ever worry about the effects of too much caffeine?' I asked when I returned.

She tugged at her nose stud and smiled. 'Nah, I'm hoping to smoke myself to death first.'

There was something very likable about Ali Wynn, despite the veneer of Siouxsie and the Banshees–era cool. The sunlight made her eyes sparkle and the right side of her mouth was permanently raised in an amused, faux-cynical grin. She was all front; the cigarette smoke didn't stay in her mouth long enough to give a gnat a nicotine buzz and her makeup was too carefully applied to be truly scary. I guessed that she probably inspired fear, lust, and irritation in her male classmates, all in roughly equal measure. Ali Wynn could have wrapped the world around her little finger if she'd had the self-confidence to do it. It would come, in time.

'You were telling me about Grace,' I prompted, as much to get myself back on track as Ali.

'Yeah, sure. There's not much more to tell. It was like the whole family history thing was draining her, sucking the life from her. It was all "Elizabeth" this and "Lyall" that. She became a real drag. She was obsessed by Elizabeth Jessop. I don't know, maybe she thought Elizabeth's spirit had entered into her or something.'

'Did she think Elizabeth was dead?'

Ali nodded.

'Did she say why?'

'She just had a feeling, that was all. Anyway, like I said, it was all getting too heavy. I told her she couldn't stay anymore because my roomie was complaining, which was, like, a total lie. That was in February. She stopped coming and we didn't really talk much between then and . . .' She let the end of the sentence hang, then stubbed the cigarette out angrily.

'I suppose you think I'm a bitch,' she said softly when the last trace of smoke had disappeared.

'No, I don't think you're a bitch at all.'

She didn't look at me, as if afraid that my expression might give the lie to my words. 'I was going to go up to the funeral but . . . I didn't. I hate funerals. Then I was going to send a card to her dad – he was a nice old guy – but I didn't do that either.'

At last, she raised her eyes and I was only half surprised to see that they were wet. 'I prayed for her, Mr. Parker, and I can't remember the last time I ever prayed. I just prayed that she'd be okay and that whoever was on the other side – God, Buddha, Allah – would look after her. Grace was a good person.'

'I think she probably was,' I said as she lit a final cigarette. 'Did she take drugs?'

Ali shook her head vehemently. 'No, never.'

'Apart from getting overinvolved with her thesis, did she seem depressed or anxious?'

'No more than any of us.'

'Was she seeing anyone?'

'She'd had a couple of flings, but nothing serious for at least a year. She would have told me.'

I watched her quietly for a time, but I knew she was

telling the truth. Ali Wynn hadn't been in the car with Grace on the night that she died. More and more, Marcy Becker was looking like the most likely candidate. I sat back and examined the crowds entering and leaving the T, the tourists and locals with bags of wine and candies from Cardullos, Black Forest ham and exotic teas from Jackson's of Picadilly, bath salts and soaps from Origins. Grace should have been among them, I thought. The world was a poorer place for her passing.

'Has that helped you?' asked Ali. I could see that she wanted to leave.

'It's cleared a few things up.' I handed her my card, after writing my home telephone number on the back. 'If you think of anything more, or if someone else comes around asking about Grace, maybe you'll give me a call.'

'Sure.' She picked up the card and placed it carefully in her purse. She was about to move away when she paused and placed her hand lightly on my arm.

'You think somebody killed her, don't you?' Her red lips were pressed tightly together but she couldn't control the trembling of her chin.

'Yes,' I answered. 'I think somebody did.'

Her grip tightened momentarily and I felt the heat of her penetrating to my skin. 'Thanks for the coffee,' she said, and then she was gone.

I spent the rest of the afternoon buying some clothes for my depleted wardrobe before heading back to Copley and the Starbucks on Newbury to read the newspaper. Reading the *New York Times* on a near-daily basis was a habit I hadn't lost, although buying it in Boston made me feel kind of guilty, as if I had just rolled up the newspaper and used it to slap the mayor.

I didn't even notice the start of the story on the far right of the front page until I came to its continuation on page seven and saw the photograph accompanying it. A man stared out at me in black-and-white, a black hat on his head, and I recalled the same man nodding to me from a darkened Mercedes as I approached Jack Mercier's house – and sitting uneasily with three other people in a framed photograph in Mercier's study. His name was Rabbi Yossi Epstein, and he was dead.

According to the police report, Rabbi Yossi Epstein left the Eldridge Street shul at 7:30 P.M. on a cool Tuesday evening, the flow of traffic on the Lower East Side changing, altering in pitch, as commuters were replaced by those whose reasons for being in the city had more to do with pleasure than business. Epstein wore a black suit and a white shirt, but he was far from being the traditionalist that his exterior suggested. There were those in the shul who had long whispered against him; he tolerated homosexuals and adulterers, they said. He was too ready to take his place before the television cameras, they argued, too quick to smile and pander to the national media. He was too concerned with the things of this world and too little concerned with the promise of the next.

Epstein had made his name in the aftermath of the Crown Heights disaster, pleading for tolerance, arguing that the Jewish and black communities should put aside their differences, that poor blacks and poor Jews had more in common with each other than with the wealthier members of their own tribes. He had been injured in the riots that followed, and a picture of him in the *Post*, blood streaming from a wound in his head, had brought him his first taste of celebrity due to the photo's unfortunate, and unintended, similarity to representations of the suffering Christ.

Epstein had also been involved with the B'Nai Jeshurun Temple up on Eighty-ninth Street and Broadway, founded by Marshal T. Meyer, whose mentor had been the conservative firebrand Abraham Yoshua Heschel. It was easy to see why someone with Epstein's views might have been attracted to Meyer, who had fought with the Argentine generals in his efforts to find disappeared Jews. Since Meyer's death, in 1993, two Argentine rabbis had continued his work in New York, including the provision of a homeless shelter and encouraging the establishment of a gay congregation. B'Nai Jeshurun was even twinned with a congregation in Harlem, the New Canaan Baptist Church, whose preacher sometimes spoke at the synagogue. According to the *Times*, Epstein had fallen out with B'Nai Jeshurun and had taken to holding twice-monthly services at the old Orensanz Center on the Lower East Side.

One of the reasons for the split with B'Nai Jeshurun appeared to be Epstein's growing involvement in anti-Nazi groups, including the Center for Democratic Renewal in Atlanta and Searchlight in Britain. He had established his own organization, the Jewish League for Tolerance, staffed mainly by volunteers and run from out of a small office on Clinton Street, above a disused Jewish bookstore.

According to the *Times*, Epstein was believed to have received considerable funding in recent weeks to enable him to commence a series of investigations into organizations suspected of anti-Semitic activities, among them the usual suspects: fanatics with 'Aryan' prominent in their names and splinter groups from the Klan who had left because the Klan now frowned on burning down synagogues and chaining blacks to the back axles of pickup trucks.

Whatever his critics might have said about him, Yossi Epstein was a brave man, a man of conviction, a man who worked tirelessly to improve the lives not only of the city's Jews but of his other fellow citizens. He was found dead in his apartment at 11 P.M. on Wednesday night, apparently after suffering some kind of seizure. The apartment, in which he lived alone, had been ransacked and his wallet and address book were missing. Foul play was suspected, according to the report, a suspicion increased by another incident earlier that night.

At 10 P.M., the office of the Jewish League for Tolerance was firebombed. A young volunteer, Sarah Miller, was working there at the time, printing off addresses for a mailing the following day. She was three days short of her nineteenth birthday when the room around her became an inferno. She was still on the critical list, with burns over 90 percent of her body. Epstein was due to be buried at Pine Lawn Cemetery in Long Island that day, following the prompt autopsy.

There was one more detail that caught my attention. In addition to his work on right-wing organizations, Epstein was reported to be preparing a legal challenge to the religious tax exemption given by the IRS to a number of church groups. Most of the names were unfamiliar to me, except for one: the Fellowship, based in Waterville, Maine. The law firm employed by Epstein to handle the case was Ober, Thayer & Moss of Boston, Massachusetts. It was hardly a coincidence that the firm also took care of Jack Mercier's legal affairs and that Warren Ober's son was soon to be married to Mercier's daughter.

I read through the piece again, then called Mercier's home. A maid took the call, but when I gave my name and asked to be put through to Mr. Mercier, another female voice came on the line. It was Deborah Mercier.

'Mr. Parker,' she said. 'My husband is not available. Perhaps I can help you?'

'I don't think so, Mrs. Mercier. I really need to speak to your husband.'

There was a pause in the conversation long enough to make our feelings about each other clear, and then Deborah Mercier concluded:

'In that case, perhaps you'd be kind enough not to phone the house again. Jack is not available at present, but I'll make sure he hears that you called.'

With that she hung up, and I got the feeling that Jack Mercier would never know that I had called him.

I had never met Rabbi Yossi Epstein and knew nothing more about him than what I had just read, but his activities had awakened something, something that lay curled in its web until Epstein caused one of the strands to twitch and the sleeping thing roused itself and came after him, then tore him apart before it returned to the dark place in which it lived.

In time, I would find that place.

Chapter Nine

I returned to Rachel's apartment, showered, and in an effort to cheer myself up for the evening ahead, put on some of my sharp new purchases: a black Joseph Abboud coat that made me look like I was auditioning for the second remake of *Nosferatu*, black gabardine pants, and a black DKNY v-neck. Screaming 'fashion victim,' I walked down to the Copley Plaza Hotel and into the Oak Bar.

Outside, the traffic on Copley melted away, the sound of horns and engines smothered by the red curtains of the Oak. The four big ceiling fans scythed the air and the ice in the raw bar glittered in the dim light. Louis was already sitting at a table by the window, his long frame folded into one of the bar's comfortable red chairs. He was wearing a black wool suit with a white shirt and black shoes. His dark head was no longer shaven and he had grown a small, vaguely satanic beard, which, if anything, rendered him even more intimidating than before. In the past, when he had been bald and devoid of facial hair, people crossed the street to avoid him. Now they probably felt the urge to book a trip somewhere safe and quiet, like Kosovo or Sierra Leone.

There was a Presidential Martini on the table before him, and he was smoking a Montecristo No. 2. That was about $55 worth of vices. He blew a stream of blue smoke at me in greeting.

I ordered a virgin cocktail and shrugged off my coat, ostentatiously showing Louis the label as I did so.

'Yeah, very impressive,' he said unconvincingly. 'Not even last season's. You so cheap, your hourly rate probably got ninety-nine cents at the end.'

'Where's the insignificant other?' I asked, ignoring him.

'Buying some clothes. Airline lost his bag.'

'They're doing him a favor. You pay them to lose it?'

'Didn't have to. Baggage handlers probably refused to touch it. Piece of shit practically walked to La Guardia by itself. How you doin'?'

'Pretty good.'

'Still huntin' pen pushers?' Louis didn't entirely approve of my move into the area of white-collar criminals. He felt that I was wasting my talents. I decided to let him go on thinking it for a while.

'The money's okay and they don't tend to kick up a fuss,' I replied, 'although one of them called me a bad name once.'

Close to the door, heads began to turn and one of the waiters almost dropped a tray of drinks in shock. Angel entered, dressed in a yellow-and-green Hawaiian shirt, a yellow tie, a powder blue jacket, stonewashed jeans, and a pair of red boots so bright they throbbed. Conversations died as he passed by, and a few people tried to shield their eyes.

'Off to see the wizard?' I asked when the red boots finally reached us.

Louis looked like someone had just splashed paint on his car. 'Shit, Angel, the hell you think you are? Mardi Gras?'

Angel calmly took a seat, ordered a Beck's from a distressed-looking waiter, then stretched out his legs to admire his new boots. He straightened his tie, which did nothing to help in the long term but obscured some of his shirt for a while.

'You have the good taste of a seasoned meths drinker,' I told him.

'Man, I didn't even know Filene's Basement *had* a basement,' said Louis. 'Must be where they keep the real shit.'

Angel shook his head and smiled. 'I'm making a statement,' he said, like a teacher explaining a lesson to a pair of slow children.

'I know the kind of statement you makin',' replied Louis as Angel's beer arrived. 'You sayin', "Kill me, I got no taste."'

'You should carry a sign,' I advised. '"I will work for fashion tips."'

It felt good to be here with them. Angel and Louis were just about the closest friends I had. They had stood by me as the confrontation with the Traveling Man drew closer, and had faced down the guns of a Boston scumbag named Tony Celli in order to save the life of a girl they had never met. Their gray morality, tempered by expediency, was closer to goodness than most people's virtue.

'How's life in the sticks?' asked Angel. 'Still living in the rural slum?'

'My house is not a slum.'

'It don't even have carpets.'

'It's got timber floors.'

'It's got *timbers*. Just cause they fell on the ground don't make them a floor.'

He paused to sip his beer, allowing me to change the subject.

'Anything new in the city?' I asked.

'Mel Valentine died,' said Angel.

'Psycho Mel?' Psycho Mel Valentine had been working his way through the A-to-Z of crime: arson, burglary, counterfeiting, drugs . . . If he hadn't died, then pretty soon the Bronx Zoo would have been mounting a guard on its zebras.

Angel nodded. 'Always thought the "Psycho Mel" thing was kinda unfair. Maybe he'd have been psychotic if they quietened him down some, but "Psycho" seemed like kind of an underestimation of his abilities.'

'How'd he die?'

'Gardening accident in Buffalo. He was trying to break into a house when the owner killed him with a rake.'

He raised his glass to the memory of Psycho Mel Valentine, gardening victim.

Rachel appeared a few minutes later, much earlier than expected, wearing a yellow coat that hung to her ankles. Her long red hair was tied up at the back of her head and held in place by a pair of wooden skewers.

'Nice hair,' said Angel. 'You pick up all the channels with those things, or just local?'

'Tuning must be off,' she replied. 'I can still hear you.'

She pulled the sticks from her hair and let it hang loose on her shoulders. It brushed my face as she kissed me gently before ordering a Mimosa and taking a seat beside me. I hadn't seen her in almost two weeks and I felt a pang of desire for her as she folded one stockinged leg over the other, her short black skirt rising above midthigh level. She wore a man's shirt, white and with only one button undone. She always wore her shirts that way: if any more buttons were opened, the scars left by the Traveling Man on her chest became visible. As she sat she placed a large Neiman Marcus bag by her feet. Inside was something red and expensive.

'Needless Markup,' whistled Louis. 'You givin' away money, can I have some?'

'Style costs,' she replied.

'That's the truth,' he said. 'Try telling it to the other fifty percent of the group.'

The 25 percent that was Angel searched through the big NM bag until he found the receipt, then dropped it quickly and rubbed his fingers like they'd just been burned.

'What she buy?' asked Louis.

'A house,' he said. 'Maybe two.'

She stuck her tongue out at him.

'You're early,' I said.

'You sound disappointed. I disturb a conversation on football or monster trucks?'

'Stereotyping,' I replied. 'And you a psychologist.'

We talked for a time, then crossed the street to Anago at the Lenox and spoke about nothing and everything for a couple of hours over venison and beef and oven roast salmon. Then, when the coffee arrived and while the other three sipped Armagnacs, I told them about Grace Peltier, Jack Mercier, and the death of Yossi Epstein.

'And you think these old guys are right, that Grace Peltier didn't kill herself?' asked Angel when I had finished.

'Things just don't fit. Mercier could probably put pressure on the investigation through Augusta, but that would draw attention to himself and he doesn't want that.'

'Which is why he hired you,' said Angel. 'To stir things up.'

'Maybe,' I replied, but I felt that there was more to it than that, although I couldn't say what.

'So what do you think happened to Grace?' asked Rachel.

'Speculating, I'd say that Marcy Becker might have been the other person in the car with Grace for most of her trip north. But Marcy Becker is missing, and she left in enough of a hurry to forget a pack of cigarettes that was probably sitting on the dashboard in front of her.'

'And maybe left her bag of coke as well,' said Angel.

'That's possible, but I don't think so. The coke looks like a plant, a way of making Grace appear a little less clean than she was. Drugs, pressure of study, takes her own life with a gun that seems to have popped up out of nowhere.'

'What was the piece?' he asked.

'Smith & Wesson Saturday Night Special.'

Angel shrugged. 'Not hard to lay your hands on one of those, you know who to ask.'

'But I don't think Grace Peltier *would* have known who to ask. According to her father, she didn't even like guns.'

'Do you think Marcy Becker could have killed her?' asked Rachel.

I toyed with my water glass. 'Again, it's possible, but they were friends and it hardly seems likely that this girl could frame a pretty good imitation of a suicide. If I had to guess – and Lord knows, I've done enough of that already –

I'd say that Marcy Becker might have seen something, possibly whoever killed her friend, while she was away from the car for some reason. And if I can figure out that Grace wasn't alone in the car for most of her journey, then someone else can figure it out too.'

'Which means you got to find Marcy Becker,' said Louis.

'And talk to Carter Paragon, whose secretary says that Grace never showed for their meeting.'

'And how does Epstein's death fit into all this?'

'I don't know, except that he and Mercier shared legal advisers and Mercier obviously knew Epstein well enough to bring him out to his house and hang a picture of him on his wall.'

Finally, I told them about Al Z and Harvey Ragle, and Mr. Pudd and the woman who had accompanied him to my house.

'You telling us he poisoned you with his business card?' said Angel incredulously.

Even I was embarrassed by the possibility, but I nodded. 'I got the sense that he had come to see me because that was what was expected of him, not because he thought that I'd actually back off,' I explained. 'The card was part of that, a means of goading me to take action, just like letting me see that I was being watched.'

Louis looked at me from over the top of his glass. 'Man wanted to take a look at you,' he said quietly. 'See what he was up against.'

'I waved my gun at him,' I replied. 'He went away.'

Louis's eyebrow rose a notch. 'Told you you'd be glad of that gun someday.'

But he didn't smile when he said it, and I didn't smile either.

Rachel and I walked back to her apartment after dinner, holding hands but not speaking, content simply to be close to each other. We talked no further of Grace Peltier or the case. When we were inside her bedroom I slipped off my shoes and lay on her bed, watching her move through the soft yellow glow of her night-light. Then she stood before me and removed a small package from the larger Neiman Marcus bag.

'Is that for me?' I asked.

'Kind of,' she replied.

She tore open the package to reveal a tiny white lace bra and panties, an even more delicate suspender belt, and a pair of sheer silk stockings.

'I don't think they'll fit me,' I said. 'In fact, I'm not even sure that they'll fit you.'

Rachel pouted, unzipped her skirt, and let it fall to the ground, then slowly began to unbutton her shirt. 'Don't you even want me to try?' she whispered.

Call me weak, but stronger men than I would have buckled under that kind of pressure.

'Okay,' I said hoarsely as the blood left my head and headed south for the winter.

Later that night I lay beside her in the darkness, listening to the sounds of the city beyond the window. I thought she was asleep, but after a time she brushed her head against my chest and I felt her eyes upon me.

'Penny for them,' she said.

'I'm holding out for more.'

'Penny and a kiss.' She placed her lips softly against mine. 'It's Grace Peltier, isn't it?'

'Her, the Fellowship, Pudd,' I replied. 'It's everything.'

I turned to her and found the whites of her eyes

'I think I'm afraid, Rachel.'

'Afraid of what?'

'Afraid of what I might do, of what I might have to do.'

Her hand reached out to me, a pale ghost moving through the void of the night. It traced the sockets of my eyes, the bones at my cheeks, following the lineaments of the skull beneath the skin.

'Afraid of what I've done in the past,' I concluded.

'You are a good man, Charlie Parker,' she whispered. 'I wouldn't be with you if I didn't believe that.'

'I've done bad things. I don't want to do them any longer.'

'You did what you had to do.'

I gripped her hand tightly and felt her palm rest itself against my temple, the fingers lightly brushing my hair.

'I did more than that,' I answered.

It seemed that I was floating in a black place, with endless night above and below me, and only her hand was stopping me from falling. She understood, for her body moved closer against me and her legs wrapped around mine as if to tell me that if I was to fall, then we would fall together. Her chin burrowed into my neck and she was quiet for a time. In the silence, I could feel the weight of her thoughts.

'You don't know that the Fellowship was responsible for her death, or for anyone else's,' she said at last.

'No, I don't,' I admitted. 'But I sense that Mr. Pudd is a violent man, and maybe something worse. I could feel it when he was close, when he touched me.'

'And violence begets violence,' whispered Rachel.

I nodded. 'I haven't fired a gun in almost a year, Rachel, not even on a range. I hadn't even held one in my hand until two days ago. But I have a sense that if I involve myself further in this, I may be forced to use it.'

'Then walk away. Give Jack Mercier his money back and let someone else deal with it.' But even as she said it, I knew that she didn't mean it; that in a way, I was testing myself through her and she knew it.

'You know I can't do that. Marcy Becker could be in trouble, and I think someone murdered Grace Peltier and tried to cover it up. I can't let that slide.'

She moved in even closer to me, and her hand moved across my cheek and my lips. 'I know you'll do what's right, and I think you'll try to avoid violence if you can.'

'And if I can't?'

But she didn't respond. After all, there was only one answer.

Outside, the traffic hummed and people slept and a sliver of moon hung in the sky like a knife slash in the heavens. And while I lay awake in the bed of the woman I loved, old Curtis Peltier sat in his kitchen, drinking hot milk in an effort to help himself sleep. He wore blue pajamas and bedroom slippers, with his tattered red robe hanging open above them. He sipped his milk, then left the glass on the table and rose to return to his bed.

I can only guess at what happened next, but in my head I can hear the back door opening, can see the shadows lengthen and move toward him. A gloved hand clasps itself over the old man's mouth while the other twists his arm up behind his back with such force that the shoulder immediately dislocates and the old man briefly loses consciousness. A second pair of hands grab his feet and they carry him up the stairs to the bathroom. There comes the sound of water gurgling and bubbling into the bath as, slowly, it fills. Curtis Peltier regains consciousness to find himself kneeling on the floor, his face against the tub. He watches the water rise and knows he is about to die.

'Where is it, Mr. Peltier?' says a detached male voice beside his ear. He cannot see the face, nor can he see the second person, who stands farther back, although their shadows shift on the tiles before him.

'I don't know what you're talking about,' he replies, scared now.

'Yes, you do, Mr. Peltier. I know you do.'

'Please,' he says, just before his head is plunged into the water. He has no time to take a breath and the water enters his mouth and nostrils instantly. He struggles, but his shoulder is convulsed with pain and he can only beat futilely at the water with his left hand. They pull his head up and he gasps and splutters, coughing bathwater onto the floor.

'I'll ask you one more time, Mr. Peltier. Where is it?'

And the old man finds that he is crying now, crying with

fear and pain and regret for his lost daughter, for she cannot protect him just as he could not protect her. He feels a force at his shoulder, fingers digging into the injured joint, and he loses consciousness again. When he awakens, he is in the bath, naked, and a redheaded man is hovering over him. There is a sharp pain in his arms, gradually grower dimmer and dimmer. He feels sleepy and struggles to keep his eyes open.

He looks down. There are long slashes from his wrists to his elbows and the bathwater has turned to blood. The shadows watch over him as slowly, slowly the light dies, as his life seeps away and he feels his daughter embrace him at last, carrying him away with her into the darkness.

Chapter Ten

In every case, according to Plato, the principle is to know what the investigation is about.

Jack Mercier had hired me to find out the truth about Grace Peltier's death. While out at his house, I had seen Yossi Epstein, who appeared to be involved in moves against the Fellowship that were sponsored by Mercier. Yossi Epstein was now dead, and his offices had been burned to the ground. Grace Peltier had been studying the history of the Aroostook Baptists, who had since emerged from beneath a cloak of mud by the shores of St. Froid Lake. She had, for some reason, found it necessary to try to contact Carter Paragon in the course of her research, once again raising the specter of the Fellowship. Lutz, the detective who was investigating the Peltier case, was close enough to the Fellowship to haul his ass out to Waterville and warn me against irritating Paragon. If I were to connect these occurrences together and add in the figure of Mr. Pudd, the investigation now appeared to be about the Fellowship.

Rachel left early on Saturday morning to attend the continuation of her college meeting. She brought with her a small plastic bag containing Mr. Pudd's business card, which someone had promised to examine before lunch. I showered, made a pot of coffee, and then, wearing only a towel, began to work the phone. I called Walter Cole, my former partner in Homicide while I was with the NYPD, and he made some calls. From him I got the name of one of the detectives involved with the Major Case Squad investigating Epstein's death and the arson attack on his office. The detective's name was Lubitsch.

'Like the movie director,' he explained when he at last came to the phone. 'Ernst, you know?'

'Any relation?'

'No, but I directed traffic a couple of times.'

'I don't think it counts.'

'You used to be a bull?'

'That's right.'

'How does the PI world pay?'

'Depends how fussy you are. There's plenty of work out there if you're prepared to follow errant husbands and wives. Most of it doesn't pay too well, so you have to do a lot of it to make ends meet. Why, don't you like being a cop?'

'Sure, I like it okay, but it pays shit. I'd make more money emptying garbage cans.'

'Different version of the same job.'

'You said it. You asking about Epstein?'

'Anything you can give.'

'I ask why?'

'Trade?'

'Sure.'

'I'm investigating the suicide of a girl who may or may not have had some contact with Epstein in the past.'

'Name?'

'Grace Peltier. CID III up in Machias have it.'

'When did she die?'

'About two weeks ago.'

'What links her to Epstein?'

I didn't see any harm in turning up the heat under the Fellowship, if I could. Anyway, Lutz's interview with Paragon was contained in the case records.

'The Fellowship. It was one of the organizations Epstein was making moves against. Grace Peltier may have met with its figurehead, Carter Paragon, shortly before she died.'

'That it?'

'There may be more. I just got started on it. Listen, if I can help at all, I will.'

There was a pause for at least thirty seconds. I thought the phone had gone dead.

'I'll trust you, but just once.'

'Once is all I need.'

'Officially, it's homicide. We've ruled out robbery as a motive, and a possible connection to the firebombing of the Jewish League for Tolerance is currently under investigation.'

'Neat. What are you leaving out?'

Lubitsch lowered his voice. 'Postmortem found a puncture wound in Epstein's armpit. They're still trying to get confirmation of what was injected into him, but the latest guess is some kind of venom.' There came the sound of papers shuffling. 'I'm reading here, okay, but it's neurotoxic, which means that it blocks transmission of nerve impulses to the muscles, overstimulating the transmitters' – he stumbled on the next words – 'acetylcholine and noradrenaline, causing paralysis of both the' – more stumbles – 'sympathetic and parasympathetic nervous systems, resulting in sudden and severe stress on the body.'

Lubitsch took a deep breath.

'In layman's terms, the venom caused acceleration of heartbeat, increase in blood pressure, breathing difficulties, and muscle paralysis. Epstein suffered a massive heart attack within two minutes. He was dead within three. Symptoms – and this is strictly on the QT, you understand? – are systemic, usually associated with spiders. Basically, unless someone comes up with a better theory, the perp took Yossi Epstein down, squatted on his chest, then injected him with a huge dose of spider venom. They're guessing black widow, but the tests aren't complete. Plus, the perp took a patch of skin from his lower back, a couple of inches wide. Now is that weird shit, or is that weird shit?'

I put down my pen and looked at the garbled notes I had written on Rachel's telephone message pad. 'Anyone else interested in this?' I asked.

'What is that sound?' replied Lubitsch. 'Why, it's the sound of somebody stretching the bounds of professional courtesy.'

'Sorry,' I said, 'but I take it that's a yes.'

Lubitsch sighed. 'Minneapolis PD. Possible connection to the death of a doctor named Alison Beck one week ago. She was found with black widow spiders sealed up inside her mouth.'

'My God.'

'Uh-huh.'

Lubitsch seemed to enjoy my response, because he continued: 'ME reckons the spiders were subdued with carbon dioxide, then inserted into her mouth as they were starting to revive. Only one widow survived: the rest bit each other, and bit her. She died of respiratory failure.'

'They have any leads?'

'She performed abortions, so they're rounding up the local crazies while trying to keep most of the details from the press. Seems like they had a bitch of a job getting her out of the car.'

'Why?'

'Whoever killed her filled it with recluses.'

Pudd.

I thanked him, promised him a return call, and hung up. I logged on to the Internet and in less than two minutes a picture of Alison Beck was on the screen in front of me. She looked younger than she had in the photograph in Jack Mercier's study; younger and happier. The reporters had done a pretty good job of nailing deep background sources, even to the extent of speculating that Alison Beck's death might have been caused by a spider bite. It's hard to keep details like that quiet.

I turned off the computer and called Rachel, since the meeting was due to break for coffee at eleven. 'Anyone have time to look at that card yet?' I asked.

'Well, a big affectionate good morning to you too,' she replied. 'Truly, the love is gone.'

'It's not gone, it's just distracted. Well?'

'They're still looking at it. Now go away before I forget why I'm with you.'

She hung up, which left me with a choice. Either do nothing, or try my luck with the Minneapolis PD. Unfortunately, I had no contacts over there and I didn't think that my natural charm would get me very far. I tried calling Mercier again but got the brush-off from the maid. With nothing else to do until later that evening, when Rachel and I were due to attend *Cleopatra* at the Wang, I dressed, took a Harlan Coben novel from Rachel's shelf, and headed down the stairs to kill some time along Newbury Street. There was a comic book store on Newbury, I recalled. I thought it might be worth a visit.

Al Z, it emerged, had already made the arrangements for our meeting. As soon as I stepped into the street, a car door opened and a huge shape emerged from a green Buick Regal parked across the street.

'Nice wheels, Tommy,' I remarked. 'Planning to take the boys to Disney World?'

Tommy Caci grinned. He was wearing a sleeveless black T-shirt and skin-tight black jeans. His trapezius muscles were so huge he looked like he'd swallowed a coat hanger, and his massive shoulders tapered to a tiny waist. All things considered, Tommy Caci resembled a walking martini glass, but without the fragility.

'Welcome to Boston,' he said. 'Al Z would appreciate a courtesy call. Get in the car. Please.'

'You mind if I make my own way?' I asked. Nothing would persuade me to get in the back of that Buick, no matter how much Tommy smiled. I'd prefer to walk blindfolded down the fast lane of the interstate. I didn't like to think of some of the trips people had taken in that car.

Tommy's smile didn't falter. 'Easier this way. Al don't like to be kept waiting.'

'I'm sure. Still, how about I take some air and follow you on over?'

Tommy shrugged. It wasn't worth getting rough over. 'You want to take some air, that's fine with us,' he said resignedly.

So I walked over to Al Z's office on Newbury Street. Admittedly, the Buick shadowed me every step of the way, never going above a couple of miles an hour, but it made me feel kind of wanted. When I arrived at the comic book store, Tommy waved at me and the Buick shot away, scattering tourists from its path. I rang the buzzer, gave my name, then pushed the door and walked up the bare stairs to Al Z's office.

It hadn't changed a whole lot since the last time I was there. It was still bare boards and peeling paint. There were still two gunmen inside the door, and there was still nowhere to sit apart from a worn red sofa against one wall and the chair behind Al Z's desk, a chair currently occupied by Al Z himself.

He wore a black suit, a black shirt and a black tie, and his gray hair was slicked back from his skull, making his thin face look even more cadaverous than it usually did. A pair of hearing aids were visible in his small, pointed ears. Al Z's hearing had been failing in recent years. It must have been all those guns going off around him.

'I see you broke out your summer wardrobe,' I said.

He looked down at his clothes as if seeing them for the first time. 'I was at a funeral,' he said.

'You arrange it?'

'Nah, just paying my last respects to a friend. All my friends are dying. Soon I'll be the only one left.' I noticed that Al Z seemed pretty certain he was going to outlive his friends. Knowing Al Z, I figured he was probably right.

He gestured at the sofa. 'Take a seat. I don't get so many visitors.'

'Can't understand why, this place looking so welcoming and all.'

'I got Spartan tastes.' He smiled and leaned back in his chair. 'Well, this is just my lucky day. First a funeral, then it turns out I'm a stop on the Charlie Parker Goodwill Tour. Next thing you know, my dick will drop off and my plants will die.'

'I'll be sorry to see your plants go.'

Al Z stretched his long body in his chair. It was like watching a snake uncoil. 'And how is the elusive Louis? We don't hear much about him now. Seems like the only person he kills for these days is you.'

'The only person he ever killed for was himself,' I replied.

'Whatever. The only reason you can still take the subway when you visit New York is because your associate will whack anyone who makes a move on you. I think he'd even whack me if he had to, and I consider myself to be a pretty nice guy, all things considered. Well, most things considered.' He shook his head in bemusement. 'Now what can I do for you, apart from letting you walk out of here alive?'

I hoped he didn't mean it. Al Z and I had had our run-ins in the past; at one point he'd given me twenty-four hours to live if I didn't find some money that had been stolen from under the nose of the underboss Tony Celli. I found the money, so I was still alive, but Tony Clean was dead. I had watched Al Z kill him. The only aspect of it that bothered Al Z was the cost of the bullet. A lot of Tony's men had died in Dark Hollow, due in no small part to the efforts of Louis and me, but Tony was the only made man to be killed, and since Al Z had killed him that took a lot of heat off us. We in turn had taken the heat off Al Z by returning the money Tony had stolen, with interest. My relationship with Al Z could have been used to define 'complicated' in the dictionary.

Since the end of the Celli affair, Al Z had been keeping tabs on me. He knew enough about my business to learn that I was investigating the Fellowship and that, somehow, the man named Mr. Pudd was tied into its workings.

'As I recall,' I pointed out gently, 'you invited me along.'

Al Z pretended to be taken aback. 'So I did. It must have been a moment of weakness.' He immediately dispensed with the small talk. 'I hear that you may be sticking your nose into the affairs of the Fellowship.'

'Why would that be of interest to you?'

'A lot of things are of interest to me. How did you enjoy meeting Mr. Ragle?'

'He's a worried man. He thinks somebody is trying to kill him.'

'I fear Mr. Ragle may be about to suffer grievously for his art.'

He gestured at the two gunmen. They left the room and closed the door behind them.

Al Z stood and walked to the window, then stared down on the tourists shopping on Newbury, his basilisk glare flicking from face to face. Nobody died.

'I like this street,' he said, almost to himself. 'I like its normality. I like the fact that I can step out onto the sidewalk and the people around me are worrying about their mortgages, or the cost of coffee beans, or whether they just missed their train. I walk down there, and I feel normal by association.' He turned around to look at me. 'You, on the other hand, you *seem* normal. You dress like any other mook. You don't look no better or no worse than a hundred other guys on the street. But you step in here, and you make me nervous. I swear, my fucking palms itch when I see you. Don't get me wrong; I respect you. I may even like you a little. But I see you and I get this sense of impending doom, like the fucking ceiling is about to cave in. The presence of your pet killers in Boston doesn't make me sleep any easier. I know you got a woman here, and I know too that you were eating with your friends at Anago last night. You had the beef, by the way.'

'It was good.'

'For thirty-five bucks, it better be real good. It better sing a fucking song while you chew on it. You talk business, or pleasure?'

'A little of both.'

He nodded. 'That's what I thought. You want to know why I pointed Ragle toward you, why I'm interested in this man who calls himself Pudd? Maybe I figure, what can I do for Charlie Parker? Whose life can I turn to shit by letting you dig around in it?'

I waited. I wasn't sure where the conversation was going but the turn that it suddenly took surprised me.

'Or maybe it's something else,' he continued, and the tone of his voice changed. It now sounded a little querulous. It was an old man's voice. Al Z turned away from the window and walked over to the sofa, seating himself only a few feet away from me. His eyes, I thought, were haunted.

'You think one good action can make up for a lifetime of evil acts?' he asked.

'That's not for me to judge,' I replied.

'A diplomatic answer, but not the truth. You judge, Parker. That's what you do, and I respect you because you act on your judgment, just like me. We're two of a kind, you and I. Try again.'

I shrugged. 'Maybe, if it's an act of genuine repentance, but I don't know how the scales of judgment are weighted.'

'You believe in salvation?'

'I hope for it.'

'Then you believe in reparation too. Reparation is the shadow cast by salvation.'

He folded his hands in his lap. They were very white and very clean, as if he spent hours each day scraping the dirt from the wrinkles and cracks on his skin.

'I'm getting old. I looked around at the graveside this morning and I saw dead men and women. Between them all, they had maybe a couple of years to live. Pretty soon, we're all going to be judged, and we'll all be found wanting. The best we have to hope for is mercy, and I don't believe you get mercy in the next life if you haven't shown it in this one.

'And I'm not a merciful man,' he concluded. 'I have never been a merciful man.'

I waited, watching as he twisted the wedding ring on his finger. His wife had died three years before, and he had no children. I wondered if he had hopes of meeting her again, in some other life.

'Everybody deserves a chance to make amends for his life,' he said softly. 'Nobody has the right to take that away.'

His eyes flicked back to the window, drawn by the light. 'I know something of the Fellowship, and of the man it sends to do its business,' he said.

'Mr. Pudd.'

'You've met him?' There was surprise in Al Z's voice.

'I've met him.'

'Then your days may be numbered,' he said simply. 'I know about him because it's my business to know. I don't like unpredictability, unless I figure that it's worth gambling on it to use for my own ends. That's why you're still alive. That's why I didn't kill you when you came looking for Tony Clean, and that's why I didn't kill you even after you and your friends took out most of Tony's crew in that snow-hole town two winters ago. What you wanted and what I wanted—' He moved his right hand, palm down, in a balancing motion. 'Plus, you found the money, and that bought you your life.

'Now, maybe I figure that we could have another meeting of minds on Pudd. I don't care if he kills you, Parker. I'd miss you, sure. You brighten things up, you and your friends, but that's as far as it goes. Still, if you kill him, then that would be a good thing for everybody.'

'Why don't you kill him yourself?'

'Because he hasn't done anything to bring himself to the immediate attention of me or my associates.' He leaned forward. 'But that's like noticing a black widow in the corner of the room and figuring that you'll leave it alone because it hasn't bitten you yet.'

The spider analogy, I knew, was deliberate. Al Z was an interesting man.

'And there's more to this than Pudd. There are other people, people in the shadows. They need to be flushed out too, but if I go against Pudd for no reason other than the fact that I think he's evil and dangerous – and that assumes that I could find him and that the people I sent after him could kill him, which I doubt – then the others in the background would move against me, and I'd be dead. I don't doubt it for one second. In fact, I think that the moment I made a move against Pudd, he'd kill me. That's how dangerous he is.'

'So you'll use me to flush him out.'

Al Z actually laughed. 'Nobody uses you, I think, unless you want it. You're going after Pudd for your own reasons, and nobody in my organization will stand in your way. I've even tried to point you in the right direction with our pornographer friend. If you corner this man, and we can assist you in finishing him off without drawing any attention to ourselves, then we will. But my advice to you is to move everybody you care about out of his reach, because he will kill them, and then he will try to kill you.'

He smiled conspiratorially.

'But I also hear that you may have some competition in trying to finish off Pudd. It seems that some old Jews have got tired of torchings and killings, and that the death of the rabbi in New York this week was the last straw. I tell you, don't mess with the fucking Jews. Maybe it ain't like the days of Bugsy Siegel no more but those people, they know how to bear a grudge. You think the fucking Sicilians are bad? The Jews, they've had thousands of years of experience of bearing grudges. They are to grudges what the Chinese are to gunpowder. These fucking people invented the grudge, excuse my language.'

'They've hired someone?' I asked.

Al Z shook his head. 'Money isn't the prime motivator where this man is concerned. He calls himself the Golem. He's Eastern European–Jewish, naturally. Never met him, which is probably a good thing. Way I understand it, anyone who meets him winds up dead. The day I see him, I'm gonna be kissing St. Peter's ring and apologizing for having an attack of selective amnesia where the ten commandments were concerned.'

He twisted at his own wedding ring again, the light from the window reflecting on it and sending tiny spears of golden light shooting across the wall.

'The guy you want to talk to is Mickey Shine, Michael Sheinberg. We called him Mickey the Jew. He's retired now, but he used to be part of Joey Barboza's crew until Joey started ratting people out. I heard that maybe he was the one killed Joey in San Francisco in seventy-six. He ended up working for Action Jackson for a time, then got tired of the whole racket and bought a flower shop in Cambridge.' He took a pen and scribbled an address on a piece of paper, tore it from the pad, and handed it to me.

'Mickey Shine,' he said. His eyes were distant and there was a sepia tint of nostalgia to his voice. 'You know, we went drinking, summer of sixty-eight, started out in Alphabet City, and I don't remember anything else until I woke up in this Turkish bath wearing only a towel. I was lying on a slab, surrounded by tiles. I swear, I thought I was in the fucking morgue. Mickey Shine. When you talk to him, you tell him I remember that night.'

'I will,' I said.

'I'll ask someone to call ahead,' said Al Z. 'Barboza was hit four times with a shotgun. You go waltzing in there with a gun at your shoulder asking about Mickey Shine's past, you're likely to find out how Barboza felt, if you get my meaning.'

I thanked him, then stood up to leave. By the time I reached the door, he had resumed his seat at his desk, his hand still toying with the gold band.

'We're two of a kind, you and I,' he repeated as I paused at the door.

'What kind is that?'

'You know what kind,' he replied.

'One good act,' I said gently, but I wasn't sure that would be enough. Al Z's business was based on drugs and whores, porn and theft, intimidation and wasted, blighted lives. If you believe in karma, then those things add up. If you believe in God, then maybe you shouldn't be doing those things in the first place.

I, too, had done things that I regretted. I had taken lives. I had killed an unarmed man with my bare hands. Maybe Al Z was right: perhaps we were two of a kind, he and I.

Al Z smiled. 'As you say, one good act. I will help you, in this small way, to find Mr. Pudd and put an end to him and those around him. You step lightly, Charlie Parker. There are still people listening for you.'

When I left, he had resumed his seat and his hands were once again steepled beneath his chin, his face hovering over them like that of some malicious, pitiless god.

Chapter Eleven

Mickey Shine was about five-six, bald, with a silver ponytail and a silver beard, both of which were designed to distract from the fact that he didn't have more than six hairs above the level of his ears. Unfortunately, when your name is Mickey Shine and the bright lights of your store reflect the dazzling brilliance of your skull, then cultivating a goatee and opting to grow your hair long at the back aren't exactly fail-safe options in the distraction stakes.

'You ever hear the joke about the two legionnaires walking through the desert?' I asked him, as the jangling of the bell above the door on Kendall Square faded away. 'One turns to the other and says, "Y'know, if her name hadn't been Sandra I'd have forgotten her by now."'

Mickey Shine looked at me blankly.

'Sand,' I said. 'Sand-*ra*.'

'You want to buy something already?' asked Mickey Shine. 'Or did somebody send you here to brighten up my day?'

'I guess I'm here to brighten your day,' I said. 'Did it work?'

'Do I look brightened up?'

'I guess not. Al Z gave me your name.'

'I know. A guy called. He didn't say nothing about you being a comedian, though. You want to lock the door, turn the sign to *Closed*?'

I did as I was asked, and followed Mickey Shine into the back of the store. There was a wooden table with a cork bulletin board above it. On the board were pinned the floral orders for that afternoon. Mickey Shine began pulling orchids from a black bucket and laying them out on a sheet of clear plastic.

'You want I should stop?' asked Mickey. 'I got orders, but you want I should stop, I'll stop.'

'No,' I replied. 'It's okay.'

'Help yourself to coffee,' he said. There was a Mr. Coffee machine on a shelf, beside a bowl filled with nondairy creamer and packets of sugar. The coffee smelled like something had crawled into the pot to die, then spent its final minutes percolating.

'You're here about Pudd?' he asked. He seemed intent upon the orchids, but his hands faltered as he said the name.

'Yes.'

'So it's time, then,' he said, more to himself than to me. He continued arranging the flowers in silence for a few minutes, then sighed and abandoned the task. His hands were shaking. He looked at them, held them up so I could see them, then thrust them into his pockets, the orchids now forgotten.

'He's a foul man, Mr. Parker,' he began. 'I have thought much about him in the last five years, about his eyes and his hands. His *hands*,' he repeated softly, and shuddered. 'When I think of him, I imagine his body as a frame, a hollow thing to carry around the evil spirit that resides inside. Maybe this sounds like madness to you?'

I shook my head and recalled my first impression of Mr. Pudd, the way his eyes peered out from behind their hoods of flesh, the strange, unconnected movements of his fingers, the hair below the joints. I knew exactly what Mickey Shine meant.

'I think, Mr. Parker, he is *dybbuk*. You know *dybbuk*?'

'I'm sorry, I don't.'

'*Dybbuk* is the spirit of a dead man that enters the body of another living being and possesses it. This Mr Pudd, he is *dybbuk*: an evil spirit, base and less than human.'

'How do you know of him?'

'I took a contract, is how I know. It was after I left, when the old ways started to fall apart. I was a Jew, and Jews do not make the book, Mr. Parker. I was not a made man, so I thought I would walk away, let them fight to the death like animals. I did one last favor, then left them to die.' He risked a glance at me, and I knew that Al Z had been correct; it was Mickey Shine who had pulled the trigger on Barboza in San Francisco in 1976, the last favor that allowed him to walk away.

'I bought my store, and things were good until about eighty-six. Then I got sick and had to close up for a year. New stores opened, I lost customers, and so and so . . .' He puffed up his cheeks and let his breath out in one loud, long exhalation.

'I heard that there was a paper on a man, a strange, thin man who killed out of some . . . misguided religious purpose, or so they said. Doctors in abortion clinics, homosexuals, even Jews. I don't believe in abortion, Mr. Parker, and the Old Testament is clear on . . . such men.'

He tried not to catch my eye, and I guessed that Al Z had told him a little about Angel and Louis, warning him to watch his mouth.

'But killing these people isn't the answer,' he resumed, with all the assurance of a man who has killed for a living. 'I took the paper. I hadn't fired a gun in many years, but the old instincts, you know, they die hard.'

He was rubbing at his arm again, I noticed, and his eyes had grown distant, as if he was drawing back from the memory of some ancient hurt.

'And you found him,' I said.

'No, Mr. Parker, he found me.' The frequency and force of the rubbing increased, harder and harder, faster and faster. 'I found out he was based somewhere in Maine, so I traveled up there to look for traces of him. I was in a motel in

Bangor. You know the city? It's a dump. I was asleep and I woke to a noise in the room. I reached for my gun but it wasn't there, and then something hit me on the head, and when I came to I was in the trunk of a car. My hands and feet were tied with wire, and there was tape on my mouth. I don't know how long we drove, but it felt like hours. At last the car stopped, and after a time the trunk opened. I was blindfolded, but I could see a little beneath the fold. Mr. Pudd was standing there, in his mismatched, old man's clothes. There was a light in his eyes, Mr. Parker, like I have never seen. I—'

He stopped and put his head in his hands, then ran them back over his bald head, as if all he had intended to do in the first place was smooth down whatever straggling hairs remained there. 'I almost lost control of my bladder, Mr. Parker. I am not ashamed to tell you this. I am not a man who scares easily, and I have faced down death many times, but the look in this man's eyes, and the feel of his hands on me, his nails, it was more than I could take.

'He lifted me from the car – he is strong, very strong – and dragged me along the ground. We were in dark woods, and there was a shape beyond them, like a tower. I heard a door open, and he pulled me into a shack with two rooms. The first had a table and chairs, nothing more, and there were bloodstains on the floor, dried into the wood. There was a case on the table, with holes in the top, and he picked it up as he passed and carried it with him. The other room was tiled, with an old bathtub and a filthy, busted toilet. He put me in the tub, then hit me again on the head. And while I lay stunned, he cut my clothes with a knife, so that the front of my body, from my neck to my ankles, was exposed. He smelled his fingers, Mr. Parker, and then he spoke to me.

'"You stink of fear, Mr. Sheinberg," was all he said.'

The store around us receded and disappeared. The noise of the traffic faded away, and the sunlight shining through the window seemed to dim. Now there was only the sound of Mickey Shine's voice, the stale, damp smell of the old hut, and the soft exhalations of Mr. Pudd's breath as he sat on the edge of the toilet bowl, placed the case on his lap and removed the lid.

'There were bottles in the box, some small, some large. He held one up in front of me – it was thin, and the stopper had small holes – and I saw the spider inside. I hate spiders, always have, ever since I was a boy. It was a little brown spider, but to me, lying in that tub and smelling of my own sweat and fear, it looked like an eight-legged monster.

'Mr. Pudd, he said nothing, just shook the jar, then unscrewed the top and dropped the spider on my chest. It caught in the hairs and I tried to shake it off, but it seemed to cling there, and I swear, I felt the thing bite me. I heard glass knocking on glass, and another little spider dropped beside the first, then a third. I could hear myself moaning, but it was like it was coming from somebody else, like I wasn't making the sound. All I could think of was those spiders.

'Then Mr. Pudd snapped his fingers and made me look up at him. He was choosing containers from the box and holding them up in front of me so I could see what was in them. One had a tarantula squatting on the bottom. There was a widow in a second one, crouched under a leaf. A third had a little red scorpion. Its tail twitched.

'He leaned forward and whispered in my ear: "Which one, Mr. Sheinberg, which one?" But he didn't release them. He just put them back in the box and took an envelope from inside his jacket. In the envelope were photographs: my ex-wife, my son, my daughters, and my little granddaughter. They were black-and-whites, taken while they were on the street. He showed me each one in turn, then put them back in the envelope.

' "You're going to be a warning, Mr. Sheinberg," he said, "a warning to anyone else who thinks he can make some easy money by hunting me down. Perhaps you'll survive tonight, and perhaps you won't. If you live, and go back to your flower store and forget about me, then I'll leave your family alone. But if you ever try to find me again, this little baby girl

– Sylvia, isn't that what they named her? – well, little Sylvia will quickly be lying where you are now, and what's about to happen to you will happen to her. And I guarantee you, Mr. Sheinberg, that she won't survive."

'Then he got up, stood by my legs, and pulled out the plug from the bath. "Get ready to make some new friends, Mr. Sheinberg," he whispered.

'I looked down and spiders started climbing from the drain. It was like there were hundreds of them, all fighting and twisting against each other. I think some of them were already dead and were just being carried along by the tide, but the rest of them . . .'

I looked away from him, a memory from my youth flashing briefly in my head. Someone had once done something similar to me when I was a boy: a man named Daddy Helms, who tormented me with fire ants for breaking some windows. Daddy Helms was dead now, but for that fleeting instant his spirit peered malevolently from behind the hoods of Mr. Pudd's eyes. I think, when I looked back at Mickey, that he must have seen something of that memory in my face, because the tone of his voice changed. It softened, and some of the anger he felt toward me for forcing him, through Al Z, to make this confession seemed to dissipate.

'They were all over me. I screamed and screamed and no-one could hear me. I couldn't see my skin, there were so many of them. And Pudd, he just stood there and watched while they crawled all over me, biting. I think I must have fainted because, when I came to, the bath was filling with water and the spiders were drowning. It was the only time I saw anything but joy in the sick fuck's face; he looked regretful, as if the loss of those fucking horrors really troubled him. And when they were all dead, he pulled me from the bath and took me back to the trunk of the car and drove me away from that place. He left me by the side of a street in Bangor. Somebody called an ambulance and they took me to a hospital, but the venom had already started to take effect.'

Mickey Shine stood up and began to unbutton his shirt, finishing with his cuffs. He looked at me, then opened the shirt and let it fall from his body, his hands holding on to the ends of the sleeves.

My mouth went dry. There were four chunks of flesh, each about the size of a quarter, missing from his right arm, as if some kind of animal had taken a bite from it. There was another cavity at his chest, where his left nipple had once been. When he turned, there were similar marks on his back and sides, the skin at the edges mottled and gray.

'The flesh rotted away,' he said softly. 'Damnedest fucking thing. This is the kind of man you're dealing with, Mr. Parker. If you decide to go after him, then you make sure you kill him because, if he gets away, you'll have nobody left. He'll kill them all, and then he'll kill you.'

He pulled his shirt back over his body and began to fix the buttons.

'Do you have any idea where he might have taken you?' I asked when he had finished.

Mickey shook his head. 'I think we went north, and I could hear the sea. That's all I remember.' He stopped suddenly, and wrinkled his brow. 'And there was a light up high, off to my right. I saw it as he pulled me in. It could have been a lighthouse, I guess.

'He said something else. He told me that if I came after him again, all of our names would be written. We would be written, and then we would be damned.'

I felt my brow furrow.

'What did he mean?'

Mickey Shine seemed about to answer, but instead he looked down and concentrated on rebuttoning his cuffs. He was embarrassed, I thought, ashamed at what he saw as his weakness in the face of Mr. Pudd's sadism, but he was also scared.

'I don't know what he meant,' he said, and his lips pursed at the taste of the lie in his mouth.

'What did you mean earlier when you said it was time?' I asked.

'Only Al Z ever heard that story before,' he answered. 'You and him, you're the only ones who know. I was supposed to be a mute witness to what Pudd could do, what he *would* do, to anyone who came after him. I wasn't supposed to talk, I was just supposed to *be*. But I knew that a day would come when it might be possible to make a move against him, to finish him off. I've been waiting a long time for it, a long time to tell that story again. So that's what I know; he's north of Bangor, on the coast, and there's a lighthouse close by. It's not much, but it's all I can give. Just make sure that it stays between us; between you, me, and Al Z.'

I wanted to press him on what he was leaving out, on what the threat of a name being 'written' might mean, but already I felt him closing up on me.

'I'll keep it that way,' I replied.

He nodded. 'Because if Pudd finds out that we talked, that we're moving against him, we're all dead. He'll kill us all.'

He shook my hand and turned from me.

'You going to wish me luck?' I asked.

He looked back at me, shaking his head. 'If you need luck,' he said softly, 'you're already dead.'

Then he went back to his orchids and said no more.

Part Two

Judge not the preacher, for he is thy Judge.

George Herbert, 'The Church-Porch'

The Search for Sanctuary

Extract from the postgraduate thesis of Grace Peltier

There are few surviving photographs of Faulkner (certainly none taken after 1963) and few records of his past, so our knowledge of him is largely limited to the evidence of those who heard him speak or encountered him in the course of one of his healing missions.

He was a tall man with long dark hair and a high forehead, blue eyes beneath dark, straight eyebrows, and pale, almost translucent skin. He dressed in the garb of a working man – jeans, rough cotton shirts, boots – except when he was preaching. At those times he favored a simple black suit with a white collarless shirt buttoned to the neck. He wore no jewelry and his only concession to religious adornment was an ornate gold crucifix that hung around his neck as he spoke. Those who had the opportunity to examine it closely describe it as extremely finely made, with tiny faces and limbs carved into the body of the cross. The face of the Christ figure was almost photographically detailed, with the sufferings of the crucified man so clear and minutely rendered as to be disturbing, his agony beyond doubt.

I have been able to find no record of Faulkner in any of the established schools of divinity, and inquiries to churches, major and minor, have also failed to yield any clue as to the origins of his religious education, if any. His earlier life is barely documented, although we do know that he was born Aaron David Faulkner, the illegitimate son of Reese Faulkner and Embeth Thule of Montgomery, Alabama, in 1924. He was an undersized child, with seriously impaired sight in his left eye that would later render him unsuitable for military service, but he began to grow quickly in his mid-teens. According to those neighbors who remember him this physical growth was accompanied by a similar development in his personality, from shy and somewhat awkward to dominant and imposing. He lived alone with his mother until her death shortly before his sixteenth birthday. Following her funeral, Aaron Faulkner left Montgomery and never returned.

The next four years, up to the time of his marriage, are a blank, with some possible exceptions. An Aarn [sic] Faulkner was charged with assault in

Columbia, South Carolina in 1941, following an incident in which a prostitute named Elsa Barker was apparently pelted with rocks, sustaining injuries to her head and back. Barker failed to appear in court to give evidence, and her statement to the police being deemed unreliable, the case was dismissed. No trace of Elsa Barker was ever found again.

One other incident is worthy of note. In 1943, a family of three named Vogel from Liberty, Mississippi, went missing from their farm. They were found, two days after the search began, buried in a shallow grave one mile from their property. Quicklime had been used on the bodies. According to police reports, a young drifter had been staying with them in the days prior to their disappearance. The Vogels had taken him in because he seemed to be a religious man. None of the neighbors ever saw him or met him, but they recalled his name: Aaron. After their deaths, it was found that the Vogels were unmarried and their daughter was illegitimate. Among those questioned in the course of the investigation was Aaron Faulkner, following his apprehension at a motel in Vicksburg. He was released after three days due to lack of evidence.

(While there is no direct link between the deaths of the Vogels and the attack on, and subsequent disappearance of, the prostitute Elsa Barker, it is my contention that both incidents display signs of a violent response to perceived sexual transgression, possibly linked to sublimated sexual desire: respectively, the Vogels' unmarried relationship and the birth of their illegitimate daughter, with its echoes of Faulkner's own parentage, and the activities of Barker. I believe that Faulkner's later attempts to restrain and regulate sexual relationships at the Eagle Lake community represent a similar pattern of behavior.)

Following his marriage in 1944, Faulkner worked with a printer named George Lemberger in Richmond, Virginia, and remained with him for the next twelve years while earning a reputation as an untrained preacher. A dispute over his preaching activities, combined with allegations that Faulkner had forged Lemberger's signature on a check, eventually led to his departure from Lemberger's printing firm in early 1957, and he subsequently went north, accompanied by his wife and two children. For some time between 1958 and 1963, he eked out a living as an itinerant preacher, eventually establishing small congregations of worshipers in the Maine towns from which the original group of sixteen was drawn. He supplemented his income by working, at various times, as a printer, a laborer, and a fisherman.

Faulkner initially made his headquarters in a rooming house on Montgomery Street in Portland, Maine, owned by a cousin of the Jessops. He conducted services in the dining room, sometimes preaching to as many as thirty people. It was as a result of those first, lengthy, sermons that his reputation spread, leading to Faulkner enjoying a small but extremely devoted following.

Faulkner was not a preacher in the hellfire-and-brimstone mode. Instead, he drew his listeners to him with a tone of quiet insinuation, gradually worming his way into their consciousness. (If this description appears unnecessarily perjorative, it should be noted that the retrospective recollections of those to whom I spoke are largely negative where Faulkner is concerned. While it is clear that he exerted a great influence while he spoke, and that there were enough people willing to follow him to enable him to establish a much bigger community than the original Eagle Lake settlement, had he chosen to do so, there were those who felt an uneasiness around him.)

His wife, Louise, was by all accounts a strikingly beautiful woman, with dark hair only marginally longer than that of her husband. She did not associate with the Preacher's congregation: if he was approached after the service, she would remain standing behind him, listening to what passed between the Preacher and the supplicant, without passing comment or participating in any way. It seems to have been her constant unspeaking presence at her husband's side that made people wary of her, although two witnesses spoke of her intervening physically when her husband was accused of perpetrating acts of fraud during a healing service in Rumford, Maine, in 1963. She did so entirely in silence, but her strength and the nature of her intervention was sufficient to enable those who saw it to recall it in detail almost forty years later. Nevertheless, she always deferred to her husband and exhibited no signs of disobedience toward him, in line with fundamentalist religious doctrine.

Louise's own family, the Dautrieves, originally came from east Texas and were Southern Baptists. According to the recollection of family members, they appear to have been largely supportive of her decision to marry Faulkner, who was only nineteen when they met, regarding him as a man of good faith although he was not himself a Baptist. After their marriage there was little direct contact between Louise and her family, and surviving relatives say that there was no contact at all once she left for Eagle Lake.

Privately, most believe that she is now dead.

Chapter Twelve

Rachel was already back in her apartment when I returned from my encounter with Mickey Shine. She greeted me with a peck on the lips.

'You have a good day?' she asked.

Under the circumstances, 'good' was probably a relative concept.

'I found out some stuff,' I replied neutrally.

'Uh-huh. Good stuff, or bad stuff?'

'Um, kind of bad, but nothing I hadn't suspected already.'

She didn't ask if I wanted to talk more about it. Sometimes it struck me forcefully that Rachel knew me very well while I hardly seemed to know her at all. I watched her open her bag and produce one of her wire-rimmed notebooks, from which she removed a single printed page.

'I don't think that what I have to tell you qualifies as good news either,' she said. 'Some folks at the chemistry department examined that business card. They e-mailed me the results. I guess they thought it might be a little technical to explain over the phone.'

'And?'

'The card was infused with a fluid called cantharidin, concentrated cantharidin,' she continued. 'It's sometimes used in medical procedures to produce blistering. One portion of the top right-hand corner had been lightly waxed, presumably so this Mr. Pudd could hold it without affecting his own skin. As soon you took it in your hand, your body heat and the moisture on your fingers activated the cantharidin and you started to blister.'

I thought about it for a moment.

'So he used some kind of medical product on the card . . .' I began, but Rachel shook her head.

'No, I said it was *used* for medical purposes, but the substance on the card was a very specific form of the toxin, produced, according to the research assistant who examined it, only by "certain vesicating arthropods." It's blister beetle venom. The man who gave it to you must have harvested the venom, concentrated it, then applied it to the card.'

I recalled Mr. Pudd's smile as I held the card in my hand.

You're also irritating, but it doesn't say that on your card either.

Oh, but it does, in its way.

I also thought of Epstein, and the substance that had been injected into him.

'If he harvested beetle venom, then I suppose he could harvest other types as well?' I asked Rachel.

'Such as?'

'Spider venom, maybe?'

'I called the lab after I received the message to clarify one or two details about the procedure, so I don't see why not. As I understand it, the beetle venom could have been extracted using some form of electric shock to provoke the insect into releasing the toxin. Apparently, the harvesting of spider venom is a little trickier. The spider has to be sedated, usually by cooling it with carbon dioxide, then put under a microscope. Each time it's shocked, it produces a tiny amount of venom, which can then be collected. You can usually shock an individual spider three or four times before it has to be put out to pasture.'

'So you'd need a whole lot of spiders to produce a reasonable amount of venom?'

'Probably,' she replied.

I wondered how many spiders had been milked in order to kill Yossi Epstein. I also wondered why anyone would bother. After all, it would have been far easier, and less conspicuous, simply to have killed Epstein in a more conventional way. Then I remembered Alison Beck, and how she must have felt as the widows struggled in her mouth and the recluses moved around her in the small, enclosed space of the car. I recalled the look in Mickey Shine's eyes as he spoke of the spiders in the bathtub, and the wounds gouged in his skin by their bites. And I thought of my own feelings as the blisters appeared on my skin, and the sensation of Mr. Pudd's thin, hairy fingers brushing against my own.

He did it because it was fun, because he was genuinely curious about the effects. He did it because to be preyed upon by a small, dark, consuming creature, multilegged and many-eyed, terrified his victims in ways that a bullet or a knife could not, and gave a new intensity to their sufferings. Even Epstein, who endured death by injection, felt something of this pain as his muscles spasmed and cramped, his breathing began to fail, and his heart at last gave way under the pressure on his body.

It was also a message. I was certain of that. And the only person for whom that message could be meant was Jack Mercier. Epstein and Beck were in the photograph on his wall, and Warren Ober's law firm had been handling Epstein's legal challenge to the IRS tax exemption granted to the Fellowship. I knew then that I had to return to Maine, that somehow Grace Peltier's death was linked to moves that her father and others had been making against the Fellowship. But how could Pudd and those who aided him have known that Grace Peltier was Jack Mercier's daughter? There was also the question of how a woman who was researching the history of a long-departed religious group ended up trying to corner the leader of the Fellowship. I could only find one answer: someone had pointed Grace

Peltier in the direction of the Fellowship, and she had died because of it.

I tried calling Mercier again as Rachel went to take a shower, but I got the same maid and a promise that Mr. Mercier would be told that I had called. I asked for Quentin Harrold and was similarly informed that he was not available. I was tempted to throw my cell phone to the ground and stamp on it, but I figured I might need it, so I contented myself with tossing it in disgust on Rachel's couch. It wasn't as if I had anything to tell Mercier anyway, or certainly nothing that he didn't already know. I just didn't like being kept in the dark, especially when Mr. Pudd was occupying space in that same darkness.

But there was another reason that I had yet to learn for Mr. Pudd's killing methods, a tenet that had its roots in the distant past and in other, older traditions.

It was the belief that spiders were the guardians of the underworld.

The Wang Center, on Tremont, was just about the most beautiful theater on the upper East Coast, and the Boston Ballet was, given my limited experience, a great company, so the combination was pretty hard to resist, especially on a first night. As we walked past Boston Common, a band played in the window of Emerson College's WERS radio station, the crowds heading to the theater district pausing briefly to examine the contorted face of the singer. We collected our tickets at the box office and walked into the ornate marble and gold lobby, past the booths hawking *Cleopatra* memorabilia and souvenir books. We had seats in the front row, far left, of the orchestra box – close to the back of the theater and slightly raised above the rows of seats ahead, so that nobody could obscure our view. The red-and-gold of the theater was almost as opulent as the stage design, giving the whole affair an air of restrained decadence.

'You know, when I told Angel we were coming here he asked me if I was sure I wasn't gay,' I whispered to Rachel.

'What did you say?'

'I told him I wasn't dancing the damn ballet, I was just going to watch it.'

'So I'm just a means of reassuring you about your heterosexuality?' she teased.

'Well, a very pleasurable means . . .'

Above and to my right, a figure entered one of the boxes on the level above ours, toward the front of the theater. He moved slowly, easing himself gently into his chair before adjusting his hearing aids. Behind him, Tommy Caci folded Al Z's coat, then poured a glass of red wine for his boss before taking the seat directly behind him.

The Wang is an egalitarian theater; there are no closed boxes, but some sections are more private than others. The area where Al Z sat was known as the Wang box; it was partially shielded by a pillar, although it was open to the aisle on the right. The adjacent seats were empty, which meant that Al had booked the entire section for the first-night show.

Al Z, I thought, you old romantic.

The lights went down as the audience grew quiet. Rimsky-Korsakov's music, arranged for the ballet by the composer, John Lanchbery, filled the huge space as the evening's entertainment commenced. Handmaidens danced around Cleopatra's bedchamber while the queen slept in the background and her brother Ptolemy and his confidant Pothinus plotted her downfall. It was all brilliantly done, yet I found myself drifting during the whole first half, my mind occupied by images of crawling things and the final, imagined moments of Grace Peltier's life. I kept seeing:

A gun close to her head, a hand buried in her hair to hold her steady as the finger tightened on the trigger. It is her finger on the trigger, but pressed against it is another. She is dazed, stunned by a blow to the temple, and cannot fight as her arm is maneuvered into position. There is no blood from the blow, and anyway the entry wound will tear apart the skin and bone, disguising any earlier injury. It is only when the cold metal touches her skin that she realizes, finally, what is happening. She strikes out and opens her mouth to scream . . .

There is a roar in the night, and a red flame bursts from her temple and sheds itself over the window and the door. The light dies in her eyes and her body slumps to the right, the smell of burning in the air as her singed hair hisses softly.

There is no pain.

There will never be pain again.

I felt a pressure on my arm and found Rachel looking at me quizzically, the ballet onstage reaching its preinterval climax. In her bedchamber, Cleopatra was dancing for Caesar, seducing him. I patted Rachel's hand and saw her scowl at the patronizing nature of the gesture, but before I could explain, a movement to my far right attracted my attention. Tommy Caci had risen, distracted, and reached inside his jacket. Before him, Al Z continued watching the ballet, apparently unaware of what was going on behind. Tommy moved away from his seat and disappeared into the aisle.

Onstage, the assassin, Pothinus, appeared in the wings, looking for his moment to strike at the queen, but Cleopatra and Caesar danced on, oblivious. The music swelled as a figure took the seat behind Al Z, but it was not Tommy Caci. Instead, it was thinner, more angular. Al Z remained engrossed in the action, his head moving in time to the music, his mind filled with images of escape as he sought briefly to forget the darker world he had chosen to inhabit. A hand moved, and something silver gleamed. Pothinus shot out from the wings, sword in hand, but Caesar was quicker and his sword impaled Pothinus through the stomach.

And in the box above, Al Z's body tensed and something red shot from his mouth as the figure leaned over him, one hand on his shoulder, the other close to the base of his skull. From behind, it would appear as if they were talking, nothing more, but I had seen the blade flash, and I knew what had happened. Al Z's mouth was wide open, and as I watched, Mr. Pudd's gloved hand closed upon it and he held him as he shook and died.

Then Mr. Pudd seemed to stare down to where I sat before draping Al Z's coat across the old man's shoulders and receding into the shadows.

Onstage, the curtain was falling and the audience had burst into applause, but I was already moving. I climbed over the edge of the orchestra box and ran up the aisle, the doors flying open noisily before me. To my left, a flight of stairs, topped by the eagle clock, led up to the next level. I took them two at a time, brushing aside an usher as I drew my gun.

'Call an ambulance,' I said as I passed. 'And the police.'

I heard the sound of his footsteps echoing on the marble as I reached the top of the stairs, my gun raised ahead of me. An exit door stood open and the counter-weighted fire escape, which descended under body weight, was rising back up. Below me was a loading dock, from which a car was already speeding, a silver Mercury Sable. Its side faced me as it turned onto Washington Street, so I didn't get the license number, but there were two figures inside.

Behind me, the seats were emptying for the intermission, and one or two people glanced out the open door. These doors were all alarmed, so security would be up here soon to find out who had opened them, and why. I retreated inside and moved to the area where Al Z still sat. His head hung down, his chin on his chest, the coat draped loosely across his shoulders to hide the bulge of the blade's handle. The handle anchored him to his seat, preventing him from falling facedown. Blood flowed from his mouth and drenched the front of his white dress shirt. Some of it had fallen into his wineglass in a final, terrible act of consecration. I couldn't see Tommy Caci.

Behind me, two Wang Center security staff appeared, but they backed off at the sight of the gun in my hands.

'You call the police?'

They nodded.

Across the aisle to my right, a door stood slightly ajar. I gestured to it. 'What's in there?'

'VIP lounge,' one of the security guards answered.

I looked down to the base of the door and saw what looked like the toe of a shoe in the gap. Gently, using my elbow, I pushed it open.

Tomy Caci lay facedown on the floor, his head to one side and the edge of the wound at his throat clearly visible. There was a lot of blood on the floor and on the walls. He had probably been taken from behind when he left his seat and entered the lounge. Beyond him was a bar, with some couches and chairs, but the room looked empty.

I stepped back into the aisle as two blue uniforms appeared behind me, advancing with their weapons drawn. I heard the order to drop my gun amid the audience's cries of surprise and fear. I immediately did as I was told and the two cops descended on me.

'I'm a private detective,' I said as one of them pushed me against the wall and frisked me while the other checked out Tommy Caci, then moved toward the body in the front row.

'It's Al Z,' I told him, when he came back, and I felt a kind of sadness for the old thug. 'He won't be bothering you again.'

I was interviewed at the scene by a pair of detectives named Carras and McCann. I told them all that I had seen, although I didn't tell them what I knew of Mr. Pudd. Instead, I described him in as much detail as I could and said that I had recognized Al Z from a previous case.

'What case would that be?' asked McCann.

'Some trouble last year in a place called Dark Hollow.'

When I mentioned Dark Hollow, the scene of Tony Celli's death at the hands of the man now dead beside us, their faces cleared, McCann even offering to buy me a drink at some unspecified date in the future. Nobody mourned Tony Celli's passing.

I stood beside them at the main door of the theater as the audience was fed through a rank of policemen, each person being asked if he or she had seen anything before being told to supply an ID and telephone number. At police headquarters I gave a statement sitting beside McCann's messy desk, then left my cell phone number and Rachel's address in case they needed to speak to me again.

After they let me go, I tried calling Mickey Shine at the florist's but there was no reply and I was told that his home number was unlisted. Another call and five minutes later, I had a home telephone number and address for one Michael Sheinberg at Bowdoin Street, Cambridge. There was no reply from that number either. I left a message, then hailed a cab and took a ride out to Cambridge. I asked the cab to wait as I stepped out onto the tree-lined street. Mickey Shine lived in a brownstone apartment block, but there was no answer when I tried his bell. I was considering breaking and entering when a neighbor appeared at a window. He was an elderly man in a sweater and baggy blue jeans and his hands shook from some nervous condition as he spoke.

'You lookin' for Mickey?'

'Yes, I am.'

'You a friend of his?'

'From out of town.'

'Well, sorry, but he's gone. Left about an hour ago.'

'He say where he was going?'

'No sir, I just saw him leave. Looks like he may be gone for a couple of days. He had a suitcase with him.'

I thanked him and got back in the cab. The news of Al Z's death would have traveled fast and there would be a lot of speculation as to who might have been behind it, but Mickey knew. I think he knew what would happen from the moment he received the call that I was coming and realized that it was, at last, time for the reckoning.

The cab dropped me back at Jacob Wirth's on Stuart, where Rachel was waiting along with Angel and Louis. There was a sing-along in progress around the piano as people who had been deaf since birth mugged "The Wanderer." We left them to it and made our way a few doors up the street to Montien, where we sat in a booth and picked uneasily at our Thai food.

'He's good,' said Louis. 'Probably been keeping tabs on you since you arrived.'

I nodded. 'Then he knows about Sheinberg, and you two. And Rachel. I'm sorry.'

'It's a game with him,' said Louis. 'You know that, don't you? The business card, the spiders in the mailbox. He playin' with you, man, testin' you. He know who you are, and he like the idea of goin' up against you.'

Angel nodded in agreement. 'You got a reputation now. Only surprise is that every psycho from here to Florida hasn't caught a bus and headed for Maine to see just how good you really are.'

'That's not very reassuring, Angel.'

'You want reassurance, call a priest.'

Nobody spoke for a time, until Louis said, 'I guess you know we be joinin' you in Maine.'

Rachel looked at me. 'I'll be coming too.'

'My guardian angels,' I said. I knew better than to argue with any of them. I was glad, too, that Rachel would be close. Alone, she was vulnerable. Yet once again I found this beautiful, empathetic woman reading my thoughts.

'Not for protection, Parker,' she added. Her face was serious, and her eyes were hard. 'I'm coming because you'll need help with Marcy Becker and her parents, and maybe the Merciers too. If the fact that I'm with you and the odd couple makes you feel better, then that's a plus, nothing more. I'm not here just so you can save me.'

Angel smiled at her with both admiration and amusement. 'You're so butch,' he hissed at Rachel. 'Give you a gun and a vest and you could be a lesbian icon.'

'Bite me, stubby,' she replied.

It seemed to have been decided. I raised a glass of water, and they each lifted their beers in response.

'Well,' I said, 'welcome to the war.'

Chapter Thirteen

The next morning, the front page of the *Herald* was dominated by a pretty good picture of Al Z slumped in his seat at the Wang, beside the headline 'Gangland Leader Slain.' There are few words that newspaper sub-editors like better than 'gangland' and 'slain,' except maybe 'sex' and 'puppy,' and the *Herald* had opted to display them in a point size so large there was barely enough room for the story.

Tommy Caci's throat had been cut from left to right. The wound was so deep that it had severed both of the common carotid arteries and the external and internal jugulars, virtually decapitating him. Mr. Pudd had then stabbed Al Z through the back of the head with a long, thin blade, which punctured his cerebellum and sliced into his cerebral cortex. Finally, using a small, very sharp knife, he had made an angled incision about three quarters of the way up the middle finger of Al Z's right hand and sliced off the top joint.

I learned this not from the *Herald,* but from Sergeant McCann, who rang me on my cell phone as I sat at Rachel's breakfast table reading the newspapers. Rachel was in the bathtub, humming Al Green songs out of key.

'Guy had some balls, taking out two men in a public place,' commented McCann. 'There are no cameras on the fire exits, so we got no visual apart from your description. Some guy in the loading bay took the license; came from an

Impala stolen two days ago in Concord, so zilch there. The killer had to gain access to the VIP lounge using a key card, so we figure he came prepared with one he made himself. It's not that hard to run one up, you know what you're doing. Al Z went to every first night – he may have been a mean, crooked son of a bitch, but he had class – and he always sat in or near those seats, so it wasn't too difficult to guess where he'd be. As for the missing finger joint, we're guessing it's a calling card and we're checking VICAP for equivalent MOs.'

He asked me if I remembered anything else from the previous night – I knew it wasn't simply a courtesy call – but I told him that I couldn't help him. He asked me to stay in touch, and I assured him that I would.

McCann was right; Pudd had taken a huge risk to get to Al Z. Maybe he had no choice. There was no way to get at Al Z in his office or his home, because he was always surrounded by his people and his windows were designed to repel anything smaller than a warhead. At the theater, with Tommy behind him and hundreds of people around him, he could have been forgiven for feeling secure, but he had underestimated the tenacity of his killer. When the opportunity presented itself, Pudd seized it.

It struck me that Pudd might also be tying up loose ends, and there were only so many reasons why someone felt compelled to do that. Primary among them was as a preparation for disappearance, to ensure that there was nobody left to continue the hunt. My guess was that if Pudd chose to disappear, then nobody would ever find him. He had survived this long even with a price on his head, so he could vanish like dew after sunrise if he chose.

Something else bothered me; it looked like bugs weren't the only things that Pudd liked to collect. He also wanted skin and bone, removing joints and sections of skin from each of his victims. His taste in souvenirs was distinctive, but Pudd didn't strike me as the kind of man who would mutilate dead bodies just so he could put the pieces in jars and admire them. There had to be a better reason.

I sat at the breakfast table, the newspapers now abandoned, and wondered if I should simply turn over all I knew to the police. Not that what I knew was a great deal, but the deaths of Epstein, Beck, Al Z, and Grace Peltier were all connected, linked either to the Fellowship itself or to actions that Grace's biological father, Jack Mercier, was taking against it. It was about time for a serious face-to-face talk with Mr. Mercier, and I didn't think that either of us was going to enjoy it very much. I was about to pack my bag in preparation for my return to Scarborough when I got my second call of the morning, and from a not entirely unexpected source. It was Mickey Shine. Caller ID could only tell me that the number he was calling from was private, and concealed.

'You see the papers?' he asked.

'I was there,' I told him.

'You know who did it?'

'I think it was our mutual acquaintance.'

There was a silence on the other end of the line. 'How did he find out about your meeting with Al?'

'He may have been keeping tabs on us,' I conceded. 'But it could also be that he was aware of Al Z's interest in him for some time, and that my investigation precipitated a course of action he'd been planning for some time.' He had learned from his pets that if something starts tugging at the farthest reach of your web, then it's a good idea to find out what that might be and, if you can, to make it stop.

'You weren't out at your apartment last night,' I continued. 'I checked up on you.'

'I left town as soon as I heard. Somebody called me about Al's death, a friend from way back, and I knew it had to be Pudd. Nobody else would dare make a move like that against Al Z.'

'Where are you?'

'New York.'

'Think you can lose yourself there, Mickey?'

'I have friends down here. I'll make some calls, see what they can do for me.'

'We need to talk some more before you disappear. I get the feeling you haven't told me all that you know.'

I thought he would demur. Instead, he admitted: 'Some I know, some I'm just guessing.'

'Meet me. I'll come down to you.'

'I don't know . . .'

'Mickey, are you going to keep running from this guy for the rest of your life? That doesn't sound like much of an existence.'

'It's better than being dead.' He didn't sound too sure.

'You know what he's doing, don't you?' I asked him. 'You know what the threat of "being written" means. You've figured it out.'

He didn't reply immediately, and I half expected to hear the connection being ended.

'The Cloisters,' he said suddenly. 'Ten tomorrow. There's an exhibition in the Treasury you might want to take a look at before I get there. It'll answer some of your questions, and I'll try to fill in the gaps. But you're not there at ten and I walk away. You'll never see me again.'

With that, he hung up.

I booked a ticket on the Delta shuttle to La Guardia, then called Angel and Louis at the Copley. Rachel and I met them for coffee in the Starbucks on Newbury before I caught a cab to Logan. I was in New York by 1:30 P.M. and checked into a double room in the Larchmont on West Eleventh Street in the Village. The Larchmont wasn't the kind of place Donald Trump was likely to be frequenting but it was clean and inexpensive, and unlike most New York budget hotels, its double rooms weren't so small that you had to step outside to change your mind. In addition, it had a security-locked front entrance and a doorman the size of the Flatiron Building, so unwanted visitors would be kept to a minimum.

The city was stiflingly hot and humid, and I was soaked in sweat by the time I reached the hotel. The weather was due to break that night, but until then the A/C would be on full-blast throughout the city, while those too poor to afford it made do with cheap fans. After a quick shower in a shared bathroom, I caught a cab uptown to West Eighty-ninth Street. B'Nai Jeshurun, the synagogue with which Yossi Epstein had until recently been involved, had an office on West Eighty-ninth, close by the Claremont Riding Academy, and it seemed that while I was in Manhattan it might be useful to try to find out a little more about the murdered rabbi. The noise of children leaving P.S. 166 echoed in my ears as I walked to the synagogue's office, but it was a wasted trip. Nobody at B'Nai Jeshurun seemed able to tell me much more than I already knew about Yossi Epstein, and I was referred instead to the Orensanz Center on Norfolk Street on the Lower East Side, where Epstein had relocated after his falling-out with the Upper West Side congregation.

To avoid the rush hour traffic I took the subway from Central Park West as far as Broadway and East Houston, which left me sweating again, then strolled along Houston, past Katz's Deli and storefront operations selling garbage masquerading as antiques, until I came to Norfolk Street. This was the heart of the Lower East Side, a place that had once been full of scholars and yeshivas, of anti-Hasidic Lithuanians and the rest of the first wave of Russian Jews, who were regarded by the already settled German Jews as backward Orientals. It was said that Allen Street used to belong to Russia, there were so many Russian Jews there. People from the same town formed associations, became tradespeople, saved so their kids could go to college and better themselves. They shared their neighborhoods uneasily with the Irish, and fought with them on the streets.

Now those times were largely gone. There was still a workers' co-op on Grand Street, a few Jewish bookstores and skullcap manufacturers between Hester and Division, one or two good bakeries, Schapiro's kosher wines, and of course, Katz's, the last of the old-style delis, now staffed almost entirely by Dominicans; but most of the Orthodox Jewish community had moved to Borough Park and Williamsburg, or to Crown Heights. The ones who were left were mainly too poor or too stubborn to retreat to the outer boroughs or Miami.

The Orensanz Center, the oldest surviving synagogue in New York, once known as the Anshe Chesed, the People of Kindness, seemed to belong to another, distant time. Built by the Berlin architect Alexander Saeltzer in 1850 for the German Jewish congregation, and modeled on the cathedral of Cologne, it dominated Norfolk Street, a reminder of the past still alive in the present. I entered through a side door, walked along a dark entrance lobby, and found myself in the main, neo-Gothic hall among elegant pillars and balconies. Dim light filtered in through the windows, turning the interior to the color of old bronze and casting shadows over flowers and white ribbons, the remnants of a wedding held some days earlier. In one corner, a small man with white hair, dressed in blue overalls, was sweeping paper and broken glass into a corner. He stopped his work as I walked over to him. I produced my ID and asked if there was anybody who might be willing to talk about Yossi Epstein.

'Nobody here today,' he said. 'Come back tomorrow.' He resumed his sweeping.

'Maybe there's somebody I can call?' I persisted.

'Call tomorrow.'

I wasn't getting very far on looks and charm alone. 'Mind if I take a look around?' I asked and, without waiting for a reply, began to walk toward a small flight of stairs leading down to the basement. I found a locked door with a card pinned to it expressing sorrow at the death of Epstein. A bulletin board to one side listed times of services and Hebrew classes, as well as a series of lectures on the history of the area. There wasn't much more to see so, after ten minutes or so of unsuccessful snooping around the rest of the basement, I brushed the dust from my jacket and walked back up the stairs.

The old guy with the broom had disappeared. Instead, there were two men waiting for me. One was young, with a red skullcap that looked too small for his head and a head that looked too small for his shoulders. He wore a dark shirt and black jeans and, judging by his expression, wasn't one of the people of kindness. The man beside him was older, with thinning gray hair and a thick beard. He was dressed more traditionally than his friend – white shirt and black tie beneath a black suit and overcoat – but didn't look significantly kinder.

'Are you the rabbi?' I asked him.

'No, we are not connected with the Orensanz Center,' he replied, before adding: 'You think everyone who dresses in black is a rabbi?'

'Does that make me anti-Semitic?'

'No, but carrying a gun into a synagogue might.'

'It's nothing personal, or even religious.'

The older man nodded. 'I'm sure it's not, but it pays to be careful with such matters. I understand you are a private detective. May I see some form of identification, please?'

I raised my hand and slowly reached into my inside pocket for my wallet. I gave it to the young guy, who handed it in turn to the older man. He examined it for a good minute, then folded it and handed it back to me.

'And why is a private detective from Maine asking about the death of a New York rabbi?'

'I think Rabbi Epstein's death may be connected to a case I'm investigating. I hoped that somebody might be able to tell me a little more about him.'

'He's dead, Mr. Parker. What more do you need to know?'

'Who killed him would be a start, or doesn't that concern you?'

'It concerns me a great deal, Mr. Parker.' He turned to the younger man, nodded, and we watched as he walked from the hall, closing the door softly behind him. 'What is this case you are investigating?'

'The death of a young woman. She was a friend of mine, once.'

'Then investigate her death and leave us to do our own work.'

'If her death is connected to that of the rabbi, it might be in both of our interests for you to help me. I can find the man who did this.'

'The *man*,' he repeated, emphasizing the second word. 'You seem very certain that it was a man.'

'I know who he is,' I said simply.

'Then we both know,' he replied. 'The matter is in hand. Steps have been taken to deal with it.'

'What steps?'

'An eye for an eye, Mr. Parker. He will be found.' He drew closer to me, and his eyes softened slightly. 'This is not your concern. Not every unlawful death is fuel for your anger.'

He knew who I was. I could see it in his face, my past reflected back upon me in the mirrors of his eyes. There had been so much newspaper coverage of the deaths of Susan and Jennifer, and the final violent end of the Traveling Man, that there would always be those who remembered me. Now, in this old synagogue, I felt my personal loss exposed once again, like a mote of dust caught in the sunlight pouring through the windows above.

'The woman is my concern,' I said. 'If the rabbi's death is connected, then that becomes my concern too.'

He shook his head and gripped my shoulder lightly.

'Do you know what *tashlikh* is, Mr. Parker? It is a symbolic act, the casting of bread crumbs onto the water, symbolizing the sins of the past, a burden with which one no longer chooses to live. I think you must find it in yourself to lay aside your burdens before they kill you.'

He began to walk away, and was almost at the door when I spoke.

'"This was said by my father, and I am the atonement for where he rests."'

The old man stopped and stared back at me.

'It's from the Talmud,' I said.

'I know what it is,' he almost whispered.

'This isn't about revenge.'

'Then what is it about?'

'Reparation.'

'For your father's sins, or your own?'

'Both.'

He seemed to lose himself in thought for a few moments, and when the light returned to his eyes a decision had been made.

'There is a legend told of the Golem, Mr. Parker,' he began, 'an artificial man made of clay. The Rabbi Loew created the first Golem in Prague, in fifty-three forty. The rabbi formed him from mud and placed the *shem*, the parchment bearing the name of God, in his mouth. The rabbi is justified in legend for creating a creature capable of defending Jews against the pogroms, against the wrath of their enemies. Do you believe that such a creature can exist, that justice can be served by its creation?'

'I believe that *men* like him can exist,' I replied. 'But I don't think justice always plays a part in their creation, or is served by their actions.'

'Yes, perhaps a man,' said the old Jew softly. 'And perhaps justice, if it is divinely inspired. We have dispatched our Golem. Let the will of God be done.' In his eyes I could see the ambivalence of his response to what had been set in train; they had sent one killer to track another, unleashing violence against violence, with all of the risks that such an act entailed.

'Who are you?' I asked.

'My name is Ben Epstein,' he answered, 'and I am the atonement for where my son rests.'

The door closed gently behind him, its sound in the empty synagogue like a breath exhaled from the mouth of God.

* * *

Lester Bargus is alone behind the counter of the store on the day he dies, the same day on which I meet Yossi Epstein's father. Jim Gould, who works for Bargus part-time, is out back fieldstripping a pair of stolen H&K semiautomatics, so there is nobody in the rear storeroom, where a pair of TV screens show the interior of the store from two angles, one from a visible camera above the door, the other from a lens hidden inside the shell of a portable stereo kept on a shelf beside the register. Lester Bargus is a careful man, but not careful enough. His store is miked, but Lester Bargus doesn't know that. The only people who know are the ATF agents who have been monitoring Bargus's illegal gun operation for the best part of eleven days.

But on this particular day business is slow, and Bargus is idly feeding crickets to his pet mantid when the door opens. Even on the oddly angled black-and-white recordings made by the cameras, the new arrival seems strangely out of place. He is dressed in a black suit, shiny black shoes, and a thin black tie over a white shirt. On his head he wears a black hat, and a long black coat hangs to the middle of his calves. He is tall, six-two or six-three, and well built. His age is harder to gauge; he could be anything from forty to seventy.

But it is only when the few clear images obtained by the cameras are frozen and enhanced that his strangeness becomes truly apparent. The skin is stretched taut on his face and he appears to be almost entirely without flesh, the striations of the tendons in his jaw and neck clearly visible through his skin, his cheekbones like shards of glass below dark eyes. He has no eyebrows. The ATF agents who later examine the tape suspect at first that he may simply be so fair that his hair does not show up, but when the images are enhanced they reveal only slightly roughened skin above his eyes, like old scar tissue.

His appearance obviously shocks Lester Bargus. On the tape, he can be seen taking a step back in surprise. He is wearing a white T-shirt with a Smith & Wesson logo on the back, and blue jeans with a lot of room around the crotch and the ass. Maybe he is hoping to grow into them.

'Help you?' His voice on the recording is cautious but hopeful. Especially on a slow day, a sale is a sale, even if it does come from a freak.

'I am looking for this man.' The accent makes it clear that English is only a second language, possibly even a third. He sounds European; not German, but Polish maybe, or Czech. Later, an expert will identify it as Hungarian, with Yiddish inflections to certain words. The man is a Jew, originally from Eastern Europe but with some time spent in the west of the continent, probably France.

He takes a photograph from his pocket and pushes it across the counter toward Lester Bargus. Lester doesn't even look at the photograph. All he says is: 'I don't know him.'

'Look at it.' And his tone tells Lester Bargus that it doesn't matter what he does or does not say from now on, because nothing can save him from this man.

Lester reaches out and touches the photograph for the first time, but only to push it away. His head does not move. He still has not looked at the photograph, but while his left hand is in sight his right is moving to grasp the shotgun that rests on the shelf beneath the counter. He has almost reached it when the gun appears. Firearms will later identify it as a Jericho 941, made in Israel. Lester Bargus's right hand returns to the counter alongside his left, and both hands start to tremble in unison.

'For the last time, Mr. Bargus, look at the photograph.'

This time, Lester does look down. He spends some time staring at the photograph, weighing up his options. It's obvious that he knows the man in the picture and that the gunman is aware of this fact because the gunman wouldn't be there otherwise. On the tape, it's almost possible to hear Lester gulp.

'Where do I find this man?' During the whole encounter, the expression on the gunman's face has not altered. It is as if the skin is so tight across his skull that merely to talk requires a huge effort. The palpable menace of the man is obvious even from the black-and-white recording. Lester Bargus, forced to deal with him face-to-face, is terrified beyond belief. It is audible in his voice when he speaks what will be his second-to-last sentence on this earth.

'He'll kill me if I tell you,' says Bargus.

'I will kill you if you don't.'

Then Lester Bargus says his last words, and they reveal a prescience that I didn't think Lester would ever have. 'You're going to kill me anyhow,' he says, and something in his voice tells the gunman that this is all he is ever going to get out of Lester.

'Yes,' says the gunman, 'I am.'

The shots sound incredibly loud after the conversation that has just taken place, but also distorted and muted as the sound levels fail to cope with them. Lester Bargus jolts as the first bullet takes him in the chest, then keeps bucking and spasming as the rest of the shots tear into him, the static-ridden thunderclaps coming again and again until it seems that they will never end. There are ten shots, then there is a noise and a movement from the left of the picture as part of Jim Gould's body appears in the frame. Two more shots come and Gould falls across the counter as the gunman springs across it and darts into the rear of the store. By the time the ATF agents reach the scene, he is gone.

On the counter, now soaked with Lester Bargus's blood, the photograph remains. It is a picture of a group of demonstrators outside an abortion clinic in Minnesota. There are men and women holding placards, some obviously screaming their protests as police try to hold them back while others stand openmouthed in shock. To the right of the picture, the body of a man lies slumped against a wall as medics crowd around him. There is black blood on the pavement and on the wall behind him. At the fringe of the group another man has been caught in the act of walking away, his hands in the pockets of his overcoat, tiny hoods of skin shrouding his eyes as he looks back toward the dying man, his face inadvertently revealed to the camera. A red circle has been drawn around his head.

In the photograph, Mr. Pudd is smiling.

The man who killed Lester Bargus had flown into Logan Airport one day earlier and entered the country on a British passport, claiming to be a businessman interested in buying stuffed animals. The address he gave to Immigration officials was later revealed to be the site of a recently demolished Chinese restaurant in Balham, south London.

The name on the passport was Clay Dæmon.

He was the Golem.

Chapter Fourteen

That night, as the bodies of Lester Bargus and Jim Gould were taken to the morgue, I headed over to Chumley's on Bedford, the Village's best bar. Technically it was between Barrow and Grove, but even people who'd been going there for the best part of a decade still had trouble finding it on occasion. There was no name outside, just a light over the big door with the metal grate. Chumley's had started life as a speakeasy during Prohibition, and it had maintained its low profile for over seventy years. On weekends it tended to attract the kind of young bankers and dot-communists who all wore blue shirts with their suits, on the grounds that nonconformists like them had to stick together, but during the week Chumley's was still recognizable as the bar that Salinger, Scott Fitzgerald, Eugene O'Neill, Orson Welles, and William Burroughs used to frequent as a change from the White Horse or Marie's Crisis.

The clouds hung low over the Village as I walked, and there was a terrible stillness in the air that seemed to communicate itself to the people on the streets. Laughs were subdued; couples bickered. The crowds emerging from the subway wore tense, fractious expressions, their shoes too tight, their shirts too thick. Everything felt damp to the touch, as if the city itself were slowly perspiring, expelling filth and waste through every crack in every sidewalk, every fissure in every wall. I looked to the sky and waited for the thunder, but none came.

Inside Chumley's, the Labradors lounged uneasily on the sawdust-strewn floor and people stood at the tiny bar or disappeared into the darkened alcoves at the far end of the room. I took a seat at one of the long benches by the door and ordered a hamburger and a Coke – hamburgers, ribs, and deep-fried fish being what Chumley's did best.

It seemed like a long time since I had been back in the Village, as if decades rather than years had passed from the day that I left my apartment to travel back to Maine. Old ghosts waited for me on these corners: the Traveling Man at the corner of St. Marks in the East Village, the phone booth still marking the place where I had stood after he sent me my daughter's remains in a jar; the Corner Bistro, where Susan and I used to meet when we were dating; the Elephant & Castle, where we had brunch on Sundays in the early months of our relationship, heading uptown afterward to walk in Central Park or browse in the museums.

Even Chumley's was not immune, for were these not the same dogs that Susan used to stroke while she waited for her drink, the same dogs that Jennifer once held after her mother told her how beautiful they were and we took her to meet them as a treat? All of these places were potential bubbles of hurt waiting to be pricked, releasing the memories sealed within. I should have felt pain, I thought. I should have felt the old agony. But instead, I experienced only a strange, desperate gratitude for this place, for the two fat old dogs and for the unsullied memories with which they had left me.

For some things should never be allowed to fade away. It was both good and proper that they should be recalled, that a place should be found for them in the present and the future so that they became a precious part of oneself, something to be treasured instead of something to be feared. To remember Susan and Jennifer as they once were, and to love them for it, was no betrayal of Rachel and of what she meant to me. If that was true, then to find a way to live a life in which lost loves and new beginnings could coexist was not to besmirch the memory of my wife and child. And in the quiet of that place I lost myself for a time, until one of the Labradors waddled sleepily over and nosed at my hand for attention, his dog jowls shedding warm spit on my pants and his soft eyes closing happily beneath the weight of my hand.

I had found a copy of the *Portland Press Herald* in Barnes & Noble at Union Square, and while I ate, I scanned the pages for reports on Eagle Lake. There were two: one was a description of the ongoing difficulties in uncovering the remains, but the main piece announced the suspected identities of two of the dead. They were Lyall Cornish and Vyrna Kellog, and they were both homicide victims. Lyall Cornish had died from a gunshot wound to the back of the head. Vyrna Kellog's skull had been crushed, apparently with a rock.

Slowly, the truth about the fate of the Aroostook Baptists was being revealed. They had not dispersed, scattering themselves to the four winds and taking with them the seeds of new communities. Instead they had been murdered and consigned to a mass grave on a patch of undeveloped land; and there they had remained, trapped in a forgotten cavity of the honeycomb world, until spring daylight had found them.

Was that why Grace had died – because in breaking through the dead layers obscuring the past, she had found out something about the Aroostook Baptists that nobody was ever supposed to discover? More and more I wanted to return to Maine, to confront Jack Mercier and Carter Paragon. I felt that my pursuit of Mr. Pudd was drawing me away from the investigation into Grace's death, yet somehow Pudd and the Fellowship had a part to play in all that had occurred. He was linked to her passing in some way, of that I was certain, but he wasn't the weak link. Paragon was, and he would have to be confronted if I was to understand what had driven someone to end Grace's life.

But first, there was Mickey Shine. I had checked the

Village Voice and found the exhibition listings. The Cloisters, which housed the Metropolitan Museum's medieval collection, was hosting a visiting exhibition on artistic responses to the Apocalypse of St. John. An image of Jack Mercier's bookshelf flashed before my eyes. It seemed that the Met and Mercier currently shared an interest in books and paintings about the end of the world.

I left Chumley's shortly after ten, patting the sleeping dogs one last time for luck as I went. The warm, damp smell of them was still on my hands as I walked beneath the shrouded sky, the noise of the city seeming to rebound back on itself from above. A shadow moved in a doorway to my right, but I paid it no heed and allowed it to move unchallenged behind me.

I passed through the streetlights, and my footsteps echoed hollowly on the ground beneath my feet.

Bone is porous; after years of burial, it will assume the same color as the soil in which it has been interred. The bones by St. Froid Lake were a rich brown, as if the Aroostook Baptists had become one with the natural world around them, an impression reinforced by the small plants that grew between the remains, fed by decay. Rib cages had become trellises for creeping roots, and the concavity of a skull acted as a nursery for small green shoots.

Their clothing had largely rotted away, since most of it had been made from natural fibers and could not survive decades of burial in the manner of synthetic materials. Water stains on the surrounding trees indicated that the land had flooded on occasion, adding extra layers of mud and rotting vegetation, compressing the bones of the dead farther and farther into the soil. The field recovery, the separation of bone from earth, human from animal, child from adult, would be a painstaking process. It would be completed on hands and knees, with aching backs and cold fingers, all supervised by the forensic anthropologist. State police, sheriff's deputies, wardens, even some anthropology students were called in to assist with the dig. Since the ME's office had only one vehicle, a Dodge van, with which to transport remains, local undertakers and the National Guard were drafted in to assist in the removal of the bodies to nearby Presque Isle, from where Bill's Flying Service would take take them down to Augusta.

At St. Froid Lake, orange aluminum arrows, the trademark of the deputy chief ME, had been used to create an archaeological square, enclosed and protected by lengths of string. An array of seemingly primitive but ultimately necessary equipment had been brought to bear on the scene: line levels to measure the depth of the remains below the surface; flat-bladed shovels and trowels with which to dig, aware always that the soft bones could be damaged by a careless movement; handheld screens for sifting small pieces of evidence – a quarter-inch mesh screen first, followed by a standard window screen; tapes; graph paper for drawing a site map depicting the area as seen from above, the position of the remains being added to the map as they were uncovered; plastic bags, bright blue heavy-duty body bags, and waterproof pens; metal detectors to search for guns or other metallic debris; and cameras, to photograph items and artifacts as they were revealed.

As each artifact was uncovered it was photographed, then marked and sealed, an adhesive label attached to the container detailing the case number, the date and time of discovery, a description of the item, its location, and the signature of the investigator who had recovered it. The item was then transported to a secure evidence storage facility, in this case the offices of the ME in Augusta.

Soil samples were taken from the carefully piled earth and bagged. Had the soil by the lake been only slightly more acidic, the remains might simply have vanished and the only sign that they had ever been there would have come from the flourishing plant life above, nourished by flesh and bone. As it was, animal predation, erosion, and scattering had resulted in missing and damaged limbs, but sufficient evidence remained to be examined by the specialists assembled by the ME's office. They included – in addition to the forensic anthropologist, the ME's own permanent staff, and the scientists at the state lab in Augusta – an anatomist, three dental teams to act as forensic odontologists, and the radiologist at the Maine General Medical Center in Augusta. Each would bring to bear his or her own specialist knowledge to assist in a formal identification of the remains.

The remains had been identified as human by an examination of the intact bones, and the sex of the victims would be confirmed by further examinations of the skull, pelvis, femur, sternum, and teeth, where teeth could be found. Age estimates of those victims under the age of twenty-five, accurate to within one year or so, would be made from teeth, where teeth remained, and from the appearance and fusion of the ossification centers and epiphyses, the end parts of the long bones, which grow separately from the shaft in early life. In the case of older bones, radiological examinations of the trabecular pattern in the head of the humerus and femur, which remodels with age, would be used, in addition to changes in pubic symphysis.

Height would be calculated by measuring the femur, tibia, and fibula of the victims, arm bones being less reliable in such cases. Dental remains would be used to make a preliminary racial determination, dental characteristics associated predominantly with particular races enabling the likelihood of the victims being Caucasoid, Negroid, or Mongoloid to be assessed.

Finally, dental records, radiological examination of the remains for evidence of fractures, and comparative DNA tests would all be brought to bear in an effort to make positive identifications of the personal identities of the victims. In this case, facial reconstruction and photosuperimposition (the overlaying of a photograph of the suspected victim over a transparency of the skull, now largely done on-screen) might have assisted the investigation, since photographs existed of the suspected victims, but the state had made no budgetary provisions for photosuperimposition techniques, mainly because those with their hands on the purse strings didn't really understand what it was. They didn't understand the mechanics of DNA testing either, but then, they didn't have to; they just knew that it worked.

But in this case, the investigators had assistance from an unexpected and bizarre source. Around the neck of each victim was found the remains of a wooden board. Some had decayed badly, although it was believed that electronic scanners, electrostatic detection apparatuses, or low-angle light could reveal traces of whatever had been indented on the wood. But others, particularly on the higher ground, were still semi-intact. One of them lay below the head of a small boy buried beside a fir tree. The roots of the tree had grown through and around his remains, and his recovery would be one of the most difficult to achieve without damaging the bones. Beside him was another, smaller skeleton, preliminarily identified as a female of about seven years, for the metopic suture along the frontal bone of her skull had not yet fully disappeared. The bones of their hands were intermingled, as if they had clasped each other in their final moments.

The boy's bones lay semiexposed, the skull clearly visible, the mandible detached and lying to one side. There was a small hole where the occipital and parietal bones met at the back of his head but no corresponding exit wound in the frontal bone, although a small fragment appeared to have been dislodged from the supraorbital foramen, the ridge of bone above the right eye, by the emerging bullet.

The indentation on the block of wood by his skull, hacked into the grain with a child's hand, read:

James Jessop
Sinner

The Search for Sanctuary

Extract from the postgraduate thesis of Grace Peltier

It is unclear when the first signs of difficulty began to appear in the new settlement.

Each day, the community rose and prayed at first light, then assisted in the completion of the houses and farm structures for the settlement, some of which were built of clapboard from old Sears, Roebuck mail-order kits originating from the 1930s. Faulkner retained control of the finances, and food was limited, since the Preacher believed in the benefits of fasting. Prayers were said four times daily, with Faulkner preaching one sermon at breakfast and a second following the main meal in the evening.

Details of day-to-day life for the Aroostook Baptists were obtained by talking to local people who had some limited contact with the community, and from occasional letters sent by Elizabeth Jessop, Frank Jessop's wife, to her sister, Lena, in Portland. These letters were, in effect, smuggled out of the settlement. Elizabeth reached an agreement with the landowner whereby, for a small fee, he would check the hollow of an oak tree at the verge of the settlement every Tuesday and ensure that whatever mail found there was posted. He also agreed to collect and deliver any responses received.

Elizabeth paints a picture of a harsh but joyful first three months, filled with a sense that the Aroostook Baptists were like the pioneers of another age, creating a new world where there had once been wilderness. The houses, although basic and somewhat drafty, were built quickly, and the families had brought some simple furnishings with them in trailers. They raised pigs and chickens and had five cows, one of which was with calf. They grew potatoes – this area of Aroostook was prime potato-growing country – broccoli, and peas, and harvested apples from the trees on the property. They used rotting fish to fertilize the land and stored the produce they had brought with them in underground caverns dug beneath the banks, where the springwater kept the air at the same low temperature all year round, acting as a natural refrigerator.

The first signs of tension arose in July, when it became apparent that the Faulkners and their children were keeping themselves apart from the other families. Faulkner took a larger share of the produce as the leader of the community and he refused to release any of the funds that the families had brought with them, a sum amounting to at least $20,000. Even when Laurie Perrson, the daughter of Billy and Olive Perrson, took seriously ill with influenza, Faulkner insisted that she be treated within the community. It was left to Katherine Cornish, who had some rudimentary medical skills, to treat the girl. According to Elizabeth's letters, Laurie barely survived.

Animosity grew toward the Faulkners. Their children, whom Faulkner insisted should be called only Adam and Eve, bullied the younger members of the community; Elizabeth refers darkly to random acts of cruelty perpetrated on both animals and humans by the Faulkner children. Clearly, her reports caused her sister concern, for in a letter dated August 7, 1963, Elizabeth attempts to reassure Lena, arguing that their difficulties 'are as nothing compared to the sufferings endured by the *Mayflower* pilgrims, or those hardy souls who journeyed west in the face of hostility from the Indians. We trust in God, who is our savior, and in the Reverend Faulkner, who is our guiding light.'

But the letter also contains the first reference to Lyall Kellog, with whom it appears that Elizabeth was becoming infatuated. It seems that the relationship between Frank Jessop and his wife was predominantly nonsexual, although whether as a result of marital strife or some physical incapacity is not known. In fact, the affair between Lyall and Elizabeth may already have begun by the time of the August letter, and had certainly progressed enough by November for Elizabeth to describe him to her sister as 'this wonderful man.'

It is my view that this affair, and its repercussions once it became known within the community, contributed greatly to the disintegration of the settlement. What is also clear, from the subsequent letters of Elizabeth Jessop, is that Louise Faulkner played a major role in this disintegration, a role that appears to have surprised Elizabeth and may, in the end, have brought Louise into bitter conflict with her own husband.

Chapter Fifteen

The passenger elevator at the 190th Street subway station was decorated with pictures of kittens and puppies. Two potted plants with Stars and Stripes sprouting from the soil hung from the ceiling and a small stereo unit played relaxing music. The elevator operator, Anthony Washington, who was responsible for the unusual ambience of the 190th Street elevator, sat at a small desk in a comfortable chair and greeted many of the passengers by name. The MTA once tried to make Anthony strip his elevator of its decorations, but a campaign by the press and the public forced the Transit Authority to back down. The paint flaked from the ceiling of the 190th Street station, it smelled of urine, and there was a steady stream of dirty water running between the tracks. All things considered, those who used the subway were pretty grateful for Anthony's efforts and felt that the MTA should be pretty damn grateful too.

It was just after 9:15 A.M. when Anthony Washington's elevator reached ground level and I emerged at the entrance to Fort Tryon Park. The weather had broken. The thunder had commenced shortly after dawn, the rains following within the hour. It had now been falling continuously for almost four hours, warm, hard rain that had caused umbrellas to sprout up like mushrooms across the city.

There was no bus waiting at the curb to take visitors to the Cloisters, although it hardly mattered, since I seemed to be the only person heading in that direction. I wrapped my coat around me and began to walk up Margaret Corbin Drive. Outside the small café on the left of the road, a group of sanitation men huddled together, sheltering from the rain while drinking cups of coffee. Above them loomed the remains of Fort Tryon, which defended itself against Hessian troops during the War of Independence with the aid of Margaret Corbin herself, the first American woman to take a soldier's part in the battle for liberty. I wondered if Margaret Corbin was tough enough to stand against the troops of junkies and muggers who now roamed the scene of her triumph, and figured that she probably was.

Seconds later, the bulk of the Cloisters was before me, the New Jersey shoreline to my left, traffic streaming across the George Washington Bridge. John D. Rockefeller Jr. had given this land to the city and reserved the hilltop for the construction of a museum of medieval art, which was eventually opened in 1938. Portions of five medieval cloisters were integrated into a single modern building, itself reminiscent of medieval European structures. My father had first taken me there as a child, and it had never ceased to amaze me since. Surrounded by its high central tower and battlements, its arches and pillars, you could briefly feel like a knight-errant, as long as you ignored the fact that you were looking out at the woods of New Jersey, where the only damsels in distress were likely to be robbery victims or unwed mothers.

I walked up the stairs to the admissions area, paid my $10, and stepped through the entrance door into the Romanesque Hall. There were no other visitors in the rooms; the comparatively early hour and the bad weather had kept most of them away, and I guessed that I was one of only a dozen or so people in the whole museum. I passed slowly through the Fuentidueña Chapel, pausing to admire the apse and the huge crucifix hanging from the ceiling, then made my way through the St.-Guilhem and Cuxa Cloisters toward the Gothic Chapel and the stairs to the lower level.

I had about ten minutes before I was due to meet Mickey Shine, so I headed for the Treasury, where the museum stored its manuscripts. I entered through the modern glass doors and stood in a room ringed by panels from the choir stalls at Jumièges Abbey. The manuscripts were stored in glass cases and opened at particularly fine examples of the illuminator's art. I stopped for a time at a beautiful book of hours, but most of my attention was reserved for the visiting exhibits.

The book of Revelation had been the subject of manuscript illumination since the ninth century, and while Apocalypse cycles had originally been produced for monasteries, they were also being made for wealthy secular patrons by the thirteenth century. Some of the finest examples had been gathered together for this exhibition, and images of judgment and punishment filled the room. I spent some time looking at various medieval sinners being devoured, torn apart, or tormented on spikes – or in the case of the Winchester Psalter depiction of Hell Mouth, all three at once, while a dutiful angel locked the doors from the outside – before passing on to examples of Dürer's woodcuts, Cranach's work for Martin Luther's German translation of the New Testament, and Blake's visions of red dragons, until I eventually reached the item at the center of the display.

It was the Cloisters Apocalypse, dating from the early part of the fourteenth century, and the illustration on the opened page was almost identical to that which I had found on the Fellowship's literature. It depicted a multi-eyed beast with long, vaguely arachnid legs slaughtering sinners with a spear while Christ and the saints looked on impassively from the right-hand corner of the page. According to the explanatory note in the case, the beast was killing those whose names did not appear in the Lamb of God's Book of Life. Below it was a translation of an illustrator's note added in Latin in the margins: 'For if the names of the saved are to be recorded in the Book of Life, shall not also the names of the damned be written, and in what place may they be found?'

I heard the echo of the threat made by Mr. Pudd against Mickey Shine and his family: their names would be written. The question, as the illuminator had posed, was, written where?

It was now ten, but I could see no sign of Mickey Shine. I left the Treasury, walked through the Glass Gallery, and opened a small unmarked door that led out into the Trie Cloister. The only sound, apart from the fall of the rain, came from the trickling of water in the fountain at the center of the marble arcades, dominated in turn by a limestone cross. To my right, an opening led out to the exposed Bonnefont Cloister. When I stepped through it, I found myself in a garden, the Hudson River and the New Jersey shoreline in front of me, the tower of the Gothic Chapel to my far right. To my left was the main wall of the Cloisters itself, a drop of maybe twenty feet leading to the grass below. The other two sides of the square consisted of pillared arcades.

The garden had been planted with shrubs and trees common in medieval times. A quartet of quince trees stood in the middle, the first signs of its golden fruit now appearing. Valerian was overshadowed by the huge leaves of black mustard; nearby grew caraway and leek, chive and lovage, madder and Our-Lady's-bedstraw, the last two constituent ingredients in the dyes used by artists for the manuscripts on display in the main body of the museum.

It took me seconds to notice the new addition to the garden. Against the far wall, beside the entrance to the tower, grew an espaliered pear tree, its shape resembling a menorah. The bare branches were like hooks, six of them growing out from the main artery of the tree. Mickey Shine's head had been impaled on the very tip of that central artery, turning him to a creature of both flesh and wood. Tendril-like trails of coagulating blood hung from the neck, and the rain damped the pallor of his features as water pooled in the sunken sockets of his eyes. Tattered skin blew softly in the wind, and there was blood around his mouth and ears. His ponytail had been severed during the removal of his head and the loose hair now stuck lankly to his gray-blue skin.

I was already reaching for my gun when the thin, spiderlike shape of Mr. Pudd emerged from the shadow of the arcade to my right. In his hand he held a Beretta fitted with a suppressor. My hand froze. He told me to toss my gun away, slowly. I did.

'So here we are, Mr. Parker,' he said, and the eyes behind their dark hoods gleamed with a hostile intensity. 'I hope you like what I've done with the place.'

His gun hand gestured to the tree. Blood and rain pooled at its base, creating a dark reflection of what lay above. I could see Mickey Shine's face shimmer as the raindrops fell, seeming to add life and expression to his still features.

'I found Mr. Sheinberg in a nickel-and-dime Bowery hotel,' he continued. 'When they discover what's left of him in his bathtub, I fear it will be merely a nickel hotel.'

And still the rain fell. It would keep the tourists away, and that was what Mr. Pudd wanted.

'The idea was mine,' he said. 'I thought it was appropriately medieval. The execution – and it *was* an execution – was the work of my . . . *associate*.'

Farther to my right, still sheltered by the arcade, the woman with the mutilated throat stood against a pillar, an open rucksack on the stone before her. She was watching us impassively, like Judith after disposing of the head of Holofernes.

'He struggled a great deal,' elaborated Mr. Pudd, almost distractedly. 'But then, we did start from the back. It took us some time to hit the vertebral artery. After that, he didn't struggle quite so much.'

The weight of the Smith & Wesson beneath my coat pressed against my skin, like a promise that would never be fulfilled. Mr. Pudd returned his attention fully to me, raising the Beretta slightly as he did so.

'The Peltier woman stole something from us, Mr. Parker. We want it back.'

I spoke at last. 'You were in my house. You took everything that I had.'

'You're lying. The old man didn't have it, but I think you might. And even if you don't, I suspect you know who does.'

'The Apocalypse?' It was a guess, but a good one. Mr. Pudd's lips twitched once, and then he nodded. 'Tell me where it is, and you won't feel a thing when I kill you.'

'And if I don't tell you?' From the corner of my eye I saw the woman produce a gun and aim it at me. As she moved, so too did Mr. Pudd. His left hand, which had been concealed in the pocket of his coat until then, appeared from the folds. In it, he held a syringe.

'I'll shoot you. I won't kill you, but I will disable you, and then . . .' He raised the syringe and a stream of clear liquid issued from the needle.

'Is that what you used to kill Epstein?' I asked.

'No,' he answered. 'Compared to what you will endure, the unfortunate Rabbi Epstein passed comfortably into the next world. You're about to experience a great deal of pain, Mr. Parker.'

He angled the gun so that it was pointing at my belly, but I wasn't looking at the gun. Instead, I watched as a tiny red dot appeared on Mr. Pudd's groin and slowly began to work its way upward. Pudd's eyes dropped to follow my gaze and his mouth opened in surprise as the dot continued its progress over his chest and neck before stopping in the center of his forehead.

'You first,' I said, but he was already moving. The first bullet blew away a chunk of his right ear as he loosed off a shot in my direction, the rain hissing beside my face as the heat of the slug warmed the air. Then three more shots came, tearing black holes in his chest. The bullets should have ripped through him, but instead he lurched backward as if he had been punched hard, the impact of the shots sending him tumbling over the wall.

Shards of stone sprang up close to my left leg and I heard the dull sound of the suppressed shots echoing around the arcade. I retrieved my gun, dove for the cover of the chapel tower and fired at the pillar where the woman had been standing, but she had stooped low and was scuttling toward the door to the Glass Gallery, her gun bucking as gunfire came at her from two directions: from the wall where I stood and from the arcade, where Louis's dark form was moving through the shadows to intercept her. The door to the gallery opened behind her and she disappeared inside. I was about to follow when a bullet whistled past my ear and I dove to the ground, my face buried in the clump of Our-Lady's-bedstraw. Across from me, Louis leaped over the wall of the arcade as I raised myself up and crawled behind the main wall. I took a deep breath and peered over.

There was nobody there. Pudd was already gone, a smear of blood on some flattened grass the only indicator of his former presence.

'Follow the woman,' I said. Louis nodded and ran to the gallery, his gun held discreetly by his side. I climbed onto the wall and then jumped, landing heavily on the grass and rolling down the slope. I sprang up quickly when I came to a stop, the gun outstretched, but Pudd was nowhere to be seen. I moved west, following the trail of blood along the main wall of the Cloisters, until somewhere at the far side of the building I heard a shot fired, then another, followed by the squealing of tires. Seconds later, a blue Voyager sped down Margaret Corbin Drive. I ran to the road, hoping for a clear shot, but an MTA bus turned the corner at the same time and I held my fire for fear of hitting the bus or its passengers. The last thing I saw as the Voyager disappeared was a figure slumped forward on the dashboard. I wasn't certain, but I thought it was Pudd.

Brushing the grass from my pants and coat, I put my gun away and walked swiftly around to the main entrance. A gray-suited museum guard lay slumped against the wall, surrounded by a crowd of newly arrived French tourists. There was blood on his right arm and leg, but he was conscious. I heard the sound of footsteps on the grass behind me and turned to see Louis standing in the shade of the wall. He had obviously made a full circuit of the complex after pursuing the woman in order to avoid passing through the museum again.

'Call nine-one-one,' he said, staring up the road the Voyager had taken. 'That's one nasty bitch.'

'They got away.'

'No shit. Got myself tangled up in the damn tourists. She shot the guard to make them panic.'

'We hurt Pudd,' I said. 'That's something.'

'I hit him in the chest. He should be dead.'

'He was wearing a vest. The shots blew him off his feet.'

'Shit,' he hissed. 'You planning on staying around?'

'To explain Mickey Shine's head on a tree? I don't think so.'

We climbed onto the MTA bus, its driver oblivious to the furore at the main door, and sat in separate seats as he pulled away. For a brief moment, as he turned onto the main road, he was able to see the entrance to the Cloisters and the crowd around the fallen guard.

'Something happen?' he called back to us.

'I think somebody fainted,' I said.

'Place ain't that pretty,' he replied, and he said nothing more until he dropped us at the subway station. There was a cab turning at the curb, and we told the driver to head downtown.

I dropped Louis off at the Upper West Side, while I continued down to the Village to collect my overnight bag. When I was done, I dropped into the Strand Book Store on Broadway and found a companion volume for the Cloisters exhibition. Then I sat in Balducci's coffee shop on Sixth Avenue, leafing through the illustrations and watching the people go by. Whatever Mickey Shine had guessed or suspected had died with him, but at least I now knew what Grace Peltier had taken from the Fellowship: a book, a record of some kind, which Mr. Pudd acknowledged to be an Apocalypse. But why should a Biblical text be so important that Pudd was willing to kill to get it back?

Rachel was still in Boston, and would join me in Scarborough the following day. She had refused an offer of protection from Angel and an offer of a Colt Pony Pocketlite from Louis. Unbeknownst to her, she was being discreetly watched by a gentleman named Gordon Buntz and one of his associates, Amy Brenner. They'd given me a professional discount, but they were still eating up Jack Mercier's advance. Meanwhile, Angel was already in Scarborough; he had checked into the Black Point Inn at Prouts Neck, which gave him the freedom to roam around the area without attracting the attention of the Scarborough PD. I'd given him a National Audubon Society field guide to New England; armed with a pair of binoculars, he was now officially the world's least likely bird-watcher. He had been monitoring Jack Mercier, his house, and his movements since the previous afternoon.

Outside Balducci's, a black Lexus SC400 pulled up to the curb. Louis was sitting in the driver's seat. When I opened the door, Johnny Cash was solemnly intoning the words to Soundgarden's 'Rusty Cage.'

'Nice car,' I said. 'Your bank manager recommend it?'

He shook his head sorrowfully. 'Man, I tell you, you need class like a junkie need a hit.'

I dumped my bag on the leather backseat. It made a satisfyingly dirty sound, although it was nothing compared to the sound Louis made when he saw the mark it left on his upholstery. As we pulled away from the curb, Louis took a huge contraband Cuban cigar from his jacket pocket and proceeded to light up. Thick blue smoke immediately filled the car.

'Hey!' I said.

'Fuck you mean, "Hey"?'

'Don't smoke in the car.'

'It's my car.'

'Your secondary fumes are a danger to my health.'

Louis choked on a mouthful of smoke before raising one carefully plucked eyebrow in my direction. 'You been beaten up, shot twice, drowned, electrocuted, frozen, injected with poisons, three of your damn teeth been kicked out of your head by an old man everybody thought was dead, and you worried about secondary smoke? Secondary smoke ain't no danger to your health. *You* a danger to your health.'

With that, he returned his attention to his driving.

I let him smoke the cigar in peace.

After all, he had a point.

The Search for Sanctuary

Extract from the postgraduate thesis of Grace Peltier

Faulkner's main claim to fame, apart from his association with Eagle Lake, was as a bookbinder, and particularly as a maker of Apocalypses, ornately illustrated versions of the book of Revelation, the last book of the New Testament, detailing St. John's vision of the end of the world and the final judgment. In creating these works, Faulkner was part of a tradition dating back to the Carolingian period – to the ninth and tenth centuries, when the earliest surviving illustrated Apocalypse manuscripts were created on the European continent. In the early thirteenth century richly illuminated Apocalypses, with texts and commentaries in Latin and French vernacular, were made in Europe for the powerful and wealthy, including high churchmen and magnates. They continued to be created even after the invention of printing, indicating a continued resonance to the imagery and message of the book itself.

There are twelve 'Faulkner Apocalypses' extant, and according to the records of Faulkner's supplier of gold leaf, it is unlikely that Faulkner made more than this number. Each book was bound in hand-tooled leather, inlaid with gold, and illustrated by hand by Faulkner, with a distinctive marking on the spine: six horizontal gold lines, set in three sets of two, and the final letter of the Greek alphabet – **Ω**, for omega.

The paper was made not from wood but from linen and cotton rags beaten in water into a smooth pulp. Faulkner would dip a rectangular tray into the pulp and take up about one inch of the substance, draining it through a wire mesh in the base of the tray. Gently shaking the tray caused the matted fibers in the liquid to interlock. These sheets of partially solidified pulp were then squeezed in a press before being dipped in animal gelatin to size it, thereby enabling it to hold ink. The paper was bound in folios of six to minimize the buildup of thread on the book's spine.

The illustrations in Faulkner's Apocalypses were drawn largely from earlier artists, and remain consistent throughout. (All twelve are in the private ownership of one individual, and I was permitted to examine them at length.) Thus, the earliest of the Apocalypses is inspired by Albrecht Dürer (1471–1528), the second by medieval manuscripts, the third by Lucas Cranach the Elder (1472-1553), and so on, with the final extant book featuring six illustrations based on the work of Frans Masereel (1889-1972), whose Apocalypse cycle drew on images from World War II. According to those who had dealings with him, it appears that Faulkner was attracted to apocalyptic imagery because of its connotations of judgment, not because he believed it foretold a Second Coming or a final reckoning. For Faulkner, the reckoning had already begun; judgment and damnation were an ongoing process.

Faulkner's Apocalypses were created strictly for wealthy collectors, and the sale of them is believed to have provided much of the seed funding for Faulkner's community. No further versions made by Faulkner's hand have appeared since the date of the foundation of the Eagle Lake settlement.

Chapter Sixteen

Louis dropped me at my house before heading for the Black Point Inn. I checked in with Gordon Buntz to make sure Rachel was okay, and a quick call to Angel confirmed that nothing out of the ordinary had occurred at the Merciers', with the exception of the arrival of the lawyer Warren Ober and his wife. He had also spotted four different types of tern and two plovers. I arranged to meet up with both Angel and Louis later that night.

I had been checking my messages pretty regularly while in Boston and New York, but there were two new ones since that morning. The first was from Arthur Franklin, asking if the information his pornographer client, Harvey Ragle, had proffered was proving useful. In the background, I could hear Ragle's whining voice: 'I'm a dead man. You tell him that. I'm a *dead* man.' I didn't bother to return the call.

The second message came from ATF agent Norman Boone. Ellis Howard, the deputy chief over in the Portland PD, once told me that Boone smelled like a French whore, but with none of the associated charm. He had left his home and cell phone numbers. I got him at home.

'It's Charlie Parker. How can I help you, Agent Boone?'

'Why, thank you for returning my call, Mr. Parker. It's only been . . .' At the other end of the line, I could imagine him ostentatiously checking his watch. 'Four hours.'

'I was out of town.'

'You mind telling me where?'

'Why, did we have a date?'

Boone sighed dramatically. 'Talk to me now, Mr. Parker, or talk to me tomorrow at One City Center. I should warn you that I'm a busy man, and my patience is likely to be more strained by tomorrow morning.'

'I was in Boston, visiting an old friend.'

'An old friend, as I understand it, who ended up with a hole in his head halfway through a performance of *Cleopatra*.'

'I'm sure he knew how it ended. She dies, in case you hadn't heard.'

He ignored me. 'Was your visit connected in any way to Lester Bargus?'

I didn't pause for a second, although the question had thrown me.

'Not directly.'

'But you visited Mr. Bargus shortly before you left town?'

Damn.

'Lester and I go way back.'

'Then you'll be heartbroken to hear that he is no longer with us.'

' "Heartbroken" maybe isn't the word. And the ATF's interest in all this is . . . ?'

'Mr. Bargus made a little money selling spiders and giant roaches and a lot of money selling automatic weapons and other assorted firearms to the kind of people who have swastikas on their crockery. It was natural that he would come to *our* attention. My question is, why did he come to *your* attention?'

'I was looking for somebody. I thought Lester might have known where he was. Is this an interrogation, Agent Boone?'

'It's a conversation, Mr. Parker. If we did it tomorrow, face-to-face, then it would be an interrogation.'

Even with a telephone line separating us, I had to admit that Boone was good. He was closing in on me, leaving me with almost no room to turn. I was not going to tell him about Grace Peltier, because Grace would bring me on to Jack Mercier, and possibly the Fellowship, and the last thing I wanted was the ATF going Waco on the Fellowship. Instead, I decided to give him Harvey Ragle.

'All I do know is that a lawyer named Arthur Franklin called me and asked me to speak to his client.'

'Who's his client?'

'Harvey Ragle. He makes porn movies, with bugs in them. Al Z's people used to distribute some of them.'

It was Boone's turn to be thrown. 'Bugs? The hell are you talking about?'

'Women in their underwear squashing bugs,' I explained, as if to a child. 'He also does geriatric porn, obesity, and little people. He's an artist.'

'Nice types you meet in your line of work.'

'You make a pleasant change from the norm, Agent Boone. It seems that an individual with an affinity for bugs wants to kill Harvey Ragle for making his sicko porn movies. Lester Bargus had supplied the bugs and also seemed to know something about him, so I agreed to approach him on behalf of Ragle.'

The improbability of it was breathtaking. I could feel Boone wondering just how far he was being taken for a ride.

'And who is this mysterious herpetologist?'

Herpetologist. Agent Boone was obviously a Scrabble fan.

'He calls himself Mr. Pudd, and I think that strictly speaking he may be an arachnologist, not a herpetologist. He likes spiders. I think he's the man who killed Al Z.'

'And you approached Lester Bargus in the hope of finding this man?'

'Yes.'

'But you got nowhere.'

'Lester had a lot of anger in him.'

'Well, he's a lot calmer now.'

'If you had him under surveillance, then you already know what passed between us,' I said. 'Which means there's something else that you want from me.'

After some hesitation, Boone went on to explain how a man traveling under the name of Clay Dæmon had walked in to Lester's store, demanded details of an individual in a photograph, and then shot Lester and his assistant dead.

'I'd like you to take a look at the photograph,' he said.

'He left it?'

'We figure he's got more than one copy. Hired killers tend to be pretty good that way.'

'You want me to come in? It could be tomorrow.'

'How about now?'

'Look, Agent Boone, I need a shower, a shave, and sleep. I've told you all I can. I want to help, but give me a break.'

Boone relented slightly. 'You got e-mail?

'Yes, and a second line.'

'Then stay on this one. I'll be back.'

The line went quiet, so I turned on my desktop and waited for Boone's e-mail to arrive. When it did, it consisted of two pictures. One was the photograph of the abortion clinic slaying. I spotted Mr. Pudd immediately. The other was a still taken from the video camera in Lester Bargus's store, showing the killer Clay Dæmon. Seconds later, Boone was back on the line.

'You recognize anyone in the first picture?'

'The guy on the far right is Pudd, first name Elias. He came out to my house, asking why I was nosing around in his business. I don't know the man in the video still.'

I could hear Boone clicking his tongue rhythmically at the other end of the line, even as I gave him the contact number I had for Ragle's lawyer. 'I'll be talking to you again, Mr. Parker,' he said at last. 'I have a feeling you know more than you're telling.'

'Everybody knows more than they're telling, Agent Boone,' I replied. 'Even you. I have a question.'

'Uh-huh?'

'Who's the injured man in the first photograph?'

'His name was David Beck. He worked for an abortion clinic in Minnesota, and he's a *dead* man in that photograph. The killing forms part of the VAAPCON files.'

VAAPCON was the code name for the joint FBI-ATF investigation into abortion-related violence, the Violence Against Abortion Providers Conspiracy. The ATF and the FBI have a poor working relationship; for a long time the FBI had resisted involving itself in investigating attacks on doctors and abortion clinics, arguing that it didn't fall within their guidelines, which meant that the investigation of allegations of a conspiracy of violence was left in the hands of the ATF. That situation changed with the formation of VAAPCON and the enactment of new legislation empowering the FBI and the Justice Department to act against abortion-related violence. Yet tensions between the FBI and the ATF contributed to the comparative failure of VAAPCON; no evidence of a conspiracy was found, and agents took to dubbing the investigation CRAPCON, despite signs of growing links between right-wing militias and antiabortion extremists.

'Did they ever find his killer?' I asked.

'Not yet.'

'Like they haven't found his wife's killer.'

'What do you know about it?'

'I know she had spiders in her mouth when she was found.'

'And our friend Pudd is a spider lover.'

'The same Pudd whose head is circled in this photograph.'

'Do you know who he's working for?'

'Himself, I'd guess.' It wasn't quite a lie. Pudd didn't answer to Carter Paragon, and the Fellowship as the public knew it seemed too inconsequential to require his services.

Boone didn't speak for a time. His last words to me before he hung up were, 'We'll be talking again.'

I didn't doubt it.

I sat in front of the computer screen, flicking between both images. I picked out a younger Alison Beck holding her dead husband, her face contorted with grief and his blood on her shirt, skirt, and hands. Then I looked into the small, hooded eyes of Mr. Pudd as he slipped away through the crowd. I wondered if he had fired the shots or merely orchestrated the killing. Either way, he was involved, and another small piece of the puzzle slipped into place. Somehow, Mercier had found Epstein and Beck, individuals who, for their own reasons, were prepared to assist him in his moves against the Fellowship. But why was Mercier so concerned about the Fellowship? Was it simply another example of his liberalism, or were there other, deeper motives?

As it turned out, a possible answer to the question pulled up outside my door thirty minutes later in a black Mercedes convertible. Deborah Mercier stepped, alone and unaided, in a long black coat, from the driver's seat. Despite the encroaching darkness she wore shades. Her hair didn't move in the breeze. It could have been hair spray, or an act of will. It could also have been that even the wind wasn't going to screw around with Jack Mercier's wife. I wondered what excuse she had come up with for leaving her guests back at the house; maybe she told them they needed milk.

I opened the door as she reached the first step to the porch. 'Take a wrong turn, Mrs. Mercier?' I asked.

'One of us has,' she replied, 'and I think it might be you.'

'I never catch a break. I see those two roads diverging in a forest, and damn if I don't take the one that ends at a cliff edge.'

We stood about ten paces apart, eyeing each other up like a pair of mismatched gunfighters. Deborah Mercier couldn't have looked more like a WASP if her coat had been striped with yellow and her eyes had been on the side of her head. She removed her glasses and those pale blue eyes held all the warmth of the Arctic Sea, the pupils tiny and receding like the bodies of drowned sailors sinking into their depths.

'Would you like to come inside?' I asked. I turned away and heard her footsteps on the wood behind me. They stopped before they reached the door. I looked back at her and saw her nostrils twitch a little in mild distaste as her gaze passed over my house.

'If you're waiting for me to carry you over the threshold, I ought to warn you that I have a bad back and we might not make it.'

Her nostrils twitched a little more and her eyes froze over entirely, trapping the pupils at the size of pinpoints. Then, carefully, the heels of her black pumps making a sound like the clicking of bones on the floorboards, she followed me into the house.

I led her to the kitchen and offered her coffee. She declined, but I went ahead and started making a pot anyway. I watched as she opened her coat, revealing a tight black formal dress that ended above her knees, and sat down. Her legs, like the rest of her, looked good for forty-something. In fact, she would have looked good for forty, and not bad for thirty-five. She removed a pack of cigarettes from her bag and lit up with a gold Dunhill lighter. She took a long drag on the cigarette, then blew a thin stream of smoke through her pursed lips.

'Feel free to smoke,' I said.

'If I was concerned, I'd have asked.'

'If I was concerned, I'd make you put it out.'

Her head turned a little to one side, and she smiled emptily. 'So you think you can make people do what you want?'

'I believe we may have that in common, Mrs. Mercier.'

'It's probably the only thing we do have in common, Mr. Parker.'

'Here's hoping,' I replied. I brought the coffee pot to the table and poured myself a cup.

'On second thoughts, I will have some of that coffee,' she said.

'Smells good, doesn't it?'

'Or maybe everything else in here smells so bad. You live alone?'

'Just me and my ego.'

'I'm sure the two of you are very happy together.'

'Ecstatic.' I found a second cup and filled it, then took a carton of skimmed milk from the refrigerator and placed it between us.

'I'm sorry, I don't have any sugar.'

She reached into her bag again and produced a packet of Sweet'n'Low. She added it to the coffee and stirred it before tasting it carefully. Since she didn't fall to the floor clutching her throat and gasping, I figured it was probably okay. She didn't say anything for a time; she just sipped and smoked.

'Your house needs a woman's touch,' she said at last, as she took another drag on her cigarette. She held in the smoke until I thought it would come out her ears.

'Why, you do cleaning as well?'

She didn't reply. Instead, she finally released the smoke and dropped the remains of the cigarette into the coffee. Classy. She didn't learn that at the Madeira School for Girls.

'I hear you were married once.'

'That's right, I was.'

'And you had a child, a little girl.'

'Jennifer,' I replied, keeping my tone as neutral as possible.

'And now your wife and child are dead. Somebody killed them, and then you killed him.'

I didn't respond. My silence didn't appear to concern Mrs. Mercier.

'That must have been very hard for you,' she continued. There was no trace of sympathy in her voice but her eyes were briefly thawed by what might have been amusement.

'Yes, it was.'

'But you see, Mr. Parker, I still have a marriage, and I still have a child. I don't like the fact that my husband has hired you, against my wishes, to investigate the death of a girl who has nothing to do with our lives. It is disturbing my relationship with my husband, and it is interfering with the preparations for my daughter's wedding. I want it to stop.'

I noticed the emphasis on 'my' daughter but didn't comment. For the final time, she took something from her handbag. It was a check.

'I know how much my husband paid you,' she said, passing the folded check across the table toward me, her red nails like eagle's talons dipped in a rabbit's blood. 'I'll pay you the same amount to walk away.'

She withdrew her hand. The check lay on the table between us, looking lonely and unloved.

'I don't believe you're so wealthy that you can afford to turn down that kind of money, Mr. Parker. You were willing to take it from my husband, so you should have no difficulty in accepting it from me.'

I made no move for the check. Instead, I poured myself some fresh coffee. I didn't offer any to Mrs. Mercier. I guessed from the floating cigarette butt that she'd had enough.

'There's a difference. Your husband was buying my time, and whatever expertise I could offer. You, on the other hand, are trying to buy *me*.'

'Really? Then, under the circumstances, my offer is particularly generous.'

I smiled. She smiled back. From a distance – a really long distance – we might have looked like we were having a good time. It seemed like the right moment to put an end to that misapprehension.

'When did you find out that Grace was your husband's child?' I asked. I experienced a brief surge of satisfaction as her face paled, and her head rocked back a little as if she'd been slapped.

'I don't know what you're talking about,' she replied, but she didn't sound convincing.

'For a start, there's the breakup of your husband's partnership with Curtis Peltier seven months before her birth and his willingness to spend a significant amount of money employing me to investigate the circumstances of her death. Then, of course, there's the resemblance. It must have been like a kick in the guts every time you saw her, Mrs. Mercier.'

She stood up and grabbed the check from the table. 'You're a mean bastard,' she hissed.

'That might hurt a little more if it came from somebody else, Mrs. Mercier, but not from you.' I reached forward suddenly and clamped her wrist tightly in my right hand. For the first time, she looked scared.

'It was you, wasn't it? It was you who told Grace about the Fellowship. Did you set her on their trail knowing what they would do to her? I don't believe that your husband said anything to her about it, and her thesis dealt with the past, not the present, so there was no reason for her to start prying into the organization. But you must have been aware of what your husband was doing, of the moves he was making against them. What did you say to her, Mrs. Mercier? What information did you give her that led those people to kill her?'

Deborah Mercier bared her teeth at me and her fingernails raked across the back of my hand, immediately drawing blood. 'I'll make sure my husband ruins your life for what you just said to me,' she snarled, as I released her hand.

'I don't think so. I think when he finds out that you sent his daughter to her death, then it's your life that won't be worth living.'

I stood as she snatched up her bag and started for the hallway. Before she could reach the kitchen door, I blocked her with my arm.

'There's one more thing you should know, Mrs. Mercier. You and your husband have set in motion a chain of events that you can't control. There are people out there who are prepared to kill to protect themselves. So you should be glad that your husband is paying me because, as of now, I'm the best chance you have of finding those people before they come after both of you.'

She stared straight ahead as I spoke. When I had finished, I lowered my hand and she walked quickly to the door. She left it open behind her, and I watched as she started the Mercedes and turned it quickly onto the road. I looked down at my hand and the four deep parallel lines she had left on it. Blood ran down my fingers and pooled at the nails and I thought, for a moment, that they looked a lot like Deborah Mercier's. I cleaned the cuts under the faucet, then put on my jacket and a pair of leather gloves to cover the wound, grabbed my keys, and headed out to my car.

I should have asked her for a ride, I thought, as I followed the lights of her car all the way to Prouts Neck. I kept far enough back so as not to arouse her suspicion, but I was still close enough to make the security barrier before it closed behind her.

There were five or six cars in the parking lot when I pulled up and stepped from the car. Mrs. Mercier had already disappeared into the house and the porn star with the mustache was lumbering forward from the porch. He was wearing an earpiece and he had a radio mike attached to his lapel. I guessed that security had been stepped up somewhat after Epstein's death.

'This is a private party,' he said. 'You'll have to leave.'

'I don't think so,' I replied.

'Then I'll have to make you leave,' he said. He looked happy at the prospect, and poked a finger into my chest to emphasize the point.

I grabbed the finger with my left hand, gripped his wrist tightly with my right, and pulled. There was a soft pop as the finger dislocated, and the porn star's mouth opened wide in pain. I turned him around, pulling his arm behind his back, and shoved him hard into the side of the Mercedes. His head banged emptily against it and he collapsed on the ground, holding his uninjured hand against his scalp.

'If you're a good boy, I'll fix your finger on my way out,' I said.

A couple of other security guards were moving toward

me when Jack Mercier appeared on the steps and called them off. They stopped and formed a loose circle around me, like wolves waiting for the signal to fall upon their prey.

'It seems like you've invited yourself to my party, Mr. Parker,' said Mercier. 'I guess you'd better come in.'

I walked up the steps and followed him through the house. It didn't look like much of a party. There was a lot of expensive booze floating around on trays and a handful of people stood about in nice clothes, but nobody seemed to be having a very good time. A man I recognized as Warren Ober put down his champagne flute and started to follow us.

Mercier led me into the same book-lined room in which we had sat the previous week, the rhombus of sun now replaced by a thin shard of pale moonlight. The bug was gone, probably already devoured by something bigger and meaner than it could ever be. There were no coffee cups brought this time. Jack Mercier wasn't offering me his hospitality. His eyes were red rimmed and he had shaved himself badly, so that patches of bristle showed under his chin and below his nostrils. Even his white dress shirt looked wrinkled, and sweat patches showed beneath his armpits when he took off his jacket. His bow tie was slightly crooked, and beneath his cologne I thought I detected a sour smell.

I walked straight to the photograph of Mercier and Ober with Beck and Epstein, and removed it from the wall. I threw it to him and he caught it awkwardly in his arms. 'What haven't you told me?' I said, as the door opened and Ober entered. He closed it behind him and both of us looked at Mercier.

'What do you mean?'

'I mean, Mr. Mercier, what were the four of you doing that could have drawn these people down on you? How do *you* think Grace became involved?'

He recoiled visibly at the question.

'And why did you hire me, because you must have known who was responsible for her death?'

He didn't say anything at first, just sat down heavily in an armchair across from me and put his head in his hands. 'Did you know that Curtis Peltier was dead?' he asked me, in tones so soft they were almost inaudible.

I felt an ache in my stomach and leaned back against the table to steady myself.

'Nobody told me.'

'He was only found this evening. He'd been dead for days. I was going to call you as soon as my guests left.'

'How did he die?'

'Somebody broke into his house, tortured him, then slit his wrists in his bathtub.'

He looked up at me, his eyes demanding pity and understanding. In that instant, I almost struck Jack Mercier.

'He never knew, did he?' I said. 'He didn't know anything about the Fellowship, about Beck or Epstein. The only thing that mattered to him was his daughter, and he gave her everything he could. I saw the way he lived. He had a big house that he couldn't keep clean, and he lived in his kitchen. Do you even know where your kitchen is, Mr. Mercier?'

He smiled. It wasn't a nice smile. There was no compassion in it, no kindness. I doubted if any voter had ever seen Jack Mercier smile like that. '*My* daughter, Mr. Parker,' he growled. 'Grace was *my* child.'

'You're deluded, Mr. Mercier.' I couldn't keep the disgust from my voice.

'I stayed out of her life because that was what we all agreed, but I was always concerned for her. When she applied to the scholarship fund, I saw a chance to help her. Hell, I'd have given her the money even if she wanted to take surfing at Malibu Tech. She intended to study religious movements in the state during the last fifty years, and one in particular. I encouraged her to do that in order to have her near me while she studied the books in my collection. It was my fault, my mistake.

'Because we didn't know about the link, not then,' he

said, and the weight of his guilt fell upon him like an executioner's blade.

'What link?'

Behind us, Warren Ober coughed. 'I have to advise you, Jack, not to say anything more in Mr. Parker's presence.' He was using his best, five hundred-dollar-per-hour voice. As far as Ober was concerned, Grace's death was immaterial. All that mattered was ensuring that Jack Mercier's guilt remained private, not public.

The gun was in my hand before I even knew it. Through a red haze I saw Ober backing away and then the muzzle of the gun was buried in the soft flesh beneath his chin. 'You say one more word,' I whispered, 'and I won't be held responsible for my actions.'

Despite the fear in his eyes, Ober spat the next six words. 'You are a thug, Mr. Parker,' he said.

'So are you, Mr. Ober,' I replied. 'The only difference is that you're better paid than I am.'

'*Stop!*'

It was the voice of an emperor, a voice used to being obeyed. I didn't disappoint it. I removed the gun from Ober's chin and put it away.

'Safety was on,' I told him. 'Can't be too careful.'

Ober adjusted his bow tie and started calculating the man-hours required to ruin me in court.

Mercier poured himself a brandy and another for Ober. He waved the decanter at me, but I declined. He handed Ober his glass, took a long sip, then resumed his seat and began talking as if nothing had happened.

'Did Curtis tell you about our respective familial connections to the Aroostook Baptists?'

I nodded. Behind me, a cloud passed over the moon and the light that had shone into the room was suddenly lost in its depths. 'They were lost for thirty-seven years, until now,' he said softly. 'I believe that the man responsible for their deaths is still alive.'

* * *

The first hint that Faulkner was alive had come in March, and it arrived from an unlikely source. A Faulkner Apocalypse was offered for auction, and Jack Mercier had acquired it, just as he had successfully acquired the twelve other extant examples of Faulkner's work. While he spoke, he removed one from his cabinet and handed it to me. Faulkner had the talent of a medieval illuminator, using decorated letters interweaved with fantastic animals to begin each chapter. The ink was iron gall, the same mix of tannins and iron sulphate used in medieval times. Each chapter contained illustrations drawn from ornate works similar to the Cloisters Apocalypse, images of judgment, punishment, and torment executed in a detail that bordered on the sadistic.

'The illustrations and calligraphy are consistent throughout,' explained Mercier. 'Other Faulkner Apocalypses are inspired by later illustrators, such as Meidner and Grosz, and the script is correspondingly more modern, although in some ways equally beautiful.'

But the thirteenth Apocalypse acquired by Mercier was different. An adhesive had been used on the pages before stitching because the weight of the paper was lighter than before and the binder appeared to have experienced some difficulty in applying the stitches. Mercier, a bibliophile, had spotted traces of the adhesive shortly after his purchase and had sent the book to be examined by a specialist. The calligraphy and brush strokes on the illustrations were authentic – Faulkner had created the Apocalypse, without doubt – but the adhesive was of a type that had been in production for less than a decade, and had been used in the original construction of the book and not during any later repairs.

Faulkner, it seemed, was alive, or at least he had been until comparatively recently, and if he could be found then an answer to the riddle of the disappearance of the Aroostook Baptists might at last be within reach.

'To be honest, my interest was in the books, not the

people,' said Mercier dismissively, an admission that hardened my growing dislike for him. 'My familial connections to Faulkner's flock added an extra frisson, but nothing more. I found the nature of his work fascinating.'

It was the source of the thirteenth Apocalypse that led Mercier to the Fellowship; it emerged, after investigation, that it had been sold through a firm of third-rate Waterville lawyers by Carter Paragon, to cover his gambling debts. But rather than pounce on Paragon, Mercier decided to wait and put pressure on his organization by other means. He found Epstein, who had already suspected that the Fellowship was far more dangerous than it appeared and was willing to be the nominal challenger of its tax-exempt status. He found Alison Beck, who had witnessed the killing of her husband years before and who was now pressing for the case to be reopened and a full investigation made into a possible link to the Fellowship, based on threats received from its minions in the months before David Beck's death. If Mercier could tear apart the front that was the Fellowship, then what was behind it might at last be revealed.

Meanwhile, Grace's work on the Aroostook Baptists had continued. Mercier had largely forgotten about it, until her life was ended in the sound of a gunshot that sent owls shooting from the trees and small animals scurrying into the undergrowth. Then Peltier had come to him, and the bond that linked them both to Grace had drawn them uneasily together.

'She went after the Fellowship, Mr. Parker, and she died for it.' He looked at me, and I saw his eyes desperately try to veil themselves in ignorance. 'I don't know why she went after them,' he continued, a denial of an accusation that had not yet been made. Something bubbled in his voice, as if he was struggling to keep his bile down.

'I think you do,' I said. 'I think that's why you hired me – to confirm what you already suspected.'

And at last I saw the veils tear and fall from his eyes in flames. He seemed about to utter some further denial, until a female voice was heard outside the door and the words melted like snowflakes on his tongue.

Deborah Mercier burst into the room. She looked at me in shock, then at her husband.

'He followed me here, Jack,' she snarled. 'He broke into our house and assaulted our staff. Why are you sitting there drinking with him?'

'Deborah . . .' Mercier began, in what might, in other circumstances, have been soothing tones but now sounded like the whispered assurances of an executioner to a condemned man.

'*Don't!*' she screamed. 'Just don't. Have him arrested. Have him thrown out of the house. I don't care if you have him killed, but get him out of our lives!'

Jack Mercier stood and walked over to his wife. He held her firmly by the shoulders and looked down, and for the first time she seemed smaller and less powerful than he.

'Deborah,' he repeated, and drew her to him. Initially it seemed like a gesture of love, but as she struggled in his grip it became the opposite. 'Deborah, what have you done?'

'I don't know what you mean,' she said. 'What do you mean, Jack?'

'Please, Deborah,' he said. 'Don't lie. Please don't lie, not now.'

Instantly, her struggles ceased and she began to cry.

'We have no further need of your services, Mr. Parker,' said Mercier, as her body shook. His back was to me as he spoke, and he made no effort to turn. 'Thank you for your help.'

'They'll come after you,' I said.

'We'll deal with them. I intend to hand the Faulkner Apocalypse over to the police after my daughter's wedding. That will be an end to it. Now, please, leave my house.'

As I walked from the room, I heard Deborah Mercier whisper, over and over again, 'I'm sorry, Jack, I'm sorry.' Something in her voice made me look back, and the glare from a single cold eye impaled me like a butterfly on a pin.

The porn star wasn't anywhere to be found as I left, so I couldn't reset his finger. I was about to get in my car when Warren Ober walked down the steps behind me and stood in the shell of light from the open door.

'Mr. Parker,' he called.

I paused and watched as his features tried to compose themselves into a smile. They gave up the struggle at the halfway point, making him look like a man who has just tasted a bad piece of fish.

'We'll forget about that little incident in the study, so long as you understand that you are to take no further part in investigating Grace Peltier's death or any incidents connected with it.'

I shook my head. 'It doesn't work that way. As I already explained to Mrs. Mercier, her husband just bought my time and whatever expertise I could bring to the case. He didn't buy my obedience, he didn't buy my conscience, and he didn't buy *me*. I don't like walking away from unsolved cases, Mr. Ober. It raises moral difficulties.'

Ober's face fell, his carefully ordered features crumbling under the weight of his disappointment. 'Then you'd better find yourself a good lawyer, Mr. Parker.'

I didn't reply. I just drove away, leaving Ober standing in the light like a solitary angel waiting to be consumed by the darkness.

Jack Mercier hadn't hired me to find out who had killed Grace, or that was not his primary reason for hiring me. He wanted to find out why she had been looking into the Fellowship to begin with, and I think he had suspected the answer all along, that he had seen it in his wife's eyes every time Grace was mentioned. Deborah wanted Grace to go away, to disappear. She and Jack already had a daughter together; he didn't need another. Through her husband, she knew just how dangerous those involved in the Fellowship could be, and she fed Grace to them.

I parked in the guest lot of the Black Point Inn and joined

Angel and Louis in the big dining room, where they were sitting at a window, their table littered with the remains of what looked like a very enjoyable, and pretty expensive, dinner. I was happy to see them spending Mercier's money. It was tainted by its contact with his family. I ordered coffee and dessert, then told them all that had taken place. When I had concluded, Angel shook his head.

'That Deborah Mercier, she's some piece of work.'

We left the table and moved into the bar. Angel, I couldn't help but notice, was still wearing the red boots, to which he had added a pair of substandard chinos and a white shirt with a twisted seam. He caught me looking at the shirt and smiled happily.

'TJ Maxx,' he said. 'Got me a whole new wardrobe for fifty-nine ninety-five.'

'Pity you didn't climb into it and throw yourself in the sea,' I replied.

They ordered beers, and a club soda for me. We were the only people in the bar.

'So what now?' asked Louis.

'Tomorrow night we pay a long overdue visit to the Fellowship,' I replied.

'And until then?'

Outside, the trees whispered and the waves broke whitely on Crescent Beach. I could see the lights of Old Orchard floating in the darkness like the glowing lures of strange, unseen sea creatures moving through the depths of black oceans. They called me to them, these echoes of the past, of my childhood and my youth.

Like those nightmarish, colorless predators, the past could devour you if you weren't careful. It had consumed Grace Peltier, its dead hand reaching out from the mud and silt of a lake in northern Maine and pulling her down. Grace, Curtis, Jack Mercier: all of them linked together by the dreams, disappearance, and eventual exhumation of the Aroostook Baptists. Grace wasn't even born when they vanished, yet part of her had always been buried with them, and her short life had been blighted by the mystery of their disappearance.

Now, a misstep, a minor accident, had revealed the truth about their end. They had emerged into the world, breaking through the thin crust that separated present from past, life from death.

And I had seen them.

'I'm going north,' I said. 'Somehow, this is all connected with the Aroostook Baptists. I want to see the place where they died.'

Louis looked at me. Beside him, Angel was silent.

It was happening again, and they knew it.

The Search for Sanctuary

Extract from the postgraduate thesis of Grace Peltier

The precise nature and extent of Lyall and Elizabeth's relationship must remain, perforce, largely unknown, but it is reasonable to assume that it included a significant element of sexual attraction. Elizabeth was a pretty woman, aged thirty-five at the time she joined the community. It is hard to find early pictures of her in which she is not smiling, although later photographs find her a more somber presence beside the unsmiling form of her husband, Frank. Elizabeth came from a small, poor family but appears to have been a bright young woman who, in a more enlightened (or liberal) community, and under less constrained financial circumstances, might have been given the space that she needed to grow. Instead, she made her match with Frank Jessop, fifteen years her senior but with some land and money to his name. It does not appear to have been a particularly happy union, and Frank was troubled with ill health in the years following the birth of their first child, James, which created a further rift between husband and wife.

Lyall Kellog was two years Elizabeth's junior and seventeen years younger than her own husband. Pictures that remain of Lyall show him to have been a stocky individual of medium height with slightly blunt features – in other words, by no means a conventionally handsome man. From all accounts he seems to have been quite happily married, and Elizabeth Jessop must have exerted an unusually strong influence on him for him not only to risk his marriage and the wrath of the Reverend Faulkner but to contravene his own strong religious beliefs.

Those who knew Lyall recall him as a gentle, almost sensitive man who could argue what sometimes seemed to others to be obscure points of religious belief with those considerably more educated than himself. He owned a large number of biblical tracts and commentaries, and was prepared to travel for a day to listen to a particularly noted speaker. It was on one of these trips that he first encountered the Reverend Faulkner.

Meanwhile, Faulkner's grip on the community had tightened by November 1963. Like Sandford before him, he demanded absolute obedience and forbade any contact with those outside the community, except for one period in the first weeks of winter when he asked each family to write to relatives in order to solicit donations of food, clothes, and money. Since most of the families were estranged from their own relatives, these letters proved largely useless, although Lena Myers did send a small sum of money.

The only relative to attempt to contact members of the community directly was a cousin of Katherine Cornish. He brought a sheriff's deputy to the settlement, fearing that some harm had befallen his kinfolk. Katherine Cornish was permitted a brief meeting with him, under Faulkner's supervision, to ease his fears. According to Elizabeth Jessop, the Cornish family was then punished by being forced to spend the night in an unheated barn, praying constantly. When they fell asleep, they were awakened by cold water thrown on them by 'Adam', Leonard Faulkner.

Letter from Elizabeth Jessop to her sister, Lena Myers, dated November 1963 (used by kind permission of the estate of Lena Myers)

Dearest Lena,

Thank you for your generosity. I am sorry I have not written sooner like I promised but things are hard here. I feel like Frank is watching me all the time and waiting for me to make a mistake. I don't think he knows for sure but I guess maybe I have been acting different.

I still see L. when I can. Lena, I have been with him again. I have prayed to God to aid me, but so help me I see him in my dreams and I want him. I feel like this cannot end well but I am powerless to stop it. It has been a long time, Lena, since a man touched me like that. Now that I have tasted the fruit I want no other. I hope that you understand.

There is bad feeling among the pilgrims. Some of them have been talking against Preacher Faulkner because of his ways. They say that he is too hard and there is even talk of asking him to return some of the money we gave him, just enough so that folks will have enough to fall back on if need be. There is trouble too with the boy and the girl. The girl has been ill, and her voice is now almost gone. She can no longer sing at suppertime, and the Preacher proposes to use some of our money to pay for a doctor for her. Laurie Perrson almost died for want of a doctor, but he will not let his own child suffer. Billy Perrson called him a hypocrite to his face.

But the boy is the worst of them. He is evil, Lena. There is no other word for him. James had a kitten. He brought it with him from Portland. It used to feed on field mice and what we could spare from our own table. It was a pretty little brown thing and he called it Jake.

Yesterday, Jake went missing. We searched the house but could find no trace of him. When the time came for James to take his daily lessons at the Preacher's house he slipped away and went looking for his kitten instead. We didn't know he had gone until Lyall heard him crying in the forest and went to see what was ailing him.

He found James standing by a shed in the woods. It used to be an old outhouse for some property that had burnt down years before and the children were told that it was out of bounds to them for fear that they might get up to badness if they were allowed near it. Lyall told me that the boy was just standing at the door to the shed, shaking and crying.

Someone had tied Jake by the neck to a nail set into the floor of the shed. The rope was only two or three inches long and the kitten almost lying flat on the floor. There were spiders all over it, Lena, little brown spiders just the size of a quarter like noone had ever seen before. They were crawling over the kitten's mouth and eyes and the kitten was scratching and mewing and damn near choking itself on the rope. Then Lyall said the kitten went into convulsions and died, just like that.

Lyall swears that he saw the boy Adam hanging around that shed where he had no business being and he told the Preacher so. But the Preacher spoke the commandments to him and warned him of the punishments of bearing false witness against his neighbor. The menfolk supported Lyall and the Preacher warned them against setting their hearts against him. All the time the boy Adam just watched and didn't speak a word but Lyall says the boy smiled at him and Lyall thought that maybe if the boy could have found a way to tie him to a nail and let the spiders feed on him as well then he would have.

I don't know what will happen here, Lena. Winter is coming on and I can only see things getting harder for us, but with the Lord's help we will prevail. I will pray for you and yours. My love to you all.

Your sister,

Elizabeth

P.S. I enclose a newspaper clipping. Make of it what you will.

Victim of Drowning Tragedy to be Buried Today

EAGLE LAKE. Edie Rattray, who died at St. Froid Lake, Aroostook, Wednesday, will be buried today. The body of Edie, 13, was found floating in the lake by Red River Road, close to the town of Eagle Lake. The body of her puppy was found nearby.

According to the only witness, Muriel Faulkner, 15, Edie got into difficulties attempting to rescue the dog when it fell from the bank, and drowned before Ms. Faulkner could summon help.

Edie was a prominent member of the choir of St. Mary's Church, Eagle Lake, and the choir will sing at her funeral mass. Ms. Faulkner is a member of the small religious community known locally as the Aroostook Baptists. Her father, Aaron, is the pastor of the community.

State police say they are treating the death as accidental, although they remain puzzled as to how Edie drowned in comparatively shallow water.

This week, candles will remain lit in every house in the town for the girl whose beautiful singing voice led her to be called the 'Nightingale of Eagle Lake'.

(from the Bangor Daily News, October 28, 1963)

Part Three

To the legion of the lost ones, to the cohort of the damned . . .

Rudyard Kipling, 'Gentleman Rankers'

Chapter Seventeen

The next morning I awoke to a throbbing at the back of my hand, a souvenir of the encounter with Deborah Mercier. I was no longer working for her husband, but there were still calls to be made. I checked in once again with Buntz in Boston, who assured me that Rachel was safe and sound, before calling the Portland PD.

I wanted to see the place in which the Aroostook Baptists had been interred. I could, I supposed, have been accused of morbid curiosity, but it was more than that; everything that had occurred – all of the deaths, all of the tainted family histories – was tied up with these lost souls. The burial ground at St. Froid was the epicenter for a series of shock waves that had affected generations of lives, touching even those who had no blood connection with the people buried beneath its cold, damp earth. It had united the Peltiers and the Merciers, and that unity had found its ultimate expression in Grace.

I had a vision of her, scared and miserable, standing on Higgins Beach while a selfish young man cast stones on the water, concerned only for the opportunities that would be lost to him if he became a father at such an age. I blamed her, I knew: for wanting me, for allowing me to be with her, for taking me inside her. As the stones fell I sank with them, dropping slowly to the seabed, where the rush of the waves drowned out her voice, and the sound of her tears and the adult world, with its torments and betrayals, was lost in a blur of green and blue.

She must have known, even then, about her family's past. Maybe she felt a kind of kinship with Elizabeth Jessop, who had departed for a new existence many years before and was never seen again. Grace was a romantic, and I think she would have wanted to believe that Elizabeth had found the earthly paradise for which she had been searching, that she had somehow remade her life, sealing herself off from the past in the hope that she could start afresh. Except that something inside her whispered that Elizabeth was dead: Ali Wynn had told me as much.

Then Deborah Mercier fed Grace the knowledge that Faulkner might still be alive, and that through him the truth of Elizabeth Jessop's disappearance might be revealed to her. It seemed certain that Grace then approached Carter Paragon, who, through his own weakness and the sale of a recently created Faulkner Apocalypse, had allowed the possibility of the Preacher's continued existence to be exposed. Following that meeting, Grace had been killed and her notes seized along with one other item. That second item, I suspected, was another Apocalypse that had somehow come into Grace's possession. How that had come to pass would require renewed pressure on the Beckers to find out if their daughter, Marcy, could fill in the blanks. That would be tomorrow's work. For today, there was Paragon, and St. Froid Lake, and one other visit that I had chosen not to mention to Angel and Louis.

PIs don't usually get access to crime scenes, unless they're the first to arrive at them. This was the second time in less than eighteen months that I had asked Ellis Howard, the deputy chief in charge of the Portland PD's Bureau of Investigation, for his help in bending the rules a little. For a time, Ellis had tried to convince me to join the bureau, until the events in Dark Hollow conspired to make him reconsider his offer.

'Why?' he asked me when I phoned him and he eventually agreed to take my call. 'Why should I do it?'

'Don't even say hello.'

'Hello. Why? What's your interest in this?'

I didn't lie to him. 'Grace and Curtis Peltier.'

There was silence on the other end of the line as Ellis ran through a list of possible permutations and came up cold. 'I don't see the connection.'

'They were related to Elizabeth Jessop. She was one of the Aroostook Baptists.' I decided not to mention the other blood link, through Jack Mercier. 'Grace had been preparing a thesis on the history of the group before she died.'

'Is that why Curtis Peltier died in his bath?'

That was the trouble with trying to deal with Ellis; eventually, he always started to ask the difficult questions. I tried to come up with the most nebulous answer possible, in an effort to obscure the truth instead of lying outright. Eventually, I knew, the lies I was telling, both directly and by omission, would come back to haunt me. I had to hope that by the time they did I would have accumulated enough knowledge to save my hide.

'I think that someone may have believed that he knew more than he did,' I told Ellis.

'And who might that person be, do you think?'

'I don't know anything but his name,' I replied. 'He calls himself Mr. Pudd. He tried to warn me off investigating the circumstances surrounding Grace Peltier's death. He may also be connected with the killing of Lester Bargus and Al Z down in Boston. Norman Boone over in ATF has more on it, if you want to talk to him.'

I'd kept Curtis Peltier's name out of my conversation with Boone, but now Curtis was dead and I wasn't sure what debt of confidentiality I owed to Jack Mercier. Increasingly, I was coming under pressure to reveal the true connections to the Fellowship. I was lying to people, concealing possible evidence of a conspiracy, and I wasn't even sure why. Part of it was probably some romantic desire to make up for the small adolescent pain I had caused Grace Peltier, a pain she had probably long forgotten. But I was also aware that Marcy Becker was in danger, and that Lutz, a policeman, was somehow connected with the death of her friend. I had no proof that he was involved, but if I told Ellis or anyone else what I knew, then I would have to reveal Marcy's existence. If I did that, I believed that I would be signing her death warrant.

'Were you working for Curtis Peltier?' said Ellis, interrupting my thoughts.

'Yes.'

'You were looking into his daughter's death?'

'That's right.'

'I thought you didn't do that kind of work anymore.'

'She used to be a friend of mine.'

'Bullshit.'

'Hey, I have friends.'

'Not many, I'll bet. What did you find out?'

'Nothing much. I think she spoke to Carter Paragon, the sleazebag who runs the Fellowship, before she died, but Paragon's assistant says she didn't.'

'That's it?'

'That's it.'

'And they pay you good money for this?'

'Sometimes.'

His voice softened a little. 'The investigation into Grace Peltier's death has been . . . *reenergized* since her father's murder. We're working alongside the state police to assess possible connections.'

'Who's the liaison for state CID?'

I heard the rustling of paper. 'Lutz,' said Ellis. 'John Lutz, out of Machias. If you know anything about Grace Peltier's death, I'm sure he'd like to talk to you.'

'I'm sure.'

'And now you want to look at a mass grave in northern Maine?'

'I just want to see the site, that's all. I don't want to drive all the way up there and have some polite state trooper turn me back half a mile from the lake.'

Ellis released a long breath. 'I'll make a call. I can't promise you anything. *But . . .*'

I knew there would be a 'but.'

'When you get back, I want you to talk to me. Anything you give me will be treated in confidence. I guarantee it.'

I agreed. Ellis was an honorable, decent man, and I wanted to help him in any way that I could. I just wasn't sure how much I could say without blowing everything apart.

I had one stop to make before I went north, a step back into my own past and my own failings.

I had to visit the Colony.

The approach to the community known as the Colony was much as I remembered it. From South Portland I headed west, through Westbrook and White Rock and Little Falls, until I found myself looking out on Sebago Lake. I followed the lakeshore into the town of Sebago Lake itself, then took the Richville Road northwest until I came to the turning for Smith Hill Road. There was water on both sides of the road, and the spires of the evergreens were reflected in the flooded marshland. Dutchman's breeches and trout lilies unfurled their leaves, and dogwood flowered in the damp earth. Farther ahead the road was carpeted in birch seeds that had fallen from the drying cones above. Eventually the road became little more than a dirt track, twin tire ruts with grass growing along the median, until it lost itself in a copse of trees about a hundred yards away. There was nothing to indicate what lay behind the trees, except for a small wooden sign by the side of the road engraved with a cross and a pair of cupped hands.

At my lowest point, after the deaths of Susan and Jennifer, I had spent some time at the Colony. Its members had discovered me huddled in the doorway of a boarded-up electronics store on Congress Street, stinking of booze and despair. They had offered me a bed for the night, then placed me in the back of a pickup and taken me out to the community.

I stayed with them for six weeks. There were others there like me. Some were alcoholics or addicts. Others were men who had simply lost their way and had found themselves cast adrift by family and friends. They had made their way to the community, or had been referred there by those who still cared about them. In some cases, like my own, the community had found them and had extended a hand to them. Every man was free to walk away at any time, without recrimination, but while they were a part of the community they had to abide by its rules. There was no alcohol, no drug use, no sexual activity. Everybody worked. Everybody contributed to the greater good of the community. Each day, we gathered for what could be termed prayer but was closer to meditation, a coming to terms with our own failings and the failings of others. Occasionally, outside counselors would join us to act as facilitators or to offer specialized advice and support to those who needed it. But for the most part we listened to one another and supported one another, aided by the founders of the community, Doug and Amy Greaves. The only pressure to remain came from the other members; it was made clear to each of us that we were not only helping ourselves but, by our presence there, helping our brothers.

I think, looking back, that I was not yet ready for what the Colony had to offer. When I left, a confused, self-pitying man had been replaced by one with a purpose, a clear aim: I would find the man who killed Susan and Jennifer, and I would kill him in turn. And in the end, that is what I did. I killed the Traveling Man. I killed him, and I tore apart anyone who tried to stand in my way.

As I passed through the trees, the house came into view. It had whitewashed walls, and close by, there were barns and storage buildings, also white, and stables that had been converted into dormitories. It was after 9 A.M, and the members of the community had already commenced their daily tasks. To my right, a black man walked among the chicken coops collecting eggs, and I could see shapes moving in the small greenhouses beyond. From one of the barns came the sound of a buzz saw, as those with the necessary skills helped to make the furniture, the candlesticks, and the children's toys, that were sold to help support the community's activities. The rest of its funding came mainly from private donations, some from those who had, over the years, passed through the Colony's gates and, in doing so, had taken the first steps toward rebuilding their lives. I had sent them what I could afford, and had written to Amy once or twice, but I had not returned to the community since the day I turned my back on it.

As I drew up outside the house, a woman appeared on the porch. She was small, a little over five feet tall, with long gray hair tied up loosely on her head. Her broad shoulders were lost beneath a baggy sweatshirt, and the frayed cuffs of her jeans almost obscured her sneakers. She watched me step from the car. As I approached her, her face broke into a smile and she dropped down into the yard to embrace me.

'Charlie Parker,' said Amy, half in wonder. Her strong arms enclosed me and the scent of apples rose from her hair. She moved back and examined me closely, her eyes locking on to mine. Her thoughts flickered across her face, and in the movement of her features I seemed to see the events of the last two and a half years reenacted. When at last she looked away, concern and relief collided in her eyes.

She held my hand as we walked onto the porch and moved inside the house. She guided me to a chair at the long communal breakfast table, then disappeared into the kitchen before returning with a mug of decaf coffee for me and some mint tea for herself.

And then, for the next hour, we spoke of my life since I had left the community, and I told her almost everything. To the east, the flooded land sparkled in the morning sun. Men occasionally passed by the window and raised a hand in greeting. One, I noticed, seemed to be having trouble walking. His gut hung over his belt, and despite the cold, his body gleamed with sweat. His hands shook uncontrollably. I guessed that he had been at the Colony for no more than a day or two, and the withdrawal was tormenting his system.

'A new arrival,' I said, when at last I had finished unburdening myself to her. I felt light headed, a simultaneous sense of elation and terrible grief.

'You were like that once,' said Amy.

'An alcoholic?'

'You were never an alcoholic.'

'How do you know?'

'Because of the way you stopped,' she replied. 'Because of why you stopped. Do you think about drinking?'

'Sometimes.'

'But not every day, not every hour of every day?'

'No.'

'Then you've answered your own question. It was just a way to fill a hole in your being, and it could have been anything: sex, drugs, marathon running. When you left here, you simply substituted something else for alcohol. You found another way to fill the hole. You found violence, and revenge.'

Amy was not one to sugar pills. She and her husband had built a community based on the importance of absolute honesty: with oneself and, from that, with others. 'Do you believe that you have the right to take lives, to judge others and find them wanting?'

I heard echoes of Al Z in her words. I didn't like it.

'I had no choice,' I replied.

'There's always a choice.'

'It didn't seem that way at the time. If they'd lived, then I'd have died. Other people would have died as well, innocent people. I wasn't going to let that happen.'

'The necessity defense?'

The necessity defense was an old English common law concept that held an individual who breaks a minor law to achieve a greater good should he be declared innocent of the lesser charge. It was still invoked occasionally, only to be knocked out of the ballpark by any judge worth his salt.

'There are only two consequences to taking a life,' Amy continued. 'Either the victim achieves salvation, in which case you have killed a good man; or you damn him to hell, in which case you have deprived him of any hope of redemption. Afterward, the responsibilty lies with you, and you bear the weight.'

'They weren't interested in redemption,' I answered her evenly. 'And they didn't want salvation.'

'And you do?'

I didn't answer.

'You won't achieve salvation with a gun in your hand,' she persisted.

I leaned forward. 'Amy,' I said softly, 'I've thought about these things. I've considered them. I thought I could walk away, but I can't. People have to be protected from the urges of violent men. I can do that. Sometimes I'm too late to protect them, but maybe I can help to achieve some measure of justice for them.'

'Is that why you're here, Charlie?'

A noise came from behind me and Doug, Amy's husband, came into the room. I wondered for a moment how long he had been there. He held a large bottle of water in his hand. Some of it had dripped from his chin and soaked the front of his clean white shirt. He was a big man, six-two at least, with pale skin and hair that was almost entirely white. His eyes were remarkably green. When I stood to greet him, he held my shoulder for a time and perused me in much the same way that his wife had examined me earlier. Then he took a seat beside Amy and they both waited in silence for me to answer Amy's question.

'In a sense,' I said at last. 'I'm investigating the death of a woman. Her name was Grace Peltier. Once, a long time ago, she was a friend of mine.'

I took a breath and looked out once again at the sunlight. In this place whose only purpose was to try to make the lives of those who passed its way a little better, the deaths of Grace and her father and the figure of a child out of time, his wounds hidden behind cheap black tape, seemed somehow distant. It was as if this little community was invulnerable to the encroachments of violent men and the consequences of acts committed long ago and far away. But the apparent simplicity of the life here, and the clarity of the aims it espoused, masked a strength and a profound depth of knowledge. That was why I was here; it was, in its way, almost the antithesis of the group I was hunting.

'This investigation has brought me into contact with the Fellowship, and with a man who appears to be acting on its behalf. He calls himself Mr. Pudd.'

They didn't respond for a time. Doug looked to the ground and moved his right foot back and forth over the boards. Amy turned away from me and stared out at the trees, as if the answers I sought might somehow be found deep in their reaches. Then, at last, they exchanged a look, and Amy spoke.

'We know about them,' she said softly, as I knew she would. 'You make interesting enemies, Charlie.'

She sipped her tea before continuing. 'There are two Fellowships. There is the one that appears in the public form of Carter Paragon, the one that sells prayer pamphlets for ten dollars and promises to cure the ailments of those who touch their television screens. That Fellowship is mendacious and shallow and preys on the gullible. It's no different from any of a hundred other similar movements; no better than them, but certainly no worse.

'The second Fellowship is something entirely different. It is a force, an entity, not an organization. It supports violent men. It funds killers and fanatics. It is powered by rage and hate and fear. Its targets are anything and everything that is not of, or like, itself. Some are obvious: gays, Jews, blacks, Catholics, those who assist in the provision of abortion or family planning services, those who would encourage peaceful coexistence between people of different races and different creeds. But in reality, it hates humanity. It hates the flawed nature of men, and is blind to the divine that exists in even the most humble among us.'

Beside her, her husband nodded in agreement. 'It moves against anything that it perceives to be a threat to itself or its mission. It starts with polite advances, then progresses to intimidation, property damage, physical injury, and finally, if it deems such action necessary, murder.'

Around us, the air seemed to change, for a wind had blown up from across the lake. It brought with it the scent of still water and decay.

'Who's behind it?' I asked.

Doug shrugged, but it was Amy who answered. 'We don't know. We know what you know; its public face is Carter Paragon. Its private face remains hidden. It is not a large organization. It is said that the best conspiracy is a conspiracy of one; the fewer who know about something, the better. Our understanding is that there are no more than a handful of people involved.'

'Policemen?'

Her eyes narrowed. 'Perhaps. Yes, almost certainly one or two policemen. It sometimes uses them to cover its tracks, or to stay in touch with any legal moves against it. But its primary instrument is a man, a thin man with red hair and a fondness for predation. Sometimes he has a woman with him, a mute.'

'That's him,' I said. 'That's Pudd.'

For the first time since we had begun to talk of the Fellowship, Amy reached out to her husband. Her hand found his and gripped it tightly, as if even the mention of Pudd's name might invoke his presence and force them to face him together.

'He goes by different names,' she continued, after a pause. 'I've heard him referred to as Ed Monker, as Walter Zaren, as Eric Dumah. I think he was Ted Bune once, and Alex Tchort for a time. I'm sure there were others.'

'You seem to know a lot about him.'

'We're religious, but we're not naive. These are dangerous people. It pays to know about them. Do those names mean anything to you at all?'

'I don't think so.'

'Do you know anything about demonology?'

'Sorry, I canceled my subscription to *Amateur Demonologist*. It was scaring the mailman.'

Doug permitted himself the ghost of a smile. 'Tchort is the Russian Satan, also known as the Black God,' he said. 'Bune is a three-headed demon who moves bodies from one grave to another. Dumah is the angel of the silence of death, and Zaren is the demon of the sixth hour, the avenging genius. Monker is the name he uses most frequently. It seems to have a particular resonance for him.'

'And Monker is a demon as well?'

'A very particular demon, one of a pair. Monker and Nakir are Islamic demons.'

A picture flashed in my mind: Pudd's fingers gently brushing the mute's cheek and softly whispering.

My Nakir.

'He called the woman his Nakir,' I told them.

'Monker and Nakir examine and judge the dead, then assign them to heaven or hell. Your Mr. Pudd, or whatever you wish to call him, seems to find the demonic associations funny. It's a joke.'

'It seems like kind of specialized humor,' I said. 'I can't see him making it onto Letterman.'

'The name Pudd has a particular meaning for him as well,' said Doug. 'We found it on an arachnology Web site. Elias Pudd was a pioneer in the field of American arachnology, a late contemporary of Emerton and McCook. He published his most famous work, *A Natural History of the Arachnid*, in 1933. His speciality was recluses.'

'Spiders.' I shook my head. 'They say people start to look like their pets, in time.'

'Or they pick the pet they most resemble,' answered Doug.

'You've seen him, then.'

He nodded. 'He came out here once, himself and the woman. They parked over by the chicken coops and waited for us to come out. As soon as we did, Pudd threw a sack from the car, then backed up and drove away. We never saw them again.'

'Do I want to know what was in the sack?'

Amy answered. 'Rabbits.' She was looking at the floor so I couldn't see the expression on her face.

'Yours?'

'We used to keep them in a hutch out by the coops. One morning we came out and they were just gone. There was no blood, no fur, nothing to suggest that they'd been taken by a predator. Then, two days later, Pudd came and dumped the sack. When we opened it, it was filled with the remains of the rabbits. Something had bitten them. They were covered in gray-brown lesions, and the flesh had begun to rot. We took one to the local vet, and he told us they were recluse bites. That's how we discovered the significance of the name Pudd for him.

'He was warning us to stay out of his business. We had been making inquiries about the Fellowship. We stopped after the visit.'

She raised her face and there was no indication of how she felt, apart from a slight tension around her mouth.

'Is there anything more that you can tell me?'

'Rumors, that's all,' said Doug, raising the water bottle to his lips.

'Rumors about a book?'

The bottle paused, and Amy's grip tightened on his hand.

'They're recording names, aren't they?' I continued. 'Is that what Mr. Pudd is – some kind of infernal recording angel, writing down the names of the damned in a big black book?'

They didn't reply, and the silence was suddenly broken by the sound of the men filing into the house for their midmorning break. Doug and Amy both stood, then Doug shook my hand once again and left to make arrangements for the meal. Amy guided me away from the dining room and walked me to my car.

'As Doug said, the book is just a rumor,' she told me, 'and the truth about the Fellowship still remains largely hidden. Nobody has yet managed to link its public face with its other activities.'

Amy took a deep breath, steeling herself for what she had to say next.

'There is something else I should tell you,' she began. 'You're not the first to have come here asking about the Fellowship. Some years ago, another man came, from New York. We didn't know as much about the Fellowship then, and we told him less than we knew, but it still provoked the warning. He moved on, and we never saw or heard of him again . . . until two years ago.'

The world around me faded into shadow, and the sun disappeared. When I looked up, I saw black shapes in the sky, descending in spirals, the beating of their wings filling the morning air and blocking out the light. Amy's hand reached out to take mine but all of my attention was focused on the sky, where the dark angels now hovered. Then one of them drew closer and his features, which had previously only been a chiaroscuro of light and shade, grew clear.

And I knew his face.

'It was him,' whispered Amy, and the dark angel smiled at me from above, his teeth filed to points, his huge wings feathered with night. A father, a husband, killer of men, women, and children now transformed by his passage into the next world.

'It was the Traveling Man.'

I sat on the hood of my car until the sickness had passed. I recalled a conversation in New Orleans some months after Susan and Jennifer had died, a voice telling me of its belief that somehow, the worst killers could find one another and sometimes connect, that they were sensitized to the presence of their own kind.

They sniff each other out.

He would have found them. His nature, and his background in law enforcement, would have ensured it. If he came hunting for the Fellowship, then he would have tracked them down.

And he would have let them live, because they were his own kind. I remembered again his obscure biblical references, his interest in the Apocrypha, his belief that he was some kind of fallen angel sent to judge humanity, all of whom he found wanting.

Yes, he had found them, and they had helped to fan his own flame into being.

Amy reached out and took both of my hands in her own.

'It was seven or eight years ago,' she said. 'It didn't seem important, until now.'

I nodded.

'You're going to continue looking for these people?'

'I have to, especially now.'

'Can I say something to you, something you may not want to hear?'

Her face was grave. I nodded.

'In all that you have done, in all that you have told me, it seems that you have been intent on helping the dead as much as the living. But our first duty is to the living, Charlie, to ourselves and those around us. The dead don't need your help.'

I paused before replying. 'I'm not sure I believe that, Amy.'

For the first time, I saw doubt appear in her face. 'You can't live in both worlds,' she said, and her voice was hesitant. 'You must choose. Do you still feel the deaths of Susan and Jennifer pulling you back?'

'Sometimes, but not just them.'

And I think that she saw something in my face, or caught something in my tone, and for a brief moment, she was in me, seeing what I saw, hearing what I heard, feeling what I felt. I closed my eyes and felt shapes move around me, voices whispering in my ears, small hands clutching at mine.

We've all been waiting for you.

A small boy with an exit wound for an eye, a woman in a summer dress that shimmered in the darkness, figures that hovered at the periphery of my vision – all of them, each and every one, told me that it wasn't true, that somebody had to act for those who could no longer act for themselves, that some measure of justice had to be achieved for the lost and the fallen. For an instant, as she held my hands, Amy Greaves had some inkling of this, some fleeting perception of what waited in the depths of the honeycomb world.

'Oh my God,' she said.

And then her hands released mine and I heard her move away and disappear into the house. When I opened my eyes I was alone in the summer sunshine, the smell of rotting pine carrying to me on the wind. Through the trees a blue jay flew, heading north.

And I followed.

The Search for Sanctuary

Extract from the postgraduate thesis of Grace Peltier

Letter from Elizabeth Jessop to her sister, Lena Myers, dated December 11, 1963 (used by kind permission of the estate of Lena Myers)

Dearest Lena,

This has been the worst week I can ever recall. The truth about Lyall and me is out and now we are both being shunned. The Preacher has not been seen for two days. He is asking the Lord to guide him in his judgment upon us.

It was the boy that found us, the Preacher's son. I think he had been watching us for a long time. We were in the woods together, Lyall and I, and I saw Leonard in the bushes. I think I screamed when I saw him but when we went to find him he was already gone.

The Preacher was waiting for us at supper. We were refused food and told to go back to our houses while the others ate. When Frank returned that night he beat me and left me to sleep on the floor. Now Lyall and me are kept apart. The girl Muriel watches over him, while Leonard is like my shadow. Yesterday he threw a stone at me and drew blood from my head. He told me that was how the Bible said whores should be punished and that his father would deal with me the same way. The Cornishes saw what he did and Ethan Cornish struck him before he could throw a second stone. The boy pulled a knife on Ethan and cut his arm. The families have all argued for forgiveness for the sake of the community, but Lyall's wife will not look at me and one of his children spat on me when I passed her.

Last night there were voices raised in the Preacher's house. The families were putting their case to the Preacher but he was unmoved. There is bitterness among us now – at me and Lyall, but more at the Preacher and his ways. He has been asked to account for the money he holds in trust for us, but he has refused. I fear that Lyall and I will be forced from the community or that the Preacher will make us all leave and start again in another place. I have asked the Lord to forgive us our trespass against him and have prayed for help but part of me would not be sorry to leave if Lyall was beside me. But I cannot abandon my children and I feel sadness and shame for what I have done to Frank.

Ethan Cornish told me one more thing. He says that the Preacher's wife asked him to deal mercifully with us and he has refused to speak with her since. There is talk that he will scatter us to the four winds, where each family will make up for the sins of the community by spreading the word of God to new towns and cities. Tomorrow, the men, the women, and the children are to be divided into separate groups and each group will pray alone for guidance and forgiveness.

I have asked Ethan Cornish to place this note in the usual place and pray that you receive it in good health.

I am your sister,

Elizabeth

Chapter Eighteen

When I was fourteen years old, my father took me on my first airplane trip. He got a good deal from a man he knew at American Airlines, a neighbor of ours whom my father had helped out when one of his sons got picked up for possession of some stolen radios. We flew from New York to Denver and from Denver to Billings, Montana, where we hired a car and spent a night in a motel before driving east early the following morning.

The sun shone on the hills, burnishing the green and beige with touches of silver before melting into the waters of the Little Bighorn River. We crossed the river at the Crow Agency and drove in silence to the entrance to the Little Bighorn Battlefield. It was Memorial Day and a platform had been erected at the cemetery, before which a small crowd occupied rows of lawn chairs while the few who could not find seats stood amid the small gravestones and listened to the words of the service. Above them, the Stars and Stripes flapped in the morning breeze, but we did not stay to listen. Instead, fragments came to us as we climbed toward the monument, words like 'youth,' 'fallen,' 'honor,' and 'death' fading and then growing once again in volume, echoing across the shifting grass as if they were being spoken both in the present and in the distant past.

This was where Custer's five cavalry troops, young men mostly, were annihilated by the combined forces of the

Lakota and Cheyenne. The battle took place over the space of one hour, but the soldiers probably couldn't even see the enemy for much of that time; they lay hidden in the grass and picked off the cavalrymen one by one, biding their time.

I looked out over the hills and thought that the Little Bighorn was a bleak place to die, surrounded by low hills of green and yellow and brown fading to blue and purple in the distance. From any patch of raised ground, you could see for miles. The men who died here would have known without question that noone was coming to rescue them, that these were their final moments on earth. They died terrible, lonely deaths far from home, their bodies subsequently mutilated and left to lie scattered on the battlefield for three days before finally receiving burial in a mass grave atop a small ridge in eastern Montana, their names carved on a granite monument above them.

In that place, I closed my eyes and imagined that I felt their ghosts crowding around me. I seemed to hear them: the horses neighing, the gunshots, the grass breaking beneath their feet, the cries of pain, of fury, of fear.

And for an instant I was there with them, and I understood.

There are places where years have no meaning, where only a hairsbreadth of history separates the present from the past. Standing there on that bleak hillside, a young man in a place where other young men had died, it was possible to feel a connection to that past, a sense that in some place further back on the stream of time these young men were still fighting, and still dying, that they would always be fighting this battle, in this place, over and over again, with ever the same end.

It was my first glimpse of the honeycomb world, my first inkling that the past never truly dies but is strangely, beautifully alive in the present. There is an interconnectedness to all things, a link between what lies buried and what lives above, a capacity for mutability that allows a good act committed in the present to rectify an imbalance in times gone by. That, in the end, is the nature of justice: not to undo the past but, by acting further down the line of time, to restore some measure of harmony, some possibility of equilibrium, so that lives may continue with their burden eased and the dead may find peace in a world beyond this one.

Now, as I headed north, I thought again of that day on the battlefield, my father standing silently beside me as the wind tousled our hair, a day of remembrance for the dead. This would be another pilgrimage, another acknowledgment of the debt owed by the living to the dead. Only by standing where the families had once stood, only by placing myself amid the memories of their final moments and listening for the echoes, could I hope to understand.

This is a honeycomb world. At St. Froid Lake, its interior lay exposed.

As I drove, I called in a long-standing favor. In New York, a woman's voice asked me my name, there was a pause, and I was put through to the office of Special Agent in Charge Hal Ross. Ross had recently been promoted and was now one of three SACs in the FBI's New York field office, operating under an assistant director. Ross and I had crossed swords the first time we met, but in the aftermath of the Traveling Man's death our relationship had gradually become more congenial. The FBI was now reviewing all cases with which the Traveling Man had been involved as part of its ongoing investigation into his crimes, and a room at Quantico had been devoted to relevant material from law enforcement agencies around the country. The investigation had been given the codename 'Charon', after the ferryman in Greek mythology who carried lost souls to Hades, and all references to the Traveling Man carried that name. It was a long process and one that was still far from complete.

'It's Charlie Parker,' I said, when Ross came on the line.

'Hey, how you doing? Social call?'

'Have I ever paid you a social call?'

'Not that I can remember, but there's always a first time.'

'This isn't it. You remember that favor you promised me?'

There was a long pause. 'You sure cut to the chase. Go ahead.'

'It's Charon. Seven or eight years ago he came up to Maine to investigate an organization called the Fellowship. Can you find out where he went and the names of anyone to whom he might have spoken?'

'Can I ask why?'

'The Fellowship may be connected to a case I'm investigating; the death of a young woman. Any information you can give me about them would help.'

'That's quite a favor, Parker. We don't usually hand over records.'

Impatience and anger crept into my voice and I had to struggle against shouting. 'I'm not asking for the records, just some idea of where he might have gone. This is important, Hal.'

He sighed. 'When do you need it?'

'Soon. As soon as you can.'

'I'll see what I can do. You just used up your ninth life. I hope you realize that.'

I gave a mental shrug. 'I wasn't doing a whole lot with it anyway.'

I drove through avenues of trees, their branches green with new growth, to this place of failed hopes and violent death, and sunlight dappled my car as I went. I stayed on I-95 all the way to Houlton, then took U.S.1 north to Presque Isle and from there drove through Ashland, Portage, and Winterville, until at last I came to the edge of the town of Eagle Lake. I drove by a WCSH truck and gave my name to the state trooper who was checking traffic along the road. He waved me through.

Ellis had called me back with the name of a detective from the state trooper barracks at Houlton. His name was

John Brouchard, and I found him waist deep in a muddy hole beneath the big tarp erected to protect the remains, digging with a spade in a steady, unhurried rhythm. That was how it worked up here; everybody played his or her part. State police, wardens, sheriff's deputies, ME's staff, all of them rolled up their sleeves and got their hands dirty. If nothing else it was overtime, and when you've got kids going to college, or alimony payments to meet, then time and a half is always welcome, whatever way it has to be earned.

I stayed behind the crime scene line and called his name. He waved a hand in acknowledgment and climbed from the hole, unfolding a frame that was at least six-six or six-seven in height. He towered over me, his head blocking out the sun. His nails were black with mud, and beneath his overalls his shirt was drenched in sweat. Damp earth clung to his work boots, and dirt streaked his forehead and cheeks.

'Ellis Howard tells me you're assisting them in an investigation,' he said, after we had shaken hands. 'You want to tell me why you're up here if your investigation is centred on Portland?'

'You ask Ellis that?'

'He told me to ask you. He said you had all the answers.'

'He's being optimistic. Curtis Peltier, the man who was murdered in Portland at the weekend, was related to Elizabeth Jessop. I think her remains were among those found here. Curtis's daughter was Grace Peltier. CID III is looking into the circumstances of her death. She was doing graduate work on the people buried in that hole.'

Brouchard eyeballed me for a good ten seconds, then led me to the mobile crime scene unit, where I was allowed to view the video tour of the crime scene on a portable TV borrowed for the duration of the field recovery. He seemed grateful for the excuse to rest, and poured us both coffee while I sat and watched the tape: mud, bones, and trees; glimpses of damaged skulls and scattered fingers; dark water; a rib cage shattered and splintered by the impact of a shotgun blast; a child's skeleton, curled in foetuslike upon itself.

When the tape had concluded I followed him across the road to the edge of the grave.

'Can't let you go beyond here,' he said apologetically. 'Some of the victims are still down there, and we're searching for other artifacts.'

I nodded. I didn't need to go inside. I could see all that I needed to see from where I stood. The scene had already been photographed and measured. Above holes in the mud, pieces of card had been attached to wooden spikes, detailing the nature of the remains discovered. In some cases the holes were empty, but in one corner I saw two men in blue overalls work carefully around a piece of exposed bone. When one of them moved away, I saw the curved reach of a rib cage, like dark fingers about to clasp in prayer.

'Did they all have their names around their necks?'

The details of the names written on the wooden boards had appeared in a report in the *Maine Sunday Telegram*. Given the nature of the discovery, it was a wonder that the investigators had managed to keep anything at all under wraps.

'Most of them. Some of the wood had rotted pretty bad, though.' Brouchard reached into his shirt pocket and produced a piece of folded paper, which he handed to me. Typed on the page were seventeen names, presumably obtained by checking the original identities of the Baptists against the names discovered on the bodies. DNA samples were to be taken from surviving relatives, where dental records were not available. Stars beside some names indicated those for whom no positive identification had yet been made. James Jessop's name was the next to last on the list.

'Is the Jessop boy's body still down there?'

Brouchard looked at the list in my hand. 'They're taking him away today, him and his sister. He mean anything to you?'

I didn't reply. Another name on the page had caught my

eye: Louise Faulkner, the Reverend Faulkner's wife. Faulkner's name, I noticed, was not on the list. Neither were those of his children.

'Any idea yet how they died?'

'Won't know for certain until the autopsies are done, but all of the men and two of the women had gunshot wounds to the head or body. The others seem to have been clubbed. The Faulkner woman was probably strangled; we found additional fragments of cord around her neck. Some of the children have shattered skulls, like they were hit with a rock, or maybe a hammer. A couple have what look like gunshot wounds to the head.' He stopped talking and looked away toward the lake. 'I guess you know something about these people.'

'A little,' I admitted. 'Judging by the names on this list, you have at least one suspect.'

Brouchard nodded. 'The preacher, Faulkner, unless somebody planted those boards to throw us off the trail and Faulkner is lying there dead with the rest of them.'

It was a possibility, although I knew that the existence of the Apocalypse bought by Jack Mercier made it unlikely.

'He killed his own wife,' I said, more to myself than to Brouchard.

'You got any idea why?'

'Maybe because she objected to what he was going to do.' The article Grace Peltier had written for *Down East* magazine had mentioned that Faulkner was a fundamentalist. Under fundamentalist doctrine, a wife has to submit to the authority of her husband. Argument or defiance was not permitted. I guessed also that Faulkner probably needed her admiration and her validation for all that he did. When that was withdrawn, she ceased to have any value for him.

Brouchard was looking at me with interest now. 'You think you know why he killed them all?'

I thought of what Amy had told me of the Fellowship, its hatred for what it perceived as human weakness and fallibility; of Faulkner's ornate Apocalypses, visions of the final judgment; and of the word hacked beneath James Jessop's name on a length of dirt-encrusted wood. *Sinner*.

'It's just a guess, but I think they disappointed him in some way, or turned on him, so he punished them for their failings. As soon as they stood up to him they were finished, cursed for rebelling against God's anointed one.'

'That's a pretty harsh punishment.'

'I guess he was a pretty harsh kind of guy.'

I also wondered if, in some dark place inside him, Faulkner had always known that they would fail him. That was what human beings did: they tried and failed and failed again, and they kept failing until either they got it right at last or time ran out and they had to settle for what they had. But for Faulkner, there was only one chance: when they failed it proved their worthlessness, the impossibility of their salvation. They were damned. They had always been damned, and what happened to them was of no consequence in this world or the next.

These people had followed Faulkner to their deaths, blinded by their hopes for a new golden age, a desire for conviction, for something to believe in. Nobody had intervened. After all, this was 1963; communists were the threat, not God-fearing people who wanted to create a simpler life for themselves. Fifteen years would pass until Jim Jones and his disciples blew Congressman Leo Ryan's face off before organizing the mass suicide of 900 followers, after which people would begin to take a different view.

But even after Jonestown, false messiahs continued to draw adherents to them. Rock Theriault systematically tortured his followers in Ontario before tearing apart a woman named Solange Boilard with his bare hands in 1988. Jeffrey Lundgren, the leader of a breakaway Mormon sect, killed five members of the Avery family – Dennis and Cheryl Avery, and their young daughters Trina, Rebecca and Karen – in a barn in Kirtland, Ohio in April 1989 and buried their remains under earth, rocks and garbage. Nobody came looking for them until almost one year later, following a tip-off to police from a disgruntled cult member. The LeBaron family and their disciples in the breakaway Mormon Church of the Firstborn murdered almost thirty people, including an eighteen-month-old girl, in a cycle of violence which lasted from the early seventies until 1991.

And then there was Waco, which demonstrated why law enforcement agencies have traditionally been reluctant to intervene in the affairs of religious groups. But in 1963, such incidents were almost beyond imagining; there would have been no reason to fear for the safety of the Aroostook Baptists, no need to doubt the intentions of the Reverend Faulkner, and no cause for his disciples to fear to walk with him in the valley of the shadow of death.

The ME's Dodge arrived while we stood silently by the lakeshore, and preparations began for the transportation of more bodies to the airfield at Presque Isle. Brouchard was tied up with the details of the removal, so I walked to the edge of the trees and watched the figures move beneath the canvas. It was approaching three o'clock and it was cool by the river. The wind blowing off the water tossed the hair of the ME's men as they carried a body bag from the scene, strapped onto a stretcher to prevent any further damage to the bones. From the north, the hybrids sang.

Not all of them had died here, of that I was certain. This land wasn't even part of the parcel originally leased to them. The fields they had worked were over the rise, behind the kennels; and the houses, now long gone, were farther back still. The adults would have been killed at or near the settlement; it would have been difficult to get them to come to the place intended for their burial, harder still to control them once the slaughter started. It made sense to bury them away from the center of the community in case, at some future date, suspicion mutated into action and a search of the property took place. Safer, then, to dispose of them by the lake.

According to Grace's article, the community had apparently dispersed in December 1963. The evidence of the burial would have been masked by the winter snows. By the time the thaws came and the ground turned to mud, there would be little to distinguish this patch of land from any other. It was solid ground; it should not have collapsed, but it did.

After all, they had been waiting for a long, long time.

I closed my eyes and listened as the world faded around me, trying to imagine what it must have been like in those final minutes. The howling became muted, the noise of the cars on the road beyond transformed itself into the buzzing of flies, and amid the gentle brushing of the branches above my head . . .

I hear gunshots.

There are men running, caught as they work in the fields. Two have already fallen, bloody holes gaping ragged in their backs. One of those still alive turns, a pitchfork clutched in his hands. Its center disintegrates as the shot tears through it, wood and metal entering his body simultaneously. They pursue the last one through the grass, reloading as they go. Above them, a murder of crows circles, calling loudly. The cries of the last man to die mingle with them, and then all is quiet.

I heard a sound in the trees behind me, but when I looked there were only branches moving slightly, as if disturbed by the passage of some animal. Beyond, the green faded to black and the shapes of the trees became indistinct.

The women are the next to die. They have been told to kneel and pray in one of the houses, to think upon the sins of the community. They hear the gunshots but do not understand their significance. The door opens and Elizabeth Jessop turns. A man is silhouetted against the evening light. He tells her to look away, to turn to the cross and beg for forgiveness.

Elizabeth closes her eyes and begins to pray.

Behind me the noise came again, like gentle footfalls slowly growing closer. Something was emerging from the darkness, but I did not turn.

The children are the last to die. They sense that something is wrong, that something has happened that should not have occurred, yet they have followed the Preacher down to the lake, where the grave is already dug and the waters are still before them. They are obedient, as little ones should always be.

They too kneel down to pray, the mud wet beneath their knees, the wooden boards heavy around their necks, the ropes burning against their skin. They have been told to hold their hands against their breasts, the thumbs crossed as they have been taught, but James Jessop reaches out and takes his sister's hand in his own. Beside him, she starts to cry and he grips her hand tighter.

'Don't cry,' he says.

A shadow falls over him.

'Don't—'

I felt a coldness in my right hand. James Jessop was standing beside me in the shade of a yellow birch tree, his small hand curled around mine. Sunlight reflected from the single clear lens of his glasses. From the covered area below, two figures emerged carrying another small bundle on a stretcher.

'They're going to take you away from here, James,' I said.

He nodded and moved closer to me, the presence of him chilling my leg and ribs.

'It didn't hurt none,' he said. 'Everything just went dark.'

I was glad that he didn't feel any pain. I tried to press his hand, to give him some sign, but there was nothing there, only cold air.

He looked up at me. 'I have to leave now.'

'I know.'

His single eye was brown, flashes of yellow at its center eclipsed by the dark moon of his pupil. I should have seen my face reflected in his eye and in the lens of his eyeglasses, but I could detect no trace of myself. It was as if I were the unreal one, the phantasm, and James Jessop who was flesh and blood, skin and bone.

'He said we were bad, but I was never bad. I always did what I was told, right up to the end.'

The chill faded from my fingers as he released my hand and began to walk back into the forest, his knees raised high so that he would not brush through the briers and the long grass. I didn't want him to leave.

I wanted to comfort him.

I wanted to understand.

I called his name. He stopped and stared back at me.

'Have you seen the Summer Lady, James?' I asked. A tear dropped onto my cheek and rolled down to the corner of my mouth. I savored it with my tongue.

He nodded solemnly.

'She's waiting for me,' he said. 'She's going to take me to the others.'

'Where is she, James?'

James Jessop raised his hand and pointed into the darkness of the forest, then turned and walked into the tangles and trees, until the shadows of the branches embraced him and I could see him no more.

Chapter Nineteen

As I drove down to Waterville to meet Angel and Louis, my hand tingled from the touch of a lost child. St. Froid Lake had seemed indescribably desolate. I still heard the howls of the hybrids ringing in my ears, a perpetual chorus of mourning for the dead. Pictures of flapping canvas and piles of earth, of cold water and old brown bones flashed through my mind before coalescing into a single image of James Jessop receding into the hidden reaches of the forest, where an unseen woman in a summer dress waited to take him away.

I felt a surge of gratitude that there was somebody waiting for him at the edge of the darkness, that he would not have to make that journey alone.

I just hoped that there was somebody waiting for us all.

In Waterville, I parked outside the Ames mall and waited. It was almost an hour before the black Lexus appeared, turning onto the main street and parking at its far end. I watched Angel get out and walk casually to the corner of Main and Temple, then turn into the back lot of the Fellowship's building at the junction with the Hunan Legends Chinese restaurant when he saw that the street was clear. I locked the Mustang, met Louis, and together we walked down to Temple to join Angel. He stood in the shadows and handed us each a pair of gloves. His own hands were already concealed and holding the handle of the newly opened door.

'I think I'm gonna add Waterville to the list of places I'm never gonna retire to,' remarked Angel as we stepped into the building. 'Along with Bogota and Bangladesh.'

'I'll break the sad news to the Chamber of Commerce,' I told him. 'I don't know how they'll cope.'

'So where you planning on retiring to?'

'Maybe I won't live long enough for it to become an issue.'

'Man, you sure going the right way about it,' said Louis. 'Grim Reaper probably got your number on speed dial.'

We followed Angel up the thinly carpeted stairs until we arrived at a wooden door with a small plastic sign nailed to it at eye level. It read simply: *The Fellowship*. There was a bell on the doorframe to the right, in case anyone somehow managed to sneak in the front door without Ms. Torrance turning on them like a hungry Rottweiler. I slipped out my mini Maglite and shined it on the lock. I had taken the precaution of wrapping some duct tape around the top so that only a thin beam of light about half the size of a dime showed. Angel took a pick and a tension tool from his pocket and opened the door in five seconds flat. Inside, the lights from the street shone on a reception area with three plastic chairs, a wooden desk with a telephone and blotter on top, a filing cabinet in one corner, and some vaguely inspirational pictures on the walls featuring sunsets and doves and small children.

Angel jiggled the lock on the filing cabinet and when it clicked, pulled open the top drawer. Using his own flashlight, he illuminated a pile of conservative and religious tracts published by the Fellowship itself and other groups of which the Fellowship presumably approved. They included *The Christian Family; Other Races, Other Rules; Enemies of the People; Jewry: The Truth About the Chosen People; Killing the Future: The Reality of Abortion;* and *Daddy Doesn't Love Me Anymore: Divorce and the American Family*.

'Look at this one,' said Angel. '*Natural Laws, Unnatural Acts: How Homosexuality Is Poisoning America*.'

'Maybe they've smelled your aftershave,' I replied. 'Anything in the other drawers?'

Angel went through them quickly. 'Looks like more of the same.'

He opened the door into the main office. This was more elegantly furnished than the reception area; the desk was marginally more expensive, with a high-backed imitation leather chair behind it and a pair of couches in the same material against two of the walls, a low coffee table between them. The walls were covered with photographs of Carter Paragon at various events, usually surrounded by people who didn't know any better than to be happy around him. The sunlight had shone directly onto these walls for a long time. Some of the photographs had faded or turned yellow in the corners, and a coating of dust added a further element of dullness. In the corner, beneath an ornate crucifix, stood another filing cabinet, stronger and sturdier than the one in the reception area. It took Angel a couple of tries to get it open, but when he did his brow furrowed in surprise.

'What is it?' I said.

'Take a look,' he replied.

I walked over and shined my light into the open drawer. It was empty, apart from a thick coating of dust. Angel opened the other drawers in turn, but only the bottom drawer contained anything: a bottle of whiskey and two tumblers. I closed the drawer and reopened the one above it: there was only dust, and dust that obviously had not been disturbed for a long time.

'Either this is special holy dust,' said Angel, 'which would explain why it has to be locked up safe at night, or there's nothing here and there never was.'

'It's just a front,' I said. 'The whole thing is just a front.' Just as Amy had told me, the Waterville organization was simply a mask to fool the unwary. The other Fellowship, the one with the real power, existed elsewhere.

'There must be records of some kind,' I said.

'Maybe he keeps them out at his house,' suggested Angel.

I looked at him. 'You got anything better to do?'

'Than burgle a guy's house? No, not really.' He took a closer look at the lock on the filing cabinet. 'Tell you something else; I think someone tried to get this open before we did. There are marks around the lock. They're small, but it was still a pretty amateur job.'

We relocked the doors and headed downstairs. At the back door, Angel paused and checked the lock with the aid of his pocket light. 'Back door's been opened from outside,' he said. 'There are fresh scratches around the keyhole, and I didn't make them. Guess I didn't see them because I wasn't looking for them.'

There was nothing else to say. We weren't the only people interested in finding out what was in Carter Paragon's files, and I knew that we weren't the only ones hunting Mr. Pudd. Lester Bargus had learned that too, in his final moments.

Carter Paragon's house was quiet as we drove past. We parked our cars off the road, in the shadows cast by a stand of pine trees, and followed the boundary wall of the property around to a barred security gate at the back of the house. There were no video cameras visible, although there was an intercom on the gatepost, just as there was at the main entrance to the house. We climbed over the wall, Angel and I going first, Louis joining us after what seemed like a very reluctant pause. When he hit the soft lawn, he looked in dismay at the marks left by the white wall on his black jeans but said nothing.

We skirted the house, staying within the cover of the trees. A single light burned in a curtained room on the upper floor at the western side. The same battered blue car was parked in the drive, but its hood was cool. It hadn't been driven that evening. The Explorer was nowhere to be seen. The curtains on the window were drawn tight, so it was impossible to see inside.

'What do you want to do?' asked Angel.

'Ring the doorbell,' I replied.

'I thought we were going to burgle him,' hissed Angel, 'not try to sell him the *Watchtower*.'

I rang the bell anyway and Angel went quiet. Nobody answered, even when I rang it again for a good ten seconds. Angel left us and disappeared around the back of the house. A couple of minutes later he returned.

'I think you need to take a look at this,' he said.

We followed him to the rear of the house and entered through the open back door into a small, cheaply furnished kitchen. There was broken glass on the floor where someone had smashed a pane to get at the lock.

'I take it that isn't your handiwork?' I asked Angel.

'I won't even dignify that with an answer.'

Louis had already drawn his gun, and I followed his lead. I looked into a couple of the rooms as we passed but they were all virtually empty; there was hardly any furniture – no pictures on the walls, no carpet on the floor. One room had a TV and VCR, faced by a pair of old armchairs and a rickety coffee table, but most of the house appeared to be unoccupied. The front room was the only one that held anything significant: hundreds and hundreds of books and pamphlets recently packed into boxes, ready to be taken away. There were American underground training manuals and improvised weapon guides; instructions for the creation of homemade munitions, timers, and detonators; catalogs of military suppliers; and any number of books on covert surveillance. In the box nearest the door lay a stack of photocopied, crudely bound volumes; stenciled on the cover of each were the words *Army of God*.

The name Army of God had first cropped up in 1982, when the abortion doctor Hector Zevallos and his wife were kidnapped in Illinois and their kidnappers used the name in their dealings with the FBI. Since then, Army of God calling cards had been left at the scene of clinic bombings, and the anonymously published manual I was holding in my hand had become synonymous with a particular brand of religious extremism. It was a kind of *Anarchists' Cookbook* for religious nuts, a guide to blowing up property and, if necessary, people for the greater glory of the Lord.

Louis was holding a thick photocopied list in his hand, one of a number piled on the floor. 'Abortion clinics, AIDS clinics, home addresses for doctors, license plate numbers for civil rights activists, feminists. Guy here on page three, Gordon Eastman, he a gay rights activist in Wisconsin.'

'There's a job you don't want,' whispered Angel. 'Like selling dildos in Alabama.'

I tossed the Army of God manual back in the box. 'These people are exporting low-level chaos to every cracker with a grudge and a mailbox.'

'So where are they?' asked Angel.

In unison, the three of us glanced at the ceiling and the second floor of the house. Angel groaned softly.

'I had to ask.'

We climbed the stairs quietly, Louis in the lead, Angel behind him, while I brought up the rear. The room with the light was at the very end of the hallway, at the front of the house. Louis paused at the first doorway we reached and checked quickly to make sure it was empty. It contained only a bare iron bedstead and a suitcase half full of men's clothing, while the adjoining rooms had been stripped bare of whatever furniture had been there to begin with.

'Maybe he had a yard sale,' suggested Louis.

'He did, then someone wasn't happy with his merchandise,' responded Angel solemnly. He was standing close to the doorway of the single illuminated room, his gun by his side.

Inside was a bed, an electric heater, and a set of Home Depot shelves filled with paperback books and topped by a potted plant. There was a small closet containing some of Carter Paragon's suits, more of which lay on the bed. A wooden chair, one of a pair, stood beside a dressing table. A portable TV sat silent and dark on a cheap unit.

Carter Paragon sat in the second wooden chair, blood on

the carpet around him. His arms had been pulled behind him and secured with cuffs. He had been badly beaten; one eye had been reduced to pulp by a punch and his face was swollen and bruised. His feet were bare and two of the toes on his right foot were broken.

'Take a look here,' said Angel, pointing to the back of the chair.

I looked, and winced. Four of his fingernails had been torn out. I tried for a pulse. There was nothing, but the body was still warm to the touch.

Carter Paragon's head was inclined backward, his face to the ceiling. His mouth hung open, and amid the blood lay something small and brown. I took a handkerchief from my pocket, then reached in and removed the object, holding it up to the light. A string of bloody saliva dripped from it and fell to the floor.

It was a shard of clay.

Chapter Twenty

We drove back to Scarborough that night, Angel and Louis going on ahead while I stopped briefly in Augusta. From a public phone I called the office of the *Portland Press Herald*, asked to be put through to the news desk, and told the woman who answered that there was a body in the house of Carter Paragon in Waterville but that the police didn't know about it yet. Then I hung up. At the very least, the *Herald* would check with the cops, who would in turn head out to knock on Paragon's door. In the meantime, I had avoided the possibility of enhanced 911, which would have pinpointed my location and raised the possibility of being intercepted by the nearest patrol car, or of my voice being recorded using RACAL or any similar procedure. Then I drove on in silence, thinking of Carter Paragon and the clay that had been deposited in his mouth as a message for whoever found him.

Angel and Louis were already making themselves at home by the time I got back to the Scarborough house. I could hear Angel in the bathroom, making the place untidy. I banged on the door.

'Don't make a mess,' I warned him. 'Rachel's coming up, and I just cleaned it specially.'

Rachel didn't like untidiness. She was one of those people who got a kind of satisfaction out of scrubbing away dust and dirt, even other people's. Whenever she stayed with me in Scarborough, I would be sure to find her advancing on the bathroom or kitchen in rubber gloves with a determined look on her face.

'She cleans *your* bathroom?' Angel once asked, as if I had told him that she regularly sacrificed goats or played women's golf. '*I* don't even clean my bathroom, and I sure as hell ain't gonna clean no stranger's bathroom.'

'I'm not a stranger, Angel,' I explained.

'Hey,' he replied, 'when it comes to bathroom stuff, *everybody's* a stranger.'

In the kitchen, Louis was squatting in front of the fridge, discarding items on the floor. He checked the expiry date on some cold cuts.

'Damn, you buy all this food at auction?'

I wondered, as I called out for a pizza delivery, if agreeing to let them inside my door had been such a good idea after all.

'Who is this guy?' asked Louis. We were sitting at my kitchen table, discussing the shard of clay left by Paragon's killer while we waited for our food to arrive.

'Al Z told me he calls himself the Golem, and Epstein's father confirmed it. That's all I know. You ever hear of him?'

He shook his head. 'Means he's very good, or an amateur. Still, cool name.'

'Yeah, why can't you have a cool name like that?' asked Angel.

'Hey, Louis *is* a cool name.'

'Only if you're the king of France. You think he got much out of Paragon?'

'You saw what he did to him,' I replied. 'Paragon probably told him everything he could remember since grade school.'

'So this Golem knows more than us?'

'Everybody knows more than us.'

There came the sound of a car pulling up at the front of the house.

'Pizza boy,' I said.

Nobody else at the table made a sudden move for his wallet. 'Guess dinner's on me, then.'

I went to the door and took the two pizza boxes from the kid. As I gave him the cash, he spoke quietly to me.

'I don't want to worry you, man, but you got a guy over there watching your house.'

'Where?' I asked.

'Over my right shoulder, in the trees.'

'Don't look at him,' I said. 'Just drive away.'

I tipped him an extra ten, then glanced casually to my left as his car pulled away. Among the trees, something pale hung unmoving in the darkness: a man's face. I stepped back into the hallway, drew my gun, and called back quietly: 'Boys, we've got company.'

I walked out to the porch, the gun at my side. Angel was behind me, his Glock in his hand. Louis was nowhere to be seen, but I guessed that he was already moving around the back of the house. I stepped slowly from the porch and moved forward, the gun held low, until I got a clearer view of the watcher. I saw his hairless scalp and face, his pale skin, his thin mouth and dark eyes. His hands were held slightly out from his sides, so that I could see they were empty. He wore a black suit with a white shirt and black tie under a long black overcoat. In every respect, he resembled the man who had taken out Lester Bargus and probably Carter Paragon as well.

'Who is he?' hissed Angel.

'I'm guessing he's the guy with the cool name.'

I leaned down, placed my gun on the ground, and walked toward him.

'Bird,' said Angel, a note of warning in his voice.

'He's on my property,' I said, 'and he knows it's mine. Whatever he has to say, he's here to say it to my face.'

'Then keep to the right,' he said. 'He makes a move, maybe I can take him out before he kills you.'

'Thanks. I feel safer already.' But I kept to the right as I had been told.

When I was within a few feet of him he raised one white hand. 'That's close enough, Mr. Parker.' The accent was unusual, with odd, European inflections. 'I suggest that your friend also halt his advance through the woods. I'm not going to harm anyone here.'

I paused, then called out. 'Louis, it's okay.'

From about fifteen feet to my left, a dark figure separated itself from the trees, his gun held steadily in front of him. Louis didn't lower the gun, but he didn't make any further move either.

Up close, the man was startlingly white, with no color to his lips or his cheeks and only the faintest of dark smudges beneath his eyes. They were a washed-out blue, almost lifeless. Combined with the absence of hair on his face, they made him appear like a wax model that had been left incomplete. His scalp was deeply scarred, as were the places where his eyebrows should have been. I noticed one other thing about him: his face was dry and flaking in places, like a reptile discarding its skin.

'Who are you?' I asked.

'I think you know who I am.'

'Golem,' I said.

I expected him to nod, maybe even to smile, but he did neither. Instead he said: 'The Golem is a myth, Mr. Parker. Do you believe in myths?'

'I used to discount them, but I've been proved wrong in the past. Now I try to keep an open mind. Why did you kill Carter Paragon?'

'The question is really, why did I *hurt* Carter Paragon? For the same reason that you broke into his house an hour later: to find out what he knew. His death was a consequence, not an intention.'

'You killed Lester Bargus too.'

'Mr. Bargus supplied weapons to evil men,' he responded simply. 'But no longer.'

'He was unarmed.'

'So was the *rabbi*.' He pronounced it 'raebbee.'

'An eye for an eye,' I said.

'Perhaps. I know something of you too, Mr. Parker. I don't believe you are in a position to pass judgment on me.'

'I'm not judging you. Lester Bargus was a lowlife and nobody will miss him, but I've found in the past that people willing to strike at unarmed men tend not to be too particular about whom they kill. That concerns me.'

'Once again, I do not plan to harm you or your friends. The man I want calls himself Pudd. You know of him, I think.'

'I've encountered him.'

'Do you know where he is?'

For the first time, a note of eagerness crept into his voice. I guessed that either Paragon had died before he could tell all, or, more interestingly, that he had been *unable* to tell his killer where Pudd had his lair because he didn't know.

'Not yet. I intend to find out, though.'

'Your intentions and mine may conflict, then.'

'Maybe we both have similar aims,' I suggested.

'No, we do not. Yours is a moral crusade. Those who engaged me for this task have a more specific purpose.'

'Revenge?'

'I do only what is required of me,' he said. 'No more.' His voice was deep and the words seemed to echo inside him, as if he were a hollow man without substance, only form. 'I came to give you a message. Do not come between me and this man. If you do, I will be forced to take action against you.'

'That sounds like a threat.'

I didn't even see him move. One moment he was in front of me, his hands empty, the next he was close by my side and a small center-fire derringer was at my throat, the twin barrels pointing upward to my brain. From out of the darkness, the Beamshot laser sight on Louis's gun projected its light as he tried to find a clear shot, but my body and the darkness of the Golem's clothes shielded him from both Louis and Angel.

'Tell them to back off, Mr. Parker,' he whispered, his head behind mine. 'I want you to walk me to my car. You have two seconds.'

I shouted out the warning immediately, and Louis killed the beam. The Golem pulled me back through the trees, guiding my footsteps. The sleeve of his overcoat had rolled up on his arm and I could see the first of the small blue numbers etched on his skin. He was a concentration camp survivor. I also saw that he had no fingerprints. Instead, the skin and flesh appeared to have collapsed inward, creating a puckered, indented scar at the tip of each finger. Fire, I thought. It was fire that did this to him; fire that scarred his head, fire that took away his fingerprints,

How do you create a clay demon?

You bake it in an oven.

When we reached his car, he made me stand in front of the driver's door, the gun at my spine, as he lowered himself into the driver's seat.

'Remember, Mr. Parker,' he said to my back. 'Do not interfere with my work.'

Then, his head low, he sped away.

Louis and Angel appeared from the trees. I was shaking as I reached up and felt the twin marks where the derringer had been pushed into my flesh.

'You think you could have hit him before he killed me?' I asked, as his lights faded away.

Louis thought for a moment. 'Probably not. You think he'd have bled?'

'No. I think he'd just have cracked.'

'What now?' said Angel.

'We eat,' although I wasn't sure how steady my stomach was. We began to walk back to the house.

'You sure pick colorful people to fall out with,' said Louis as he fell in beside me.

'Yes,' I said. 'I guess I do.'

All three of us heard the car approaching from behind at the same time. It turned into the yard at speed and we were frozen in its headlights, our guns raised and our eyes wide. Instantly, the driver killed the beams, and still blinking, we scattered left and right. There was silence for a moment, then the driver's door opened and Rachel Wolfe's voice said:

'Okay, no more coffee for you guys. Ever.'

After we had eaten, Rachel went off to take a shower. While Angel sipped his beer by the window, Louis sat at my table finishing a bottle of wine. It was Flagstone sauvignon blanc, from some new winery in Cape Town, South Africa. Louis had two mixed cases imported especially twice yearly and had brought two bottles with him in the trunk of his car. He and Rachel had spent so long cooing over it that I thought one of them must have given birth to the bottle.

'If you're a private eye,' asked Angel at last, 'how come you ain't got no office?'

'I can't afford an office. If I had an office, I'd have to sell the house and sleep on my desk.'

'Wouldn't be such a big stretch. You got next to nothing in this old house anyway. You ever worry about burglars?'

'Burglars in general, or just the one who happens to be standing in my kitchen right now?'

He scowled. 'In general.'

'I don't have anything worth stealing.'

'That's what I mean. You ever think of the effect a big empty place like this is going to have on some guy who goes to the trouble of breaking into it. You better hope he ain't agoraphobic, else you're gonna have a lawsuit on your hands.'

'What are you, some kind of organizer for Burglars' Local three-oh-two?'

'No, just a fly on the wall. One of many, judging by the state of your kitchen.'

'What are you implying?'

'What am I always implying? You need some company.'

'I was thinking of getting a dog.'

'That wasn't what I meant, and you know it. How long you planning on keeping her at arm's length? Till you die? You know, they don't bury you side by side. You won't be touching under the ground.'

'Opportunity only knock once, man,' drawled his partner. 'It don't knock, knock again, then leave a note asking you to give it a call back when you got your shit together.'

Behind us there came the sound of bare feet on boards. Rachel stood at the door, drying her hair. Louis glanced at me, then rose and placed his empty bottle in the recycling bin.

'Time for my bed,' he said. He jerked his chin at Angel as he reached the door. 'You too.' He kissed Rachel on the cheek and headed out to the car.

'You two kids don't be staying up late smoochin' and all,' smiled Angel, then followed Louis into the night.

'Brought together by a pair of gun-toting gay matchmakers,' I said as we heard their car pull away. 'It'll be something to tell the grandchildren.'

Rachel looked at me, as if trying to determine if I was being flippant or not. Frankly, I wasn't sure myself.

She immediately cut to the chase. 'Did you hire people to watch over me in Boston?' she asked.

'You spotted them?' I was impressed with her, although I got the feeling that it wasn't mutual.

'I guess I was on my guard. I called in the license plate of their car when I saw them change shifts. One of them followed me all the way to your front gate.' Rachel's brother had been a policeman, killed on duty some years back. She still had friends on various forces.

'I was worried about you.'

Her voice rose. 'I told you, I don't want you feeling you have to protect me.'

'Rachel,' I said, 'these people are dangerous. I was concerned for Angel too, but at least he carries a gun. What would you have done if they came for you? Thrown plates at them?'

'You should have told me!' She slapped her hand hard on the table. There was real anger in her eyes.

'If I had, would you have let it go ahead? I love you, Rach, but you're stubborn enough to head up the Teamsters.'

Some of the fury in her eyes died and the hand on the table curled into a small tight fist that shook as the tension gradually eased from her.

'How can we be together if you're always afraid of losing me?' she asked gently.

I thought of the dead of St. Froid, crowding a narrow street in Portland. I thought of James Jessop and the figure I had glimpsed leaning over him, the Summer Lady. I had seen her before: in a subway train; outside the Scarborough house; and once, reflected in the window of my kitchen, as if she were standing behind me, but when I turned to look there was nobody there. Sitting in Chumley's only a few nights before, it seemed that an accommodation with the past might be possible. But that was before Mickey Shine's head was impaled on a tree, before James Jessop emerged from a dark forest and took my hand. How could I bring Rachel into that world?

'I can't compete with the dead,' she said.

'I'm not asking you to compete with the dead.'

'It's not a question of asking.' She sat across from me, cupped her chin in her hands, and looked sad and distant.

'I'm trying, Rachel.'

'I know,' she said. 'I know you are.'

'I love you. I want to be with you.'

'How?' she whispered, lowering her head. 'On weekends in Boston, or weekends here?'

'How about just here?'

She looked up, as if unsure of what she had heard.

'I mean it.'

'When? Before I'm old?'

'Old*er*.'

She slapped at me playfully and I reached out to touch her hair. She gave a small smile.

'We'll get there,' I said and felt her nod against my hand. 'And sooner rather than later. I promise.'

'We'd better,' she said, so quietly that it was almost as if I had heard her thoughts. I held her, sensing somehow that she had more to say, but nothing came.

'What kind of dog were you planning to get?' she asked after a time, as the warmth of her spread across me.

I smiled down at her. She had probably heard my entire conversation with Angel and Louis. I think she had been meant to.

'I hadn't decided. I thought you might help me pick one from the pound.'

'That's a very couply thing to do.'

'Well, we are a couple.'

'But not a normal one.'

'No. Louis would never forgive us if we were.'

She kissed me, and I kissed her back. Past and future receded from us like creditors temporarily denied their demands, and there was only the brief, fleeting beauty of the present to hold us. That night, I held her in my arms as she slept and tried to imagine a future for us together, but I seemed to lose us in tangles and weaves. Yet when I awoke my fist was clenched tightly closed, as if I had grasped something vital in my dreams and now refused to let it go.

Chapter Twenty-one

I lay with Rachel and listened to the rising wheeps of a flycatcher from high in the trees. His stay in New England would be short; he had probably arrived in the past week, and would be gone by the end of September, but if he managed to avoid the hawks and the owls, then his little yellow belly would soon be filled with a smorgasbord of insects as the bug population exploded. Already the first of the horseflies were circling, their large green eyes glittering hungrily. They would quickly be joined by greenheads and locusts, ticks and deerflies. At Scarborough Marsh, clouds of golden salt marsh mosquitoes would converge, the males sipping on plant juices while the females scoured the waters and the roadsides for meatier pickings.

And the birds would feed, and the spiders would grow fat upon them.

Beside me, Rachel murmured softly in her sleep, and I felt the warmth of her back against my stomach, the line of her spine beneath her pale skin like a stone path blanketed by new-fallen snow. I raised myself gently to look at her face. Strands of red hair had caught between her lips, and carefully, I brushed them away. She smiled, her eyes still closed, and her fingers softly grazed my thigh. I kissed her gently behind the ear and she leaned her head into the pillow, exposing her neck to me as I followed its lines down to her shoulder and the small hollow at her throat. Her body arched as she pressed herself against me, and all other thoughts were lost in sunlight and birdsong.

It was almost midday when I left Rachel singing in the bathroom while I went out for bagels and milk, conscious still of the weight of the Smith & Wesson in its holster beneath my arm. It made me uneasy how quickly I had slipped back into the old routine of arming myself before I left the house, even for something as simple as a trip to the store.

It was, by then, late in the morning, but today I hoped to find Marcy Becker. Circumstances had forced me to postpone the hunt for her, but more and more, I was convinced that she was the key to what had taken place on the night Grace Peltier died, one more piece of a greater picture whose dimensions I was only now beginning to understand. Faulkner, or something of him, had survived. He, in collusion with others, had slaughtered the Aroostook Baptists and his own wife, then disappeared, eventually reemerging veiled by the organization known as the Fellowship. Paragon had merely been a front, a dupe. The real Fellowship, the substance behind the shadow, was Faulkner, and Pudd was his sword.

I parked the car and took the bag of groceries from the front seat. I was still rearranging my thoughts, shifting possibilities, as I reached the kitchen door. I pushed it open and something white lifted from the floor and tumbled in the air, carried upward by the draft.

It was a sugar wrapper.

Rachel was standing at the entrance to the hallway, Pudd at her shoulder pushing her into the kitchen. She was gagged with a scarf, and her arms were secured at her back.

Behind her, Pudd froze.

I dropped the bag and reached for my gun. Simultaneously, Rachel twisted in Pudd's grip and, with a single movement, slammed her head back into his face, connecting with the bridge of his nose. He staggered backward, swiping at Rachel with the back of his hand. My fingers were already brushing the grip of the Smith & Wesson when something struck me hard on the side of the head and I went down, bright white pain erupting in my brain. I felt hands at my side and then my gun was gone and red droplets were exploding like sunbursts in the spilt milk. I tried to get up, but my hands slipped on the wet floor and my legs felt heavy and awkward. I raised my eyes to see Pudd's fist raining down blows on Rachel's head as she sank to the floor. There was blood on his face and palm. Then a second impact connected with my head, followed by a third, and I didn't feel anything else for what seemed like a very long time.

I came to in slow, arduous steps, as if I was struggling through deep red water. I was vaguely conscious of Rachel sitting on a kitchen chair by the table, still wearing her white cotton robe. Her teeth were visible where the scarf had been pulled tightly into her open mouth, and her hands were tied behind her back. There was bruising to her cheek and left eye, and blood on her forehead. Some of it had run down to stain the gag. She looked at me imploringly and her eyes flicked frantically to my right, but when I tried to move my head I was struck again and everything went black.

I drifted in and out like that for a while. My arms had been tied separately, each wrist bound to one of the spars of the chair by what felt like cable ties. They bit into my skin when I tried to move. My head ached badly, and there was blood in my eyes. Through the mists I heard a voice say:

'So this is the man.'

It was an old man's voice, faded and scratched like a recording heard through an old radio. I tried to lift my head and saw something move in the shadows in the hallway of the house: a slightly hunched figure, wrapped in black. Another, taller shape moved beside it, and I thought that it might be a woman.

'I think that perhaps you should leave now,' said a male

voice. I recognized the careful, composed rhythms of Mr. Pudd's speech.

'I would prefer to stay,' came the reply as the voice drew closer to me. 'You know how I like to watch you work.'

I felt fingers on my chin as the old man spoke, and smelled salt water and leather. The stench of internal decay was on his breath. I made an effort to open my eyes fully but the room was spinning and I was conscious only of his presence, of the way his fingers clutched at my flesh, testing the bone structure beneath my skin. His hand moved to my shoulder, then my arms and my fingers.

'No,' said Pudd. 'It was unwise of you to come at all, on this of all days. You must leave.'

I heard a weary exhalation of air. 'He sees them, you know,' said the old voice. 'I can feel it from him. He is an unusual man, a tormented man.'

'I will put him out of his misery.'

'And ours,' said the old man. 'He has strong bones. Don't damage his fingers or his arms. I want them.'

'And the woman?'

'Do what you have to do, but a promise to spare her might encourage her lover to be more cooperative.'

'But if she dies . . . ?'

'She has beautiful skin. I can use it.'

'How much of it?' asked Pudd.

There was a pause.

'All of it,' said the old man.

I heard footsteps on the kitchen floor beside me. The red film over my eyes was fading now as I blinked away the blood. I saw the strange, nameless woman with the scarred neck gazing down at me with narrow, hateful eyes. She touched my cheek with her fingers, and I shuddered.

'Leave now,' said Mr. Pudd. She stayed beside me for another moment or two, then moved away almost regretfully. I saw her blend into the shadows, and then two figures moved through the half-open front door and into the yard. I tried to keep them in sight until a slap to my cheek brought me back and someone else moved into my line of vision, a woman dressed in a blue sweater and pants, her hair loose on her shoulders.

'Miss Torrance,' I said, my mouth dry. 'I hope you got a reference from Paragon before he died.'

She hit me on the back of my head. It wasn't a hard slap. It didn't have to be. She caught me right on the spot where the earlier blows had landed. The pain was almost visible to me, like lightning flashes in the night sky, and I grew nauseous with pain. I let my head hang down, my chin on my chest, and tried to keep myself from retching. From the front of the house came the sound of a car pulling away, and then there was movement ahead of me and a pair of brown shoes appeared at the kitchen door. I followed the shoes up to the cuffs of the brown pants, then the slightly stretched waistband, the brown check jacket, and finally, the dark, hooded eyes of Mr. Pudd.

He looked considerably worse than when we had last met. The remains of his right ear were covered in gauze, and his nose had swollen where Rachel's head had impacted upon it. There were still traces of blood around his nostrils.

'Welcome back, sir,' he said, smiling. 'Welcome indeed.'

He gestured to Rachel with one gloved hand. 'We had to make our own entertainment while you were gone, but I don't believe there was much that your whore could tell us. On the other hand, Mr. Parker, I believe you may know considerably more.'

He stepped forward so that he stood over Rachel. With one movement he tore the sleeve of her robe, exposing the whiteness of her arm, speckled here and there with small brown freckles. Miss Torrance, I noticed, now stood in front of me and slightly to my right, her own Kahr K9 leveled on me while my Smith & Wesson lay in its holster on the table. The remains of my cell phone were scattered across the floor and I saw that the wire to the telephone in the kitchen had been pulled out.

'As you know, Mr. Parker, we are looking for something,' began Pudd, 'something that was taken from us by Ms. Peltier. That item is still missing. So too, we now believe, is a passenger who may have been in the car with the late Ms. Peltier shortly before she died. We think that individual may have the item we are looking for. I would like you to confirm who that person is so that we can retrieve it. I would also like you to tell us all that passed between you and the late Mr. Al Z, everything of which you and Mr. Mercier spoke two nights ago, and all that you know of the man who killed Mr. Paragon.'

I didn't reply. Pudd remained silent for about thirty seconds, then sighed. 'I know that you are a very stubborn man. I think you might even be willing to die rather than give me what I want. It's very laudable, I admit, to give up one's life to save another. It is, in a sense, what brings us to this point. After all, we are all the fruit of one man's sacrifice, are we not? And you *will* die, Mr. Parker, regardless of what you tell me. Your life is about to end.'

He leaned over Rachel's shoulder and grasped her chin in his hand, forcing her to look at me. 'But are you willing to sacrifice the life of *another* to protect Grace Peltier's friend, or to fuel your strange crusade? That is the real test: how many lives is this person worth? Have you even met the individual in question? Can someone whom you do not know be worth more to you than the life of this woman? Do you have the right to give up Ms. Wolfe here to safeguard your own principles?'

He released his grip on Rachel's jaw and shrugged. 'These are difficult questions, Mr. Parker, but rest assured we will shortly have answers to them.' From the floor he lifted a large plastic case, its surface covered in tiny perforations. He placed it on the table beside his own Beretta, then opened it so that it faced me. Inside lay five plastic containers. Three of them were boxes of four or five inches in length, while the other two were simply small containers for herbs and spices adapted to his purpose.

He withdrew the two spice jars, the reusable kind with a

perforated lid. In each of them, something small and multi-legged tested the glass with a tiny raised limb. Pudd placed one of the jars on the table, then walked over to me with the other, holding it gently between his thumb and forefinger so that my view of its contents was unobscured.

'Do you recognize this?' he asked. Inside the jar, the light brown recluse spider raised itself up against the glass, revealing its abdomen before it slid back down, its stringy legs probing at the air. On its cephalothorax was the small, dark brown, violin-shaped mark that gave the spider its common name of fiddleback.

'It's a recluse, Mr. Parker, *Loxosceles reclusa*. I've been telling it what you did to its brothers and sisters in your mailbox. You burnt them alive. I don't consider that to be very sporting.'

He held the jar an inch from my eye, then shook it gently. Inside, the spider grew increasingly agitated, tearing around the confined space, its palps constantly moving.

'Some people consider recluses to be nasty, verminous arachnids, but I rather admire them. I find them to be remarkably aggressive. I sometimes feed them black widows, and you would be surprised at how quickly a widow can become a tasty snack for a family of recluses.

'But the most interesting aspect of all, Mr. Parker, is the venom.' His eyes glowed brightly beneath their hoods and I caught a trace of a faint smell rising from him, an unpleasant, chemical scent, as if his body had begun to produce its own toxin as his excitement grew. 'The venom it uses to attack humans is not the same as that which it uses to paralyze and kill its insect prey. There is an extra component, an additional toxin, in the venom it uses against us. It is as if this little spider is aware of us, has always been aware of us, and has found a way to hurt us. A most unpleasant way.'

He moved away until he was, once again, beside Rachel. He brushed the jar against her cheek. She shrank from the touch, and I saw that she had begun to tremble. Tears ran from her eyes. Mr. Pudd's nostrils flared, as if he could smell her fear and disgust.

But then she looked at me, and shook her head gently once.

'The venom causes necrosis. It makes the white blood cells turn against their own body. The skin swells, then starts to rot, and the body is unable to repair the damage. Some people suffer greatly. Some even die. I heard of one man who died within an hour of being bitten. Amazing, don't you think, that all of this suffering could be caused by such a tiny spider? The late Mr. Shine was given an intimate revelation of its workings, as I'm sure he told you before he died.

'But then, some people are not affected at all. The venom simply has no effect on them. And that's what makes this little test so interesting. Unless you tell me what I need to know, I am going to apply the recluse to the skin of your whore. She probably won't even feel its bite. Then we will wait. The antidote to recluse venom must be administered within half an hour for it to be effective. If you are unhelpful, then I am afraid we will be here for much longer than that. We will start with her arms, then move on to her face and her breasts. If that proves unsuccessful in moving you, we may have to progress to some of my other specimens. I have a black widow in my case, and a sand spider from South Africa of which I am particularly fond. She will be able to taste it in her mouth as she dies.'

He raised the little jar.

'For the last time, Mr. Parker, who was the second passenger, and where is that person now?'

'I don't know,' I said. 'I haven't figured that out yet.'

'I don't believe you.' Slowly, Pudd began to unscrew the top of the jar.

I twisted in my chair as he held the jar close to Rachel once again. Pudd took the movement as a sign of my discomfort, and his excitement grew. But he was wrong. These were old chairs. They had been in this house for the best part of fifty years. They had been broken, then repaired and broken again. Using the pressure of my shoulders and by twisting my hand, I could feel the spar in the back of my chair loosening. I pushed up with my shoulders and heard a faint crack. The spar rose about a quarter of an inch as the frame of the chair started to come apart.

'I mean it,' I said. 'I don't know.'

I gripped harder with my right hand and felt the spar turn in its hole. It was almost free. Beside me, Miss Torrance's attention was focused on Rachel and the spider. Pudd flipped off the lid and tipped the jar over, trapping the recluse on the skin of Rachel's arm. I saw the spider respond as he shifted the jar slightly, provoking it into a bite. Rachel's eyes grew large and she gave a muffled cry from behind the gag. Beside her, Pudd opened his mouth and emitted a small gasp as the spider bit, then stared at me with absolute, perverse joy.

'Bad news, Mr. Parker!' he cried, as the spar came free in my hand and I spun my wrist, pushing the spear of wood with all the force I could muster into the left side of the woman. I felt brief resistance before it penetrated the skin between her third and fourth ribs and shot through. She screamed as I rose. My forehead impacted with her face and she lurched back against the sink. Simultaneously, Rachel shifted her weight in the chair, causing it to topple backward and forcing Pudd away from the table. With the chair still dangling from my left hand, I reached for my gun and fired two shots at Pudd's body. Splinters flew from the door frame as he dived into the hallway.

Beside me, the woman pawed at my legs. I kicked out at her and felt my foot connect. The pawing stopped. I shrugged the remains of the chair from my arm and reached the hallway just in time to see the front door slam open and Pudd's long brown frame disappear to the right. I sprang down the hall, risked a quick glance from the doorway, and pulled my head in quickly as the shots came. He had a second gun. I took a breath, then rolled out onto the porch and started firing, the Smith & Wesson bucking in my right hand. Pudd disappeared into the trees and I followed, increasing my pace as I heard the car start. Seconds later, the Cirrus burst from cover. I kept firing as it shot down the drive and onto Mussey Road, the rear window shattering and one of its back lights exploding as the gun locked empty. I let him go, then ran back to the house and untied Rachel. She immediately retreated into the hall, curling in on herself and rubbing again and again at the spot where the recluse had bitten her.

The woman was crawling to the back door, the spar still buried in her side and a trail of black blood following her across the floor. Her nose was broken and one eye had been closed by the kick to her head. She looked blearily at me as I leaned over her, her vision and her life already fading.

'Where has he gone?' I hissed.

She shook her head and spat blood in my face. I gripped the spar and twisted. Her teeth gritted in agony.

'*Where has he gone?*' I repeated. Miss Torrance beat at the ground with one hand. Her mouth opened to its fullest extent as she squirmed and writhed then went into spasm. I released my hold on the spar and stepped back as her eyes rolled back into her head and she died. I patted her down but there was no ID on her body, no indication of where Pudd might be based. I kicked once at her legs in impotent rage, then reloaded my gun with a spare mag before walking Rachel to my car.

Chapter Twenty-two

I called Angel and Louis from the Maine Medical Center, but there was no reply from their room at the inn. I then placed a call to the Scarborough PD. I told them that a couple had broken into my house, assaulted my girlfriend, and one of them was now lying dead on my kitchen floor. I also gave them a description of the Cirrus Mr. Pudd had driven away from the house, complete with smashed rear windshield and busted back light.

The Scarborough PD was equipped with QED, or computer-enabled despatch, which meant that the nearest patrol car would be immediately assigned to the house. They would also alert neighboring departments and the state police in an effort to find Pudd before he ditched the car.

At Maine Medical they dosed Rachel with antivenin after she had replied to a barrage of questions to which I was not privy, then put her on a gurney in a curtained-off section to rest up. By then Angel and Louis had got my message, and Angel was now seated beside her, talking to her gently, while Louis waited outside in the car. There were still people with questions to ask about the events in Dark Hollow the previous winter, and Louis was considerably more conspicuous than Angel.

Rachel had not spoken during the ride to the hospital. Instead, she had simply held her hand over the area where the spider had bitten her, shaking softly. She had also suffered some cuts and bruises to the head, but there was no concussion and she was going to be okay. I was X-rayed and then given ten stitches to close up the wound in my scalp. It was already midafternoon, and I was still feeling dazed and numb when Ramos, one of the detectives out of Scarborough, arrived, accompanied by the department's detective, Wallace MacArthur, and a whole cartload of questions. Their first question was: who was the injured woman? More to the point, *where* was she?

'She was lying there when I left,' I said.

'Well, she wasn't lying there when the first patrol got to your place. There was a hell of a lot of blood on your kitchen floor, and more outside in the yard, but there was no dead woman.'

He was seated across from me in a small private room usually used to comfort relatives of recently deceased patients. 'You sure she was dead?' he asked.

I nodded and sipped at my lukewarm coffee. 'I stuck a piece of chair halfway into her body, right between numbers three and four, and I pushed up hard. I saw her die. There's no way she got up and walked away.'

'You think this guy, this Mr. Pudd, came back for her?' he asked.

'You find a suitcase full of spiders on my kitchen table?'

MacArthur shook his head.

'Then it was him.'

It was a huge risk for him to take; he probably had only a few minutes to retrieve her. 'I think he's trying to keep the waters as muddy as he can,' I said. 'Without the woman, there's no positive ID, nothing that can link her to him. Or to anyone else,' I added.

'You know who she is?'

I nodded. 'I think her name is Torrance. She was Carter Paragon's secretary.'

'The late Carter Paragon?' MacArthur sat back, opened a fresh page in his notebook, and waited for me to begin. From across the hall, I heard Rachel calling for me.

'I'll be back,' I told MacArthur. For a second or two he looked like he might be tempted to sit on me and shake me by the throat until I gave up what I knew. Instead, he nodded reluctantly and let me leave.

Angel stood and discreetly walked to the window as I approached her. Rachel was pale, and there was sweat on her brow and upper lip, but she gripped my hand tightly as I sat on the edge of her bed.

'How you doing?'

'I'm tougher than you think, Parker.'

'I know how tough you are.'

She nodded. 'I guess you do.' She looked past me to the room where Ramos and MacArthur waited.

'What are you going to tell them?'

'Everything that I can.'

'But not everything that you know?'

'That would be unwise.'

'You're still going to see the Beckers, aren't you?' she asked softly.

'Yes.'

'I'm going with you. Maybe I can succeed in convincing them where you couldn't. You and Louis go walking in on those people in your current mood and you're likely to scare them to death. And if we do find Marcy, a friendly face will help.'

She was right. 'Okay,' I said. 'Rest up for a while, and then we'll leave. Nobody's going anywhere without you.'

She gave me a satisfied smile and released my hand. Angel resumed his seat beside her bed. His Glock was in an IWB holster at his waist, concealed by his long shirt.

From the room in which I had left MacArthur and Ramos came the sound of raised voices. I saw Ramos emerge from the room at a sprint. MacArthur was right behind him, but he stopped when he saw me.

'What's up?' I asked.

'Trawler spotted Jack Mercier's yacht drifting a couple of

miles out. Tide's carrying it in to shore.' MacArthur swallowed. 'Captain says there's a body lashed to the mast.'

The cruiser, named the Revenant, *had docked at the Portland marina five days earlier. It was a twenty-five-foot Grady White Sailfish 25, with twin 200-horsepower Suzuki outboards, and its owner paid $175 in advance for one week's mooring, at the standard rate of $1 per foot per night. The name, address, phone number, and boat registration number he gave to Portland Yacht Services, administrators of the marina, were all false.*

He was a small man, cross-eyed, with a tightly shaven skull. He spent most of his time in or near his boat, sleeping in its single compartment. By day he sat on the deck with a pair of binoculars in one hand, a cell phone in the other, and a book on his lap. He didn't speak, and rarely left the boat for longer than fifteen minutes. His eyes seemed almost permanently fixed on the waters of Casco Bay.

Early on the morning of the sixth day, a group of six people – two women, four men – boarded a yacht on the bay. The boat was the Eliza May, *a seventy-footer built three years earlier by Hodgdon Yachts in East Boothbay. Its deck was teak, its body epoxy, glass, and mahogany over Alaska cedar. As well as the Doyle sail on its eighty-foot mast, it had a 150-horsepower Perkins diesel engine and could sleep seven people in luxury. It was equipped with a forty-mile radar, GPS, LORAN, and WeatherFax, as well as VHF and single sideband radio and an EPIRB emergency system. It had cost Jack Mercier over $2.5 million and was too big to moor at Scarborough, so it had a permanent berth at Portland.*

The Eliza May *left Portland for the last time shortly after 9:00* A.M. *There was a northwest wind blowing, superb weather for yachting, and the wind tossed Mercier's white hair as he steered her into Casco Bay. Deborah Mercier sat apart from her husband, head down. By then, the cross-eyed man had been joined by two other people, a woman in blue and a slim red-haired man dressed in brown, both carrying tuna rods. As the* Eliza May *headed out into deep waters, the* Revenant *left the harbor and shadowed it, unseen.*

★ ★ ★

I caught up with MacArthur at the elevator.

'Mercier's involved in this,' I told him. There was no point in keeping Mercier's role secret any longer.

'The hell . . . ?'

'Believe me. I've been working for him.'

I could see him considering his options, so I decided to preempt him. 'Take me along,' I said. 'I'll tell you what I know on the way.'

He paused and gave me a long, hard look, then nodded and reached out his hand. 'You can come as far as Pine Point. Hand over the gun, Charlie,' he said.

Reluctantly, I gave him the Smith & Wesson. He ejected the magazine and checked the chamber, then handed it back to me. 'You can leave it with your friend,' he said.

I nodded, walked into Rachel's room, and handed the gun to Angel. As I turned to leave I felt a light tug at my waistband, and the coolness of his Glock sliding against my skin. I took my jacket from the chair, nodded politely to Angel, then followed MacArthur down the hallway.

Mercier's last log entry recorded that the Revenant *contacted the* Eliza May *shortly after 9:30 A.M, about forty miles out from port. The northwest wind might have been ideal for yachting, but it could also carry a cruiser in distress out to sea, and the* Revenant *was in trouble. The* Revenant*'s distress call came in on VHF but the* Eliza May *was the only boat to hear it, despite the fact that there were other boats two and three miles away. The radio had been set to low range, maybe one watt, to prevent anyone else hearing the signal and answering. The* Revenant*'s batteries were almost dead, and it was drifting. Mercier adjusted his course, and went at speed to his death.*

I told MacArthur almost everything, from my first meeting with Jack Mercier to that morning's encounter with Mr. Pudd. The omissions were few, but crucial: I left out Marcy Becker, Mickey Shine's murder, and our unscheduled early viewing of Carter Paragon's body. I also made no mention of the fact that I suspected that someone in the state police, possibly Lutz, Voisine, or both, was involved in Grace Peltier's death.

'You think this Pudd killed the Peltiers?'

'Probably. The Fellowship, or at least what the public saw of it, is just a front for someone or something else. Grace Peltier found out what that was, and it was enough to get her killed.'

'And whatever Grace knew, this Pudd thought Curtis Peltier also knew, and now he thinks you might know too?'

'Yes,' I said.

'But you don't.'

'Not yet.'

'If Jack Mercier's dead, there'll be hell to pay,' said MacArthur fervently. Beside him, Ramos nodded silently in agreement as MacArthur leaned back to look at me.

'And don't think you'll get away without picking up your share of the check,' he added.

We drove along U.S.1 south before turning left onto 9 and heading for the coast, past the redbrick Baptist Church and the white bell tower of St. Jude's Catholic Church. At the Pine Point Fire Department on King Street, seven or eight cars were parked in the lot and the doors were wide open. A fireman in jeans and a Fire Department T-shirt waved us on toward the Pine Point Fishermen's Co-op, where *Marine 4* was already in the water.

The Scarborough PD used two boats for marine duty. *Marine 1* was a seventy-horsepower inflatable based at Spurwink, to the north of Pine Point, and launched from Ferry Beach. *Marine 4* was a twenty-one-foot Boston Whaler powered by a 225-horsepower Johnson, based at the Pine Point Co-op and berthed, when not required, in the Fire Department. It had a crew of five, all of whom were already on board as we pulled up at the gray-and-white co-op building. The harbormaster's boat was alongside the Whaler, and there were two Scarborough PD officers on board. Both carried 12-gauge Mossberg shotguns, the standard arms kept in Scarborough PD patrol cars. There were two more policemen in the Whaler carrying M-16s. All wore blue windbreakers. From the jetty, curious fishermen looked on.

Both Ramos and MacArthur shook on their waterproofs as I followed them to the boat. MacArthur was climbing down to the Whaler when he saw me.

'The hell do you think you're going?'

'Come on, Wallace,' I pleaded. 'Don't do this. I'll stay out of the way. Mercier was my client. I don't want to be waiting here like an expectant parent if something has happened to him. You don't let me go with you, I'll just have to bribe a fisherman to take me out and then I'll really be in the way. Worse, I might just disappear and then you'll have lost a crucial witness. They'll have you back directing traffic.'

MacArthur glanced at the other men on the boat. The captain, Ted Adams, shrugged.

'Get in the damn boat,' hissed MacArthur. 'You even stand up to stretch and I'll feed you to the lobsters.'

I followed him down, Ramos behind me. There were no more windbreakers so I pulled my jacket tight around me and huddled on the plastic bench, my hands in my pockets and my chin to my chest, as the Whaler pulled away from the dock.

'Give me your hand,' said MacArthur.

I extended my right hand and he slapped the cuffs on it, then locked me to the rail of the boat.

'What happens if we sink?' I asked.

'Then your body won't drift away.'

The boat surged through the dark, gray waters of Saco Bay, white foam erupting as it went. MacArthur stood beside the covered cockpit looking back to Scarborough, the horizon bobbing merrily with the movement of the boat on the sea.

In the wheelhouse, Adams was responding to someone

on the radio. 'Still drifting,' he said to MacArthur. 'Only two miles out now, heading to shore.' I looked out past the seated policemen, past the crew at the cockpit, and imagined that I saw, like a tiny rip in the sky, the long, thin mast of the yacht. Something clawed at my insides, the last desperate scratchings of a cat left to drown in a bag. The prow dipped and sent a fine spray lashing over the deck, soaking me. I shivered as gulls glided above the surface of the water, calling noisily over the sound of the engine.

'There she is,' said Adams. His finger pointed to a small green dot on the radar screen while, simultaneously, the half-seen needle of the mast joined a dark spot on the horizon. Beside me, Ramos checked the safety on his Glock .40.

Slowly the shape acquired definition: a white seventy-footer with a tall mast, drifting on the waves. A smaller boat, the lobster fisherman out of Portland that had first spotted the yacht, shadowed it from a distance. From the north came the sound of *Marine 1* approaching. The two boats always responded to a call together for safety reasons.

Marine 4 turned to the south and came around so that it was on the yacht's eastern side, its lines silhouetted before the setting sun. As the Whaler circled it, there was blood visible on the deck that even the salt water hadn't managed to fully erase, and the wood was pitted with what looked like bullet holes. Close to the bow of the boat was a black scorch mark where a flare appeared to have ignited on the deck.

And at the top of the mast, partially concealed by the furled sail, a body hung with its arms outstretched and tied to the crossbeam. It was naked but for a pair of white boxers, now stained black and red. The legs were white, the feet tied together, a second rope around its chest lashing it to the mast before heading down taut at an angle, tied off to one of the rails. The body was scorched from the stomach to the head. Most of its hair was gone, its eyes were now dark hollows, and its teeth were bared in a rictus of pain, but still I knew that I was looking at the remains of Jack Mercier.

The Whaler hailed the yacht and, when no response came, drew up off the port side while a young crewman climbed on board the *Eliza May* and tied *Marine 4* off. Ramos and MacArthur joined him, pulling on protective gloves before they stepped shakily on board.

'Detectives,' the crewman called from the cockpit. They headed toward him, trying not to touch anything with their hands as the boat rocked gently in the waves. The crewman pointed to where a long, dark trail of blood followed the steps down. Someone had been dragged, dead or dying, belowdecks. MacArthur knelt down and examined the steps more closely. The end of a long, blond hair curled out of the blood. He rummaged in his pockets and removed a small evidence bag, then carefully lifted the hair and stored it away.

'You stay here,' he said to the crewman as Ramos moved behind him. From the deck of the two police boats, guns were trained on the other two of the yacht's three entryways belowdecks. Then MacArthur took the lead, using the very edges of the steps, the only parts not covered in blood, to make his way below.

This is what they found.

There was a small, dark passageway, with the head to the immediate right and a quarter berth to the left. The head was empty and smelled of chemicals; a shower curtain was pulled back, revealing a clean white shower stall. The quarter berth was unoccupied. The passageway was carpeted, and the material squelched beneath their feet as they walked, blood bubbling up from between the fibers. They passed the galley and a second pair of facing doors that led into two sleeping compartments, both fitted with small double beds and closets big enough to take only two pairs of shoes set side by side.

The door leading into the main salon was closed and no sounds came from behind it. Ramos looked at Wallace and shrugged. Wallace retreated back into one of the bedrooms, his gun in his hand. Ramos moved into the other and called out: 'Police. If there's anybody in there, come out now and keep your hands up.'

There was no response. Wallace stepped back into the passage, reached for the handle of the door and, keeping his back against the wall, slowly pulled it open.

There was blood on the walls, on the ceiling, and on the floor. It dripped from the light fittings and obscured the paintings between the portholes. Three naked bodies hung upside down from the beams in the ceiling: two women, one man. One woman had gray-blond hair that almost touched the floor; the other was small and dark. The man was bald, apart from a thin circle of gray hair, which was mostly soaked red with his blood. The throat of each had been cut, although the blonde also had stab wounds to her stomach and legs. It was her blood on the steps and soaked into the carpet. Deborah Mercier had tried to run, or to intervene, when they took her husband.

The smell of blood was overpowering in the confined space, and the bodies swayed and bumped against one another with the rocking of the boat. They had been killed facing the door, and the spray from their arteries had hit only three sides of the cabin.

But there was still some blood behind them. It formed a pattern that could be seen between the moving bodies. MacArthur reached forward and stopped the swaying of Deborah Mercier's corpse. She hung to the left of the others, so that by stilling her the others also grew still. She was cold, and he shuddered at the touch, but now he could see clearly what had been written behind them in bright, red arterial blood.

It was one word:

SINNERS

Chapter Twenty-three

What harm can it do?

Jack Mercier's words, spoken on the day he first asked me to look into Grace's death, came back to me as I learned of what had been found in the main salon of the *Eliza May*, its decks stained with red and Jack Mercier's crucified form hanging from the mast. They came back to me as I saw the pictures of the yacht in the following day's papers, smaller photographs beside it of Jack and Deborah Mercier, and of the attorney Warren Ober and his wife, Eleanor.

What harm can it do?

I recalled myself sitting, wet and shivering, in the bow of *Marine 4*, surrounded by the cries of gulls as arrangements were made to tow the *Eliza May* back to shore. I was there for over two hours, the lineaments of Jack Mercier's body slowly fading and growing indistinct as evening fell. MacArthur was the only one who spoke to me, and then only to detail the discovery of the bodies and the word written in blood upon the wall behind them.

Sinners.

'The Aroostook Baptists,' I said.

MacArthur grimaced. 'Little early for a copycat, don't you think?'

'It's not a copycat killing,' I answered. 'It's the same people.'

MacArthur sat down heavily beside me. Seawater swirled around his black leather shoes. 'The Baptists have been dead for over thirty years,' he began. 'Even if whoever killed them was still alive, why would he – or they – start again now?'

I was too tired to go on hiding things, much too tired.

'I don't think they ever stopped killing,' I told him. 'They've always been doing it, quietly and discreetly. Mercier was closing in on them, trying to put pressure on the Fellowship through the courts and the IRS. He wanted to draw them out, and he succeeded. They responded by killing him and those who were prepared to stand alongside him: Yossi Epstein in New York, Alison Beck in Minneapolis, Warren Ober, even Grace Peltier.'

Now, their countermeasures were almost complete. The word on the wall indicated that, a deliberate echo of the slaughter with which they had begun and that had only recently been revealed. There was now one final act left to perform: the recovery of the missing Apocalypse. Once that was accomplished, they would disappear, vanishing below the surface to lie dormant in some quiet, dark cavern of the honeycomb world.

'Who are they?' asked MacArthur.

'The Faulkners,' I replied. 'The Faulkners are the Fellowship.'

MacArthur shook his head. 'You're in a shitload of trouble,' he said.

The sound of *Marine 1* approaching us disturbed my thoughts. 'They're going back to pick up the local ME, have the victims declared dead at the scene,' said MacArthur, unlocking the cuffs. 'You go back with them. Someone will take you to the department. I'll follow on within the hour and we'll pick up this discussion where we left off.'

He watched me as I stepped carefully from the Whaler into the smaller boat. It turned in a broad arc and headed for the shore, leaving the *Eliza May* behind. The sun was setting, and the waves were afire. Jack Mercier's body hung dark against the red sky like a black flag set in the firmament.

At the Scarborough Police Department I sat for a time in the lobby and watched the dispatchers behind their protective screen. My clothes were soaked and I couldn't seem to get warm again. I found myself reading, over and over, warnings against rabies and DUI posted on the bulletin boards. I felt like I was coming down with a fever. My head ached and the skin on my scalp seemed to be constricting around the stitches.

Eventually I was led into the general-purpose briefing room. The command staff had just broken up their meeting in the smaller conference room, where MacArthur had been chewed out for letting me on board the Whaler. I was trying to draw in some heat through a cup of coffee, a patrol officer at the door to make sure I didn't try to steal one of the canine trophies stored in the cabinet, when MacArthur joined me, accompanied by Captain Bobby Melia, one of two captains in the force who were second in command to Chief Byron Fischer. MacArthur carried a tape recorder with him. They sat across from me, the door behind them closed, and asked me to take them through it all again. Then Norman Boone arrived from the ATF, and Ellis Howard from the Portland PD.

And I went through it again.

And again.

And again.

I was tired, cold, and hungry. Each time I told them what I knew, it got harder and harder to remember what I had left out, and their questions became more and more probing. But I couldn't tell them about Marcy Becker, because if the Fellowship did have connections among the police, then telling anyone in law enforcement about her would be tantamount to signing her death warrant. They were threatening to charge me as an accessory to Mercier's murder, in addition to witholding evidence, obstructing justice, and anything else that the law allowed. I let the waves of their anger break over me.

Two bodies were missing from the boat: those of the porn star and Quentin Harrold, both of whom had gone out on the yacht to guard the Obers and the Merciers. The Scarborough PD suspected they had died in the first burst of gunfire. Jack Mercier had tried unsuccessfully to fire off a flare but had instead ignited his own clothing. There was a Colt revolver in the cabin where the bodies were found, but it had not been fired. Cartridges were scattered on the floor beside it where someone had made a last, desperate effort to load.

What harm can it do?

I wanted to get away from there. I wanted to talk to the Beckers, to force them – at gunpoint if necessary – to tell me where their daughter was hiding. I wanted to know what Grace Peltier had found. I wanted to sleep.

Most of all, I wanted to find Mr. Pudd, and the mute, and the old man who had wanted Rachel's skin: the Reverend Faulkner. His wife was among the dead of St. Froid but he was not, and neither were his two children. A boy and a girl, I remembered. What age would they be now: late forties, early fifties? Ms. Torrance had been too young, as was Lutz. Unless there were others hidden elsewhere, which I doubted, that left only Pudd and the mute: they were Leonard and Muriel Faulkner, dispatched, when required, to do their father's bidding.

They gave me a ride back to my car after eleven that night, threats of retribution still ringing in my ears. Angel and Louis were with Rachel when I got back, drinking beer and watching television with the volume almost muted. All three of them left me alone while I stripped and showered, then pulled on a pair of chinos and a sweater. A new cell phone lay on the kitchen table, the memory card salvaged from the wreckage of the old phone and reinstalled. I took a bottle of Pete's Wicked Ale from the fridge and twisted it open. I could smell the hops and the distinctive fruity scent. I raised it to my mouth and took one mouthful, my first sip of alcohol in two years, then held it for as long as I was able. When at last I swallowed, it was warm and thick with saliva. I poured the rest into a glass and drank half of it back, then sat looking at what remained. After a time, I took the glass to the sink and poured the beer down the drain.

It wasn't exactly a moment of revelation, more a confirmation. I didn't want it, not now. I could take it or leave it, and I chose to let it go. Amy had been right; it was just something to fill the hole, and I had found other ways to do that. But for now, nothing in a bottle was going to make things better.

I shivered again. Despite the shower and the change of clothes, I still hadn't been able to get warm. I could taste the salt on my lips, could smell the brine in my hair, and each time I did I was back on the waters of the bay, the *Eliza May* drifting slowly before me and Jack Mercier's body swaying gently against the sky.

I placed the bottle in the recycling box and looked up to see Rachel leaning against the door.

'You're not finishing it?' she said softly.

I shook my head. For a moment or two, I couldn't speak. I felt something breaking up inside of me, like a stone in my heart that my system was now ready to expunge. A pain at the very center of my being began to spread throughout my body: to my fingers and toes, to my groin, to the tips of my ears. Wave after wave of it rocked me, so that I had to hold on to the sink to stop myself from falling. I squeezed my eyes closed tightly and saw:

A young woman emerging from an oil barrel by a canal in Louisiana, her teeth bared in her final agony and her body encased in a cocoon of transformed body fats, dumped by the Traveling Man after he had blinded her and killed her; a little dead boy running through my house in the middle of the night, calling me to play; Jack Mercier, burning with a desperate flame as his wife was dragged bleeding belowdecks; blood and water mixing on the pale, distorted features of Mickey Shine; my grandfather, his memory fading slowly away; my father sitting at a kitchen table, ruffling my hair with his great hand; and Susan and Jennifer, splayed across a kitchen chair – lost to me and yet not lost, gone and yet forever with me . . .

The pain made a rushing sound as it passed through me, and I thought I detected voices calling me over and over as, at last, it reached its peak. My body tensed, my mouth opened, and I heard myself speak.

'It wasn't my fault,' I whispered.

Her brow furrowed. 'I don't understand.'

'It – wasn't – my – fault,' I repeated. There were huge gaps between the words as I retched each one up and spat it, blinking, into the light. I licked my upper lip and tasted, again, salt and beer. My head was pounding in time to my heart, and I thought I was going to burn up. Past and present twisted and intertwined with each other like snakes in a pit. New deaths and old, old guilts and new, the pain of them white hot even as I spoke.

'None of it,' I said. My eyes were blurring, and now there was fresh salt water on my cheek and lips. 'I couldn't have saved them. If I'd been with them, I'd have died too. I did everything that I could. I'm still trying to do it, but I couldn't have saved them.'

And I didn't know about whom I was speaking. I think I was talking about them all: the man on the mast; Grace and Curtis Peltier; a woman and child, a year earlier, lying on the floor of a cheap apartment; another woman, another child, in the kitchen of our home in Brooklyn a year before that again; my father, my mother, my grandfather; a little boy with a bullet wound for an eye.

All of them.

And I heard them calling my name from the places in which they lay, their voices echoing through burrows and pits, caverns and caves, hollows and apertures, until the honeycomb world vibrated with the sound of them.

'I tried,' I whispered. 'But I couldn't save them all.'

And then her arms were around me and the world collapsed, waiting for us to rebuild it again in our image.

Chapter Twenty-four

I slept a strange, disturbed sleep in her arms that night, twisting and clawing at unseen things. Angel and Louis were in the spare room and all of the doors were locked and bolted, so we were safe for a time, but she had no peace beside me. I imagined I was sinking into dark waters where Jack Mercier waited for me, his skin burning beneath the waves, Curtis Peltier beside him, his arms bleeding black blood into the depths. When I tried to rise they held me back, their dead hands digging into my legs. My head throbbed and my lungs ached, the pressure increasing upon me until at last I was forced to open my mouth and the salt water flooded my nose and mouth.

Then I would wake, over and over, to find her close beside me, whispering softly, her hands moving in a slow rhythm across my brow and through my hair. And so the night passed.

The next morning we ate a hurried breakfast, then prepared to separate. Louis, Rachel, and I would head for Bar Harbor and a final confrontation with the Beckers. Angel had repaired the phone at the house and would stay there so we would have room for maneuver if needed. When I checked my cell phone messages on the way to the car, there was only one: it came from Ali Wynn, asking me to call her.

'You told me to contact you if somebody started asking about Grace,' she said, when I reached her. 'Somebody did.'

'Who was it?'

'A policeman. He came to the restaurant yesterday. He was a detective. I saw his shield.'

'You get his name?'

'Lutz. He said he was investigating Grace's death. He wanted to know when I saw her last.'

'What did you tell him?'

'Just what I told you, and nothing else.'

'What did you think of him?'

She considered the question. 'He frightened me. I didn't go home last night. I stayed with a friend.'

'Have you seen him since yesterday?'

'No, I think he believed me.'

'Did he tell you how he got your name?'

'Grace's tutor. I talked to her last night. She said she gave him the names of two of Grace's friends: me, and Marcy Becker.'

It was just after 9:00 A.M., and we were almost at Augusta, when the cell phone rang. I didn't recognize the number.

'Mr Parker?' said a female voice. 'It's Francine Becker, Marcy's mother.'

I mouthed the words 'Mrs. Becker' to Rachel.

'We were just on our way to see you, Mrs. Becker.'

'You're still looking for Marcy, aren't you?' There was resignation in her voice, and fear.

'The people who killed Grace Peltier are closing in on her, Mrs. Becker,' I said. 'They killed Grace's father, they killed a man named Jack Mercier, along with his wife and friends, and they're going to kill Marcy when they find her.'

At the other end of the line I could hear her start to cry.

'I'm sorry for what happened the last time you came to see us. We were scared; scared for Marcy and scared for ourselves. She's our only daughter, Mr. Parker. We can't let anything happen to her.'

'Where is she, Mrs. Becker?'

But she was going to tell me in her own time, and her

own way. 'A policeman came, just this morning. He was a detective. He said that she was in a lot of danger, and he wanted to take her to safety.' She paused. 'My husband told him where she was. We're law-abiding people, Mr. Parker. Marcy had warned us to say nothing to the police, but he was so kind and so concerned for her. We had no reason not to trust him and we have no way of contacting Marcy. There's no phone at the house.'

'What house?'

'We have a house in Boothbay Harbor. It's just a lodge, really. We used to rent it out during the summer, but we've let it get run down these last few years.'

'Tell me exactly where it is.'

Rachel handed me a pen and a Post-it note and I wrote down her directions, then read them back to her.

'Please, Mr. Parker, don't let anything happen to her.'

I tried to sound reassuring. 'I won't, Mrs Becker. One more thing: what was the name of the detective who talked to you about Marcy?'

'It was Lutz,' she said. 'Detective John Lutz.'

I signaled right and pulled into the hard shoulder. Louis's Lexus appeared in the rearview seconds later. I got out of the car and ran back to him.

'Change of plan,' I said.

'So where we going?' he asked.

'To get Marcy Becker. We know where she is.'

He must have seen something in my face.

'And let me guess?' he said. 'Someone else know where she at too.'

'That's right.'

'Ain't that always the way?'

Boothbay Harbor used to be a pretty nice place thirty years ago, when it was little more than a fishing village. Thirty years before that the whole town probably smelled of manure, since Boothbay then was the commercial and shipping center for the fertilizer trade. If you went back far enough, it was pretty enough to provide a site for the first permanent settlement on the coast of Maine, back in 1622. Admittedly, that settlement was also one of the most wretched on the eastern seaboard, but everybody has to start somewhere.

Now, during the season, Boothbay Harbor filled up with tourists and recreational sailors, crowding a harbor front that had been brutalized by uncontrolled commercial development. It had come a long way from its wretched origins, or if you were one of the naysayers, it had come a long way to become wretched all over again.

We took 27 southeast from Augusta and made Boothbay in just over an hour, following Middle Street out until it became Barters Island Road. I had almost been tempted to ask Rachel to wait for us in Boothbay, but apart from not wanting to risk a sock to the jaw, I knew that she would provide reassurance for Marcy Becker.

At last we came to a small private road that curved up a rough, tree-lined drive to a timber house on a small hill, with a ramshackle porch and boards built into the slope to act as steps. I guessed that it couldn't contain more than two or three rooms. Trees surrounded it to the west and south, leaving a clear view of most of the road up to the house. There was no car visible at the front of the drive, but a mountain bike stood below the window to the left of the front door.

'You want to leave the cars here?' asked Louis, as we paused beside each other at the foot of the road. If we drove any farther, we would be immediately visible to anyone in the house.

'Uh-uh,' I replied. 'I want to be there and gone before Lutz arrives.'

'Assuming he ain't there already.'

'You think he rode up on his mountain bike?'

'Could be he's been and gone.'

I didn't reply. I didn't want to consider that possibility.

Louis shrugged. 'We best not arrive with our hands

hangin' by our sides.' He popped the trunk and got out of the car. I took another look at the house, then glanced at Rachel and shrugged. There didn't seem to be any activity, so I gave up looking and joined Louis. Rachel followed.

Louis had lifted the matting in the trunk, exposing the spare tire. He twisted the bolt holding it in place, then lifted the tire and handed it to me, leaving the trunk empty. It was only when he slipped a pair of concealed clasps that it struck me how shallow the trunk was. The reason became apparent a couple of seconds later when the whole floor raised up on a hinge at the rear, exposing a small arsenal of weapons fitted into specially designed compartments.

'I just know you've got permits for all these,' I said.

'Home, there's shit here they ain't even got permits *for*.'

I saw one of the Calico minisubs for which Louis had a particular fondness, two fifty-round magazines on either side of it. There was a spare Glock 9-millimeter and a Mauser SP66 sniper's rifle, along with a South African-made BXP submachine gun fitted with a suppressor and a grenade launcher, which seemed to me like a contradiction in terms.

'You know, you hit a bump in the road and you'll be the only dead hit man with a crater named after him,' I said. 'You ever worry about DWBs?'

Driving While Black was almost a recognized offense under law.

'Nah, got me a chauffeur's license and a black cap. Anybody asks, I just driving it for massa.'

He leaned in and removed a shotgun from the rear of the trunk, then handed it to me as he replaced the floor and spare tire.

I had never seen a gun like it. It was about the same length as a sawed-off, with twin barrels over a raised sight. Beneath the twins was a third, thicker barrel, which acted as a grip. It was surprisingly light, and the stock fitted easily into my shoulder as I sighted down the gun.

'Very impressive,' I said. 'What is it?'

'Neostead. South African. Thirteen rounds of spin-stablized slugs and a recoil so light you can fire it with one hand.'

'It's a shotgun?'

'No, it's *the* shotgun.'

I shook my head despairingly and handed the shotgun back to him. Behind us, Rachel leaned against the car, her mouth tightly closed. Rachel didn't like guns. She had her reasons.

'Okay,' I nodded. 'Let's go.'

Louis shook his head sadly as he climbed into the Lexus and propped the Neostead against the dashboard. 'Can't believe you don't like my gun,' he remarked.

'You have too much money,' I replied.

We headed up the drive at speed, the gravel in front of the house crunching loudly as we pulled up. I got out first, Louis seconds behind me. As he was stepping from the car, I heard the back door of the lodge slam.

We both moved at the same time, Louis to the left and I to the right. As I rounded the house, I saw a woman wearing a red shirt and jeans running downhill toward the cover of the trees, a rucksack over her shoulder. She was big and a little slow, and I caught up with her before she made it even halfway. Just inside the woodland ahead of us, I could see the shape of a motorcycle covered by a tarp.

As I got within touching distance of her back, she spun around, the rucksack held by its straps, and caught me a hard blow on the side of the head. I stumbled, my ears ringing, then shot a foot out and tripped her as she tried to get away. She landed heavily and the rucksack flew from her hands. I was on top of her before she could even think of rising. Behind me, I heard Louis slowing down and then his shadow fell across us.

'Damn,' I said. 'You nearly took my head off!'

Marcy Becker was squirming furiously beneath me. She was in her late twenties, with light brown hair and plain, blunt features. Her shoulders were large and muscular and she looked like she might once have been a swimmer or a field athlete. When I saw the expression on her face I felt a twinge of guilt for scaring her.

'Take it easy, Marcy,' I said. 'We're here to help you.' I lifted my weight from her and let her rise. Almost immediately, she tried to run again. I wrapped my arms around her, gripped her wrists in my hands, and twisted her so that she was facing Louis.

'My name is Charlie Parker. I'm a private investigator. I was hired by Curtis Peltier to find out what happened to Grace, and I think you know.'

'I don't know anything,' she hissed. Her left heel shot back and nearly caught me a nasty blow on the shin. She was a big, strong young woman, and holding her was taking quite an effort. Louis just looked at me, one eyebrow raised in amusement. I guessed that I wasn't going to get any help from that quarter. I turned her again so that she was facing me, then shook her hard.

'Marcy,' I said. 'We don't have time for this.'

'Fuck you!' she spat. She was angry and frightened, and she had good reason to be.

I felt Rachel's presence beside me and Marcy's eyes shifted to her.

'Marcy, there's a man on his way here, a policeman, and he's not coming to protect you,' said Rachel quickly. 'He found out where you were hiding from your parents. He thinks you're a witness to Grace Peltier's death, and we think so too. Now, we can help you, but only if you'll let us.'

She stopped struggling and tried to read the truth of what Rachel was saying from her eyes. Acceptance changed the look on her face, easing the lines that furrowed her brow and dousing the fire in her eyes.

'A policeman killed Grace,' she said simply.

I turned to Louis. 'Get the cars out of sight,' I said.

He nodded and ran back up the hill. Seconds later, the Lexus pulled into the yard above us, hidden from the road by the house itself. The Mustang quickly joined it.

'I think the man who killed Grace is called Lutz,' I told Marcy. 'He's the one who's coming. Are you going to let us help you?'

She nodded mutely. I picked up her bag and handed it to her. As she reached for it, I pulled it out of her grasp.

'No hitting, okay?'

She gave a little frightened smile and said, in agreement, 'No hitting.' We started up the hill to the house.

'It's not just me he wants,' she said quietly.

'What else does he want, Marcy?' I asked.

She swallowed, and that scared look darted into her eyes again. She raised the rucksack.

'He wants the book,' she answered.

As Marcy Becker packed the last of her things, the clothes and cosmetics she had abandoned as she fled from us, she told us about Grace Peltier's last hours. She wouldn't let us look in the rucksack, though. I wasn't sure that she completely trusted us yet.

'She came out of the meeting with the Paragon guy in a real hurry,' she told us. 'She ran straight up to the car, jumped in and started to drive. She was really angry, as angry as I've ever seen her. She just kept swearing all the time, calling him a liar.

'That night, she left me at the motel in Waterville and didn't come back until two or three in the morning. She wouldn't tell me where she'd been, but early the next morning we drove north. She abandoned me – *again* – in Machias and told me to knock myself out. I didn't see her for two days.

'I sat in my room most of the time, drank some beers, watched some TV. At about two A.M. on the second night, I heard this hammering on the door and Grace was there. Her hair was all damp and matted and her clothes were wet. She was really, really pale, like she had seen something that frightened the hell out of her. She told me we had to leave – quickly.

'I put on my clothes, grabbed my rucksack, and we got in the car and started driving. There was a package on the backseat, wrapped in a plastic bag. It looked like a block of dark wood.

' "What is that?" ' I asked her.

' "You don't want to know", was all she told me.

' "Okay, so where are we going?"

' "To see my father." '

Marcy stopped talking, and looked at Louis and me. Louis stood by the window, looking down on the road below.

'We better get going soon,' he warned.

I knew Lutz was on his way, but now that I had got Marcy Becker talking I wanted her to finish.

'Did she say anything else, Marcy?'

'She was kind of hysterical. She said "He's alive," and something about them taking him into town because he'd gotten sick. She'd seen him collapse on the road. That's all she would say. She told me that, for the moment, it was better if I didn't know anything else.

'We'd been driving for maybe an hour. I was dozing on the back seat when Grace shook me awake. As soon as I woke up, I knew we were in trouble. She kept looking in the rearview. There was a cop following us, with lights flashing. Grace just stepped on the gas and tore away until he was out of view, then pulled off the road and told me to get out. I tried to get her to tell me why, but she wouldn't. She just threw me my bag and then handed me the package and all of her study notes and told me to look after them until she contacted me. Then the cop appeared and I opened the door and headed into the bushes to hide. I guess something about the way Grace was acting transferred itself onto me, because now I was scared and I had no reason to be. I mean, what had we done? What had she done? And after all, this guy was a cop, right? Even if she had stolen something, she was maybe going to get in some trouble, but nothing worse.

'Anyway, I could see her trying to start the car, but the

cop walked up to her door and told her to kill the engine. He was your size, smoking a cigarette. He kept his gloves on, even while he smoked. I could hear him talking to her, asking her what she was doing, where she had been. He wouldn't let her get out of the car, just kept leaning over her. I could her him ask her, "Where is it?" again and again, and Grace telling him that she didn't know what he was talking about

'He took her car keys, then made a call on his cell phone. I think it must have been fifteen or twenty minutes before the other guy arrived. He was a big man, with a mustache.'

Marcy began to cry. 'I should have tried to help her, because I knew what was going to happen even before he took out the gun. I just knew. I felt him thinking about it. I saw him climb in and I was going to cry out. I thought he was trying to rape her, but I couldn't do anything, I was so scared. I could hear Grace crying and he hit her on the head to shut her up. After that, he searched the trunk and the rest of the car, then started checking along the road. I moved back, and once I thought he might have heard me, because he stopped and listened before he went back to what he was doing. When he didn't find what he was looking for, he slapped the hood of Grace's car and I heard him swear.'

She paused.

'Then he stepped over to the driver's side with the gun in his hand. He shouted at Grace again, pushing her head with the gun. She reached up to stop him; there was a struggle. The gun went off and the windows turned red. The other policeman started screaming at the big guy, asking him what he thought he was doing and what were they going to do now. But he just told him to be quiet.

'After that, he leaned in and did something to the back of Grace's head. When I saw him again, he had a piece of her hair in his hands and he was looking out at the trees, as if he guessed that I was out there somewhere. I crawled away on my belly. I could see Grace through the windshield, Mr. Parker. Her head was hanging to one side and there was blood all over the inside of the car. She was my friend, and I let her die.'

Rachel reached out and held her hand.

'There was nothing you could have done,' she said softly, and in her voice I heard echoes of my own from the night before. 'Nothing. This man Lutz would have killed you both, and then nobody would have known what happened. But you didn't tell anyone what you saw?'

She shook her head. 'I was going to, until I saw the book. Then I was too scared. I figured the best thing to do was to lie low and stay out of the way of the cops. If they found me, if the man who killed Grace knew what I had seen, then I was afraid that he would do the same thing to me. I rang my mom and told her that something bad had happened to Grace and that I had to stay out of everyone's way until I figured out what to do. I told her not to tell anyone where I was, not even the police. I took the first bus from Ellsworth the next morning and I've been here ever since, apart from one or two trips to the store. I rented the scooter, in case I needed to get away quickly.'

'Were you going to stay here forever, Marcy?' I asked.

She let out a long deep breath. 'I had nowhere else to go,' she said.

'Did she tell you where she had been?'

'No. She mentioned a lighthouse, that's all, but she was completely wired. I mean, she was scared and excited at the same time, you know? She wasn't making a whole lot of sense.'

'And you still have the book, Grace?'

She nodded, and pointed to her knapsack. 'It's in there,' she replied. 'I was keeping it safe.'

Then Louis called my name.

I looked at him.

'They're coming,' he said.

Lutz's white Acura roared up the gravel drive and drew up about twenty yards from the front of the house. Lutz emerged first, closely followed by a small, thin man with close-cropped hair. His eyes were crossed and he wore painter's overalls and rubber gloves. He looked like what Louis used to call a 'puppy drowner,' the kind of guy who wasn't happy unless he was hurting something smaller and weaker than himself. Both men had guns in their hands.

'Guess they want her dead or alive,' I said.

The smaller man opened the trunk of the Acura and removed an empty body bag.

'Nope,' said Louis. 'Looks like they just expressed a preference.'

We drew back as Lutz examined the windows of the house from where he stood. He gestured at the smaller man to head round the back as he started for the front door. I put my finger to my lips and indicated to Rachel that she should take Marcy Becker into the small bedroom and keep her quiet. Louis handed Rachel his SIG, and after a moment's hesitation, she took it. Then, shotgun in hand, he padded silently to the back door of the lodge, opened it, and disappeared to intercept Lutz's associate. I waited until he was outside, then slipped the safety catch on my gun and examined my options.

The front door opened straight into a blank wall. Four feet to the left, the living room began, a tiny kitchen area at the far end. To the right of the living room was the bedroom where Marcy Becker now lay huddled beneath the window with Rachel, so that anyone looking inside would be unable to see them. I raised the gun, walked to the wall where the hall ended and the living area began, and waited, shielded from anyone entering. I heard the handle on the door turn and then a noise like a cannon going off came from the back of the house. There was a thudding noise and Lutz entered fast, gun first. The noise had panicked him and he came in a little too quickly, his gun pointing into the main body of the room and away from me. I moved in hard with my left arm raised to push the gun away and knocked him back against the window, then brought the butt of the Smith & Wesson down as hard as I could on the side of his head. He staggered and I hit him again. He fired a shot into the ceiling and I hit him a third time, driving him to his knees. When he was on the floor I tore the gun from his fingers and tossed it into the kitchen before checking him for a spare. He had none, but I found his cuffs. I hit him one more time for luck, cuffed him, then dragged him outside and onto the gravel. I expected Louis to be there, and he was, but he wasn't alone.

He wasn't even armed.

Instead, he stood with his hands on his head and the big shotgun on the ground in front of him. Behind him loomed the tall, bald figure of the Golem, the Jericho two inches from Louis's head. He had a second Jericho in his left hand, pointing at me, and a length of rope hung across his arm.

'Sorry, man,' said Louis. To his left, Lutz's associate lay dead on his back, a huge hole torn in his chest.

The Golem looked at me, unblinking. 'Put your gun down, Mr. Parker, or I will kill your friend.'

I held the Smith & Wesson out at shoulder length from my body, gripping it by the trigger guard, then laid it gently on the ground before me. Lutz raised his bloodied head and stared dazedly at the bald man. I was gratified to see the look of fear that gradually spread across his face, but it was a small, fleeting pleasure. We were all at risk from this strange, hollow man.

'Now I want you to remove the detective's shoes and socks.' I did as I was told, kneeling on Lutz's legs to keep him still. With a flick of his wrist, the Golem tossed me the rope. 'Tie his legs together.'

Again, I knelt and tied him. All the while, Lutz was whispering to me: 'Don't let him take me, Parker. I'll tell you what you want to know, just don't let him take me.'

The Golem heard him. 'Be quiet, Detective. Mr. Parker and I have reached an accommodation.'

I saw Rachel moving behind the window, and shook my head slightly to indicate that she shouldn't get involved.

'Have we?' I asked.

'I will let you and your friend live, your girlfriend too, and you can take the young woman.' I should have known that nothing would get past this man. 'I take Detective Lutz.'

'No!' shouted Lutz. 'No way, man. He's going to kill me.'

I looked at the Golem, although I hardly needed confirmation that Lutz's fears were justified.

'Detective Lutz is correct,' he said, 'but first he will tell me where to find his associates. Put him in the body bag, Mr. Parker, then you and your friend will carry the bag to my car.'

I didn't move. I wasn't prepared to give up Lutz without first learning what he knew.

'We both want the same thing,' I said. 'We both want to find the people responsible for these deaths.'

The Jerichos both cocked simultaneously beneath his thumbs. There was to be no discussion.

After a struggle, we put Lutz in the body bag, stuck his socks in his mouth to silence him, and carried him down the road to where the Golem's Lincoln Continental stood. We opened the Continental's trunk and put Lutz inside before slamming the door closed on him with the hollow finality of a coffin lid being sealed. I could hear his muffled howls through the metal and the sound of his feet kicking against the sides of the trunk.

'Now, start walking back to the house, please,' said the Golem.

We stepped back and began walking slowly backward toward the house, never once taking our eyes off the bald man with the guns.

'I don't think we will be meeting again, Mr. Parker,' he said.

'I won't take it personally.'

He waited until we were fifty yards from the car, then walked quickly to the driver's door, got in, and drove away. Beside me, Louis released a long breath.

'That went well,' I said. 'Although your professional reputation took something of a beating.'

Louis scowled. 'You know, used to take me months to set up a hit. You give me five damn minutes. I ain't no James Bond.'

'Don't sweat it. He doesn't seem like the kind of guy who's going to tell.'

'Guess not. Still, cool name.'

We walked quickly back to the house. Rachel came out onto the porch to meet us. The blood had drained from her face, and I thought that she was going to faint.

'Rachel?' I said, my hands gripping her shoulders. 'What is it?'

She looked up at me.

'See for yourself,' she whispered.

I found Marcy Becker sitting in one of the big armchairs, her legs curled into her body. She was looking at the wall, tearing at one of her fingernails with her teeth. She glanced at me, then her eyes flicked to what lay on the floor before she returned her gaze quickly to the blank wall. We stayed in those positions for what seemed like a long, long time, until I felt Louis behind me and heard him swear softly as he saw what lay before us.

It was a book.

A book of bones.

Part Four

A great book is like great evil.

Callimachus (c. 305 – c. 240 B.C.)

Chapter Twenty-five

The book was about fourteen inches long and seven inches wide. Six small bones curled horizontally across its spine in three equidistant sets of two. They were slightly yellow and coated with some form of preservative that made them gleam in the sunlight. I wasn't certain, but I thought they might once have been the ends of ribs. They felt slick to the touch compared to the texture of the material upon which they lay. The cover of the book had been dyed a deep red, through which lines and wrinkles showed. Close to the top left-hand corner, a raised mole stood.

It was human skin. It had been dried, then sewn together in patches, using what appeared to be tendon and gut for stitching. When I moved my fingers gently over the cover, I felt not only the pores and lines of the derma used to construct it but also the shapes of the bones that formed the framework beneath: radius and ulna, I suspected, and probably more ribs. It was as if the book itself had once been a living thing, skin over bone, lacking only flesh and blood to make it whole again.

There was no writing on either the cover or the spine, no indication of what the book might contain. The only marking was the cover illustration, Jansenist in style with its single central motif repeated in each of the four corners. It was a spider, indented in gold leaf, its eight legs curled inward to hold a golden key.

Using only the tips of my fingers, I opened the book. Its spine was a human spine, held together with gold wire, the only material used that did not appear to have come from a human body. The pages had been attached to it using more tendon. The inside covers had not been dyed, and the differentiations in the pigments of the various skins used in its construction could be more clearly divined. From the top of the spine a bookmark curled down, constructed from lengths of human hair tightly bound, scavenged from bodies that, for reasons of discretion and concealment, could not be marked in more obvious ways.

There were about thirty pages of varying sizes in the book. Two or three were constructed from single patches of skin, twice as large as the book itself. These had been folded, then bound through the fold, creating a double page; other pages had been made up from smaller sections of skin sewn carefully together, some of them no bigger than two or three square inches. The pages varied in thickness; one was so thin that the color of my hand showed through beneath, but others were more thickly layered. Most appeared to be sections taken from the lower back or shoulders, although one page showed the strange sunken hole of a human navel and another bore, close to its center, a shrunken nipple. Like the bifolia of old, the parchments made from goatskin and calfskin used by medieval scribes, one side of the page was smooth where any remaining body hair had been rubbed off, while the other was rough. The smooth sides had been used for the illustrations and the script, so that on some double pages only the right-hand side was filled.

On page after page, in beautiful ornate script, were sections from the book of Revelation; some were complete chapters, others simply quotes used to elaborate upon the meaning of the illustrations contained in the book. The writing was Carolingian in origin, a version of the beautiful clear script inspired by the Anglo-Saxon scholar Alcuin of York, with each italic letter being given its own distinct but simple shape to aid legibility. Faulkner had worked around the natural flaws and holes of the skin, disguising them, where necessary, with a suitable letter or ornamentation. The capital letters on each page were uncials, each one an inch high and carefully created from hundreds of individual pen strokes. Animal and human grotesques cavorted around their bases and stems.

But it was the illustrations that drew the eye. There were echoes of Dürer and Duvet in them, of Blake and Cranach and later artists too: Goerg and Meidner and Masereel. They were not copies of the original illustrations, but variations on a theme. Some were painted in ornate colors, while others used only carbon black mixed with iron gall to create a dense ink that stood out from the page. A version of Hell Mouth drawn from the Winchester Psalter marked the first page, hundreds of tiny bodies twisting in what looked like the jaws of a creature half man, half fish. A greenish tint had been added to the human figures so that they stood out from the skin on which they had been inscribed, and the scales of the fish were marked individually in shades of blue and red. Elswhere, there were Cranach's four horsemen in red and black; Burgkmair's *Harvest of the World* in tones of green and gold; a vision of an arachnid beast, inspired by the twentieth-century artist Edouard Goerg, beside the words 'The beast that ascendeth out of the bottomless pit shall make war against them, and shall overcome them all, and kill them'; and a richly detailed variation on Duvet's frontispiece for his 1555 Apocalypse, depicting St. John against a backdrop of a great city, surrounded by emblems of death, including a swan with an arrow in its mouth.

I flicked forward to the last completed illustration, which accompanied a quotation from Revelation 10:10: 'And I took the little book out of the angel's hand, and ate it up; and it was in my mouth sweet as honey: and as soon as I had eaten it, my belly was bitter.' Inspired by Dürer, the illustration depicted, once again, St. John, a sword in one hand as he consumed a representation of the very book I now held in my hand, the human spine and the spider with the key clearly visible as he fed it to himself. An angel watched him, its feet pillars of fire, its head like the sun.

St. John had been drawn in black ink, and enormous effort had been expended in detailing the expression on his face. It was a representation of Faulkner as he was in his younger days and in the picture I had seen in the newspaper following the discovery of the bodies to the north. I could see the same high brow, the same sunken cheeks and almost feminine mouth, the same straight, dark brows. He was swathed in a long white cloak, his left hand raising the sword toward the sky above.

Faulkner was in every illustration. He was one of the four horsemen; he was the jaws of hell; he was St. John; he was the beast. Faulkner: judging, tormenting, consuming, killing; creating a book that was both a record of punishment and a punishment in itself; an unveiling and a concealing of the truth; a vanity and a mockery of vanities; a work of art and an act of cannibalism. This was his life's work, begun when the human weaknesses of his followers displayed themselves and he turned against them, destroying them all with the aid of his brood: the men first, then the women, and finally the children. As he had begun, so he had continued, and the fallen had become part of his great book.

In the bottom right-hand corner of each page, like marginalia, were written names. The pages constructed of a single sheet of skin bore only one name, while those made up of a number of sections contained two, three, or sometimes four names. James Jessop's name was on the third fragment of skin, his mother's on the fourth, and his father's on the fifth. The rest of the Aroostook Baptists took up the majority of the book's entries, but there were other names too, names that I did not recognize, some of them comparatively recent, judging by the color of the ink on the skin. Alison Beck's name was not among them. Neither was Al Z's, or Epstein's, or Mickey Shine's. They would all have been added later, once the book had been retrieved, just as

Grace Peltier's name would also have been written, and perhaps my own as well.

I thought back to Jack Mercier and the book I had been shown in his study, the three double spine markings now transformed from gold to bone. A craftsman like Faulkner would not simply have ceased to make the books he loved so much. The copy presented to Carter Paragon was proof of that. Now it was clear that Faulkner had a wider vision: the creation of a text whose form perfectly mirrored its subject, a book about damnation made up of the bodies of the damned, a record of judgment composed of the remains of those who had been judged.

And Grace had found him. Deborah Mercier, jealous of her husband's first daughter, had told her of the existence of the new Apocalypse and its source. By then, Jack Mercier had already commenced his moves against the Fellowship, recruiting Ober, Beck, and Epstein to his cause, but Grace couldn't have known that, because it was more than Deborah Mercier would have been willing to tell her. She would put Grace at risk, but not her husband.

Grace had confronted Paragon with her knowledge of the sale of the Apocalypse, but Paragon was simply a dupe, and Grace, clever woman, must have guessed it. He would have been afraid to tell Pudd and Faulkner that he had sold the book, but he would also have been too afraid to tell them nothing of Grace's visit. And so Grace had watched him and waited for him to panic. Did she follow him north, or wait for them to come to him? I suspected the latter if Paragon had died because he could not tell the Golem of their hiding place. Whatever had occurred, Grace had somehow found her way to the very gates of Faulkner's own, private hell. And then, when the opportunity arose, she made her way in and managed to escape with the book, a book that contained the truth about the fate of the Aroostook Baptists and, in particular, Elizabeth Jessop. Its theft had forced the Fellowship to respond quickly; while Pudd and the others searched for it, they set about eliminating all those who were moving against them and for whom the work stolen by Grace Peltier would have been a powerful weapon, a task that assumed a new urgency with the discovery of the bodies at St. Froid Lake.

I closed the book, laid it carefully in its packaging, then ran my hands under the kitchen faucet. When I had cleaned them thoroughly I picked up a towel and turned to face Rachel and Louis.

'Looks like we got a whole new definition of the word "crazy,"' muttered Louis. 'You know what that thing supposed to be?'

'It's a record,' I replied. 'A journal of deaths, and maybe more than that. It's an account of the damned, the opposite of the book of life. The Aroostook Baptists are in there, and at least a dozen other names, male and female, all used to create a new Apocalypse.

'And Faulkner made it. His remains weren't among those found at the grave site; neither were his son's or those of his daughter. They killed those people, all of them, then used parts of them to create his book. I think the other names are those of people who've had the misfortune to cross the Fellowship at some time, or who posed a threat. Eventually, parts of Grace and Curtis Peltier, Yossi Epstein, and maybe a piece of Jack Mercier and the others on the boat would have been added, once the book had been retrieved. It would have to be as complete a record as possible, otherwise it would have no meaning.'

'I take it you're using "meaning" in the loosest possible sense,' said Rachel. Her disgust was obvious.

I was rubbing my hands red on the towel yet still feeling the taint of the book upon me. 'Its meaning doesn't matter,' I said. 'This thing is a confession to murder, if it can be traced back to Faulkner.'

'If we can find him,' added Louis. 'What's going to happen when Lutz don't report back?'

'Then he'll send someone else, probably Pudd, to find out what happened. He can't let this book remain out in the world. That's assuming that our friend with the bald head doesn't get to him first.'

I thought of what I knew, or suspected, of Faulkner's hiding place. I knew now that it was to the north, beyond Bangor, close to the coast, and near a lighthouse. There were maybe sixty lighthouses on the Maine coast, most of them automated or unmanned, with a couple given over to civilian use. Of those, probably only a handful were north of Machias.

I knelt down and took the wrapped book in my hands.

'What are you going to do with it?' asked Rachel.

'Nothing,' I replied. 'Not yet.'

She moved closer to me and held my gaze. 'You want to find him, don't you? You're not prepared to let the police do it.'

'He had Lutz and Voisine working for him,' I explained, 'and Voisine is still out there somewhere. There could be others as well. If we hand this over to the police and even one of them shares Lutz's loyalties, then Faulkner will be alerted and he'll be gone forever. My guess is that he's already preparing to disappear. He's probably been planning it ever since the moment the book was lost and certainly since the discovery of the bodies at St. Froid. For that reason, and for Marcy's safety, we're going to keep this to ourselves for the present. Marcy?'

She picked up her bag and stood expectantly.

'We're going to put you somewhere safe. You can call your parents and let them know you're okay first.'

She nodded. I went outside and called the Colony on the cell phone. Amy answered.

'It's Charlie Parker,' I said. 'I need your help. I have a woman here. I need to stow her out of sight.'

There was silence on the other end of the phone. 'What kind of trouble are we talking about?'

But I think she knew.

'I'm close to him, Amy. I can bring this to an end.'

When she answered, I could hear the resignation in her

voice. 'She can stay in the house.' Women, with the obvious exception of Amy herself, were not usually admitted to the Colony, but there were spare bedrooms in the main house that were sometimes used under exceptional circumstances.

'Thank you. There will be a man with her. He'll be armed.'

'You know how we feel about guns here, Charlie.'

'I know, but this is Pudd we're dealing with. I want you to let my friend stay with Marcy until this is over. It'll be a day or two at most.'

I asked her to take Rachel in as well. She agreed, and I hung up. Marcy made a short call to her mother and then we drove away from the house and into Boothbay. There, we parted. Louis and Rachel would drive south to Scarborough, where Angel would take Marcy Becker and a reluctant Rachel to the Colony. Louis would rejoin me once Marcy and Rachel were in Angel's care. I kept the book, concealing it carefully beneath the passenger seat of the Mustang.

I drove north as far as Bangor, where I picked up a copy of Thompson's *Maine Lighthouses* at Betts Bookstore on Main Street. There were seven lighthouses in the Bold Coast area around Machias, the town in which Marcy Becker had been left while Grace went about her business: Whitlock's Mill in Calais; East Quoddy at Campobello Island; and farther south, Mulholland Light, West Quoddy, Lubec Channel, Little River, and Machias Seal Island. Machias Seal was too far out to sea to be relevant, which left six.

I called Ross in New York, hoping to light a fire under him, but got only his secretary. I was twenty miles outside Bangor when he called me back.

'I've seen CHARON's reports from Maine,' he began. 'This part of the investigation was minor stuff, pure legwork. A gay rights activist was killed in the Village in nineteen ninety-one, shot to death in the toilet of a bar on Bleecker; MO matched a similar shooting in Miami. The perp was apprehended but his phone records showed that he made seven calls to the Fellowship in the days preceding the killing. A woman called Torrance told Charon that the guy was a freak and she reported the calls to the local police. A detective named Lutz confirmed that.'

So, if the killer had been working for the Fellowship, they had a cover story. They had reported him to the police before the murder, and Lutz, already their pet policeman, had confirmed it.

'What happened to the killer?'

'His name was Lusky, Barrett Lusky. He made bail and was found dead two days later in a Dumpster in Queens. Gunshot wound to the head.

'Now, according to Charon's report, he went no farther north than Waterville during his enquiries. But there's an anomaly; his expenses show a claim for gas purchased in a place called Lubec, about a hundred and fifty miles farther north of Waterville. It's on the coast.'

'Lubec,' I echoed. It made sense.

'What's in Lubec?' asked Ross.

'Lighthouses,' I answered. 'And a bridge.'

Lubec had three lighthouses. It was also the easternmost town in the United States. From there, the FDR Memorial Bridge stretched across the water to Canada. Lubec was a good choice of location if you needed an escape route left permanently open, because there was a whole new country only minutes away by car or boat. They were in Lubec. I was certain of it, and the Traveling Man had found them there. The gas receipt was careless, but only in the context of what came later and the murders he himself committed, using a strange justification based on human frailty and inconsequence that mirrored some of Faulkner's own beliefs.

But I had underestimated Faulkner, and I had underestimated Pudd. While I closed in on them, they had already taken the most vulnerable one among us, the only one left alone.

They took Angel.

Chapter Twenty-six

There was blood on the porch, and blood on the front door. In the kitchen, cracks radiated through the plaster from a bullet hole in the wall. There was more blood in the hallway, a curving snake trail like the pattern of a sidewinder. The kitchen door had been torn almost off its hinges, and the kitchen window had been shattered by more gunfire.

There were no bodies inside.

Taking Angel was partly a precaution in case we found Marcy Becker first, but also an act of revenge against me personally. They had probably come to finish us off, and when they found only Angel, they took him instead. I thought of Mr. Pudd and the mute with their hands on him, his blood on their clothes and skin as they dragged him from the house. We should never have left him alone. None of us should ever have been alone.

They would never let him live, of course. In the end they would never let any of us live. If they escaped and disappeared from our sight I knew that one day they would reemerge and find us. We could hunt them, but the honeycomb world is deep and intricate and rich with darkness. There are too many places to hide. And so there would be weeks, months, perhaps years of pain and fear, waking from uneasy sleep to each new dawn with the thought that this, at last, might be the day on which they came.

Because, finally, we would want them to come, so that the waiting might be brought to an end.

I could hear the sound of a car engine in the background as Rachel told me all that she had seen. She was driving Marcy Becker to the Colony in her own car; now that they had Angel, she was safe for a time. Louis was on his way north and would call me within minutes.

'He's not dead,' said Rachel evenly.

'I know,' I replied. 'If he was dead they'd have left him for us to find.'

I wondered how quickly Lutz had talked and if the Golem had reached them yet. If he had, all of this might be immaterial.

'Is Marcy okay?' I asked.

'She's asleep on the seat beside me. I don't think she's slept much since Grace died. She wanted to know why you were willing to risk your life for this: Angel, Louis, me, but you especially. She said it wasn't your fight.'

'What did you tell her?'

'It was Louis who told her. He said that everything was your fight. I think he was smiling. It's kind of hard to tell with him.'

'I know where they are, Rachel. They're in Lubec.'

Her voice had tightened a notch when she spoke again. 'Then you take care.'

'I always take care,' I replied.

'No, you don't.'

'OK, you're right, but I mean it this time.'

I was just beyond Bangor. Lubec was about another 120 miles away along U.S. 1. I could do it in less than two hours, assuming no eagle-eyed lawman decided to haul me over for speeding. I put my foot on the gas and felt the Mustang surge forward.

Louis called when I was passing Ellsworth Falls, heading down 1A to the coast.

'I'm in Waterville,' he said.

'I think they're in Lubec,' I replied. 'It's on the

northern coast, close to New Brunswick. You've a ways to go yet.'

'They call you?'

'Nothing.'

'Wait for me at the town limits,' he replied. His tone was neutral. He could have been advising me not to forget to pick up milk.

At Milbridge, maybe eighty miles from Lubec, the cell phone rang for the third time. This time I noticed that the ID of the caller was concealed as I pressed the answer button.

'Mr. Parker,' said Pudd's voice.

'Is he alive?'

'Barely. I'd say hopes for his recovery are fading fast. He seriously injured my associate.'

'Good for him, Leonard.'

'I couldn't let it go unpunished. He bled quite a lot. In fact, he's still bleeding quite a lot.' He snickered unpleasantly. 'So you've worked out our little family tree. It's not pretty, is it?'

'Not particularly.'

'You have the book?'

He knew that Lutz had failed. I wondered if he knew why and if the shadow of the Golem was already almost upon him.

'Yes.'

'Where are you?'

'Augusta,' I said.

I could have cried with relief when he seemed to believe me.

'There's a private road off Route nine, where it crosses the Machias River,' said Pudd. 'It leads to Lake Machias. Be at the lakeshore in ninety minutes, alone and with the book. I'll give you whatever is left of your friend. If you're late, or if I smell police, I'll skewer him from his anus to his mouth like a spit pig.' He hung up.

I wondered how Pudd planned to kill me when I reached the lake. He couldn't let me live, not after all that had taken place. And ninety minutes wasn't enough time to reach Machias from Augusta, not on these roads. He had no intention of bringing Angel there alive.

I called Louis. It was a test of trust, and I wasn't certain how he would respond. I was closest to Lubec; there was no way that Louis could get there before Pudd's deadline ran out. If I was wrong about Lubec, then somebody would have to be at the rendezvous point to meet him. It would have to be Louis.

The pause before he agreed was barely detectable.

Chapter Twenty-seven

Three wooden lighthouses decorated the sign at the outskirts of the town of Lubec: the white-and-red Mulholland Light across the Lubec Channel in New Brunswick; the white Lubec Channel Light, a spark-plug-style cast iron structure out on the Lubec Channel; and the red-and-white striped West Quoddy Light at Quoddy Head State Park. They were symbols of stability and certainty, a promise of safety and salvation now potentially corrupted by the stain of the Faulkners' presence.

After a brief stop at the edge of the town, I drove on, past the boarded-up frame of the old Hillside Restaurant and the white American Legion building, until I came to Lubec itself. It was a town filled with churches; the White Ridge Baptists, the First Assembly of God, the Seventh Day Adventists, the Congregational Christians, and the Christian Temple Disciples had all converged on this place, burying their dead in the nearby town cemetery or erecting memorials to those lost at sea. Grace Peltier had been right, I thought; I had only glanced at the thesis notes Marcy had given me, but I had noted Grace's use of the term 'frontier' to describe the state of Maine. Here, at the easternmost point of the state and the country, surrounded by churches and the bones of the dead, it was possible to feel that this was the very end of things.

On the waterfront, seabirds sat on the dilapidated pier, its walkway sealed off with *Private Property* notices. There was a stone breakwater to the left, and to the right, a congregation of buildings, among them the old McMurdy's Smokehouse, which was in the process of being restored. Across the water, the Mulholland Light was visible, the FDR Memorial Bridge extending toward it across the water of the Lubec Narrows.

It was already growing dark as I drove up Pleasant Street, the waterfront on my left, to a dirt lot beside the town's wastewater treatment facility. From there, a small trail led down to the shore. I followed it, stepping over seaweed and rocks, discarded beer cans and cigarette packs, until I stood on the beach. It was mainly stones and marram grass, with some gray sand exposed. Beyond, the Lubec Channel Light scythed through the encroaching darkness.

Maybe half a mile to my right, a stone causeway reached into the sea. At the end was a small island covered in trees, their branches like the black spires of churches set against the lighter tones of the evening sky. A dull green light shone between the trees in places, and I could see the brighter white lights of an outbuilding close to the northern side of the island.

There were three lighthouses on Lubec's sign, for only three lighthouses were still in existence. But there had once been another: a stone structure built on the northern shore of the Quoddy Narrows by a local Baptist minister as a symbol of God's light as well as a warning to mariners. It was a flawed, imperfect structure, and had collapsed during a heavy gale in 1804, killing the minister's son who was acting as lighthouse keeper. Two years later, concerned citizens nominated West Quoddy Head, farther down the coast, as a more suitable position, and in 1806 Thomas Jefferson had ordered the construction of a rubblestone lighthouse on the spot. The Northern Light was largely forgotten, and now the island on which it lay was in private ownership.

All of this I learned from a woman in McFadden's

variety store and gas station on the way into town. She said the people on the island kept themselves pretty much to themselves, but they were believed to be religious folk. There was an old man who took ill sometimes and had to be treated by the doctor in town, and two younger people, a man and a woman. The younger man shopped in the store sometimes, but always paid with cash.

She knew his name, though.

He was called Monker.

Ed Monker.

It had begun to rain, a harbinger of the coastal storm that was set to sweep northern Maine that night, and heavy drops hammered on me as I stood watching the causeway. I got back in the car and took the road to Quoddy Head Park until I saw a small, unmarked private drive heading down to the coast. I killed my lights and followed the trail until it petered out among thick trees. I left the car and walked through the grass, using the trees for cover, until the trail ended. Ahead of me was a barred gate with high fencing on either side and a camera mounted on the gatepost. The fence was electrified. Beyond it was a small locked shack in the middle of a copse of pines. Through the branches, the Lubec Channel Light was visible. I could guess at what was in the shack: an old iron bath with a toilet beside it and the corpses of spiders decaying in the drain.

I took my flashlight from the glove compartment and, shielding the light with my hand, shadowed the fence. I spotted two motion sensors within fifty feet, the grass cropped low around them. I figured there were probably more among the trees themselves. As the rain soaked my hair and skin, I stayed with the fence until I found myself at the top of a steep incline leading back down to the shore. The tide was rolling in and the base of the causeway was now covered in water. The only way to get to the island without getting drenched, or maybe even washed away, was through those gates and along the causeway, but to take that route would be to alert those on the island to my approach.

Grace Peltier must have stood here, weeks earlier, before she scaled the gates and walked onto the causeway. She must have waited until they were gone, until she was certain that the island was unoccupied and that nobody would be returning for some time, and then crossed over. Except she had activated the sensors, alerting them to an intruder, and the system would have informed Pudd or his sister, automatically calling a pager or his cell phone. When they returned, closing off the causeway, Grace had taken to the sea. That was why her clothes had been soaked with seawater. She was a strong swimmer. She knew she could make it. But they had seen her face on the camera's tapes, maybe even spotted her car. Lutz and Voisine had been alerted, and the trap was closed on Grace.

I looked out on the dark waves, glowing whitely as they broke, and decided to take my chances with the sea. I unloaded the spare .38 at my ankle, ziplocked the bullets, then checked the safety on the Smith & Wesson beneath my arm. Something tightened in my belly, and the old feeling came over me again. The sea before me was a dark pool, the hidden place on which I had drawn time and time before, and I was about to plunge into it once more.

I waded through the water, teeth chattering as I approached the causeway. Waves rocked me and once or twice I was almost pushed back to the shore by their force. The stones and rocks that made up the causeway were slick and spotted with green algae, and the tide was already splashing almost to the level of my waist. I tried to wedge my boots into the cracks and hollows, but the rocks had been bound with cement, and after only two awkward sideways movements, my feet slid from under me and I lost my grip. I slid quickly back into the sea, the water drenching me to my chin. As I recovered from the shock, a line of white emerged to my left and I barely had time to take a breath before a huge wave lifted me off my feet and pushed me back at least five yards, salt water filling my mouth as the rain fell and seaweed twisted around me.

When the wave had passed, I began to wade again along the edge of the rocks, trying to find a point at which I could pull myself back onto the road. It took me about ten minutes and two more dousings to find a hollow where one of the stones had fallen from the concrete. Awkwardly, I placed a wet boot into the alcove, then barked my knee painfully as it slipped out. Digging my fingers around one of the highest stones, I tried again and managed to haul myself onto the road. I lay there for a moment, catching my breath and shivering. My cell phone, I discovered, was now at the bottom of the sea. I stood, let the water run out of the barrel of the Smith & Wesson, reloaded the .38, and continued on down the causeway at a crouch until I reached the island.

Thick green firs grew on either side of the road as it made its way to the remains of the lighthouse, where the road became part of a gravel courtyard that touched on the entrance to each of the island's structures. There should have been nothing more than a pile of old stones where the original lighthouse had once stood, but instead I found an edifice about thirty feet high, with an open gallery at the top surrounded by a chain-link fence, offering a clear view of the causeway and the coast itself. It was a lighthouse without a light, except for a faint illumination in one of the windows at the highest enclosed level.

To the right of the new lighthouse stood a long wooden single-story building with four square windows covered with wire frame, two on either side of the heavy door. A greenish glow emanated from it, as if the light inside was struggling to penetrate water or the leaves of plants. In front of the lighthouse, blocking my view of its entrance, was what I took to be a garage. Farther back, almost at the eastern edge of the island, was a second similar structure, possibly a boathouse. I leaned against the back of the garage and listened, but I could hear nothing except the steady falling of the rain. Staying on the grass and using the building as a shield, I began to make my way toward the lighthouse.

It was only when I cleared the garage that I saw him. Two tree trunks had been bound together to form an *X*, supported in turn by a second pair of trunks that kept the cross at an angle of sixty degrees to the ground. He was naked, and his arms and legs had been bound to the wood with wire. There was a lot of bruising to his face and his upper body, and swellings on his arms, chest, and legs that looked like the result of bites. Blood had flowed from the wounds in his femoral arteries and pooled on the ground below him. The rain washed over his pale body, dripped from the soft flesh on his arms and glistened on his bare skull and white, hairless face. A patch of skin was missing from his stomach. I moved closer to him and checked his pulse, his skin still warm to the touch. The Golem was dead.

I was about to leave him when gravel crunched to my right and the mute appeared. There was mud on her boots and her loose denim jeans, and she wore a yellow windbreaker, which hung open over a dark sweater. She held a gun in her right hand, pointing to the ground. There was no time for me to hide, even if I wanted to.

She stopped short when she saw me, her mouth opened soundlessly, and she raised her arm and fired. I dived left. Beside me, the Golem's body shuddered slightly as the bullet struck his shoulder, close to where my head had been. I knelt, sighted, and squeezed the trigger. My first shot took her in the neck, the second in the chest. She twisted, her legs wrapped themselves around each other, and she fell, loosing off two shots into the air as she hit the ground. I ran to her, keeping the gun trained on her body, and kicked her Beretta away from her right hand. Her left leg was trembling uncontrollably. She looked up at me, the scars on her neck now obscured by the blood flowing from her wound. Something rattled in her throat, her mouth opened and closed twice, and then she died.

In the outbuilding to my right, a shape distorted the flow

of green light for an instant. A thin shadow passed across the glass and I knew instinctively that Mr. Pudd was waiting inside for me. He could not have failed to have heard the shots, yet he hadn't responded. Behind me the door of the lighthouse remained securely closed, but when I looked to the top of the building, the light that had been burning was now burning no longer. In the darkness it seemed to me that something was watching me closely. Pudd would have to be dealt with first, I thought; I did not want him at my back.

Quickly, my hands brushing the wet grass, I ran to the door of the outbuilding. There was a small glass panel at about face level, criss-crossed with wire, and I stayed low as I passed beneath it. A bolt had been pulled across midway down the door, and a lock hung open beneath it. Stepping to one side, I eased my foot against the crack and pushed the door open.

Three shots sounded and the door frame exploded in showers of splinters and flaking paint. I jammed my gun into the gap and fired five times in an arcing pattern, then threw myself into the room. I could still hear glass falling as I sprinted to the far left wall, but no more shots came. Working quickly, I ejected the magazine from the Smith & Wesson and replaced it with a full clip, scanning the room while my hands worked at the gun.

The stench was incredible, a powerful smell of decay and defecation. There were no lights on the ceiling or on the walls, and the single skylight had been draped with folds of thick cotton to prevent direct sunlight from falling on the room. Instead, the only illumination came from small shielded bulbs set below the metal shelves that ran in five rows across the width of the room. The shelves had four levels, and the green tint to the light came from plants that grew in pots alongside the glass cases that rested on each shelf. Every case or cage on the shelves had a thermometer and a humidity gauge, and dimmer switches had been placed in series with the lightbulbs to reduce the intensity of their radiant heat. Aluminum foil had been used to partially shield the bulbs, protecting the spiders and insects in the terrariums from direct light, while the use of foliage further softened the glare. The bulbs were not powerful enough to penetrate to the farthest corners of the room, where thick pools of darkness lay. Somewhere among them, Pudd waited, his form hidden by the shadows and the greenery.

A sound came from close to where my hand rested on the ground, a soft tapping on the stone floor. I looked to my left and saw, resting in a small arc of green light, a dark, semicircular shape, its body perhaps an inch and a half long and its spiny legs, it seemed, at least as long again. Instinctively, I yanked my hand away. The spider tensed, then raised its first pair of legs and exposed a set of reddish jaws.

Suddenly, and with surprising speed, it moved toward me, its legs almost a blur and the rhythm of the tapping increasing. I backed away, but it kept coming as I lashed out with my foot and felt it connect with something soft. I kicked again with the toe of my boot and the spider tumbled away into the far recesses of the room, where some empty glass cases lay piled untidily upon one another.

In my panic, I had moved almost to the aisle between the first and second lines of shelves. To my right, shards of glass caught the light and the remains of a case shattered by my 10-millimeter bullets lay in pieces on the second level. A square of card, heat-sealed in plastic, was among the glass fragments on the floor. In ornate black script were written the words *Phoneutria nigriventer* and then, in English below, *Brazilian wandering spider*. I glanced back toward the shadows into which the aggressive brown spider had bounced, and shuddered.

From far to my right came the sound of something brushing against the leaves of a plant, and the shadows on the ceiling rearranged themselves briefly. Pudd now knew where I was. The sounds of my frantic kicks at the spider had alerted him. I found that my left hand was trembling, so I used it to double-grip my gun. If I couldn't see it shaking, then I could convince myself that I wasn't afraid. Slowly, I moved to the second row of shelves, took a deep breath, and glanced into the aisle.

It was empty. Beside my left eye, a shape shifted in a case. It was small, maybe just over an inch in total, with a broad red stripe running along its abdomen. White spherical egg sacs, almost as big as the spider herself, hung suspended in the web that surrounded her. *Latrodectus hasselti*, read the card: *Red-back spider*. Starting a family too, I thought. How sweet. Shame Pop probably wouldn't be alive to see the birth.

Two more cases lay shattered beside each other in the third row. Amid the sharp edges, a long green shape stood motionless. The mantid's huge eyes seemed to stare right at me as its jaws worked busily on the remains of the occupant of the adjoining case. Small brown legs moved weakly as the huge insect chomped away. I didn't feel sorry for whatever the mantid was consuming. As far as I was concerned, the sooner it finished its appetizer and got busy with some of the main courses wandering the floor, the better.

My skin was crawling, and I had to fight the urge to brush at my hair and neck, so I was partly distracted as I stepped into the next aisle. I looked to my left and saw Mr. Pudd standing at the far end, his gun raised. I threw myself forward and the bullet hit the fuse box beside the door. Sparks flew and the lights died as I rolled on the floor and came to rest against the far wall, the gun raised before me, my left hand now supporting myself on the ground for only as long as it took me to realize that something soft was crawling across it. I lifted it quickly and shook it, but not before I felt a sharp bite, like twin needles being inserted beneath my skin. I rose quickly, my lips drawn back from my teeth in disgust, and examined my hand in the dim light that filtered through the windows. Just below the knuckle of my middle finger, a small red lump was already beginning to form.

In a pair of large plastic aquariums to my right, thousands of small bodies moved. From the first aquarium came the chirping of crickets. The second contained oatmeal and bran flakes across which tiny mealworms crawled, speckled with some small black beetles that had already grown to their mature stage. To my left, arrayed along the wall in a long, multilayered display cabinet, were what looked like row upon row of plastic cups. I leaned down and made out a small black-and-red shape at the base of each cup, the remains of crickets and fruit flies lying in the ugly web beside the spider. The smell was particularly strong here, so strong that I started to gag.

This was Mr. Pudd's black widow farm.

My ears rang from the sound of the shots and there were spots before my eyes from the muzzle flare as I returned my attention to the room itself. A long shadow trailed along the ceiling, heading away from me. Through the leaves I caught a glimpse of what might have been Pudd's tan shirt, and I fired. There was a grunt of pain and the sound of glass breaking as the empty cases in that corner tumbled to the ground. I heard the glass grinding beneath his feet as he stepped over them. He was now at the far wall, close to where I had started, and I knew then what I had to do.

The shelves were not bolted to the cement floor. Instead, they rested on tripod legs, the weight of the frame and the cases it supported insurance enough against any casual impact. Ignoring the spreading pain in my hand and the possibility that the spider responsible might still be close by, I lowered myself to the ground, braced my back against the wall beside the racks of widows, and pushed at the shelf with the soles of my feet. For a moment I thought that it might just move across the floor, but then the top row tilted and the heavy frame fell slowly away from me, impacting loudly on the next shelf and creating a domino effect; two, three, four shelves fell, accompanied by the sounds of breaking glass and grinding metal, and then their combined weight collapsed on the final shelf, and I heard a sound that might have been a man's voice before it was lost in the final tumultous roar of metal and glass.

By then I was already on my feet, using the frames of the fallen shelves to keep off the floor. I was conscious of movement all around me as predatory, multilegged things began to crawl and fight, hunt and die. I reached the door and pushed it open, the feel of the sea breeze and the cold rain beautiful after the stale, rotten smell of the insects and spiders. The door slammed behind me and I jammed the bolt home, then stepped back. My hand was throbbing now and the swelling had increased in size, but it didn't feel too bad. Still, it would need a shot, and the sooner the better.

From inside the bug house, I heard sounds of movement. I raised my gun and aimed. A face appeared at the glass screen, and the door shook as Mr. Pudd hurled his body against it. His eyes were huge, one of them already filling with blood, and a muscle in his cheek was spasming. Tiny brown spiders, each only a fraction of an inch in length, crawled across his face and lost themselves in his hair as a large black spider with thin, skeletal legs pursued them relentlessly. Then Pudd's mouth opened and two legs appeared at each corner, pushing his lips apart, and I glimpsed palps moving inside and a cluster of dark eyes as the spider emerged from his mouth. I turned away for an instant and when I looked back, Pudd was gone.

A low thudding sound came from behind me, and the door to the lighthouse slammed softly against its frame. I was soaked through and starting to feel the cold desperately, but I wiped the rain from my eyes and made my way toward the lighthouse.

The floor inside the door was flagged with stone and an iron staircase wound up to the top of the structure. There were no levels between where I stood and the open platform at the top of the lighthouse, through which a small panel allowed access to the exposed gallery.

At my feet, a trapdoor stood open. It was made of heavy oak bound with iron, and below it a flight of stone steps led into a patch of bright yellow light.

I had found the entrance to the honeycomb world.

I took each step slowly, my gun aimed below me. The final step led into a concrete bunker, furnished with armchairs and an old couch. A small dining table stood in the far corner, on a worn Persian rug. To my right was a narrow galley-style kitchen, separated from the main room by a pair of saloon doors. Wire-rimmed lights hung from the ceiling. A set of shelves in one corner lay empty, a box filled with books and newspapers on the floor beside it. There was a smell of wax polish in the air. The tabletop gleamed, as did the shelves and the breakfast counter.

But it was the walls that drew the eye; every available space, every inch from corner to corner, ceiling to floor, had been illustrated. There were Kohnlike impressions of death upon a dark horse; images of war victims inspired by Dix and Goerg; cities crumbling in a fury of reds and yellows as in Meidner's apocalyptic landscapes. They overlapped one another, blurring at the edges into greens and blues where the pigments had mixed. Images taken from one artist recurred in the work of another, at once out of context yet still part of the greater vision. One of Goerg's demons fell upon the crowds fleeing Meidner's destruction; Kohn's horse wandered among Dix's battlefield corpses.

No wonder his kids were screwed up.

The next room was similarly decorated, although this time the images were medieval in origin and much more ornate. This room was larger than its neighbor, with two double beds on a linoleum floor, the beds separated by a slatted wood divider. There were books and magazines on rough shelves, two closets, and a small shower and toilet in one corner, separated from the main room by sliding glass doors. The only light came from a single bedside lamp standing on a table. Close by where I stood were two cardboard boxes filled with women's clothing and an open suitcase containing some men's suits and jackets. All of the clothes looked at least two decades out of date. The sheets had been removed from the beds and tied in two bundles. A vacuum cleaner stood in one corner, its dust bag removed and lying beside it. It seemed that all traces of the bunker's occupants were in the process of being removed.

A doorway stood half open at the entrance to the third room. I paused as a sound came from inside, a noise like the jangling of chains. I smelled blood on the air. I could sense no movement close to the doorway. Again the sound of metal on metal rang out. I pushed the door open with my foot and drew back against the wall, waiting for the shots. None came. I waited for a few seconds longer before glancing inside.

A butcher's block supported by four thick legs stood in the center of the stone floor. There was old, dried blood at its edges. Beyond it, against the far wall, was a stainless steel table with a sink attachment and a drainage pipe leading from the drain to a sealed metal container below. There were surgical implements on the table, some recently used. I saw a bone saw, and two scalpels with blood on their blades. A cleaver hung from a hook on the stone wall behind. The whole room stank of meat

It was only when I entered that I saw Angel. He was naked and attached to a metal rail above an iron tub, his arms held over the rail by a pair of handcuffs. He half stood, half knelt in the tub, its sides stained brown with old blood. His body was twisted toward me, and his mouth had been taped shut. His torso was streaked with blood and sweat, and his eyes were half-open. They closed briefly as I moved to him, and he made a small sound from behind the tape. There was bruising on his face, and a long wound to his right leg; it looked like a knife slash. It had been left to bleed.

I was about to reach around his back to support him before releasing him when the mewling sound rose in pitch. I stepped back and turned his body slightly. A patch of skin, easily a foot square, had been cut from his back, and the exposed flesh pulsed redly. Blood had pooled and dried around his feet. As I stared at the wound, Angel's legs began to shake and he started to sob. I found the keys to the cuffs hanging on a hook, then gripped him around the waist and released him, the full weight of him falling into my arms as I eased him from the tub and knelt him on the floor. I pulled the tape from his mouth as gently as I could, then took a plastic beaker from a shelf and filled it from the sink, the water sending the blood spiraling down into the drain. Angel took the cup and drank deeply, water spilling down his chin and onto his chest.

'Get me my pants,' were his first words.

'Who did this, Angel?'

'Get. Me. My. Damn. Pants. Please.'

His clothes lay in a pile by the tub. I found his chinos, then helped him ease into them as he sat on the floor, supporting himself as best he could on his weakened arms as he kept his back away from the wall.

'The old man,' he said as we hauled the pants up to his waist. Immediately, they stuck to the wound in his leg and a red stain spread across them. Every time he moved, his face creased with pain and he had to grit his teeth to keep from howling. 'There was gunfire from outside, and when I looked around he was disappearing up those stairs. He left the oven open. I might need what's inside.'

He pointed behind me, to where a steel box with a temperature dial at the top stood against the wall. A thin sheet of what might have been paper hung within, assuming paper could bleed. I turned off the dryer, then flipped the door closed with my foot.

'You meet the other two?'

I nodded.

'They're his kids, Bird.'

'I know.'

'What a fuckin' family.' He nearly smiled. 'You kill them?'

'I think so.'

'What does that mean?'

'The woman's dead. I fed Mr. Pudd to his pets.'

I left Angel and walked over to where a staircase led up from a small doorway at the back of the room. To the left of the first step was a room with another bed and a crucifix hanging from the ceiling. The walls here were covered with shelving, the weight of their books causing them to sag. Some had already been removed in preparation for flight, but many still remained; the arrival of Angel must have caused Faulkner to rearrange his priorities. I doubted that he had been allowed many live subjects on which to practise before. There was a workbench against one wall, inks, pens, knives, and nibs arrayed carefully in a metal carrying case on top of it. In an alcove opposite the bedroom, a generator hummed.

When I went back into Faulkner's preparation room, Angel had struggled to his feet and stood, slightly hunched over, at the wall, supporting himself with his hands, his injured leg raised slightly. His back had begun to bleed again.

'You think you can make it up?'

He nodded. I took his left arm, draped it around my shoulder, then held him carefully around the waist. Slowly, and with the agony etched clearly on his face, he made his way up the stone steps. He was almost at the top when his foot slipped and his back banged against the wall. It left a bright red streak as he lost consciousness, and I had to carry him the rest of the way. The stairs ended in a kind of alcove where a steel door stood open. A sheet of thick plastic lay beside it, slapping in the wind. Beside it, a shape lay rolled up in a second sheet stained inside with blood. Part of Voisine's face was exposed. I recalled Pudd's anger at the wounds inflicted by Angel on his assoicate; it looked like Voisine had since died from them.

Angel regained consciousness as I laid him, facedown, on the floor. I removed the .38 from my holster and pressed it into his hand.

'You killed Voisine.'

His eyes focused blearily on me. 'Good. Can I piss on his grave?'

'I'll make some calls, see what I can do.'

'Where are you going?'

'To find Faulkner.'

'You find him, you tell him I said "hi" before you kill him.'

The rain fell relentlessly and the ground had turned to mud as I stepped carefully onto the grass. Some fifty feet behind me, the woman still lay where she had fallen and no sound came from inside Mr. Pudd's spider house. The lighthouse was at my back, and in front of me a grass verge sloped down to the boathouse. There, in a sheltered inlet, was a small floating jetty. The door to the boathouse stood open and a boat bobbed at the end of the concrete ramp. It was a little Cape Craft runabout, with an Evinrude outboard. A figure stood on the deck, pouring diesel into the engine's fuel hatch. The rain fell on its bare skull, on the long white hair plastered to its face and shoulders, on its black coat and black leather shoes. It must have sensed me approaching, for it looked up, the diesel spilling over the deck as its concentration lapsed.

And it smiled.

'Hello, sinner,' said the Reverend Faulkner. He went for the revolver tucked into his waistband and I fired once, the can falling from his hands as he stumbled back, his shattered right arm now hanging loosely by his side. The gun dropped from his fingers to the deck of the boat, but the smile stayed where it was, trembling slightly with the pain of the wound. I fired twice and holed the outboard. Diesel sprayed from the ruptured tank.

He was, I guessed, about six feet tall, with long, white, tapering fingers and pale, elongated features. In the light from the cabin his eyes were a deep, dark blue, verging on black. His nose was exceptionally long and thin and his Cupid's bow was tiny, his almost lipless mouth seeming to begin just where his nostrils ended. His neck was scrawny and striated, and loose flesh hung in a wattle from beneath his chin.

At my feet lay a suitcase and a battered waterproof emergency pack. I kicked at it once.

'Going somewhere, Reverend?' I asked.

He ignored the question.

'How did you find us, sinner?'

'The Traveling Man led me here.'

The old man shook his head.

'An interesting individual. I was sorry when you killed him.'

'You were the only one. Your daughter's gone, Reverend, your son too. It's over.'

The old man spat into the sea and his eyes looked over my shoulder to where the woman lay dead in the rain. He betrayed no emotion.

'Step off the boat. You're going to stand trial for the deaths of your flock, for the killing of Jack Mercier and his wife and friends, for the murders of Curtis and Grace Peltier. You're going to answer for them all.'

He shook his head. 'I have nothing to answer for. The Lord did not send demons to kill the firstborn of Egypt, Mr. Parker; he sent angels. We were angels engaged in the Lord's work, harvesting the sinners.'

'Killing women and children doesn't sound like God's work.'

Blood dripped from his fingers onto the timbers of the boat. Gently, he raised his injured arm, seemingly oblivious to the pain, and showed me the blood on his hand. 'But the Lord kills women and children every day,' he said. 'He took your wife and child. If he believed that they were worthy of salvation, then they would still be alive.'

My hand tightened on the gun and I felt the trigger shift slightly.

'God didn't kill my wife and child. A man tore them apart, a sick, violent man encouraged by you.'

'He didn't need encouragement in his work. He merely required a framework for his ideals, an added dimension.'

He didn't say anything more for some time. Instead he seemed to examine me, his head to one side.

'You see them, don't you?' he asked at last.

I didn't reply.

'You think you're the only one?' That smile came again. 'I see them too. They talk to me. They *tell* me things. They're waiting for you, sinner, all of them. You think it ended with their deaths? It did not: they are all waiting for you.'

He leaned forward conspiratorially.

'And they fuck your whore while they wait,' he hissed. 'They fuck both your whores.'

I was only a finger's pressure away from killing him. When I breathed out and felt the trigger move forward, he seemed almost disappointed.

'You're a liar, Faulkner,' I said. 'Wherever my wife and child are, they're safe from you and all your kind. Now, for the last time, step off the boat.'

He still made no move.

'No earthly court will judge me, sinner. God will be my judge.'

'Eventually,' I replied.

'Good-bye, sinner,' said the Reverend Faulkner, and something struck me hard in the back, forcing me to my knees. A brown shoe stamped down hard on my fingers and the gun went off, sending a bullet into the jetty before it was kicked away from me and into the sea. Then a huge weight seemed to fall upon me and my face was pressed hard into the mud. There were knees on my upper back, forcing the air from my lungs as my mouth and nostrils filled with dirt. I dug my toes into the soft earth, pressed my left arm against the ground, and pushed upward as hard as I could, striking back with my right hand. I felt the blow connect and the weight on my back eased slightly. I tried to throw it off completely as I turned but hands closed on my neck and a knee struck me hard in the groin. I was forced flat on my back and found myself looking into the face of hell.

Mr. Pudd's features had swollen from the spider bites. His lips were huge and purple, as if they had been packed with collagen. The swelling had almost closed his nostrils, so he was forced to breath heavily through his mouth, his distended tongue hanging over his teeth. One eye was almost closed while the other had grown to twice its original size, so that it seemed about to burst. It was gray-white and partially filled with blood where the capillaries had ruptured. There were strands of silvery cobweb in his hair, and a black spider had become trapped between his shirt collar and his tumid neck, its legs flailing helplessly as it bit at him. I struck at his arms but he maintained his grip. Blood and saliva oozed from his mouth and dripped onto his chin as I reached up and dug the fingers of my right hand into his face, trying to strike at his injured eye.

From behind me, I heard the sound of the boat's engine starting and Pudd's grip shifted as his thumbs tried to crush my Adam's apple. I was tearing at his hands with my fingers, the pressure in my head increasing as my windpipe was slowly constricted. The outboard made a spluttering sound as it pulled away from the jetty, but I didn't care. My ears were filled with the roaring in my head and the labored, spit-flecked breaths of the man who was killing me. I felt a burning pain behind my eyes, a numbness spreading from my fingers. Desperately I raked at his face, but I was losing the feeling in my hands and my vision was blurring.

Then the top of Mr. Pudd's head exploded, showering me with blood and gray matter. He stayed upright for a moment, his jaw slackening and his ears and mouth bleeding, then tumbled sideways into the mud. The pressure eased on my throat and I drew in long, painful rattling breaths as I kicked Pudd's body away from me. I got to my knees and spat dirt onto the ground.

At the top of the grass verge, Angel lay on his stomach, the .38 outstretched before him in his right hand while the left used the plastic sheet to shield his injured back. I looked to the sea as the sound came to me of the runabout moving away on the dark, choppy waters. It was only thirty or forty feet from the shore, the white froth churning at the bow as

Faulkner stood at the wheel, his white face contorted with rage and grief.

The engine coughed, then died.

We stood facing each other across the waves, the rain falling on our heads, on the bodies behind me, on the dark waters of the bay.

'I'll see you damned, *sinner*.'

He raised the gun with his left hand and fired. The first shot was wild, impacting with a whine on the rocks behind me. He swayed slightly with the movement of the boat beneath him, aimed, and fired again. This time the bullet tugged at the sleeve of my coat but there was no impact. It passed straight through the wool, leaving only a faint smell of burning in its wake. The next two shots hissed through the damp air close to my head as I knelt down and flipped open the emergency pack.

The flare was a Helly-Hanson, and it felt good in my hand. I thought of Grace and Curtis, and the patch of black tape covering James Jessop's ruined eye. I thought of Susan, the beauty of her on the first day we met, the smell of pecans on her breath. I thought of Jennifer, the feel of her blond hair against mine, the sound of her breathing as she slept.

Another shot came, this time missing by a good three feet. I pointed at the waves and imagined the incandescent glow spreading across the water as the flare shot along the surface; the flash of pink-and-blue flame as the diesel fuel ignited, bursting from the waves and moving toward the man with the gun; the explosion of the outboard and then the flames scouring the deck, engulfing the figure in their midst. The heat would sear my face and the sea would be lit with red and gold, and the old man would travel, wreathed in fire, from this world to the next.

I tightened my finger on the trigger.

Click.

Out upon the waves, Faulkner rocked slightly as the hammer fell upon the empty chamber of his revolver. He tried to fire again.

Click.

I walked to the edge of the water and raised the flare gun. Once more the hollow sound came, yet the old man seemed neither to notice nor to care. The barrel of the gun followed me as I moved, as if with each pull of the trigger the empty weapon launched a fresh volley of lead that tore through my body and brought me, inch by inch, closer to death.

Click.

For an instant, the flare was level with him, its thick muzzle centered on his body, and I saw the satisfaction on his face. He would die, but I would damn myself in his destruction, and I would become like him.

Click.

Then the muzzle rose until the gun was above my head, pointing at the heavens.

'No!' cried Faulkner. 'No!'

I pulled the trigger and the flare shot forth, shedding bright light on the dark waves, turning the rain to falling silver and gold, the old man screaming in rage as a new star was born in the void.

I went to Angel. A smear of blood lay across the width of his plastic shield, where it had fallen against his wound. Carefully, I lifted it away so that it would not stick. The gun was still in his hand and his eyes were open, watching the figure out on the water.

'He should have burned,' he said.

'He will burn,' I replied.

And I held him until they came for us.

The Search for Sanctuary

Extract from the postgraduate thesis of Grace Peltier

'Truth exists,' wrote the painter Georges Braque. 'Only lies are invented.' Somewhere, the truth about the Aroostook Baptists remains to be discovered and written at last. All that I have tried to do is to provide a context for what occurred: the hopes that inspired the undertaking, the emotions that undermined it, and the final actions that swept it away.

In August 1964, letters were sent to relatives of each of the families who had joined Faulkner more than a year earlier. Each letter was written by the male or female parent of the family involved. Lyall Kellog wrote his family's letter; it was posted from Fairbanks, Alaska. Katherine Cornish's letter came from Johnstown, Pennsylvania; Frida Perrson's from Rochester, Minnesota; and Frank Jessop's, which assured his family that all was well with his wife and children, from Porterville, California. Each letter was undated, contained general good wishes, and added little more than that the Aroostook Baptists were no more and the families involved had been chosen to send out the Reverend Faulkner's message to the world like the missionaries of old. Few of the relatives involved were particularly concerned. Only Lena Myers, Elizabeth Jessop's sister, persisted in the belief that something might have happened to her sister and her family. In 1969, with the permission of the landowner, she engaged a private firm of contractors to excavate sections of land on the site of the Eagle Lake community. The search revealed nothing. In 1970, Lena Myers died as a result of injuries received in a hit-and-run accident in Kennebec, Maine. No one has ever been charged in connection with her death.

No trace of the families has ever been found in any of the towns from which their letters originated. Their names have never been recorded. No descendants have been discovered. No further contact was ever made by them.

The truth, I feel certain, lies buried.

EPILOGUE

This is a honeycomb world, each hollow linked to the next, each life inextricably intertwined with the lives of others. The loss of even one reverberates through the whole, altering the balance, changing the nature of existence in tiny, imperceptible ways.

I find myself returning again and again to a woman named Tante Marie Aguillard, her impossibly tiny child's voice coming to me from out of her immense form. I see her lying on a mountain of pillows in a warm, dark room in western Louisiana, the smell of the Atchafalaya drifting through the house; a shining, black shadow among shifting forms, heedless of the boundaries between the natural and the man-made as one world melts into another. She takes my hand and talks to me of my lost wife and child. They call to her and tell her of the man who took their lives.

She has no need of light; her blindness is less an impediment than an aid to a deeper, more meaningful perception. Sight would be a distraction for her strange, wandering consciousness, for her intense, fearless compassion. She feels for them all: the lost, the vanished, the dispossessed, the frightened, suffering souls who have been violently wrenched from this life and can find no rest in their world within worlds. She reaches out to them, comforting them in their final moments so they will not die alone, so they will not be afraid as they pass from light into dark.

And when the Traveling Man, the dark angel, comes for her, she reaches out in turn to me, and I am with her as she dies.

Tante Marie knew the nature of this world. She roamed through it, saw it for what it was, and understood her place in it, her responsibility to those who dwelt within it and beyond. Now, slowly, I too have begun to understand, to recognize a duty to the rest, to those whom I have never known as much as to those whom I have loved. The nature of humanity, its essence, is to feel another's pain as one's own, and to act to take that pain away. There is a nobility in compassion, a beauty in empathy, a grace in forgiveness. I am a flawed man, with a violent past that will not be denied, but I will not allow innocent people to suffer when it is within my power to help them.

I will not turn my back on them.

I will not walk away.

And if, in doing these things, I can make some amends, some recompense, for the things that I have done and for all that I have failed to do, then that will be my consolation.

For reparation is the shadow cast by salvation.

I have faith in some better world beyond this one. I know that my wife and child dwell within it, for I have seen them. I know that they are safe now from the dark angels and that wherever may dwell Faulkner and Pudd and the countless others who wanted to turn life to death, they are far, far from Susan and Jennifer, and they can never touch them again.

There is rain tonight in Boston, and the glass of the window is anatomized with intricate veins traced across its surface. I wake, my knuckle still sore from the treated bite, and turn gently to feel her move close beside me. Her hand touches my neck and I know somehow that, while I have been asleep, she has been watching me in the darkness, waiting for the moment to arrive.

But I am tired, and as my eyes close again,

I am standing at the edge of the forest, and the air is filled with the howling of the hybrids. Behind me, the trees reach out to one another, and when they touch, they make a sound like children whispering. And as I listen, something moves in the shadows before me.

'Bird?'

Her hand is warm upon me, yet my skin is cold. I want to stay with her, but

I am drawn away again, for the darkness is calling me and the shape still moves through the trees. Slowly, the boy emerges, the black tape masking the lens of his glasses, his skin pale white. I try to walk to him but I cannot raise my feet. Behind him, other figures shift but they are walking away from us, disappearing into the forest, and soon he will join them. The wooden board has been discarded but the burn marks from the rope remain visible at the sides of his neck. He says nothing but stands watching me for a long, long time, one hand gripping the bark of the yellow birch beside him, until, at last, he too begins to recede,

'Bird,' she whispers.

fading away, moving deeper and deeper,

'I'm pregnant.'

down, down into the depths of this honeycomb world.

ACKNOWLEDGMENTS

The following books proved invaluable in the course of writing this novel:

Wrath of Angels: The American Abortion War by James Risen and Judy L. Thomas (Basic Books, 1998); *Eagle Lake* by James C. Ouellette (Harpswell Press, 1980); *The Red Hourglass: Lives of the Predators* by Gordon Grice (Allen Lane, 1998); *The Book of the Spider* by Paul Hillyard (Hutchinson, 1994); *The Bone Lady* by Mary H. Manheim (Louisiana State University Press, 1999); *Maine Lighthouses* by Courtney Thompson (CatNap Publications, 1996); *Apocalypses* by Eugen Weber (Hutchinson, 1999); *The Apocalypse and the Shape of Things to Come*, edited by Francis Carey (British Museum Press, 1999); and *The Devil's Party* by Colin Wilson (Virgin, 2000). In addition, *Simpson's Forensic Medicine* by Bernard Knight (Arnold, 1997) and *Introduction to Forensic Sciences*, second edition, edited by William G. Eckert (CRC Press, 1997) rarely left my desk.

Much of the material relating to religious movements in Maine came from Elizabeth Ring's Introduction to her *Directory of Churches & Religious Organizations in Maine, 1940* (Maine Historical Records Survey Project); 'Till Shiloh Come' by Jason Stone (*Down East* magazine, March 1990); and 'The Promised Land' by Earl M. Benson. (*Down East* magazine, September 1953).

As each novel progresses, the depths of my ignorance become more and more apparent. I have relied on the knowledge and kindness of a great many people in researching this book, among them James Ferland and the staff of the Maine Medical Examiner's Office, Augusta; Officer Joe Giacomantonio, Scarborough Police Department; Captain Russell J. Gauvin, City of Portland Police Department; Sergeant Dennis R. Appleton, CID III, Maine State Police; Sergeant Hugh J. Turner, Maine State Police; L. Dean Paisley, my excellent guide to Eagle Lake; Rita Staudig, historian of the St. John Valley; Phineas Sprague Jr. of Portland Yacht Services; Bob and Babs Malkin and Jim Block, who helped me with Jewish New York; Big Apple Greeters; Phil Procter, theater manager of the Wang Center in Boston; Beth Olsen at the Boston Ballet; the staff of the Center for Maine History in Portland, Maine; Chuck Antony; and many others. To all of them I owe a drink, and probably an apology for all the mistakes I've made.

Finally, I wish to thank my agent, Darley Anderson, and his assistants, Elizabeth and Carrie; my foreign rights agent Kerith Biggs; my editor, Sue Fletcher; and everyone at Hodder & Stoughton for putting up with me.